TRISTAN STRONG DESTROYS THE WORLD

BOOK 2

KWAME MBALIA

RICK RIORDAN PRESENTS

Disney • HYPERION
Los Angeles   New York

Copyright © 2020 by Cake Literary

All rights reserved. Published by Disney • Hyperion, an imprint of Buena
Vista Books, Inc. No part of this book may be reproduced or transmitted
in any form or by any means, electronic or mechanical, including
photocopying, recording, or by any information storage and retrieval system,
without written permission from the publisher. For information address
Disney • Hyperion, 77 West 66th Street, New York, New York 10023.

Created in association with Cake Literary

First Hardcover Edition, October 2020
First Paperback Edition, October 2021
1 3 5 7 9 10 8 6 4 2
FAC-025438-21232

Printed in the United States of America

This book is set in Minion Pro, Hoefler Text, Courier Std/Monotype;
Astoria, Bouledoug/Fontspring

Designed by Tyler Nevins
Map illustration © 2020 by Robert Venables

Library of Congress Cataloging-in-Publication Control
Number for Hardcover Edition: 2020005493
ISBN 978-1-368-04240-6

Reinforced binding
Follow @ReadRiordan
Visit www.DisneyBooks.com

SUSTAINABLE
FORESTRY
INITIATIVE
Certified Chain of Custody
Promoting Sustainable Forestry
www.sfiprogram.org
SFI-01054
The SFI label applies to the text stock

For the stories across the Diaspora,
and the elders who carried them

CONTENTS

Bottle Tree Forest

Old Barn

1
TRICKSTERS AND WHISPERS

NOBODY LIKES GETTING PUNCHED IN THE FACE.

Call it a hunch or an educated guess. Either way, I can confirm from firsthand experience that getting punched in the face is way down on the list of enjoyable activities. It's somewhere between eating a halfway-scraped-off piece of burnt toast and giving yourself a wedgie. Nope. Don't like it. *Especially* when it's accompanied by my grandfather's trash talk.

POP!

"C'mon, boy! Keep your head moving! Unless you wanna make your living lying down on the mat. You want me to build you a house down there? I can get you a one-room studio, utilities included."

When I opened my eyes, Granddad was standing over me with his hands on his hips. Well, his mitts on his hips. He wore gray jogging sweats and a crisp white T-shirt that he had probably ironed. His afro, neatly trimmed and nearly all gray, moved from side to side as he grumbled and shook his head. He took off one mitt and held out a massive brown hand with scars on the knuckles. When I reached up with my right glove and he pulled me to my feet, I could feel the strength that had made him a legend in the boxing circuit.

"You gotta move," Granddad said. He got into a boxer's crouch and started bobbing and weaving his head. "You're too stiff in there right now, like something's holding you back. What's wrong? You asked for this, remember? You tired?"

We were inside the old barn on my grandparents' farm. The early-afternoon sun peeked through gaps in the walls, sending warm yellow rays down in stripes across the packed dirt floor. Granddad and I had been working all day—clearing out junk, sweeping, stuff like that. A makeshift boxing ring now stood in the middle of the open space, and a few other adults were setting up benches.

Why, I hear you asking, did I volunteer for this?

Well, a few days ago, Granddad had gotten a call from an old buddy he knew back on the amateur boxing circuit, now a trainer himself. A practice bout for one of his new prospects had been canceled because of a storm, and he wanted to know if Granddad knew of anyone they could spar with.

Why yes, I imagined Granddad saying, *I have the perfect sparring partner. No, don't worry, he's up for the challenge.*

That, my friends, isn't volunteering. That's called being volun-told.

So I had a sparring match in an hour or so, and I was *not* looking forward to it, but Granddad had insisted I get in one good match before I left to go back home to Chicago.

Yay.

But don't get me wrong. I wasn't backing down. I wanted the challenge. Kept me distracted. Helped suppress unwanted thoughts. Mr. Richardson, my counselor, called them *intrusive thoughts*. Busy hands, calm mind.

And when you trained with Granddad, your hands stayed busy.

"No, sir, I'm not tired." I hopped up, slammed my gloves together, and started the routine again.

Granddad held up his mitts, and I let my hands go to work.

"All right, boy," my grandfather said. "One-two."

I took a deep breath and fired off the punch combination. Sharp. Quick. Had to be better. Had to get stronger. Step forward, twist the hips, snap off a punch.

Faster.

FASTER.

FAST—

"All right, boy, all right. Don't get too worked up." Granddad backed away and dropped the mitts. I stopped in mid-jab, breathing hard. "I told you, we're warming up. What's gotten into you?"

I started to answer, then closed my mouth. I didn't know how to explain my need to improve, the weight I felt on my shoulders.

Granddad watched me closely. "Take a deep breath. You sure you ain't tired? I heard you up late last night, then early this morning. You getting enough sleep?"

I bounced on my feet. "I'm okay, Granddad. I'm ready."

"I'll tell you when you're ready. Just breathe. You look tired."

I rolled my neck, trying to loosen up, looking everywhere around the barn instead of at Granddad. Pictures and posters decorated the walls, detailing fights from years past, and faded brown boxing gloves dangled from a beam running across the high two-story ceiling. But the real eye-catcher was a giant mural depicting two men, a weary boxer with one fist up as he curled a bicep, and his cornerman, towel slung over his shoulder, standing behind him with both arms flexed.

It was Alvin Strong, my dad, the night he defended his championship for the first time, and his trainer, Walter Strong—Granddad.

I once asked Granddad why he'd chosen to commemorate that night and not the time Dad had won the belt in the first place. He'd scratched his beard, then made a fist and flexed, like Dad in the mural. "Taking the belt was a feat, I'll grant you. Somethin' hard, worthy of a mural, I suppose. But it's one thing to take the belt when don't nobody see you coming. It's another to stare down an entire country while you got a target on your back, and then beat them challengers into submission. It's hard to win a belt. . . . It's even harder to keep it."

As I shook my arms to loosen them and then slipped my mouthpiece back in, Granddad stood beneath that mural. He might have been older, skinnier, with more wrinkles and less hair, but the same strength still radiated from him. I had that strength, too. I'd used it before, and I was going to have to use it again. Because, as much as it pained me, I *had* asked to train. I needed to get stronger.

"I'm okay, Granddad. Honest," I said, pounding my gloves together again. "I'm not tired at all."

"Mm-hmm. We'll see. Here we go. One-two. One-two. Good. Hook coming in. One-two. One-two. Tuck that chin in, boy, show these hands some respect! One-two. That's it, that's the Walter Strong special. Watch it, now. Good!"

POP! POP!

I snapped lefts and rights at the mitts as Granddad called the cadence, and for a while I did good. When the hooks came in from either direction, I ducked them, and when the straights came in, I dodged them, weaving from side to side so they went sailing by. A rhythm had me bouncing on my feet and practicing the sweet science. It felt good. I got into a groove.

POP! POP!

And then it happened.

A sound drifted past my ear. Something tiny and faint. A breath of wind brushed my cheek. A chill gripped my chest, making it hard to breathe.

Tristan . . .

Someone whispered my name. And right after that, another sound reached my ears. My heart seized up. My fists dropped as I turned toward whatever—or whoever—it was.

"Tristan!"

I recovered too late.

WHAP!

The hook came again and clipped the side of my head, sending me head over heels. It didn't hurt—it just knocked me upside down—but Granddad grew upset. He took off the mitts and tossed them out of the ring.

"Now what done got into you?! What is so fascinating that you'd take a punch from your opponent just to get a peek at it? Hmm? A piece of trash on the ground? You ain't even here—you off somewhere in your head!"

I didn't answer. Something fluttered across the floor, tumbling between the feet of the adults who were trying hard to not look at us. It was a receipt, crumpled up and harmless. I let out a shaky breath. Granddad waited, then sighed and motioned for me to come over. He unlaced the gloves and pulled them off, then undid the wraps on my hands and wrists. He worked quickly, then gathered up everything and stared at the mural on the barn wall.

"Boy," he said without looking at me. "Let's take fifteen. I need to get some water in me anyway. You look exhausted, and you're chewing on something in that head of yours and need to spit it out. Whatever it is, you can't bring that into the ring. Distractions will be the end of you before your opponent throws a single punch."

He stepped out of the ring and stuffed the equipment into a giant faded-green army duffel. He strained once, then stopped and took a deep breath. With a grunt, he lifted the bag over his shoulders and headed off. "I'll be back with the body pads," he said over his shoulder. "Then we're going to start over. I expect you to be ready to get serious."

Granddad marched out and the spectators followed him, leaving me alone in the barn, staring at the balled-up receipt. Tiny. Like a small wad of cotton. That had bad associations for me. But the piece of paper wasn't the actual distraction. I just couldn't tell Granddad that. A whisper? He would've stared at me like I'd sprouted an extra armpit on my forehead. And who could blame him?

How could I tell him that, just for a second, I'd thought I heard a faint drumbeat?

A miffed, cultured voice jerked me out of my thoughts.

"You know, boy, the least you could do is remove me from

your sweaty pocket before you start prancing about in your silly outfit and gloves. Hurry up and let me breathe. Or do you plan on moping forever?"

It came from my training shorts. I rolled my eyes and pulled out a shiny black phone with a gold spider emblem on the back, sleek and brand-new. When I raised it, the screen blinked on and a splash screen appeared—a fancy box with the word STORY written inside it. The image faded away, and in its place appeared a tiny brown man stomping back and forth, hopping over glowing app icons and kicking aside the clock. He wore flip-flops, pants that were either too short or shorts that were too long, and a T-shirt with a grinning spider on it. Anansi's sense of style was somewhere between lazy dad and retro-chic teen, and I could only shake my head.

Why was Anansi, the original trickster, the master of storytelling, the weaver of tales and webs of mischief, inside my phone?

Great question!

Because a month ago a tiny loudmouth stole my dead best friend's journal.

Because in my anger I punched a hole into a different realm where Black folktale heroes and African gods walk around like you and me.

Because I accidentally brought a diabolical haint with me, stirring up an even more ancient evil.

Because I caught Anansi trying to use all the confusion

to gain power for himself instead of helping the people, and this was his punishment.

Because I am an Anansesem, a carrier and spreader of stories, and this phone is the Story Box, the vessel in which those stories are stored, and which it is my responsibility to watch over and refill.

Because I got the hookup, that's why. Now stop asking questions.

Anyway, that was a month ago. It had been thirty days since Eddie—well, his spirit, actually, since he's my dead best friend—told me good-bye for the last time. Since then I'd read aloud every word in the journal he left me and recorded it with the Listen Chile app on the SBP (Story Box Phone—give me a break, let me be lazy).

The SBP's screen went blank, and then the lock screen appeared. Anansi glanced at the Story Box logo, then sat down and leaned his back against it. He pulled a black pixel out of the background and began to toss it against the edge of the screen like a ball.

"Look," he said gently. "I know you and I haven't seen eye to eye...."

I snorted.

"And we might've gotten off on the wrong foot—"

"You tried to get the people of Isihlangu to throw us in their dungeons," I said with a raised eyebrow.

Anansi flapped his hand and waved the words away. "Stop

living in the past. We have to look toward the future. I am due for a reprieve from this prison soon, and that can't happen if you don't pay attention to incoming fists. Who will tell old Nyame I fulfilled my obligations if you're unconscious? Who will transcribe your grandmother's fantastic key lime pie recipe for me? No, no, you must focus."

I shrugged and started rewrapping my hands. Granddad would be back any minute now, and I needed to be ready. If I could just get through this match, the rest of the week would fly by, and then I'd be on my way back to Chicago. "I'll be fine."

"It appears to me you're not acting fine."

"I'm good. Relax."

Anansi raised an eyebrow. "And the nightmares?"

Whispers drifted past my ear again. A rhythm pulsed from somewhere out in the cornfield behind the barn—a fast drumbeat that sent my heart racing. I hadn't told anyone about the bad dreams that had sent me lurching up in bed every night since returning from Alke. This is why you can't leave a trickster god on your nightstand while you sleep. I tugged on my gloves, then stood. "I'll. Be. Fine."

"You can't punch your way out of everything, boy. Sooner or later you'll find someone or something that punches harder. Trust me."

Before I could respond to *that* startling piece of wisdom, the barn door creaked open. Granddad walked in; sure enough, he wasn't alone. A crowd gathered behind him, and Nana—my grandmother—stood by his side, but my eyes were on the person standing next to him.

"By my eight ashy legs," Anansi whispered. "That boy is huge!"

"Let's go, boy—up and at 'em," Granddad said. "It's time to spar."

2
THE SPARRING MATCH

LIFE ISN'T FAIR.

That's what every adult has said when I've told them something wasn't fair. You've probably heard the same thing. *Oh, nothing's fair. You have to play the cards you're dealt.* Well, why are we even playing cards? I don't even like card games!

Anyway...

What *really* wasn't fair was my sparring partner. His name was Reggie Janson, and he stood taller than most of the adults surrounding the ring. Wider, too. I mean, even his muscles had muscles. Smooth brown skin, JAWBREAKER scrawled in graffiti print on his hoodie and trunks, and a face pulled into a scowl that made him look meaner than the neighborhood dog everyone steers clear of. His legs were tree trunks and his gloves bowling balls. In short—

"You might want to rethink this," Anansi said into my ear. I was wearing my earbuds in the hope of tuning out the prefight noise and commotion, but what I got was trickster-god color commentary over some chopped-and-screwed classic hip-hop songs. Yep, apparently Anansi had discovered streaming and was currently obsessed with Houston rap.

I ignored him. He might have been right, but still, he didn't have to come out and say it. Whatever happened to false encouragement?

I continued my warm-up until Granddad came over with a water bottle and a towel. He was chewing on a blade of grass, which he only did when he was worried. "Okay," he said, "stick to the basics. A simple sparring match, three rounds, nothing serious."

The sound of a small explosion filled the barn.

We all turned to see Reggie's trainer standing over a ruptured punching bag that had hit the floor, sand spilling out. Reggie turned, saw me watching, and shrugged, then started shadowboxing.

"Sweet peaches," Anansi and I said at the same time.

Granddad chewed the blade of grass even harder, as if he were having second thoughts, but then he shook his head. "You'll be fine" was all he said.

I nodded, then someone caught my eye. A short curly-haired woman in hospital scrubs had opened the barn doors and stepped inside. She saw somebody she recognized and waved. "Who's that?" I asked.

Granddad turned and grunted. "Hmm. Ring doctor. Travels with Reggie when he spars, just to be safe."

"Reggie travels with a doctor? Is he sick?"

"The doctor isn't for him. She's here for his opponents."

My jaw dropped, but Granddad studiously avoided my eyes and spat out the blade of grass before pulling another from his pocket. Who keeps grass in their pocket? And who sets up a boxing match like this for their grandson? I wanted to protest. Maybe it wasn't too late for me to back out and take up a less threatening sport, like staring contests. But I didn't have a chance to suggest it before Granddad turned around and started clapping. "All right, let's get started. Tony, you ready?"

Reggie's trainer flashed a thumbs-up before slapping his boxer on the shoulder.

I took out my earbuds and dropped them and the SBP onto a bench in the corner. Anansi was lying on his back with his eyes closed when I left him. *Thanks for your support*, I thought as I walked away.

Reggie and I both climbed into the ring. We had on our headgear, but I felt like I needed a football helmet as extra protection.

"All right, keep it clean, but take it serious. We ain't here to hurt nobody. It's just a tune-up, right?" Tony, Reggie's trainer, looked between us with an eyebrow raised, and we both nodded. "Good. Let's show them folks how we roll down here in Alabama." He stepped out of the ropes and put a whistle in his mouth. "Touch 'em up, then wait for my whistle."

Reggie's gloves pounded into mine as we stood face-to-face. "Why so tight, little bro? It's just a sparring match."

We backed up. I bounced on my toes, ready to do this thing.

At least I thought so.

The whistle came and my fists went up, just as a right hook came howling toward the left side of my head. I ducked, and a left uppercut streaked toward my face. Somehow, at the last minute, I managed to twist my body so my shoulder took the blow.

The impact sent me flat on my butt.

"C'mon, boy, what're you doing? Get up and get in the match!" Granddad's gruff voice and the snickers from the crowd brought a flushing heat to my face. I climbed to my feet and rotated my right shoulder. It felt like a hammer had battered it.

Just a tune-up. Right.

As if he could hear my thoughts, Reggie grinned. Jeez, even his mouthpiece said JAWBREAKER. Was there anything peaceful about him?

The rest of the round was more of the same. Me ducking. Me slipping and twisting. Me trying not to die as fists the size of my face tried to punch me into another zip code.

At the end of the round, Tony the Trainer (look, it's how I remembered his name) blew his whistle and I collapsed onto the stool Granddad had waiting for me. I took a sip of water and tried to force some air into my lungs.

"You dancing or you boxing?" Granddad held up a bucket for me to spit out the water. "You know you can throw some punches, too?"

"Yes, sir," I said.

"Do you want me to call the match? Is it too much?"

"No, sir. Just—"

"Just what?"

"Just waiting for an opening."

Granddad put down the bucket and placed both hands on my shoulders. "Sometimes, boy, you gotta make your own opening. Don't wait for somebody to give you permission to do your best. You let 'em have it and leave all that other mess for the hogs. Fight for something! You got it? Grab whatever you need to grab deep down inside of yourself, whether it's pride or honor or even just the love of fighting, and you fight for it. Got me?"

"Yes, sir."

"Got me?"

"Yes, sir!"

Round two started out the same, though. As much as I wanted to, I couldn't land a blow during Reggie's barrage. The dude had punches that threw punches. He clipped me a good one on the top of the head when I didn't duck fast enough, and it felt like a cannonball had grazed my skull.

Even so, Reggie was getting frustrated with all my defense. "You planning on fighting today?" he taunted. "Scared money don't make money."

The second round ended, and Granddad didn't say much. He rubbed my shoulders and gave me a little water, but I could tell he was disappointed.

And that wasn't even the worst part.

Just before the third round started, I heard it again.

Tristan?

A voice calling my name. Even stranger, a tingling sensation rippled down the fingers of my left hand and circled my wrist. The barn door was closed, but I swore I felt a breeze swirl around me. A humming song sounded faintly in my ears, and the dull thuds of a giant drum echoed around the barn.

"Oh no," I whispered, looking around wildly to see if anyone else had noticed. But everyone seemed focused on the match. This was something only I could hear.

Well, there was one other person . . . sort of.

The SBP still lay on the bench at the edge of the ring, partially covered by a damp towel Granddad had dropped. I could just make out Anansi's worried face as he tried to peer over the edge of the screen and into the crowd. He'd felt something strange, too, and it had left him shaken.

That makes two of us, I thought as Tony the Trainer blew his whistle for the final round.

Everyone had given up on me.

Tony kept glancing at me and shaking his head as he backed up. A few of the adults who'd gathered to watch—those that still remained—were no longer paying the sparring session any attention. Even Granddad seemed uninterested. He met my eyes...then looked away.

That hurt the most.

Reggie bounced on his toes and knocked his gloves together. Every time he did, it sounded like two cinder blocks slamming together. "C'mon, man, let's get this over with. I thought the legendary Coach Strong would have some sort of prodigy for a grandson. No shade, but I guess we can't all be great."

"Yeah," I muttered. "That sorta sounds like shade to me." I wanted the match to end so I could escape to a corner somewhere. Maybe a hole. With a bag of cheese puffs and some root beer. And—

A soft fragment of a song drifted through the talking crowd to my ears.

Tristan...

I looked up, confused. Reggie danced in front of me, shaking out his arms and rocking his head from side to side. "Did you hear that?" I asked.

"The ringing?" Reggie's mouthpiece muffled his speech,

but when he tapped his glove against the side of his head, I got the message. "Don't worry, little bro, it's only gonna get WORSE." He grunted the last word as he ripped a right hook toward my temple. It missed by inches, but he followed it up with a barrage of jabs and straights that took every ounce of Granddad's training to avoid. Bob, weave, duck, backpedal. Even with all that, a few blows landed. A right slipped through my guard and grazed my ribs. An uppercut nicked my chin when I threw my head back too slowly.

I backed up, panting. This was getting out of hand. Granddad stood on the ring apron, halfway over the ropes, shouting something at me. Why couldn't I make it out? Had I lost my hearing? Was I in a daze? Reggie stalked toward me and I was raising my fists when—

Tristan . . .

There it was again! From the crowd. I could hear a voice—a different one this time. No, several.

Tristan!

Help, please!

He's coming!

So many voices. And beneath them I heard a rhythm. *The* rhythm. The one I hadn't heard in a month. Not since a giant shadow crow had flown me through a gash of roaring fire.

Something surged inside me. A feeling. A power. But why here? Why now? Bright light flashed and caught my eye. The SBP was ringing. Was I getting a call? Or was it Anansi? I felt the tingling on my wrist again, like when your foot falls asleep. It felt like I was trying to wake up. Or someone was trying to wake me up. They needed me. I was being summoned to—

Reggie dashed forward and bull-rushed me into the ropes. His head ground against mine, and he looked up, a sharklike grin exposing his custom mouthpiece.

"You're wasting my time," he snarled. "Do me a favor and stay down."

"What do y—"

Before I could finish, Reggie reared back, his right fist cocked behind him, ready to unleash fury. Then I understood. He wanted to end the fight now. His fist roared forward, a heat-seeking missile with a target lock on my face. If it connected it was game over, good night, thanks for playing.

I couldn't let that happen.

Fight for something, Granddad had said.

Fight for something. Fight for something!

"Alke," I whispered.

POP! POP!

3

TWO-PIECE SPECIAL

NO ONE MOVED.

A second passed. Two. Three. An eternity. Granddad's eyes were wide and Tony the Trainer gawked. The chatter and conversations had stopped. No one in the crowd moved a muscle. All attention was on the ring and the two fighters standing in the middle of it.

Well, one of us was still standing.

Reggie lay on his back, his eyes fixed on me, astonished. It looked as if this was the first time he'd ever been knocked down and he couldn't believe it. Slowly, a furious expression crept across his face.

"Walter Strong's two-piece special, no biscuit," I said, bouncing on my toes. "You ready to box?"

Reggie slammed his gloves into the ground, then shot to his feet with a growl. I dropped into my stance, feet wide and gloves up, ready for whatever barrage he was preparing to unleash. But before the two of us could resume our battle, Tony the Trainer hopped into the ring and grabbed Reggie around his shoulders.

"Hold it, hold it! Just a sparring match, remember? Look at me." The trainer checked Reggie's pupils, but the boy kept shifting side to side to scowl at me. "Hey, come on, let me see. You good?"

The ring doctor stepped up, too. Reggie tried to wave them both away, but they insisted on doing their due diligence and led him to the corner. A hand clapped me on the shoulder. Granddad stood behind me, a hint of a smile on his face.

"Two-piece special, huh?" he asked. "You did good, boy."

I smiled. "Thanks, Granddad."

He pulled me into a fierce one-armed hug, then pushed me to the opposite corner. "Go take a break, get some water. Let me check on them, see if they need anything. I'm pretty sure this bout is finished." He went over and crouched beside Tony and the doctor and murmured something.

I walked to the far side of the ring, nodded at a few people who congratulated me, and leaned against the ropes. My knees felt like jelly, and I let out a shaky breath.

He's coming!

The words slipped in between my thoughts and hovered at the front of my mind. I stared at my wrist. Quickly, using my teeth to loosen the Velcro straps, I pulled off my boxing gloves. I hopped out of the ring, grabbed the phone, and slipped the earbuds back into my ears. While everyone else's attention was focused on Alabama's number one Intermediate boxing prospect, I ducked out the barn door.

"Anansi," I said, "I need your help."

I was sitting on a tuft of grass around the back of the barn, slowly unwinding the wraps from my wrists as the breeze cooled the sweat on my skin. It was a gorgeous afternoon. The sun draped the farm in warm golden rays. Birds sang their late-day chorus as insects buzzed and chirped in the cornfield behind me (no crickets...best believe I double-checked that).

The SBP was propped in front of me on the ground. On the screen Anansi rolled over and kept snoring. A strand of silk from the web he'd stretched across the top corner drifted over his mouth, floated away as he exhaled, and returned once more. I poked the tiny god once, then twice.

How could he be asleep at a time like this? "Hey! Did you hear those voices back there? What do I...? Hey, wake up!" I poked the screen again, harder this time, and the trickster god sprang to his feet with a cry and pulled the belt from around his waist in a flash.

"WHO WANNA ROMP?!" he shouted, looking around wildly, twirling the belt above his head like a lasso. He was in his partial-spider form—a six-legged, two-armed man with shining brown skin and twinkling eyes. Right now he looked disheveled, and his voice boomed out of the earbuds. I winced. Alkean acoustics were pretty impressive.

"*Shh!* Stop shouting. I need your help."

Anansi blinked, then frowned when he saw it was only me. He rubbed his eyes, yawned, and put his belt back on. "Oh. It's you. Boy, don't you know it's bad form to poke a sleeping god? You're quite lucky I only let a little Diaspora out."

I frowned. "Diaspora? What does that mean?"

Anansi raised one tiny eyebrow and sniffed. "It means a group of people who originally came from one spot and then dispersed. How do you think my stories got spread? Folks carried them when they left or were stolen from their homeland and told the tales wherever they landed. I'm big all over, if you didn't realize. My stories have been shared by queens who were taken to Jamaica, and by workers in Jamaica, Queens. From Port-au-Prince, Haiti, to Paris, France, I'm—as that rhythmic poet says—good in any hood."

"Soooo..."

"So *Diaspora* means there are people who are scattered across the globe, in cities and towns and farms, but can all trace their roots back to a single source. For you and me, it means that even though we come from two different worlds, we can claim each other as kinfolk because of where we originated from."

I sat there and digested that for a second. It was a lot to

take in, and for a moment I wished my best friend, Eddie, were still alive so we could break it down. Even if I could talk to his spirit, that might help.

Help!

My head snapped up, and I sprang to my feet. "Nice lecture, but right now I need something else."

"I told you once, boy—I'm not giving you my secret fried-plantain recipe."

"I— What? No, nothing like that. I think . . . I think someone's in trouble. I sensed something strange in the barn. It looked like you did, too. The last time I felt that, I was in—"

"Alke," Anansi finished. A sly expression crossed his face, and the spider god clapped his hands and hopped up and down on his six feet. "All right, boy, stop hoarding your gourds. Let's go take a peek."

"Hoarding my gourds?" I muttered.

"Come on! Brother Anansi's got your back."

Like *that* was going to make me feel better.

"I had the feeling over there." I crouched behind the barn and aimed the SBP's camera through a loose slat. A crowd was still gathered around Reggie, but that wasn't what I was focused on.

Anansi sat on the edge of the screen and pursed his lips. "Did you use the sky god's adinkra?"

I shook my head. When I was in Alke, Nyame, the sky god, had given me a trinket with the symbol of his power: the Gye Nyame adinkra. By holding it I could actually *see* stories, the story threads that tied Alke together. It was just one of several magical charms I'd been given on my journey, and I'd worn them on a band around my wrist.

"Nah," I said. Something like that would've been really helpful right now. The only problem was... "I buried the bracelet."

Anansi stared at me like I'd started talking out of my ears. "You what?!"

I didn't meet his eyes. "I buried it. And the gloves—the ones John Henry gave me. I don't know, I just... Having them nearby and not being able to see... anyone." I almost slipped up and said *Ayanna*. "It hurt. Like homesickness, but for a place that wasn't my home. Does that make sense?"

Anansi scratched his head and muttered something that sounded a lot like *Heroes, I swear.* Then he sighed. "We'll talk about this later. Right now... Hmm. Yes, I can help, but I need a little permission."

I shrugged. "Of course. I'm the one who asked you—"

"No, you giant bag of cobwebs, I need permission from this box Nyame trapped me in. I'm not supposed to use my powers, remember? You have to allow it."

I stared at him suspiciously. "That sounds like something a trickster god would say."

Anansi flopped backward and tipped his hat over his eyes. "Fine. I was just trying to help *you*. But suit yourself. I can go back to investigating the best napping position. Personally, I think hands-folded-over-the-belly-after-a-meal is best, but I need to study it some more."

"Okay, okay," I said. "I get it. You better not be planning anything, though. Otherwise, Nyame's gonna hear about it."

Anansi raised his hands innocently. As he did, an alert popped up above his head, the kind that asks permission to access your phone's contacts list, or to know your location. Normally I'd automatically hit *yes*, but this time I felt the need to read the fine print aloud.

"'Do you grant the recipient, Kwaku Anansi, the ability to manipulate the fabric of reality...?' Wait, what? No!" I scanned the list. "'Reinvent history'? No. 'Own all stories from here on out'? No. 'Exclusive audiobook rights to *Fight for Our Lives: The Tristan Strong Story*'? NO! Definitely not."

I checked out the rest of them and tapped *yes* on the few I thought wouldn't immediately imperil the world as we knew it. I hoped.

"There. That should do it. *Now* will you please help?"

Anansi flexed his fingers, stretched his six legs, and then dropped into a seated position and began pulling glimmering spiderwebs from his pants pockets. "At last, some tools. Okay, then. Let's see what we can do."

The camera app opened, went black, then infrared, and

then bright silver. I winced and turned away. When I looked again, the searing light had faded and been replaced by a glittering cloud that drifted around the screen.

"Is that a filter?" I asked. "Like, for selfies?"

"Selkies are a different mythology."

"Not selkies . . . You know what? Never mind."

"Good. Now, show me where you heard someone," Anansi said. His voice came through the earbuds with a musical lilt, full of laughter and mischief. It filled me with a sense of joy. I shook my head, then glared at him. Just what sort of permissions had I granted?

He flapped a hand at me, and I rolled my eyes and aimed the phone's camera lens. The glitter on the screen drifted away, leaving a few bright outlines scattered about, and I gasped.

Anansi's eyes widened and he gave a low whistle. "Well, I'll be . . ."

"Anansi," I asked slowly, "why are there ghosts in my grandparents' barn?"

4

THE SPIRITS COME CALLING

SEVERAL TRANSPARENT FIGURES HOVERED ABOUT. THE FIRST —a girl—might've been my age or a little older, but not by much. Her clothes were like nothing I'd seen before. She wore pants that billowed at the bottom with a wide flourish, ending at her bare feet. Her hair was plaited into small micro-braids that fell past her shoulders; shimmering wire had been woven into each braid, making them look like rippling waves every time she moved her head. She was by far the brightest of all the ghosts. Almost a beacon. Her eyes roamed the room, and she seemed keenly interested in everything inside the barn.

The other ghosts were an old badger whose fur would probably be just as silver without the SBP's filter, a human mother and father standing close together, a small child hanging on to their legs, and a teenage brother and sister. All of them looked scared.

"Where did these ghosts come from?" I asked Anansi.

"Not ghosts, boy—spirits. You know better. At least I'd hoped so, but you've disappointed me before." Anansi dropped into a squat on the SBP's screen to study the first spirit more closely. "And I think—no, I know—that this one is not ordinary."

"There are ordinary spirits?"

"Yes. Run-of-the-mill haints and spooks. Souls lingering due to unfinished business or because their deeds are keeping them from passing on, and some because they need assistance from the living. But other spirits have a greater purpose." Anansi looked out at me. "Your friend on the bus was one of those, from what you told me."

Eddie, my dead best friend, had consistently tried to warn me that Anansi was trying to trick us all, and he'd done it while King Cotton, an evil haint, was holding him hostage. Friends, man. How many of us have them?

I swallowed the ball of sadness trying to lodge itself in my throat and nodded at the current spirit of the day, the brightest girl. "So, you're saying we have to figure out who she is and what brought her here?"

"Oh, I know who she is."

"You do?"

"Of course. She's an Alkean river spirit."

Was it my imagination, or did the girl stiffen when Anansi said that?

I nodded. "Of course. That makes perfect sense. So, how does— WAIT, WHAT? From Alke?"

Anansi nodded. "In fact, I'd say—yes, I'm pretty positive all of them are from Alke."

From Alke. The realm of stories where Black folk heroes and African gods coexisted—peacefully now, I hoped. The spirits were from Alke. . . . That statement knocked loose all my thoughts, and I tried to grab them and put them back in order. How could they be from Alke? We'd closed the hole between the worlds. Had it reopened? What else was slipping through?

Suddenly, as if my thinking about it had drawn her attention, the river spirit turned her head and looked straight at the camera. Like she knew I was there. I recognized her expression immediately. It had been on the faces of the Midfolk when they were being harassed by iron monsters in MidPass. It was on the sky god Nyame's face when he had described watching the people of the Golden Crescent being snatched away. The same expression had crossed the faces of the people of Isihlangu when the hullbeast had crashed through the doors of their mountain fortress and sent a swarm of brand flies to hunt everyone down. Oh, I knew that expression well.

Terror.

He's coming!

Help!

So these spirits were the ones I'd heard when I was

fighting. "Anansi," I said slowly, then paused and licked my lips. "What would send spirits fleeing from Alke to this world? And how can they even travel here? Didn't we close the hole in the sky?"

The spider god stood and folded his arms. He looked troubled. "I'm afraid I don't have the answers. But whatever's driving them must be terrible indeed."

I studied the spirits. The brother and sister clutched each other, cringing every time a living person passed through them. The badger had floated to the back of the barn, moving behind a stack of empty buckets to hide. Fear had driven them here . . . but fear of what?

"Tristan—" Anansi began, but I cut him off.

"Isn't there something we can do? Call the gods in Alke? Slide into their DMs?"

The spider god shook his head. "What you're asking . . . it's not impossible, but it's pretty close. And dangerous. Really dangerous. Once you open a connection, it stays open. And who knows who might pick up on the other end. No, I don't think so. And even if I wanted to, which I don't, I don't think I have the power to do it, not while stuck in this phone, anyway. Also, what's a DM? And why wouldn't someone just walk into it? Is sliding necessary? Flip-flops aren't the most athletic of footwear and, well, I have many legs, so . . ."

I zoomed out with the camera and as I did, another spirit materialized—a tall man. His faint outline wavered, but I could still see that he was holding a small child in his arms. I bit my lip. I had to do something. They'd all been drawn here for a reason—maybe it was the SBP or me, as an Anansesem. Whatever the case, I had to help them.

"We *have* to do something. Anansi, please—"

Suddenly, the camera app closed. The SBP began to vibrate, jostling Anansi off his feet and sending him falling head over six heels. Then the home screen reappeared.

A new app icon bloomed into view in the lower right of the screen: a black-and-ivory square with rounded edges and a silhouette of two people in the middle.

"'Contacts,'" I read aloud, confused. Then the realization hit me. It was a directory. I stared at it, slightly afraid, but also excited. The phone had never done that before. It was as if it had heard my needs and instantly created an app that would help me accomplish them. I love technology.

Anansi stared at the icon suspiciously. "Tristan, I don't think you should—"

"Too late," I said as I tapped it. The screen shimmered and faded to black until it looked as if Anansi were standing in empty space. Words swirled across the top of the screen.

Enter the name of video call recipient.

I quickly typed in the first person who came to mind.

Anansi groaned. "Not him," he said, but the letters were already swirling and rearranging.

I took a deep breath and propped the phone on a loose

board on the ground outside the barn. After a few seconds, a grand dining hall appeared on the screen. An incredibly long table stood in the middle, surrounded by elegant wooden chairs with beautiful images engraved on the backs. Golden statues lined the walls, and I squinted to see if I recognized any of the figures, but it was dark, like nighttime.

And there, at the head of the empty table, sat the largest man I'd ever seen. Even sitting down he seemed to fill the screen. He wore the same overalls I remembered, but the buckles were made of beaten gold, and underneath he wore a white shirt also trimmed in gold. He was bald and his dark skin gleamed even in the low light. At his feet, leaning against the edge of the chair, rested a mighty hammer, nearly as tall as I was, with a shining metal head and a carved wooden shaft. And yet . . . there was something off about the whole scene.

Bags under his eyes, head propped in one hand, his other fingers tapping on the armrest of the chair.

John Henry, leader of the gods of MidPass, looked tired.

I'd just opened my mouth to greet him when—

"What do you want?" he snapped.

My jaws clamped shut. I'd never heard him like this. Had I interrupted something important? I started to apologize when I saw Anansi waving at me out the corner of my eye. He was crouched in the very bottom right of the screen, holding a finger over his lips and shaking his head. *Don't speak,* he mouthed.

I frowned. I was about to ask him what was wrong when John Henry looked up.

"I said," the giant folk hero said in his unmistakable rumble, anger coloring his voice. "What. Do. You. Want?"

Before I could stammer out a response, the screen rippled. Someone else was in the hall with him. Heavy footsteps sounded, and then a metal-covered arm entered the screen. A clawlike finger pointed at John Henry. I gulped. Waves of... *wrongness* radiated from that hand. I couldn't explain it. But John Henry seemed to know whoever it was.

Then the shadowy figure spoke.

"You know what has to be done." That voice. Something between a hiss and a roar. It was filled with pain...barely repressed, raw, and scalding. As if every word hurt. It was so awful, even John Henry winced at it.

"And I've told you that's impossible. Foolish, I reckon."

A low growl rumbled through the hall. "What is foolish, *grum grum*, is to let ourselves be chained like this. At any moment, what happened to us before could happen again. We need to take steps to prevent it. Already the whispers are starting. The ancestors and spirits are fleeing."

Ancestors and spirits fleeing? I looked at the barn. Could it be?

"We must act," the voice continued. "Unless...you'd rather see us burn again."

CRACK!

John Henry's massive hand had slammed down on the

table. The echo filled the room and rattled my eardrums. He leaned forward, a furious expression on his face, but I also saw the exhaustion in his eyes. Wrinkles at the corners. He was dead tired, and whatever they were discussing had obviously been the source of many arguments in the past. He slid back his chair, stood up, and put his hands on his hips.

The shadowy figure came closer to the table, their cloak obscuring their features. Whoever it was, they were large. Very large. A hand reached out and touched the back of the chair where John Henry had been sitting.

The one his hammer was resting against.

An alarm sounded in my mind. I opened my mouth to yell a warning, but again Anansi held up a hand. Curiosity was written all over his face. I hesitated, then bit my lip and settled back to watch.

"You know it's true, *grum grum*. The fate of our world, our very lives, was left in the hands of an impostor. A charlatan. And he did not get the job done. What happened before can happen again. And while he flew away, reaping all the glory, you and I had to fight to rebuild and keep our people together."

Impostor? Did he mean Anansi? But we *had* gotten the job done. We'd closed the tear between the worlds. I looked at Anansi, but he seemed just as confused as I was.

John Henry was shaking his head. "I understand your pain, friend, truly I do. But what you're asking... I reckon it's not time for that. Don't rightly know if it ever will be." The massive folk hero turned around in a circle and scratched his scalp. "Something else has been bothering me, though...."

The shrouded figure raised one hand, as if in mock confusion. "Oh? *Grum grum*, what could bother the mighty John Henry? The steel-driving man, isn't that what they call you?"

I didn't like the tone in the growly voice, and the alarms going off inside my mind grew louder. Anansi put a finger to his lips to keep me quiet. Was he trying to identify the stranger?

"Well," John Henry said with a drawl, "we're on the highest floor of this here palace, protected by my powers and those of Rose and Sarah. Even old Nyame put his wards in place. Them statues? The sky god had them set up to alert me, in case something evil comes outta that sea again." He faced the visitor. "And you know what's strange? Ever since you stepped in here, *every single one of them has been screaming in my ear.*"

The folk hero leaned forward, his palms out and an odd expression on his face. Hurt? Betrayal?

"What have you done?" John Henry asked.

The other person's hand fell, and a heavy sigh sounded. For one second I thought it was a sign of remorse.

The leader of MidPass must've thought the same thing, because he lifted his hands to his face, exhaustion still weighing on him.

And at that moment, the shadowy hand moved to the handle of the hammer.

That's when I realized how wrong I was.

The only remorse that mysterious figure had was for what they were about to do.

The stranger's hand lifted the hammer high in the air, and the cloak's hood slipped off for the first time. I could see the head clearly... and I wished I hadn't. What I'd thought was armor, or a metal of some sort, was even worse. I'd seen it before, in Alke. And more recently, in my nightmares. Every night.

It was the snarling head of an iron monster. A bossling.

"JOHN HENRY!" I screamed.

The giant folk hero flinched, then looked up. His eyes met mine. "Tristan?"

A growl ripped through the phone's speaker and I realized I shouldn't have drawn John Henry's attention. I'd distracted him. Left him vulnerable. His head was turned, and now—

The monster swung the hammer down in a vicious arc, and the screen went black.

5
BURIED TRAUMA

"TRISTAN? YOU ALL RIGHT, BABY?"

He's coming.

Bosslings. Fetterlings. Brand flies. Hullbeasts.

He's coming.

I couldn't see the spirits, but their voices were still ring-ing in my head, swirling around my worry about John Henry. Was the big guy okay?

"Tristan?"

He's coming, he's coming, he's coming. Beware, beware, he's coming. The Shamble Man is coming. The Shamble Man. THE SHAMBLE MAN!

"TRISTAN!"

I looked up. Nana stood in front of me, a flour-dusted apron hanging around her neck and both hands on her hips as she waved a dough-covered spatula at me. I sat at the old wooden table in the kitchen, the SBP facedown in front of me and the smell of baking rolls in the air. A sheen of sweat gleamed on Nana's brow from the combined heat of the oven and the summer day.

"Sorry, Nana," I said. "What'd you say?"

"Hmph. I saaaid, are you all right? You sitting there like you done lost your puppy." Nana squinted at me over her glasses before she turned back to the rolls rising on the counter. She checked them, then opened the oven and slid the pan next to the two other trays browning inside. The smell washed over me and my stomach grumbled. Nana snorted. "At least your appetite is acting normal. I'm over here telling you this story, and you ain't even listening."

I'd asked Nana to help me document more stories. You know, so I could do what I was supposed to do as an Anansesem. Whenever she thought of a good one, I'd grab a seat and turn on the Listen Chile app and record our culture. It felt good to do that, you get me? Like I was helping to keep our history alive.

Unfortunately, the events of the last hour had me shook. Literally. My hands fumbled with the phone as I tried to pause the recording app.

"I'm sorry, Nana, which one were we doing?"

My grandmother started rolling out another batch of dough and pursed her lips. "Anansi and the moon. The one where his sons saved his behind after his mouth ran up a check it couldn't cash. Trouble Seer, Road Builder, River

Drinker, Skinner... Now, what were the names of those last two boys of his?"

As Nana muttered to herself, my mind wandered again. *The Shamble Man.* It sounded like someone straight out of my nightmares. I shuddered. Was that who had attacked John Henry...? How was I supposed to help? What could I do?

"Stone Thrower and Ground Pillow, that's it. Hey! You woolgatherin' again?" A piece of dough hit my forehead and I blinked. Nana was staring at me, a larger ball of the floury stuff in her hands. "What's wrong with you? Thought my grandbaby would be happy, putting that huge boy on his behind like that. Walter sure ain't stopped crowing about it. And if he don't get in here and help me with this meal, I'm gonna put him on *his* behind."

That brought a smile to my face. We were hosting Reggie and his team along with some of the neighbors for dinner, a friendly get-together for a (not so) friendly sparring match. Roasted chicken, rolls, vegetable lasagna for vegetarians, and Nana's famous and award-winning key lime pie for dessert. It should have been the highlight of the day. But...

My smile faded, and the anxiety returned.

Was John Henry okay? Who was his attacker? The image of the bossling clutching the hammer in its shackle hands sent shivers down my spine. The rusted-iron color, the jagged maw... I squeezed my eyes shut and tried to slow my breathing.

The table creaked, and when I opened my eyes, Nana sat across from me, concern on her face.

"You got something you need to talk about?" she asked.

I hesitated. What could I say? The magical world that I'd brought to the brink of disaster and then saved might be in trouble again? And I felt powerless to help?

"Tristan?"

I took a deep breath. "I . . . I've been having bad dreams, Nana. Really bad. About . . . something that happened before, and I guess I'm scared it might happen again." That wasn't exactly a lie. A generalization, maybe, but it was still true.

Nana nodded. "You wanna tell me what your nightmare is about?" I opened my mouth, then closed it, and she patted my hand. "It's all right. You don't have to if you don't want to. But talking about it with someone might help. Isn't that what your therapist back north said?"

I nodded. "Mr. Richardson. Yeah, I mean, yes. He said to talk about it slowly, or in pieces, if I wasn't ready to talk about the whole thing."

"Exactly. 'Cause it sounds like you've gone through some trauma."

"Trauma?"

Nana squeezed my hand and then got up to check the rolls in the oven. "Yes, baby. Trauma. A rough patch in your life. Something that deeply distressed you. Can be physical or emotional, or a combination of the two." She pinched off a piece of dough, rolled it between her hands until it was really long and thin, and then laid it on the flour-covered table. "Say this is how your life normally looks. Well, something traumatic can do this." She smooshed a portion of the dough snake in the middle with her thumb, so it was flat. "Or it can do this." She pulled a different section into a sharp spike. "And part of what makes trauma so difficult is the period afterward. Figuring out why you're hurting, and how you can heal.... There's no easy solution, baby. But at some point, you might have to talk about it, even if it's to yourself. Especially if it's to yourself. Sometimes we can be our own worst obstacles to healing. Understand?"

I studied the dough snake and nodded slowly. Sometimes I felt like that squashed part, as if the weight of the world—*two* worlds!—were pressing down on me. And other times were more like that spike....

"Nana," I said slowly. "Can a whole bunch of people experience trauma at the same time?"

A sad smile crossed her face. "Of course, baby. Sometimes an evil will rock a community, strip their will and feeling right from them, until they're raw and bleeding and hurting, inside and out. Tulsa, Oklahoma. Ferguson, Missouri. Oh yes, baby, a whole city can hurt all at once."

"And... how does a city like that—I mean, how do they all heal?"

Nana sighed. "Well, it's like I said, just on a larger scale. At some point, it needs to be talked about."

I thought about the spirits in the barn. The horror on

their faces. They'd fled from something—something that had affected them all. I clenched my fists. I needed to talk to them.

I was an Anansesem, after all. Finding and carrying other people's stories was sort of my thing.

"Thanks, Nana," I said, scooting back from the table, my jaw set with determination. "That really helped."

"Of course, sugar. Now, before you slink away, scrub some of these dishes. Then find your grandfather and tell him he better come and help. Ain't no maids here." Nana raised an eyebrow and I grinned.

"Yes, ma'am."

Grandmothers. They're the best.

When I reached the barn, however, the motivation I'd gained by talking to Nana faded away. A few people, including Reggie and his trainer, still lingered around the boxing ring, talking. Granddad was there, too, and I hesitated. I didn't want them to see what I planned on doing.

The tingling feeling started up again immediately after I crossed the threshold—so strong, I nearly flinched—as if imploring me to hurry up. I didn't see any spirits, but Reggie's eyes immediately locked with mine and a frown crossed his face.

"Ignore him," Anansi said. His voice spoke softly through my earbuds. "Focus, boy."

I inhaled deeply and moved to the far corner. Reggie's gaze followed me . . . until his trainer tapped his shoulder. He turned around, and I took advantage of the opportunity to duck behind a stack of crates. I pulled aside a dusty burlap sack to reveal a small spade and a patch of dirt slightly darker than the surrounding packed floor.

Anansi whistled in my ear. "You were serious. You really did bury it. I'm impressed."

"Thanks."

"I'm impressed that a so-called hero would do so much to shirk his responsibility. Astounding."

The comment stung, but I bit back the retort I wanted to make and instead grabbed the spade and started digging. I paused every few seconds to make sure no one was coming over. Not sure how I would explain this. *Oh yeah, I just buried this jewelry I received from gods in another realm, no biggie.*

THUNK!

The spade hit something solid. I widened the shallow hole, scraped away loose clods of dirt, then reached down and pulled out a cloth-covered box. When I slid the covering away, Anansi scoffed in my ear.

"Really? That was the best you could do? You receive the blessings of some of the most powerful gods in existence and you hide them, bury them, in *this*?"

"Hey," I whispered in protest. "It's all I had on such short notice. Besides, it's waterproof."

"But the insult. The disgrace!"

I brushed away a few specks of dirt from the multicolored plastic case and patted it gently. "You're just jealous. You wish you had a lunch box as glorious as this one. Now hush, you're going to get me in trouble." I unlatched the clasp and opened the old Darkwing Duck lunch box. I'd had it for years, ever since the grandson of one of Nana's friends had given it to me while snickering. Kids.

Inside, on top of a wadded-up towel I'd hoped Nana would never notice missing from her untouchable stack of "good linens," lay a corded leather bracelet with several adinkra charms fastened to it. A spider's web, representing Kwaku Anansi. It gave my stories power and also warned me when trouble was near. The crossed swords of the akofena, for when I needed to defend several places at once. Gye Nyame, the sky god's symbol, helped me tell the difference between illusion and reality. The Amagqirha's glimmering bead from Isihlangu enabled me to see spirits.

And flanking them all were the gloves John Henry had given to me. Fingerless, made of thin, worn brown leather, and branded with the sign of a hammer just below the knuckles, they didn't look like much. But they were imbued with incredible strength. I pulled them on, flexed my fingers, and smiled. Then I slid on the bracelet. The tingling sensation I'd been feeling exploded into a rippling wave of electricity that washed over me. A thunderous chorus of drums erupted in my ears. The rhythm pounded my bones and shook my soul. I grinned. It felt good. But my grin quickly faded as the spirits' rush of emotions returned even stronger. The worry. The terror. The desperation.

Please...

He's coming!

The Shamble Man is coming.

You have to help!

I had to talk to them, and quickly, before this Shamble Man, whoever he was, hurt anyone else. But where were they?

"If you're quite finished with your dramatic reveal, could we please hurry up to the part where we actually do something?" Anansi asked impatiently.

I got to my feet. "Says the god famous for being lazy. Besides, I can't do anything while Reggie—"

A voice interrupted me. "Can't do anything while Reggie what?"

"Busted," whispered Anansi.

I turned to find Reggie towering over me, glaring, his bare hands balled into loose fists. His eyes dropped to the hole in the ground, then took in the lunch box, and a scowl crossed his face.

"You talking trash behind my back while you're digging in the dirt and playing pretend? Some boxer. The world-famous Strong Gym, huh? Can't believe I wasted my time coming here. Could've shadowboxed and done better."

Hot anger swept aside my embarrassment at being caught with the lunch box. "I still knocked you down."

"Luck, that's all."

"Yeah, losers always say that."

Reggie's eyes narrowed. "What did you call me?"

I started to take a step forward, but the tingling sensation swept over me again. Right. Priorities. "Look, I don't have time for this. Why don't you go eat—my nana cooked for everyone—and we'll just forget we ever met." I tried to step past him to go where the voices seemed to be coming from, but Reggie slid over and blocked me.

He stuck a finger in my face. "I don't need your grandmother's trash cooking, and I don't need your trash hospitality. Understand?" He poked my chest.

The barn door opened. Nana stepped inside, her quilting bag in one hand, the other hand on her hip. "Walter? Y'all gonna come set the table, or am I eating by myself? Out here jibber-jabbering. Them green beans ain't gonna snap and sauté themselves, either. I told Tristan to come get you. Tristan! Didn't I tell you—?"

They're coming!

Nana suddenly stopped talking, as if she'd heard the voices as well. But I didn't have a chance to think about that, because Reggie sneered and stabbed me one more time with his finger. "Why don't *you* go eat . . . *your mudpies*," he said with a snicker.

That did it.

I shoved the larger boy in the chest with one hand. Just one hand, I swear!

Reggie flew backward across the barn, and for the second time today, landed on his backside. This time it wasn't at my feet, but a dozen yards away.

"The gloves," Anansi hissed in my ear.

Sweet peaches, I was wearing John Henry's *gloves*!

I stepped forward, ready to apologize, but it was too late. Reggie slammed his hands against the ground and climbed to his feet. With the look on his face, he could've been arrested for attempted murder. He sprinted forward with his fists up, ignoring the shouts of Tony the Trainer and Granddad. The giant boy came closer and closer until he was within striking distance, then lunged forward, his right fist arcing toward my head. I knew that if that punch connected, I was a goner. I ducked, then realized the truth.

It was a feint.

An uppercut rose through the air, aimed right at my chin.

Good-bye, world, I thought, closing my eyes and bracing for impact.

6
GHOST CATS

I WAITED AND WAITED, AND...

Nothing.

A cold wind swept through the room.

The noise faded away, like someone had turned down the volume knob on the world. I opened my eyes and looked around, confused, but what I saw didn't make any sense. Nearly everything in the barn had gone completely still. Reggie was frozen in mid-lunge, a snarl etched on his face. A mosquito hovered inches above Tony the Trainer's nose, getting ready to chow down. The man himself had his cheeks puffed out and his eyes crossed, in the middle of blowing his whistle to stop the fight after the haymaker landed. Two of the spectators were frozen in mid-laugh, both of them clutching their bellies with their heads thrown back. And one older man had his back sort of turned, shielding himself from the others, his index finger shoved so far up his nose he could probably smell his knuckle.

"What is going on?" I whispered under my breath.

Something fluttered in the corner of my eye and I sighed, thankful for *some* movement. It was the river spirit. . . . But how was I able to see her without using Anansi's filter? Wait . . . the bracelet! I must have activated the spirit bead.

The girl stared directly at me, her eyes wide and her mouth working in a silent shout. She raised her arm and pointed with the universally understood signal for *Behind you!*

A cat stood in the middle of the ring, its tail swishing angrily from side to side. No, there were two of them! They weren't ordinary cats, either. Each was as big as a rottweiler. Matted brown fur covered them from the tops of their ears to the tips of their tails, and two large fangs extended down from their upper jaws, making them look like saber-toothed tigers. But that wasn't the scariest part.

I could see right through them. They were spirits, too.

The cats had the biggest, brightest white eyes I'd ever seen. I mean they were huge, like the size of my fists. At the moment, those eyes were focused on Nana, sitting on a bench behind me. She wasn't frozen—she was . . . quilting?

I took a step forward. The cats whipped their heads around, and I stopped when I heard, "Don't. Move."

Nana's voice cracked like a whip. She was stitching so fast

it looked like she was twirling her needle like a miniature baton. The spool of thread in her lap got thinner and thinner while the quilt she was working on grew in a dazzling golden pile at her feet. The cats were mesmerized by it. Mangy tails swished, and wide, unblinking eyes followed every movement Nana made.

Wait a minute.

Nana could move? She could talk? And she could see the cats?

"Nana—" I started, but she cut me off.

"I'll explain later, child."

"But..."

"Later! Right now we've got to take care of these ole Murder Whisker twins. I can keep them distracted for now, but I'm running out of this here special thread."

I felt Nyame's adinkra pressing against my wrist. The sky god's charm helped me see the stories that made up the world around us. I hadn't used it since returning to good old Alabama, but something about Nana's "special thread" made me think...

I closed my eyes. After a second, maybe two, I opened them.

"Sweet peaches..."

Nana's thread blinded me with its dazzling brilliance. The spool was a blaze of copper and bronze, and she cradled her project in her arms as if she were swaddling the sun. Words moved along the stitches, but I couldn't look at them long enough to read them, not without three pairs of sunglasses. I closed my eyes again and shook my head to clear the after-images. I'd always known Nana was full of surprises, but—

"C'mon, child, ain't no time for dawdlin'." Nana stared at me over her horn-rimmed glasses. "I need your help."

Look, when your grandmother says she needs your help, you don't ask why or for how long. You jump to attention and get ready to go to work, no matter what she asks. That's what grandchildren are supposed to do.

She nodded at a bucket sitting on the floor just outside the ropes of the ring. "Grab a handful of them rags when I say so. Count of three, you throw them as hard as you can at those things. You hear me?"

I looked at the faded blue bucket. Granddad used the dented plastic container to hold dirty, sweaty, funky towels that boxers and trainers discarded. It was supposed to be emptied into the washer after every training session, but in all the hype and commotion around this sparring session, I guess I'd forgotten. So it was filled to the brim with damp nastiness.

"Uh..." I said.

"Don't fix your lips to say anything other than 'Yes, ma'am,'" Nana warned. "Do you hear me?"

"Yes, ma'am," I said. "Hurl funk at the felines. Got it."

"Good. Here we go, now. One. Two. THREE!"

I took off. Head down, arms pumping. I dodged the frozen spectators, avoided Reggie, then slid next to the overflowing bucket and grabbed it. I hoisted it over my head with both hands and turned around, ready to toss the contents with all my might. I didn't know how it was supposed to work, but if Nana wanted me to throw stinky laundry at the cats, then that's what I was going to do.

At least, I'd planned to.

But then Nana stood up. She reached out, sewing project in her hands, and spread her arms wide. When the quilt unfurled, I felt my heart swell. The large blanket shone with a steady light. Within glimmering squares of ivory-white fabric, Nana had used her special thread to stitch a variety of magnificent patterns. When combined, they formed an entire landscape portrait of . . .

"Our farm," I whispered.

The house stood in the middle, along with the barn we were standing in now. There was the cornfield behind it, a golden-brown color that seemed to shift the more I looked at it, like stalks blowing in the wind. A river of words circled the quilt's border. Bright blue and shining silver, they rippled as I read them.

I was born in the shallows of a mighty river,
Or in the maelstrom,
Or in the hurricane,

Or in the lakes of the people.

I am—

"Tristan!" Nana's shout dragged me back to the present, and I realized my mistake. The spirit cats had dropped into a crouch and their tails swished angrily, like twin lionesses ready to pounce. You know what I mean. That thing where a cat is ready to attack and destroy your ankle and there's nothing you can do to stop it.

Except in this case the cats were monsters/haints/ghosts/ all of the above, the size of attack dogs, and instead of an ankle, it looked like they wanted to maul my grandmother.

Not on my watch.

"Now, Tristan!"

The cats sprang forward and I flung the bucket at them. The balled-up towels tumbled out and I wrinkled my nose. Those things stank—the odor hit me like a sucker punch to the nostrils. And when they hit the cats, the spirits reacted like they'd been scalded with hot oil. They both jumped, each opening its mouth in a silent yowl, then starting to twitch in midair before collapsing on the ground.

I ran forward, eager to put the finishing stomp on the terrifying tabbies, but Nana's shout stopped me in my tracks.

"Don't, boy! This ain't over yet."

Too late.

A sudden peal of thunder shook the whole barn, just as the ghost cats flipped onto their paws and, as one, launched themselves at me. Their shining eyes pinned me in place. I screamed, expecting to feel a burst of pain at any moment as they clawed me to pieces.

Just when it appeared I was doomed, a golden blur zipped past me toward the cats, so bright I had to close my eyes. The scent of ozone—that lingering smell after a lightning strike or electric shock—floated beneath my nose.

"Sweet peaches," I muttered. "I'm getting too old for this."

I heard a groan and opened my eyes. I couldn't believe what I saw. Nana sat on the floor near the spot where the cat spirits used to be, her quilt in tatters at her feet. That explained the blur—my grandmother must have thrown the glowing blanket over those monsters.

As the quilt dimmed slowly like a dying candle, the other people in the barn came back to life. With me out of the way, Reggie lunged at nothing and fell on his face. Tony the Trainer blew his whistle while swatting at the mosquito. The spectators finished laughing abruptly, as if they'd forgotten what was so funny.

Meanwhile, Nana stared at me with a peculiar expression. Confusion? Sadness? Understanding? Frustration? Maybe a combination of all four.

"It's about time you and I had a talk," she said in a hoarse voice. She frowned at the sound of her own words, then sighed and pushed her glasses up the bridge of her nose and tried to stand. But when she got to her knees, Nana's face contorted, and she let out a hiss of pain. My heart jumped into my throat. She dropped back onto the ground, sending torn pieces of quilt scattering like dead leaves as she clutched her chest.

"Nana!" I shouted and scrambled to her side.

"Get . . . Walter," she whispered, and her eyes fluttered shut.

7
STRONG BLOOD

REGGIE'S RING DOCTOR AND GRANDDAD STEPPED OUT OF MY grandparents' bedroom. Quietly. Carefully. The way adults do when something *serious* has happened and they don't want to talk about it in front of kids, so they exchange Looks and tiptoe to another room.

The doctor was a short and stocky Afro-Latina with curly black-and-brown hair pulled into a bun. Her small medical kit had the name ALMEIDA TORRES stitched on the side, and she flashed me a warm smile before murmuring to Granddad in the hallway. I was sitting on the large fluffy couch in the middle of the living room, my fingers tracing the flowers on the dust cover, my bare feet slowly sliding back and forth over the plush area rug.

Thunder boomed in the distance. No rain or lightning yet, but with the dark clouds gathering outside, it felt like one was going to unleash its fury any minute now. As if we needed this day—evening, I guess—to get any worse.

After Nana fell, Reggie and his trainer had helped us carry her into the house on a bench. That had been several hours ago, and since then I hadn't moved from the couch. I couldn't.

"She's going to be fine," I heard Dr. Torres say quietly to Granddad. "It was more exhaustion than anything—some stress as well. She needs to rest. That's important. Lots of rest, and I put in a prescription for her blood pressure."

Granddad seemed to sink into himself. I'd never seen him look so haggard, so . . . so unsure. He kept wringing his hands slowly, carefully, as if there was something clinging to them and it was dogging him relentlessly.

"But she's gonna be all right, you said?" he asked. "I mean . . . she's gonna be fine?"

"Yes, Mr. Strong. But she needs rest. Also, have you thought of . . ."

Their voices trailed off as the two moved into the kitchen. I watched the empty hallway for a few moments, then looked at Nana's door, which was open a crack. It wasn't fair. She'd gotten hurt while trying to protect me from something I should've been able to take care of myself. I was the Anansesem; I had the adinkra bracelet from the gods of Alke. I was so upset, I started talking to myself. "If I hadn't flinched, if I hadn't frozen, if I—"

"You're doing it again," came a small voice.

The SBP rested on my lap. Anansi reclined on the Contacts app icon and swung his six legs like a child. His floppy hat was pulled down over his eyes and he was nodding gently to a beat only he could hear. When I didn't say anything, he lifted his hat with one finger and shook his head. "That thing you do where you make everything about you. It's not your fault, boy."

"But she was trying to save me," I whispered.

He shrugged. "Most people would have. Okay, I know a few who would've just watched you suffer without lifting a finger. But that's not your grandmother. She saw someone in trouble, someone she loved dearly, and she acted. I've seen you do similar things."

"Not when I needed to most," I said bitterly. "And those . . . whatever those creatures were—they could still be out there somewhere, waiting to attack us again. We need to figure out what's going on, Anansi. Everything's falling to pieces and I don't know why. If only I could've—"

"You know," Anansi said, talking right over me, "ifs are pretty powerful. You can collect them like a lazy man collects excuses. If this, if that. If I can't, if I could. Better watch it, little storyteller, or you'll build yourself a wall of ifs you can't get around. Now, ever since you gave me more permissions, I've been digging around in this here Story Box Phonogram—"

"Phone," I muttered.

"—and I've managed to cook up some interesting things. Which shouldn't come as a surprise to anyone, of course."

"Of course."

"I've got something that's going to spice up your soup, you just watch."

I wrinkled my brow suspiciously.

"Don't look at me like that," Anansi said, making an innocent face. "I'm trying to help, honest! I'm a web developer, after all."

My brow wrinkled even further. It probably looked like someone had balled up my forehead like a piece of trash.

Anansi raised his right hand. "I promise, young Anansesem, I have only the purest intentions. I just need a little more time. Let me do my thing and work my magic, and I'll have a web app hopping like ole Frog did when I told him I'd bought him a brand-new hot tub."

I rolled my eyes, then squinted. "Fine. Hey, wait... Where's your other spider-arm?"

He cleared his throat and pulled it from behind his back. I shook my head. He'd probably had his fingers crossed the whole time. You can never trust a trickster god. But at this point, who else could I rely on?

A cough sounded from Nana's bedroom. After a second, another one came, and I dropped the phone on the couch and tiptoed over to the door. I peeked inside, but couldn't see anything, because it was so dark.

"Hello?" Her feeble voice rang out, followed by another cough. "Is anyone there? I need some water. Let me just—"

I heard the bed creak, and I quickly pushed the door open wider. "Nana, you're not supposed to get up! You have to rest!"

"Tristan? Is that you?"

"Yes, ma'am. I'll get you some water, hold on." I walked to the kitchen, ready to explain what I was doing to Granddad and Dr. Torres, but it was empty. They were out on the front porch. The doctor was pointing at the sky, a worried look on her face. I grabbed a glass, filled it with some water, then hurried back to Nana.

I paused before I entered. I rarely went into my grandparents' bedroom, out of respect for their privacy. (And maybe Nana's leaning tower of hatboxes by the door scared me. Seriously. She had more hats than I had sneakers, and *that* was saying something.) It smelled of antiseptic and Granddad's aftershave. Nana sat up on their queen-size bed, pillows propping her upright as if she were sitting in a chair.

She smiled at me when I handed her the cup. "Thanks, baby," she said. When I turned to go, she reached out and touched my arm. "Set yourself down and stay awhile. I expect we need to talk about a few things."

I'd been hoping she would say that. "Really? About what?" I did my best to imitate Anansi and smiled innocently.

Nana's stare could've melted ice cream and stripped paint off a wall. "You really gon' try that on me?" she asked.

I hung my head. "No, ma'am."

"Good." She took a sip, then another, and sighed. "Used to be a couple li'l old cats weren't nothing. They should've been a breeze for me to take care of."

"I'm sorry, Nana," I said in a low voice. "They were coming for me, and I froze."

"Shoot, boy, ain't no need for you to be feeling sorry for yourself. One plat-eye is more than I expect someone to handle on their own the first time, let alone two."

"One what?"

"Plat-eye. That's what your great-grandmother called them. She was born over on the Sea Islands." Nan shifted, straightening her back, and I smothered a smile. Sick or not, she was going to tell her story.

"Plat-eyes are spirits that still need something done. Can't move on until they get it resolved. Might be treasure they buried, or a wrong they committed, or any number of things. Most of them are harmless, but you gotta be careful with them—that's why I stepped in. Them things will change shape and grow and haunt you until you can't take it no more."

"Wait. Change shape and grow? Are they Pokémon?"

Nana looked down her nose and over the top of her glasses. "Pokey-what?"

"Never mind."

She blinked, then sniffed. "As I was *saying* . . . the only way to get rid of a plat-eye, if you don't know how to solve its problem, is to keep something foul on you at all times. In the old days, folks would've used gunpowder, but it looks like a grandson's sweat towels work just as well."

"So they're gone for good?" I asked hopefully, but my shoulders slumped when Nana shook her head.

"No, child, we just shooed 'em away for a bit. If they were looking for you, they'll be back in a different form next time, but you'll recognize them." Nana tapped the side of her glasses. "The eyes. They can't change them eyes."

She leaned over the side of the bed, looked down at the fragments of her quilt in the bag on the floor, and sighed.

"I'll help you fix that," I said.

Nana smiled. "Sometimes there ain't no fixing something, baby. If you wanna rebuild, you gotta break it down and start all over. Might seem hard, but it's the only way if you wanna get it right."

I helped her sit back on her pillow. "Nana, why do you think those plat-eyes were looking for me?"

"You know why," she said. "'Cause you could see 'em, hear 'em."

"But so could you. . . ."

"There's something special about you," Nana continued, as if she hadn't heard me. "Known it since you was born, child. You got Granddad's and my blood running through your veins—Strong blood. What is it you kids say? Game recognize game."

I rolled my eyes. "No one says that anymore, Nana."

"Well, they should. Soon as I catch up to the slang, y'all go and change it. Rude children. But yes, I've always known that you were special. I also know the places you been, the people you've talked to."

"You do?"

Nana nodded and leaned closer. "Alke."

The word started as a whisper and grew into a gust that stirred the blankets. A shiver of excitement rippled down my spine. Finally, someone in this world who could understand what I'd been through, what I'd seen!

"Nana, this is incredible!" I whisper-shouted. "Have you been to the Golden Crescent? Or Isihlangu? Did they let you in the front door, or did you have to pretend to be trash, like I did? And the stories! Is that where you got your stories?"

Nana laughed. "Easy, child, easy. Yes, I got a few stories from them. Left quite a few behind, too. Can't help it—all of Alke is a story. You should know that by now. Didn't you see the special thread I was using?"

I started to ask another question, but just then the bedroom door opened and Granddad stepped in. He flicked on the light and I stood up quickly. His eyes were red and he was still wringing his hands. "Okay, Tristan, that's enough. Your grandmother needs her rest."

His tone brooked no argument, so I kissed Nana on the forehead and headed out. As I crossed the threshold, she called out to me.

"Tristan, remember what I said, now. You got Strong blood. Whatever comes calling, you remember that."

I nodded, then shut the door. I headed toward my own room and then stopped.

Strong blood. Plat-eyes. Spirits needing help.

Enough was enough.

It was time for the Anansesem to do his job.

8

THE MAN IN THE IRON-MONSTER MASK

I STEPPED INTO THE BARN WITH A FLASHLIGHT ON AND ALL MY Anansesem powers active. My ears thrummed as the world sang around me. My reflection appeared in a mirror Granddad had mounted on the wall for shadowboxing, and what I saw made me pause.

A tall Black boy, hoodie pulled over his head, with glowing golden eyes.

I shivered and then, holding the flashlight in one hand and the ancestral bead from my bracelet in the other, scanned the barn. The place was empty ... except for something shimmering in the corner. The river spirit. I'd half expected the girl to be gone like the rest, but she still floated there, staring at me with a pleading expression, and this time I didn't ignore it.

I put an overturned bucket on a bench and propped the SBP on top of it, opening the camera so Anansi could join our conversation. The more I focused on her, the brighter the spirit girl seemed to flare.

"Please," came her faint voice. "Please, he's coming. You have to save her."

A bright blue aura surrounded her transparent body. Not the blue of a clear sky, or the blue of the ripe berries that Nana baked into her pies. No, it was more of a bluish green, the color of lakes and seas and oceans, and her outline was the white of rushing rapids. Her dress and braids gently swirled around her as if she were floating in water at that very second.

"Who are you?" I finally asked, my voice barely above a whisper.

Turquoise eyes studied mine. "Ninah. I am called Ninah. And I need your help, and the help of the tiny god you've trapped."

"I'm not trapped," Anansi protested. "I'm one of them virtue assistants. Tell her, Tristan."

"You mean *virtual* assistant. But that's not important. Ninah," I said, turning back to the spirit. "How did you get here? Is there another tear between our worlds? You aren't here to steal something from me, are you?" A certain sap-covered doll baby came to my mind. "I swear, I need an Alkean alarm system."

Ninah shook her head. "River spirits do not steal, Anansesem. We give and we heal. But yes, I arrived as the others did, through a seam. But that doesn't matter. Someone has taken her, and we need you to get her back. Only you have the power and knowledge to do so."

I couldn't help it. My back straightened and I stood a bit taller.

Anansi smirked. "Pardon me, spirit of the river, but you keep mentioning 'her.' Who exactly has been taken from your home in the Grasslands? And—no offense, boy—why is Tristan uniquely equipped to perform this rescue?"

The river spirit looked surprised. "Because he holds the Story Box. He has the blessings of the gods of Alke. He is the Anansesem, and the hero of the Battle of the Bay."

"Is that what they're calling it now?" I muttered.

"Hmm." Anansi stroked his chin. "I'll come back to that undeserved praise. But you still haven't mentioned *who* was taken."

Have you ever seen a spirit sigh? Their aura fades a little. I was suddenly more aware of how faint Ninah was. It must have been taking great effort on her part to stay there and talk to me, and I felt guilty. But that emotion disappeared when she spoke again.

"The Shamble Man took my mother," she said softly.

The SBP vibrated, startling me. Anansi was pacing back and forth, and the screen was flashing. "Your mother?" he asked. His voice was loud, almost as if he were standing right next to us. "Is she—?"

Ninah shook her head again—sadly this time. "I don't know."

I looked between the two. They knew something I didn't. Anansi glanced at me with an expression that said *Later.*

I scratched my head. "I don't even know who this Shamble Man is." Again I wondered whether he was the one who had attacked John Henry. If so, I couldn't take him on by myself.... "Or where he's taken your mother. Are they in Alke? With my grandmother sick, I'm not sure I should be leaving right now...."

"But that's just it." Ninah looked from me to the phone, where Anansi sat in his web. "There's no time left."

A chill ran down my spine. "What do you mean?"

"He's on his way. The Shamble Man is coming *here.*"

Her words punched me in the gut harder than Reggie had earlier. I stumbled back a few steps and collapsed on the bench. A thundering roar filled my ears. It felt like a storm was surging around me, and my fists were clenched so hard I thought my fingernails would pierce my palms.

"Tristan."

When I raised my eyes, I saw that Anansi and Ninah were both staring at me. No, they were staring at what was floating in midair in front of me: four gleaming black boxing gloves with emblems of crossed swords. The akofena, the Swords of War, had come to life. Okay, then.

I stood and took a deep breath. "What do I have to—? OUCH!"

Something had burned my wrist, like that time I brushed against my mother's flatiron before church. Searing pain.

"Oh no." I looked down at the adinkra bracelet dangling at the end of my arm.

Anansi and Ninah hadn't been staring at the floating gloves.

The very first adinkra I'd received, the one my best friend, the dead seventh grader now known as Tupacrates, had attached to his journal, Anansi's personal symbol . . .

It was glowing.

"Iron monsters," I whispered.

My nightmare had been ripped out of my head and given life.

There were two versions. In scenario number one, I'm at some sort of public event and everyone's looking at me. Maybe it's a school assembly, or a talent show, or that one time Nana took me to her church and I had to lead the choir in singing the Black National Anthem and I forgot the words.

Forgot. The. Words.

Anyway.

No matter where I'm at, though, I'm missing something extremely important and vital.

Clothes.

That's right—I'm in front of a bunch of people in my tighty-whities.

Scenario number two is even worse. This nightmare started after I came back from Alke. I'm running after someone, someone I love. They're being taken from me, and I can't stop it. Sometimes the abductors are iron monsters—fetterlings or hullbeasts; other times it's King Cotton. I can be back in MidPass, in the Drowned Forest, or chasing after a school bus on an icy road, knowing what happens next. I never catch up to them...I always lose.

It repeats over and over until I wake up breathless, panicking. Nana called it trauma, and now I was reliving it. Granddad and Nana were in the house all alone, and something terrifying was about to attack the farm.

It felt like I couldn't run fast enough.

Wind lashed at my face, and the night insects seemed to cackle as they watched my desperate sprint across the hard-packed dirt. My hair stood on end as a jagged bolt of lightning hit the ground, followed by a bone-rattling thunderclap.

BOOM!

Wait. That wasn't thunder.

That sounded like...

I leaped up the front stairs and skidded to a stop on the wooden porch. The door had been smashed open, knocked nearly off the hinges. It was like someone had taken an ax to the farmhouse in a rage.

The lights were off inside. Shadows lurked in the hallway. I wished I hadn't left my flashlight in the barn.

"Hello?" I called.

The only response was silence. I thought I heard something moving around, but it could've just been the wind dancing past me, daring me to go in.

Thought you were a hero, big boy.

I filled my lungs with air and took a step forward. Then another. The moon peeked out from behind a cloud and faint light fell across my shoulders, adding my shadow to the others. I held my breath. Even the crickets outside had gone quiet. A floorboard creaked underfoot, and I winced. But nothing jumped out at me, so maybe—

"So . . . you are the Anansesem, *grum grum*."

I froze, my heart in my throat. The words were muffled, almost garbled, and the voice was deeper than that of anyone I knew. But I recognized it. I'd heard it during the video call with John Henry. So that *had* been the Shamble Man!

"Who's there?" I asked, hating the way my voice shook. "Come out where I can see you!"

The Shamble Man continued as if I hadn't spoken. "The hero of Alke. The savior of Isihlangu." The voice paused, then continued in a harsh growl. "The destroyer of MidPass."

An image of MidPass burning flared in my mind, friends screaming, and I closed my eyes at the sudden wave of pain.

"Yesss, the Destroyer. I like that title better, *grum grum*."
The voice grew lighter, almost playful, as the intruder sang:

"Tristan Strong punched a hole in the sky
And let the evil in.
Cities burned.
Now what did we learn?
Don't let him do it again."

I gritted my teeth, willing myself to ignore the disturbing—
and yet accurate—lyrics. "Stop hiding and come out where I
can see you. Or are you scared? You just gonna shout insults
while hiding?" I held up my left arm so Anansi's adinkra
shone in the darkness like a tiny green star, warning me that
iron monsters were near.

"'Come out,' says the little hero. 'Come out'! But does he
really want me to, *grum grum*? Little man might not like what
he seesss." The words ended in a hiss that swirled from the
far corner, where I thought the door to Nana and Granddad's
bedroom was. There, a group of shadows seemed to ripple on
top of the darkness. Something thumped on the floor, shaking the house, and I thought the refrigerator had fallen over.
But then it thumped again, and again. A chill swept over me
when I realized that what I was hearing were the footsteps
of something massive. Something...monstrous.

A figure slowly emerged. My muscles locked up and a deep
chill settled in my bones as my worst fears became reality.

Two huge feet covered in fetterling chains. Arms and legs

armored with the rotted wood of a hullbeast. The broken, jagged halves of a bossling's manacle-like head rested on either shoulder, and a long, tattered cloak was fastened to them. And in between the iron halves, I could now see a face . . .

"No," I whimpered.

On the face was a gleaming, twisted amber mask, knotted and warped, the eye and mouth holes ringed with the crumpled insect-like bodies of brand flies.

The Shamble Man moved closer, one arm tucked into his cloak, and I took a step back without thinking. He laughed, and the mask shifted slightly. I flushed in hot anger and embarrassment, and I forced myself to hold my ground and clench my fists.

"What do you want?" I shouted.

The mask tilted, as if the wearer found the question amusing. "By grum, the little hero has some courage after all. But he keeps asking questions he might not like the answers to. Look at him shake. Look at him shiver. This is the Destroyer? He is a whelp, a child, *grum grum*."

"I am not—"

"So eager to leap into battle," he continued, talking right over me. "Not knowing what he risks losing." He raised one arm to open the cloak, and in the faint light of my adinkra bracelet I saw two figures curled up in fear on the floor next to him.

Granddad and Nana.

They were holding each other, each trying their best to shield their partner in life, and when they saw me, they stiffened. Granddad struggled to his feet and put up his fists.

"Get out of my house!" he shouted at the monster.

"Walter, don't!" Nana said. "You don't know what—"

"I said, leave!" Granddad edged forward and threw a few jabs at the Shamble Man. But the masked intruder just chuckled, a harsh sound that filled the room with violent foreboding. Granddad bobbed and weaved, then rushed forward with a flurry of punches. I held my breath, hopeful.

An armored hand shoved my grandfather aside, and he collapsed against the far wall.

"Granddad!" I shouted. I started forward, then stopped. The Shamble Man was in my way.

"Finally, some fire. You see, little hero? There was still some pride in that one. But I'm sorry, *grum grum*, I'm not here for the old man. No, not here for him at all. There's another whose legend is just as strong in Alke as your false epic, little hero. Someone who taught you everything she knew. Yesss," he hissed, turning.

"No," I whispered.

The Shamble Man pointed an armored hand at Nana.

"Here we are, *grum grum*."

I didn't think. My body just acted on its own. I lunged forward, desperate to get in between my grandmother and the Shamble Man, but the huge figure sprang into my way and I was forced to throw myself backward with a yelp. Something gleamed in the darkness and a thunderous crash sounded from the spot where I'd stood only a second earlier. I clenched my fists and activated the akofena adinkra, High John the Conqueror's gift to me before the Battle of the Bay. Four obsidian black boxing gloves shimmered into view. When I swung my right fist, two of the gloves mimicked the action in a vicious hook Granddad would've been proud of. . . .

Only to be batted away like flies by a whirling metallic blur. The impact spun me in a circle, and when I turned back around, I froze in confusion.

The masked intruder held something I'd never dreamed of defending myself against. I knew it on sight, had even fought alongside its owner in battle. But that was back in Alke, not in Alabama. And the last time I'd seen it, it had been swinging toward the leader of MidPass.

"Come, little hero. Let me smash you to bits." The masked intruder held up the weapon and prepared to charge. I gulped, my eyes glued to one of the most powerful items in all Alke. A smooth wooden handle carved with symbols. Cold polished iron engraved with the adinkra symbol for strength and protection.

John Henry's hammer.

The hammer slammed down into the floor again and again as the Shamble Man attempted to crush me in my grandparents' kitchen. He didn't chase me, however, and I noticed he never moved far from the doorway. He was stalling for some reason, but I didn't exactly have the time to stop and work through that mystery.

"Why are you doing this?" I shouted as I dodged another swing. The hammer crashed into the sink, demolishing the countertop and sending water spraying into the air.

"'Why?' the little hero asks." The hammer swung again, obliterating the pantry door as I ducked the wave of splintered wood fragments. One of them glanced off my cheek, stinging, and I felt something warm run down my face. "'Why?' says the Destroyer. After burning the homes of thousands. Sending hundreds to lie in chains in the walls of a monster. 'Why?' he asks."

"That wasn't my fault—" I started to protest.

"NOT YOUR FAULT?!" the Shamble Man roared. John Henry's hammer twirled above his head before he swiped at me, the iron head barely missing as it whistled past. It was starting to glow in a familiar way, and I felt I should know what that meant. But it's hard to think when you're dodging and ducking to save your life. The hammer head swung left and right, scraping the floor and scarring the ceiling. "Everything is your fault. Everything! So now I must do what is best for my world, for Alke, and I do it gladly."

He lunged forward, the hammer raised, and I threw myself backward. But he had tricked me. As I tumbled head over heels, the masked intruder stepped into the hallway, scooped up Nana, and tossed her over his shoulder like she was as light as a pillow. She fought him. Somehow she'd grabbed her quilting bag and was smacking the Shamble Man upside the head with it. But it was all in vain.

"Put her down!" I screamed, scrambling to my feet. My akofena shadow gloves appeared again as I started to dash forward, but a swipe of the hammer sent me crashing into the cabinet beneath the kitchen sink.

The Shamble Man turned and pressed the head of the hammer, now glowing hot orange, against the floor of the hall and shoved it downward. A golden seam appeared. It was as if the air unzipped itself and an entrance to another world appeared. Now I remembered where I'd seen this before. John Henry and Brer Rabbit had done the same thing when they sent Gum Baby from Alke into my world. This was another tear, but smaller, controlled. Was this how the spirits were crossing into my world?

"Good-bye, little hero," the Shamble Man said. The hood of his cloak was pulled low, but I still saw red-orange eyes brimming with hate behind the mask he wore. They glared at me with such fury, I took a step back without thinking. "May your heart wither. May your tears fall endlessly, as mine once did."

With that, the man in the amber monster mask stepped toward the glowing seam.

"Nana!" I screamed.

My grandmother, still hammering her kidnapper upside the head, met my eyes. She mouthed something, but I couldn't understand it. My arms reached out to try to grab his swirling cloak, to try and hold him back, but the Shamble Man stepped through the seam between worlds. Behind him the golden line in the floor disappeared, leaving me stumbling to a stop.

They were gone.

9

UNSPOOLING A STORY

"TELL ME AGAIN, SLOWER THIS TIME."

Anansi's stern voice cut through my panicked breathing. I was sitting on the floor of the barn where I'd left the SBP, my head between my knees. Ninah was nowhere to be seen—probably scared off by the Shamble Man. Granddad was back in the house, hollering into the phone at the police while a large welt grew on the side of his head. I'd slipped away without him noticing. I couldn't blame him.

"Nana..." I whispered. It felt like my chest was gripped in a vise.

"Tristan," Anansi said again. The SBP vibrated in my lap to get my attention, and I looked at it through tear-blurred eyes to see the trickster god standing in his partial-spider form with two hands on his hips. "Tell me what happened."

I took a deep breath and tried to keep my voice steady. "He was here."

"Who?"

"Him. The one who attacked John Henry...the Shamble Man."

A chill swept down my arms and I shivered as I continued. "He was wearing iron monsters as armor. He destroyed the farmhouse and...and...took Nana. And he did it with John Henry's hammer."

Anansi's eyes grew wide. "He still has the hammer?" When I nodded, he rubbed his chin and shook his head. "So that's what that surge of energy was. A wave of magic slammed through this place, so powerful it knocked me into full spider form for a second and dispelled the river spirit. It was incredible." He saw the expression on my face and quickly added, "But dangerous. Very dangerous. I could tell the intent was filled with wrongness. Wielding another god's symbol is... it's unheard of. And the armor...did you by chance get a look at it with the sun god's adinkra?"

I clapped a hand to my forehead in embarrassment. "No, I didn't. Everything happened so fast."

"Hmm."

"Anansi," I said quietly.

"Yes?"

"What am I going to do? He took Nana. My grandmother! I need to go after them. I can't leave her in that monster's hands. He was so...angry, like I'd done something to him, but I've never even seen him before."

The image of my grandparents, assaulted in their farmhouse that had survived so many other tragedies, so many hard times, filled me with helpless rage. Burning tears appeared in the corners of my eyes and I cuffed them away angrily.

"Whatever *we* do, it has to be together." Anansi began pacing along the edges of the SBP's screen, walking up one side, across the ceiling, and back down the other. "This new threat is powerful. More powerful than I wanted to believe. How did he know the hammer could allow passage through the realms? What other tricks does he have up his sleeve? No, for this we need help. We need to contact the other gods and—"

"There's no time for that!" I exploded, jumping to my feet. The SBP clattered to the floor and Anansi shouted in dismay as he tumbled around the screen. "We have to go now! I need to get to Alke immediately. Nana could be hurt, and I can't sit around and wait for y'all to have a conference call! Help me get my grandmother back, please!"

Anansi sighed. "Tristan...you said that he knew everything about you. Your history, your strengths. Who your grandmother is and why she's so important to you. Have you ever stopped to think you might be doing exactly what he wants?"

"I don't care, I have to! Don't you see? I *have* to. What would you do if you were in my place?" The phone grew blurry, and I shook my head quickly to scatter my tears to the dusty floor. "Huh? Would you wait?"

"No. No, I wouldn't." Anansi rubbed his chin, and, for a brief second, a look crossed his face. An expression of remorse, or regret. Before I could ask about it, he stood up. "Okay, we'll go. But we have to be smart about this.... We're going to need help once we get there. And it's gonna take time. You need to give me a little bit more freedom—a few more unlocked doors in this here phone—if you want to move quickly after this Shamble Man." He raised an eyebrow.

I hesitated. Giving Anansi more freedom to use the Story Box, the one thing he wanted more than anything, set off a few alarm bells in my head. But then the image of Nana disappearing in the clutches of the Shamble Man reappeared, his burning, hate-filled gaze searing my brain. I swallowed my questions and nodded. I took a deep breath, then climbed to my feet and dusted myself off. There was no time to worry. If I was going to get Nana back safely, I needed to be on my game and ready for anything.

Anansi let a wide sly grin split his face and he nodded with approval. "There we go. Nothing wrong with crying, but when you're done, it's time for action. Now, here's what I'm going to need...."

"Are you sure this is the only way?"

I walked on the dusty path that wound around the farm,

circling the cornfields and heading farther and farther away from the safety and comfort of the farmhouse. It was dark outside—so dark everything looked like shadows and spilled ink. The air was cooling rapidly, and the clouds overhead were bunched on top of each other angrily, ready to send torrential rains crashing down.

That was fine.

A storm had already ripped through my life. What was a few more drops of water?

Luckily, I had the SBP on, and the glow of the screen cast a soft white light around me. I wore an old gray training hoodie, a matching pair of gray shorts, and a beat-up old pair of black-and-red Chuck Taylor sneakers. A slim backpack was slung over my shoulders, filled with water, snacks, and an old pocketknife I had found on one of the shelves in the barn. I'd even stuffed in the remains of Nana's tattered quilt—to have a part of her with me, I guess. More importantly, I wore the enchanted fingerless gloves John Henry had given me, as well as my adinkra bracelet. No way anyone was gonna catch me unprepared again.

"For the last time, boy, it's either this or nothing. Now pay attention." Anansi was crouching on the screen. He'd built a pixelated fire below the blank, rounded square of an app icon. He was in human form, and as I watched, he pulled a spool of silk from one of his pants pockets and sat down next to the fire and began to weave. Silvery thread began to spool out behind him, curling into connected shapes that gathered in piles in the corner of the phone.

"Don't just sit there, storyteller." Anansi spoke without looking away from his work. "You're the Anansesem—I'm just a god trapped in a phone. Never mind the centuries of knowledge and skill restricted by this tiny rectangular prison, just because ole Sky God couldn't take a joke." He cleared his throat. "At any rate. I'm not bitter."

"Mm-hmm," I said.

"Do your job, boy. This doesn't work without you."

"What job?" I asked, confused.

"The god—excuse me, goddess—we're attempting to summon. What, did you think I could tear open another hole between worlds? If I recall, that's *your* specialty. We're going to do things the Anansi way this time."

"Get someone else to do it?" I muttered under my breath.

"No!" the spider god snapped. Then he thought about it. "Well...actually, yes. In this case, you."

I rolled my eyes. In nearly every Anansi tale that exists, the trickster attempts to get others to do the hard work, then cheats them out of the fruit of their labors. Sometimes it's literally fruit, and other times it's fame and recognition. If there was a way Anansi could get the most while doing the least, you'd better believe he'd find it.

"I assume," Anansi continued, "you know the story of

Keelboat Annie, yes? Strongest woman on the river? Go ahead and tell the tale, and I'll collect the power of your words."

I didn't really like the sound of Anansi "collecting" any power of mine, but I didn't have a choice. "Okay. I can do that, I guess." I walked on for a little bit, trying to gather my thoughts. "Okay."

"Anytime now."

I racked my brain and licked my lips. *Come on, Tristan.* Of course I'd heard about Keelboat Annie. Everyone had. I just needed to spit it out. But for some reason, trying to gather up the story felt like collecting water with a vegetable strainer. It was like I couldn't focus. As soon as I thought I was ready, the image of the Shamble Man looming over Nana flashed in my brain, and all the words and characters and images just fell out of my mind and scattered in the wind.

Anansi looked up at me and raised an eyebrow. "You *can* tell the story, can't you?"

I kicked a rock in frustration. "Yes! It's just . . . I don't know. I . . . I'm not feeling too good at the moment. Must be something left over from the Shamble Man."

Anansi studied my expression. Surprisingly, he didn't offer any wisecrack or insult. Instead, he examined the glittering net he'd woven and pursed his lips. Then, with a flick of his wrist, the net returned to a pile of silk and he started over.

His body shimmered, and all of a sudden he had six arms instead of two. His additional hands moved in a blur, and the silvery strands curled across the screen.

"Words?" I asked, confused.

Anansi nodded. "Read the story as we walk. When we get there, summon the spell of activation for this symbol."

"You mean open the app by touching the icon? Fine. And get where? Where are we going?"

Anansi cleared his throat and, for the first time, hesitated. "That ancient forest. You know . . . the place where we emerged from Alke."

I stopped in my tracks as realization dawned on me.

"I assure you, my boy," he continued quickly, "it will be fine. We will not touch the tree, nor any of the haint traps there. In fact, we'll be on the opposite side, by the creek. Trust me. We need to be in a place of power to make this happen. It is the only way."

The only way. I started walking again, slowly. The Bottle Tree forest. We were going back to the Bottle Tree forest. I had to take several deep breaths to calm myself down. It was just a forest. Only it was like a porch light for spirits ranging from troubled ghosts to devious haints. And the forest felt alive at times, as if it were watching and judging me, like Nana when I spill spaghetti sauce down my shirt. And—

"Boy, read the story." Anansi's voice broke into my thoughts. "We're nearly there."

Sure enough, the ominous treetops of the Bottle Tree forest peeked over the sloping hill I walked up. I gulped and held the SBP in front of my face, trying to focus on the words the trickster god had woven.

"'May the stories you hear sound just as good the second time around.'" I paused and wrinkled my brow as I thought about that. Anansi kept working, but he did look up at me as his hands moved in a blur.

"You've got to open a story right, or don't tell it at all. And this won't work without some style, you understand? Some flavor. In Alke you brought forth stories that your grandmother told you, or you created your own from your memories. Right now I need you to take someone else's story and transform it into something magical. Hear me? That's also part of being an Anansesem. Listening and keeping the stories of others to tell again at a later date. Very special. Very necessary. So don't walk all over my good name."

I nodded and cleared my throat. Read the story aloud and make it my own. I could do that. Maybe it would even help get rid of whatever was preventing me from doing my thing. I took a deep breath and began to speak.

"'They say Old Man River didn't love nobody like he loved the greatest soul to sail along the waters. And that great soul loved him back. I'm talking, of course, about Keelboat Annie.'"

As I spoke, the weirdest thing began to happen—the

words untangled themselves as I said them, disintegrating into gold and copper pixels that floated over the fire onscreen before being lifted into the blank app icon above. It was like we were cooking up a tale. The story—fused with Anansi's magic, an Anansesem (me), and the power of the Story Box in its cell-phone form—built the mysterious app with every word I spoke.

And it was a doozy of a story.

10
RIVERBOAT RIDESHARE

"'THERE ARE TONS OF STORIES FLOATING UP AND DOWN OLD MAN River about Annie, some more incredible than others. But each and every one of them sprang from a seed of truth. If I had to start with one, if you twisted my arm and forced me to choose, it'd have to be the one that started it all. The one where Old Man River couldn't hold her back.'"

My feet moved on their own. Somewhere in the back of my mind I knew I was still walking, but the nighttime sounds faded away and all I could see in front of me were those swirling silver words. I knew I was still heading to the Bottle Tree forest, but the story had taken hold of me and demanded to be shared. Who was I to refuse that call?

"'They say Annie ran a keelboat up and down Old Man River all day long, sunup to sundown. She was the only worker on that boat, and she owned it outright. She took passengers when floating downstream and fought the current with nothing but her pole when she carried cargo upstream. Now, how did she manage to do something by herself that it took four others to do in the same amount of time?

"'Easy.

"'Annie was the strongest person living on that side of Old Man River.'"

I could hear something. Strange sounds. The kind that didn't belong in the middle of a farm in Alabama. It was almost like . . . a low splash of something entering water. Like an oar, or a pole.

"'One day, Annie loaded up the most cargo she'd ever carried upstream. I'm talking barrels, crates, bushels, and bundles. On top of that, several families running from trouble down in New Orleans were riding as well. All them people meant it was slow going, but progress was progress, as the old folks will tell you. That is, until the keel pole snapped in half like a twig under a boot. Oh, how the children cried. That keelboat bumped and clattered its way back downstream a ways before Annie finally got it righted.

"'But now there was a problem. She would lose good money if she couldn't deliver that cargo, and she'd lose sleep if those families didn't make it to their destination safely. That left one option.

"'Annie grabbed a rope, tied it to the front of the keelboat, then jumped into the river and waded ashore. There, she wrapped it around her wrists several times, glared at

Old Man River (who was surely chuckling over this turn of events), and began to *haul* the keelboat upriver.'"

The sounds around me grew louder and louder as I read. I could hear people cheering. I could feel vibrations as the small riverboat bumped against large logs and scraped over sandbars. My eyes stayed focused on the words of the story, however. The app Anansi was building was three-quarters of the way finished. I just had to keep going.

"'Annie pulled that boat through mud and over rocks. The waters rose and still she hauled. Old Man River battered and bruised her and tried to rip the rope from her hands, but still she pulled. She bled and she ached. She heaved and she dragged. Annie willed that heap of wood upriver until her feet were sore and her back was screaming. Just her. No one helped. Everyone else was too afraid of the dangers in the water, like snakes and the current. But not Annie. She wrapped that rope around her waist and put one foot in front of the other, moving one inch at a time.

"'Progress is progress, remember?

"'Finally, she made it into town, and she hadn't lost a single passenger or piece of cargo. Not one. The legend of Keelboat Annie had been born.'"

I stopped speaking, confused. The words Anansi had woven had all disintegrated, and the pixelated fire had died. Above it, the app icon was no longer blank. Instead, a deep blue boat glimmered in a silver circle. The label RIVERBOAT RIDESHARE hovered above it.

"Well?" Anansi leaned against the side of the phone. "You planning on pressing it? We're here."

"We are?" I looked around and my eyes grew wide. I hadn't even noticed. The wind chuckled as it curled around me, gusting through a shadowy opening in a stand of trees. A thick group of old trees as tall as buildings leaned in my direction, as if they were happy to see me. The Bottle Tree forest. But it wasn't a section I remembered. I stood in a field of grass that came up to my knees. It stretched behind me to the horizon, rolling up hills and down into valleys.

"Where—?" I began to ask, but Anansi cut me off.

"No time. If we're going to go, it has to be now. Activate the symbol and then enter the forest."

"But—"

"Tristan, that icon isn't going to last for long!"

Anansi was right. Even as I watched it, the shining boat icon began to fade, and the app began to lose its luster. Soon it would be a gray square again. If he was telling the truth— and that's always a biiiig *if* with the trickster god—my shot at getting back to Alke was disappearing fast.

"Fine," I said through gritted teeth. "But it better not be another fiery pit in the ground. I'm running out of underwear."

"What?"

"Nothing," I said, then pressed the icon and stepped into

the Bottle Tree forest. The only thing I heard was the sound of my own panicky breathing. No birds. No crickets. Everything was blanketed in a layer of silence that made me nervous beyond belief.

Squelch

That is, until I stepped into a trickling stream of water.

"Oh c'mon," I said with a groan. "Why can't I start an adventure with dry feet for once?"

I could've gone on complaining (trust me, I'm a highly skilled complainer), but just then a low roar echoed through the forest. It sounded like a freeway at rush hour. It shook the trees and rattled the ground. In the distance, between the branches and the leaves and the trunks, something glinted and sparkled like stars on a clear night.

The roar grew louder, and I took a step back.

"I wouldn't do that," Anansi said.

When I turned to look behind me, I gasped. "Where's the farm?"

The trees crowded in around me, and there was no sign of the field or the path anywhere. Just darkness.

No, wait. There was *one* new addition.

Clouds of white mist began to creep out of the forest, covering the ground and washing over the tree bottoms. It started at my ankles, climbed to my knees, and soon I was waist-deep and too worried about tripping to move.

Turns out I didn't have to. The forest was moving for me.

The trees parted as more and more mist seeped out of the ground and swirled around us. It was as if the Bottle Tree forest was clearing the way for someone—or something—to come find us.

"Seriously?" I muttered. "This is starting to become the worst adventure I've ever been on. And I've only been on two!"

The roaring grew even louder, and with it came faint singing and a *very* familiar drumbeat.

"Um, Tristan..." Anansi said, his voice filled with worry.

"Don't *Tristan* me," I said, glaring at him. "What did that app do? Where are we, exactly?"

The spider god scratched his head. "You know, I'm not sure."

"You're...you're not sure?"

"No. But, Tristan, I think you need—"

"I'm about to go Gum Baby on you."

"Turn around, NOW!"

A wave of water rushed toward us through the trees, parting the mist, ripping up the soil, and uprooting saplings. And it was wide. Wiiiiide. There was nowhere to go. The trees blocked our escape in every direction.

That was when I started screaming.

Just when it looked as if the wall of water would batter us into the trees right before it drowned us, and I was getting ready to wish my Chucks a tearful farewell, the onrushing wave dropped and sank into the ground, like someone pulled the stopper from a bathtub. It drained away until it was only ankle deep, leaving a soggy boy and a wet phone confused in a swirling mist.

"If this don't beat all," a giant voice boomed in the night.

My jaw dropped as a wooden barge as long as a bus and twice as wide emerged from the steamy fog. A woman the size of John Henry and with skin I could only describe as midnight brown stood with one foot resting on the prow, her hands on her hips and a giant smile on her face. Someone else was behind her, but I couldn't get a good look at them because the woman threw her hands wide. She wore loose pants rolled up at the ankles and her feet were bare. A blue collared shirt was unbuttoned at the very top, and its sleeves were rolled up over massive forearms. A scarf was tied around her neck.

"Well, if it ain't the ole ghost wrassler himself." The woman jumped down off the boat, causing the ground to tremble. "How do? The name's Annie. Am I right in presuming you need to hitch a ride?"

I gawked.

At Annie, yes. But also . . . was that . . . ? No, it couldn't be.

"Don't mind him," a familiar voice said. The second crewperson hopped down, splashing me in the process, but I didn't care. I couldn't help it—a big goofy smile spread across my face as a short brown girl with golden bangles on each wrist and a gold-tipped staff strapped to her back folded her arms and put on a mock glare.

"He did the same thing when I first met him," Ayanna said.

11
KEELBOAT ANNIE

KEELBOAT ANNIE WAS BIG AND PROUD OF IT. HER HAIR WAS BIG —a mass of tight curls somehow wrangled into a bun that exploded in all directions and *swished* through the air when she shook her head. Her movements were big, too. Every gesture was exaggerated, every facial expression authentic and genuine, and when she stepped forward, she did it with purpose.

But maybe the biggest thing about her was her voice.

Her laugh boomed through the forest. If her voice had a volume control, it was stuck on ten. It got down into your bones and shook them, like when you stand next to the speakers at a block party, or when your cousin with a couple of 808 speakers in the back of his Tahoe drives slowly through the neighborhood. Annie's voice was pure, loud joy.

And yet... something worried her. I could see it in the way she constantly scanned the forest. The way her eyes lingered on the shadows. Just as I was about to ask her what was wrong, she spied the light from the SBP and whistled.

"So that's where ole Web Butt snuck off to," Annie said. "We'd heard a few rumors, but seeing it up close really puts the hog on the spit, don't it? Serves him right. Serves you right!" She shouted this last sentence at Anansi, who was busy building a cocoon of silk high in the corner of the phone and hiding inside. I didn't blame him. I wouldn't want to be on Keelboat Annie's bad side, either. Her good side was scary enough. She held out her hand and I sheepishly deposited the SBP into it, and the giant woman began to give Anansi a piece of her mind, and then a few more servings.

Ayanna jabbed me in the ribs with her elbow, dragging my attention away from the booming lecture. "You too important to speak to me now? Tuh. Big heads get bigger, I see." But she smiled when she said it, robbing the comment of all its sting.

I smiled back. "Still upset you missed the big showdown?" When the Maafa, an ancient sentient slave ship, had attacked the Golden Crescent, MidPass's ace raft pilot had been unconscious and in the care of the Mmoatia, the African forest fairies. It really lifted my spirits to see her back in full health.

She cocked her head. "You still afraid of heights?"

The smile dropped from my face. "That's low."

"Any higher and you'd be afraid of it."

I made a rude gesture and she scowled at me. After a second we both dissolved into laughter. It was so good to see her again. Felt like old times. Too much, now that I thought about it, and my good humor faded. I sighed.

"Couldn't get enough of us, huh?" Ayanna asked.

"I've, uh, got some unfinished business." I wasn't sure how much I should say in front of Keelboat Annie, at least not before I consulted with Anansi, and he was busy getting the lecture of a lifetime. Maybe two lifetimes.

Ayanna raised one eyebrow, and I knew she was going to ask more questions, so I beat her to the punch.

"How is everyone?"

"Fine, I guess," she said. "Things are…well, things are fine."

It seemed like she wasn't in a sharing mood, either. "Why are you hanging out with Keelboat Annie?" I asked.

Ayanna grinned. "Work study. A few of us got to pair off with a god or goddess to help oversee the repairs to Alke and get experience. It was Thandiwe's idea. She's with High John on a mission to recruit more artists and builders from the Sands."

I was glad to hear that the princess of Isihlangu and High John the Conqueror weren't off fighting some kind of threat. I didn't need any distractions from getting Nana back home safe.

"Where's your raft?" I asked.

Ayanna's magical raft had literally saved my life when I'd first dropped into the Burning Sea. The vessel could shrink to the size of a skateboard so she could sling it over her back, and without it, I don't think we could've saved Alke. Even if she did fly it like a daredevil.

She shrugged. "Wasn't exactly useful on the boat, and it got in the way. So I lent it to Gum Baby."

I choked. "What?!"

Gum Baby, scourge of iron monsters and clean clothes everywhere. The ten-inch loudmouth had been another key person—doll?—in the fight against the Maafa, King Cotton, and the iron monsters that terrorized the land. She was all right, I guess. In small doses.

Very small doses.

"Where's the sticky menace now?" I asked.

"Helping with the rebuilding process. It's amazing—one of her sap attacks has the adhesive power of fifty nails."

I rubbed the back of my head and winced. I'd been on the receiving end of those sap attacks on many occasions. After a few moments I cleared my throat. "Who's with John Henry?" I asked as casually as I could.

She glanced over at Annie, then pulled my elbow and we began to stroll around the keelboat. It took a few moments for her to speak, and I used the time to study the boat. It was huge and flat-bottomed, built of massive planks that had been polished to a gleaming shine. When I reached out to touch the hull, my fingers thrummed as if a small jolt of electricity had shocked me.

"No one at the moment." Ayanna looked left and right, then bit her lip. "He's holed up in Nyame's palace. I'm not really supposed to talk about it, though."

"Because of the Shamble Man?"

She stopped in her tracks and grabbed my shoulder. "What did you say?"

"The Shamble Man." I twisted my head and frowned. "And how he injured John H—mmghg!"

Ayanna clapped a hand over my mouth and dragged me next to the keelboat. For a person who only came up to my shoulder, she moved me with ease. I saw the fury blazing in her eyes and gulped. Reggie had been a marshmallow in comparison.

"How do you know about that? Huh? Nobody was supposed to say anything!"

"Mmghg ffmmmg ghmmm," I said.

Ayanna removed her hand. "What?"

"I said, the Shamble Man came here. Just a few hours ago. He took..." But I couldn't finish.

Ayanna loosened her grip on my arm. "Took what?"

I inhaled, then said, "My grandmother. Said he wanted me to know how it felt."

"You two know each other?"

"NO! I don't think so...."

I quickly explained the confrontation, and with each passing second Ayanna's face grew more and more worried. When I finished, she pulled her staff off her back and squeezed the handle, staring into the carved golden face on its end. Finally, she looked up at me.

"This is bad. Really bad. First the attack on John Henry... Nyame and the Flying Ladies are trying to keep it quiet so no one panics. Then the Riverfolk. Now this. It's like we can't catch a break. I've got to tell Annie."

"The Riverfolk?" I asked, but Ayanna had already walked away. She marched back around the keelboat and I followed, confused. Annie still stood in the middle of the clearing, the towering trees of the Bottle Tree forest leaning ever so slightly away, as if scared to provoke her temper. The SBP rested in the giant palm of her hand, and Anansi was hiding behind the Contacts app.

"Messin' with people's lives like that," Annie was grumbling as we approached. Her gaze landed on us. "Now, what's eating you two? River snake nip your behinds?"

"No, but, Miss Annie—" I started to say.

"Just Annie," she interrupted. She winked. "I don't miss."

"Oh, uh..."

Ayanna rolled her eyes. "There's a problem." She explained about the Shamble Man's attacks on John Henry and my grandparents.

Keelboat Annie pursed her lips and frowned. "Sure you right, that *is* a problem. Well, we'll get to them eventually—"

"Eventually?!" I blurted. "I need to save my grand— Ow!"

Ayanna shut me up by jabbing my foot with her staff. "Don't interrupt the goddess," she hissed.

Annie's glare at me hurt even more. "As I was *saying*, first we got to finish the job we were in the middle of before Mr. Six Legs here started making with the magic. We got some more passengers to drop off. Y'all hop aboard and get yourselves settled. Old Man River ain't gonna wait forever, and I sure as shuckin' ain't gonna lay up in this place. No, ma'am. I can feel the spirits clawing at my bones."

We all climbed aboard using a ladder on the side, and Annie stood up straight and rerolled the sleeves of her shirt. Her forearms were like the tree trunks surrounding us in the Bottle Tree forest. "Hold tight, y'all, we're going cruising."

It felt like I'd joined some weird field trip. In fact, when I saw the rows of benches stretching from under the tent to the back of the boat ("The stern," Ayanna corrected), I immediately envisioned a group of kids being shuttled to some riverside school. I'm not sure what I'd expected a keelboat to be. Instead of oars or a sail, you were supposed to use a long wooden stick called a keel pole to push it along.

The giant goddess stomped by as she took a survey of

the boat, double-checking everything, then triple-checking, peering over the sides and talking to herself. "Sometimes it's something deep in the water that's stirring things up on the surface." Yep, she definitely seemed worried. Which didn't exactly make me feel any better.

I mean, if you were getting on the school bus and the driver started eyeing the steering wheel suspiciously and muttering threats at it, you'd be on edge, too. Then again, I didn't have a good history with school buses.

Meanwhile, Ayanna was coiling rope and making sure all the supplies were tied down tight. When she moved closer, I got her attention.

"Why is she so nervous?" I whispered, nodding at Annie.

Ayanna glanced over, paled, and swallowed. "I'm sure it's nothing," she said, putting a cheerful tone in her voice. "The last few trips have been a bit . . . rough."

"What do you mean 'rough'?"

"Don't worry! I'm sure she's got the trouble figured out by now."

"Trouble?" I hated the way my voice squeaked, but I also hated surprises. Especially the kind that ended up with me running—or swimming, in this case—for my life. The last time I'd taken a swim in Alkean waters, giant ships made out of bones had tried to swallow me whole and make me a permanent passenger.

Ayanna didn't elaborate, so I changed the subject.

"And what's up with her and John Henry?" I asked, keeping my voice low. "It doesn't sound like she cares about him much."

Ayanna winced. "Yeah. We haven't really talked about it, but from what I can tell, Annie doesn't think he and some of the other gods did enough to save the Midfolk from the iron monsters."

"What?!" I asked, outraged on his behalf. "He literally pulled them to safety in the Golden Crescent!"

"That was at the end. Before that, the gods of MidPass told everyone to hole up and hide in the Thicket. While Annie and a few other gods sailed up and down the rivers trying to rescue folk, like she's doing now." When Ayanna saw my face, she added, "I'm not saying I agree with her, but—"

Before she could go any further, Keelboat Annie shouted, "Hold on to your dirt-lovin' derrieres!" She lifted something from the rear of the boat and I gasped.

"Sweet peaches!" I said. "That's a whole log!"

Ayanna snickered. The log was Annie's keel pole. The thing looked like someone had uprooted a tree. I couldn't get both of my hands around it, and yet one of Annie's hands easily slipped into the finger grooves at the top. There was a seam in the middle, as if the pole had been split in two, then glued back together.

"This here pole has kept me moving along for as long as I've had this boat," Annie said proudly. "Kept more than a few varmints off my back when the going got tough, too. A whack from this and you'll think twice before sneaking up on Annie." She scowled slightly. "Now it's the only thing that ain't acting all out of sorts! But that's all right. Park your posterior anywhere you please, I gotta get Old Man River up here."

I gripped the edges of my seat as she raised the keel pole high, then jabbed it into the ground and shoved. The bottom of the boat scraped against the floor of the Bottle Tree forest and we lurched into the rolling carpet of mist that had slowly begun to build up again. I winced each time a rock or root scraped at the wood, but before long the sound changed. It sounded almost like...

"Water?" I muttered to myself. I leaned over the side. Sure enough, the pole now splashed instead of *thunk*ed. We were floating!

When Annie saw the amazement on my face, she smiled and patted the railing next to her fondly. "Old Man River and I have an arrangement. Anywhere I need to go, he gives this old barge a lift. All over Alke, as long as there's a river or stream nearby, Keelboat Annie can get you there." As Old Man River continued to swell around us, lifting the boat and easing us forward through the forest mist, Annie talked about her life on the river.

"In the days of the iron monsters, boats like this used to

carry a bunch of things across MidPass." She squinted at a chipped section of the keel pole, decided it was still sea-worthy (river-worthy?), and dusted off her hands. Annie tow-ered over me and stretched, then pointed at the rows of seats on the boat. "And folks. People, creatures, even a few spirits. For thems that couldn't sit, they stood the whole journey. You believe that? Stood. Some holding babies, some clutching everything they owned in a sack in their arms, all of them with an idea of a new beginning in their hearts. Leastways, that's what I like to think." Annie motioned for me to fol-low as she moved to the next inspection point on the boat.

The SBP was in my pocket, and I thought about some-thing Anansi had said earlier. "Annie," I asked, "did people carry stories with them, too? When they moved from one place to another, I mean."

"Shoot, of course! You bring whatever makes you com-fortable. Maybe it's your auntie's favorite skillet for biscuits, maybe it's your daddy's stories. And you know, stories are easy to carry. Don't weigh nothing. Don't cost nothing. Just a little bit of space up here," she said, tapping the side of her head. "Bit by bit, piece by piece, folks carried a little bit of home with them when they moved. And then you throw someone like you in the mix."

"Me?"

"Yessir! An Anansesem. You collect them stories, right? It

ain't just about us gods and goddesses and everyone beyond that binary! Naw, you pulling stories of families, of sisters and brothers and cousins, and taking them with you, too."

"On the phone, you mean?"

"No, inside you." A giant finger poked my chest, right above my heart. Annie raised both eyebrows. "That there Story Box thingamajig is just a tool to help you—*you*—do your job. Don't rely on that thing more than you have to. No matter what old Web Butt says. Hear me?"

I nodded, just as Ayanna called out that the river was ready. Before I could ask what that meant, Annie moved to the rear of the keelboat, leaving me to think on what she'd just said. It sort of reminded me of what Anansi had been talking about earlier, that idea of a Diaspora. Carrying stories on journeys, planting their seeds in new grounds, connecting us all. I needed to think about that some more, especially since as an Anansesem I was supposed to be doing a lot of that carrying and planting.

Responsibilities, man. They never let up.

Thump thump

Something rattled against the hull near me. I looked around. No one was close by—everyone else was occupied. Annie pushed us forward, which confused me. Where were the passengers we were supposed to drop off? Ayanna stood at the prow checking for obstacles, calling out directions so Annie could steer us around them. I didn't know how either of them could see, though. The mists had completely engulfed us now, surrounding the boat in milky-white strands of clouds that dissolved as we passed through them and re-formed behind us.

Thump thump

There was that sound again.... It came from right over the guardrail.

I got up to take a look. The noises grew more frequent. It wasn't just thumps now, but all sorts of scrapes and knocks and scratching noises, as if...as if there was something climbing up—

I peered over the rail, straight into the hollow eyes of a grinning skull.

12
TALKING SKULLS

THE SKULL AND I STARED AT EACH OTHER. MORE THUMPING AND rattling echoed across the boat, and I fought down a wave of panic as dozens—maybe hundreds!—of skulls inched up the hull. Some large, some small, all bleached white. And when they saw me, they began to shake and rattle, as if in warning. My body locked into place. They were like tiny, ghastly crabs swarming toward us. Just when I opened my mouth to either shout in horror or . . . Well, no, that was it, I was only going to shout in horror. Just then, the first skull beat me to it.

"Save me," it whispered.

The scream died on my lips. "Uh . . ." I said. We stared at each other.

"Save me," another skull said. Then another. And another. Soon all the skulls were talking, their collective whispering like a faint breeze moving through dead leaves.

"Save me. Save me. Save me."

It almost sounded like the spirits back on Nana and Granddad's farm. Their pleas grew louder as they inched closer and closer, and my body was still frozen in shock. In my mind, I saw other creatures made of bones. Larger and scarier, surging toward me. The bone ships, the haunted vessels that had roamed the Burning Sea. I fell backward while shouting a wordless warning.

"Tristan!"

Ayanna caught me before I hit the deck, and I pointed at the hull in terror. "They're back!"

"Who?" she asked.

Keelboat Annie moved past us quickly in a giant stride that rocked the boat from side to side, wielding the keel pole like a baseball bat. She peered over the side, then let out a hearty chuckle. Ayanna joined her, and—to my extreme surprise—squealed in delight.

Squealed.

I've never heard Ayanna make that sound. You would've thought she'd found some kittens, not legions of creatures that belonged in a horror movie. But she was laughing like she'd reunited with some old friends. Then, get this, she had the nerve to turn around and gesture for me to come over as if nothing was wrong.

Nope. No way. At least, I wasn't planning on it until Anansi called to me from the SBP. It had fallen out of my pocket and skidded across the deck.

"Hey, hero of MidPass, is your wrist burning?"

"What?" I asked. When I picked up the phone (no scratches, Nyame screen protectors FTW), Anansi was swinging gently in a spiderweb hammock, a straw hat tilted over his eyes. He raised an arm and tapped its wrist with the other hand.

I looked down at my wrist, confused, then felt the air *whoosh* out of my lungs as I realized what he was referring to. "Oh," I said, feeling a little foolish. The Anansi adinkra on my bracelet wasn't glowing or hot. We weren't under attack.

"Are you coming?" Ayanna called. "Don't be rude. I mean *ruder*."

I trudged over cautiously. There weren't any bone ships coming our way. Those had only been in my head. Ghosts of the past.

Once, when I was in one of my therapy sessions with Mr. Richardson, we'd talked about how our fears and memories could haunt us, even into the future. We were eating popcorn mixed with M&Ms and drinking hot cocoa when Mr. Richardson said, "Ghosts from the past are like scars. They heal, and some even fade over time, but they never truly go away. They're reminders of trauma."

There was that word again: *trauma*.

"Tristan, come on!"

When I peeked over the edge, I still saw skulls, but now their bottoms were just stuck to the side of the boat like limpets. (I looked up limpets one time. Have you ever seen one? They're like a snail that has a seashell for a hat. Amazing.)

Keelboat Annie shook her head and headed back to her position in the stern.

"Did they talk to you?" I asked Ayanna.

She raised an eyebrow and cupped a hand around her ear, pretending to listen. After a moment she shook her head. "Nope. Nothing."

I glared at her, then looked at the first skull I'd seen, the largest one. It clung to the wooden hull, silent. I tapped it gingerly with one finger, recoiling immediately in anticipation. Nothing happened. I frowned, then poked it harder. "Come on, say something. Whisper for help like you did before!"

A noise that sounded suspiciously like a muffled snicker came from behind me. When I turned around, Ayanna was trying to keep a straight face, but she burst into laughter as soon as we made eye contact. From the back of the boat came a giant "HA-HAAAAAA" as Keelboat Annie shook the vessel with her own guffaws. Even Anansi was laughing. I could feel the SBP vibrate in my pocket in time with his chuckles.

Finally, Ayanna flapped her hands and wiped the tears from her eyes. "I'm sorry," she gasped. "I'm so sorry. But it was too funny. See, it's happened to all of us."

"What?" I asked.

"The Talking Skulls. They do it to every new person they meet." She finally stopped laughing and stared quizzically at my confused expression. "You've really never heard of them? I would've thought that you of all people . . ."

I bit my lip and shook my head.

Once Ayanna mentioned it, I did recall Nana telling me a folktale about a man who found a Talking Skull on the riverbank. But when he brought others to listen to it, the skull remained silent, and everyone made fun of the man. At least that's what I could remember. I didn't want to admit that ever since Nana had been taken, I was having trouble feeling stories.

Ayanna shrugged and extended her arm over the side. The skull closest to her rattled up the hull, and she grabbed it. She walked it over to the rows of benches in the middle of the boat and set it down before repeating the process with another skull. After a second I started helping her.

We worked in silence. There had to be thirty to forty skulls hanging on as Keelboat Annie steered us through the mist. Every so often I thought I saw low shapes cruising alongside us, just out of sight. Other boats, but not bone ships, luckily. Faint snatches of song echoed across the water. Chants, maybe. A group of voices keeping time as Annie poled.

"Hup-one, hup-two, carry me on the way.
Hup-one, hup-two, lookin' for a better day."

"Do you hear *that*?" I whispered.

Ayanna nodded. "You hear it when Annie gets in a groove. She says—"

"She *says*," Keelboat Annie boomed behind us, "to stop with the jibber-jabber and get our passengers aboard! No cause to make these fine folk wait."

Ayanna scooped up five more skulls and sat them on the bench, and I grabbed the last straggler, the one that had first spoken to me, and gingerly carried it to the final seat.

Keelboat Annie nodded and said, "Now. Sounds like someone missed a tale or two about our passengers. Is that right?"

I nodded, avoiding Ayanna's stare.

Keelboat Annie lashed her pole to a rail to keep it in place and then joined us. "Well, no one knows how a Talking Skull gets where it does—it's just there when you least expect it. And if you get the fool notion to start talking in front of them...well, they're gonna chat right back. But see, that conversation is just for you. It ain't for you to go spreading. Try to involve someone else in what y'all supposed to keep betwixt yourselves, and them Talking Skulls will go silent as a stone."

Save me, the skulls had said. Save them from what? I wondered. The Shamble Man? Were they trying to flee him like the spirits back in the barn had? Or were they somehow channeling Nana...? I clenched my fists in frustration. I needed to get this ride back on course for . . . where? I didn't know, exactly.

The boat shuddered, and Keelboat Annie frowned. "Now, what's got Old Man River riled up?" We waited, but nothing happened, and she scratched her head. "That didn't feel right. Well, anyway, that's the story of them Talking Skulls. Whatever you heard them say was meant for you. It's up to you whether you wanna listen."

Meanwhile, Ayanna had been studying me the whole time. "Tristan knows all the stories. He can bring them to life when he tells them! Go on, show Annie—"

"It's fine," I interrupted. "I . . . just want to hear Keelboat Annie's stories. How did you start giving the skulls rides?"

I tried to ignore Ayanna's questioning looks. No need to tell her the Shamble Man had thrown my Anansesem abilities off-kilter. *May your heart wither. May your tears fall endlessly, as mine once did.*

Keelboat Annie cleared her throat several times, and a faraway look settled on her face. "Now, I told you I carried all sorts of folk up and down the river. Well, it just so happened that on one of them return trips, this old boat ran aground near a lake in the Grasslands."

"The Grasslands?" I interrupted. Wasn't that where Ninah was from?

Keelboat Annie nodded. "Behind Isihlangu. Whole countryside filled with lakes and cities just as pretty as can be.

Like jewels, they are. Leastways, they were once. But after I'd dropped off some folks, Old Man River took me 'round that way. He always carries me to the next pickup, but I'll be a fish out of water if he didn't leave me high and dry in an old lake, just as muddy as you please. It's like something had sucked all the water out of the Grasslands. Anyways, them Talking Skulls were scattered about in the reeds, waiting for someone to stumble on 'em and get in all sorts of trouble. Not Annie, though! Shoot, no. I, unlike some folks around here, know the score. Figured they were the passengers Old Man River wanted me to collect, so I did. And that's what I was doing when you and ole Web Butt pulled me from my job."

Anansi snorted from his spot in the hammock in the corner of the SBP, but I noticed he did it quietly. Probably didn't want another chewing-out.

"So now where are you headed?" I asked.

"Back to the Golden Crescent, I figure." Keelboat Annie returned to her post, where she loosened the pole and grinned. "Got a full load of passengers and one hero. Might as well bring 'em on home, right? Maybe you'll find what you're looking for there."

The SBP vibrated, and when I looked down Anansi gave me a thumbs-up, like we were on the right track.

Home.

Before I could truly process that word, the boat surged forward. It sliced across the surface of Old Man River like a surfer. Ayanna threw back her head and laughed, and even I grinned. Drops of water splashed on our faces and arms, and dozens of rainbows appeared like ribbons in midair. I couldn't see more than a few feet in front of the boat, but between Keelboat Annie's sure hands and Ayanna cackling next to me, it felt like—for once—things were finally looking up....

Yeah. You already know.

They weren't.

13
HERO'S WELCOME

SEVERAL THINGS WENT WRONG FROM THE VERY BEGINNING.

First, Old Man River carried us angrily out of the mist, twisting and turning through a small field of razor-sharp grass before we splashed into the sea. Keelboat Annie steered us as carefully as she could, but her frown grew more troubled each time the craft shuddered or rocked unexpectedly. I could tell she was confused as to why her traveling partner was acting out of sorts. It was like the Old Man had woken up on the wrong side of the riverbed.

(Ha-haaaaa! I'm here all week.)

Still, we made it to the coast of the Golden Crescent unharmed. Wet, but unharmed. And for a brief period, it was magical. The shining blue waters of the bay rippled as far as the eye could see. Gleaming sand dunes rose to meet the ivory walls of the marina. We were on the north side of the bay, and the coast curved away from us like a backward C.

Several large yachts with ruby-red adinkra symbols on their sails bobbed up and down in their berths. Behind them, up the gently sloping hills, palaces rose out of emerald-green forests, their golden-capped towers winking in the midday sun. It was the palaces that had given the area its name, and their beautiful splendor should have filled me with joy.

"Feels weird, doesn't it?" Ayanna asked quietly.

Waves lapped at the boat's hull as I stared at the spot where the Maafa had beached and unleashed a horde of iron monsters onto Alkean soil. It felt like only yesterday we'd all come together to battle the minions of the evil slave ship. Yet there were no lingering signs of the battle, save for the long floating wooden walkway anchored to the beach by thick pillars that stretched off toward the horizon and disappeared into the distance. John Henry had been building it the last time I'd seen him in person. He'd said it was a way to bridge the divide between MidPass and the Alkean continent.

John Henry, holed up in Nyame's palace. Was he okay? I needed to find out.

"How long has it been?" I asked, peering around to see if anyone was hiding nearby.

Ayanna knew immediately what I was talking about. "Last time we saw you was a few months ago." Time moved at different speeds in the two realms. I'd only been back in Alabama for a few weeks.

"We've been working every day," Ayanna continued as Keelboat Annie hopped into the shallows and wrapped ropes around her wrists. With what looked like very little effort, the giant goddess began to haul the boat onto the beach. "Everyone. Cleaning, rebuilding, expanding. Some folks from the Horn came up, as well as people from the Sands. They'd escaped the notice of . . . the iron monsters, but now they're all coming to our aid."

"Sounds like everyone is pitching in."

"They are. Well, except for the Grasslands. Haven't heard from them yet, but I'm sure they'll be coming soon, especially after we sent our special messenger. So, we're making it. It's been a little difficult at times, but everyone has welcomed the Midfolk without a single complaint."

"Even High John?" I asked.

High John the Conqueror, the smiling god from MidPass with a giant shadow crow for a companion, hadn't been too keen on working with the Alkeans, and he'd taken John Henry to task about it on several occasions.

Ayanna flashed a quick smile. "Yes, even him. Eventually."

I scanned the beach. Something was bothering me. I tried not to let it show, but nobody's perfect. "So . . . where is everyone?"

From the look of pity Ayanna wore, I hadn't quite managed to keep the disappointment out of my voice. But the beach was empty. No shouting crowds, no joyful celebration.

There wasn't even a banner! I mean, it wasn't like I was expecting much, you get me? But . . . I *had* helped save Alke. Okay, I also endangered it by uppercutting a magical tree, but we need to stop living in the past.

"I guess they're all busy," Ayanna said. "You know, rebuilding a country?"

After another second of glancing around hopefully, I sighed. Ayanna shook her head and turned away, probably to roll her eyes. The boat ground to a halt, and Keelboat Annie rapped on the hull. We hopped down, and the three of us—four, if you included Anansi—stared at the empty beach. The bay, which had been filled with ships of all sizes the last time I'd visited, now only had a few anchored in place.

Anansi yawned and climbed into his webbed hammock on the phone's screen. "Well, this has been a wonderful cruise. Do me a favor, will you, boy? Leave me on the boat. I'm not exactly eager to see old Shiny Eyes again. He might find a new 'task' for me to perform, and this cramped metal rectangle is just starting to grow on me."

"I don't think—" I began, but it was too late. The spider god was already fast asleep, snoring lightly as he rocked in the SBP's screen. I glared at him, mumbling something that would've gotten me in trouble in school. But he did have a point. Nyame and Anansi weren't exactly best friends. Quite the opposite. And I couldn't risk losing Anansi to the sky god. I needed the trickster to help me unravel the mystery of the Shamble Man and rescue Nana before it was too late. It worried me that he would be on the boat by himself, but Keelboat Annie solved that issue by presenting the third and final problem.

No matter how much I tried to convince her, she refused to accompany us to Nyame's palace.

"No sirree, I won't step one foot up there," she said, her large arms folded across her chest and a dark frown on her face. "They waited until the last minute to confront those iron monsters, and if they didn't want my help before, they don't need me now. Let them hem and haw all they want. Me and Old Man River will be just fine down here," she continued, jerking a thumb at the rattling skulls on the deck behind her. "Besides, I've got to get these boneheads over to their new riverside home down the bay a bit. Get it? Boneheads."

I groaned. It should be illegal for grown-ups to make puns. "Fine. Can you at least keep an eye on this for me?" I held up the SBP.

She raised an eyebrow but nodded, and I reluctantly passed over the phone. I didn't tell her the passcode, though. No sense inviting trouble from either of the gods.

While Annie climbed back onto the boat and stowed the phone away, Ayanna squinted and put a hand up to shade her eyes.

"Hey, look," she said. She pointed up the beach, where a

tall, skinny boy with golden-brown skin sprinted toward us, kicking up sand as he ran. "Looks like your welcome party is finally here."

"Ha-ha," I muttered sarcastically. I did, however, straighten my hoodie and dust the sand off my Chucks. Gotta make a good impression, no matter who's coming to thank you.

The boy skidded to a stop in front of us, spraying sand everywhere and sending us reeling backward.

"Hey," I said, shielding my face.

The boy, who was a little older than me, wore a black-and-gold woven tunic and matching black pants. His hair was plaited and decorated with what looked like silver wires, the braids pulled back into a ponytail, and his feet were in sandals. A small silver-and-gold satchel was slung across his body, and he rested one hand on it as if its contents were precious. He wasn't breathing hard, even though he'd just dashed a hundred yards, easy. A smile spread slowly across his face as he looked me up and down, raised an eyebrow, then dismissed me completely and turned to Ayanna.

"Hey, sis," he said, winking.

Sis? Was this Ayanna's brother?

She rolled her eyes, which didn't answer my question. "Junior. What do you want?"

He threw his arms wide and put on an innocent face. "Come on, now, don't be like that. I'm here to welcome you back! Everyone's been waiting for you to return. Well. You and your . . . companion." This last word he directed at me without so much as a glance.

"Hey!" I said.

Junior jerked a thumb at me. "Is that all he can say?"

I stepped forward so he had no choice but to look at me. "I can say a whole lot if it's worth my time. Ayanna, who is this clown?"

"Don't mind him," she said. "This is just Junior, one of the people I told you about. You know, the ones who are *supposed* to be helping Nyame rebuild the Golden Crescent. Instead, he just cracks jokes and gets in everybody's way. Sort of like somebody else I know around here."

Junior and I ignored her shots at us and studied each other. So this was one of the Alkeans who had escaped the wrath of the iron monsters. He seemed . . . annoying. But at least he was here now, so he couldn't be all bad, right?

I pushed my irritation down—way down—and held out my hand, forcing a smile onto my face. "Nice to meet you, Junior. My name is—"

"Yeah, yeah." The boy flapped a hand as he interrupted me. "We get it. Everyone knows who you are. The *hero*. What, did you think there'd be a parade when you arrived?" Junior shook his head. "Anyone could've done what you did if the gods were blessing them left and right."

My jaw dropped. The fact that I'd been hoping for some sort of fanfare only made his words sting more. Also, they were eerily similar to the Shamble Man's, and that made me angry. "That's not fair," I spluttered. "You don't even know me."

"Yeah, well, life isn't fair."

I glared at him as he smirked. "All right, then, where were you when people needed help? Hiding?"

"Oh-ho." He clapped a hand over his heart and pretended to stagger back. "I'm wounded."

"Not yet. Keep talking and we'll see."

"Quick with the words, huh? Is that all you're quick with? I wonder."

I folded my arms across my chest. "What's that supposed to mean?"

"We've been told all about the mighty Tristan Strong, Savior of Alke. Hero. Leader against the horrific and the terrifying, a defender of justice. But I've heard a lot of stories in my life, tall tales and outright fiction. So I think we should make sure you are who you claim to be."

"How?"

"A race. To the top of the hill. First one to the sky god's palace wins."

"How would that prove anything?" Ayanna asked, taking the words out of my mouth.

He didn't answer her, and I stared at him in disbelief. He couldn't be serious. I shook my head and started to turn around. This was ridiculous. I didn't have time for childish games. I turned to Ayanna. "Come on, let's go find John Henry and the others. We've got to warn them about the—"

Junior cleared his throat loudly. "John Henry isn't seeing anyone."

I turned around. "What?"

"You heard me. Word is he's not seeing anyone except other gods. And, last I checked, you weren't a god."

I rolled my eyes. "Fine. Miss Sarah or Miss Rose, then."

"Busy."

"High John?"

"Gone."

"He's on his recruiting mission with Thandiwe, remember?" Ayanna said.

I threw up my hands. "Fine, we'll just go see Nyame and—"

"Wow, you just don't get it, do you?" Junior squatted and began to stretch his legs, pulling the toes of one foot toward him, then repeating the same thing with his other foot. "No one's gonna meet with you. You're not important enough. We have a country to rebuild. Nyame has even placed his guardians at the entrances to his palace to keep out unwanteds while he and the other gods meet. And it seems to me you fall into the category of *unwanted*."

That got my attention. I'd seen Nyame's warrior statues in action. No way did I want to cross any of them. But I had to talk to the gods. I had to check on John Henry and see if he and the others would help me go after the Shamble Man.

My grandmother needed us! I looked at Ayanna, but she bit her lower lip and shrugged. If we'd had her raft, we might've been able to sneak into the palace from the roof, but even that would've been risky.

We were stuck.

Junior stretched his arms out wide and began twirling them in small circles to warm up his muscles. He flashed a bright smile at me. "If you beat me in the race, I'll show you a foolproof way of getting into Nyame's palace."

I stared at him. "You're lying."

He held up both hands. "I swear I'm not."

I looked around the empty beach, then sighed. "Fine. Let's just—"

"But if I win," he said with a sly look, "I get five minutes alone with the Story Box."

My hand automatically went to the pocket that normally held the SBP; then I remembered I'd given it to Keelboat Annie. And before I replied, Junior dropped the act and stood up straight. "I'm not playing games, Anansesem. No trickery, no theft. I just . . ." He paused, then cleared his throat. "The Story Box is legendary. All the stories, held forever and carried across worlds and realms? It is . . . a treasure. All I want to do is tell it a story about my father, and how much he defined me and helped motivate me. He . . . left, a long time ago. This story about him is all I have left, and I would be forever grateful if I could tell it."

A raw note of honesty had crept into his voice. I looked away, swallowed, and thought about another boy who'd wanted to record the stories of others. "No tricks?" I asked.

"None."

I hesitated, then nodded. "Okay, but you don't need to race me to do that. Why don't you just—"

Junior backed up and shook his head. "I don't take anything I haven't earned," he said, his words almost a snarl. "I will win, or you will."

I nodded. I could respect that. And either way, the only thing I'd lose was time. I wasn't going to get into Nyame's palace without Junior's help.

"Let's do it," I said. "Ayanna, you want to race, too?"

"Not a chance," she said. "You two go look silly if you want—I need to stay with Annie."

"Right. Work-study."

"Work*ing*, unlike y'all."

"You coming or not?" Junior asked me. With fierce determination on his face, he adjusted the satchel so it was on his back. The two of us lined up next to each other and jostled shoulders as we prepared to race.

"At least give us a countdown," I said to Ayanna.

"Boys," she said, shaking her head. "On your mark, get set, go!"

14
A RACE TO TROUBLE

HAVE YOU EVER SPRINTED IN THE SAND? IT'S BRUTAL. ABSOLUTELY horrendous.

So of course Granddad had made me do it a few times when he held his annual Walter Strong Winter Boxing Camp. A fancy title that meant he got to drag me and some other unlucky amateur boxers to do sand sprints. Now, most trainers would head south for the winter, but not Granddad. If there was a way to make training more uncomfortable, Walter Strong would find it. Such as running as hard as you could next to a partially frozen lake. Yes, I'm talking about Lake Michigan in Chicago. In the winter.

Like I said. Horrendous.

Now I tried to keep up with the gangly-limbed boy as he tore up the dunes and slid down to the polished marble plaza beyond them. Arms pumping, half stumbling, we charged across the wide-open space toward one of the spiraling main avenues that led to the highest hill and grandest palace in all the Golden Crescent. But just before we reached the street, Junior took a sharp right turn down a narrow brick walkway steeped in shadows.

"Wait, where are you going?" I called.

Junior glanced back at me, winked, then dipped his head and put on a burst of speed. I gaped stupidly for a moment before increasing my own pace. We sped through the dark corridor, barely dodging sharp corners as the alley twisted and turned. I gritted my teeth as I tried to keep up. This race wasn't fair! I didn't know this route. There was no way I was letting that boy out of my sight.

Suddenly Junior dipped around another corner, and we exploded into a dazzling plaza. I recognized that place! I'd been there before. It was filled with fountains as well as bushes trimmed into the shapes of giant animals—we were near the hidden gate to Nyame's palace. We'd just avoided the main avenues—which meant we'd avoided his golden sentinels. Now all I had to do was—

BOOM!

A giant golden foot, complete with a fancy golden sandal, crashed to the ground inches away from me. A towering statue of a woman holding a golden stool in one hand and a spear in the other glared down at us. Junior sprinted around it with a wild glint in his eyes. He made a face at me over his shoulder and ran toward two towering marble pillars. The air shimmered between the columns.

Nyame's gate.

Junior was getting away!

"Hi, Kumi!" I shouted up at the statue. "Bye, Kumi!" The golden woman tilted her head as I waved, running backward. I raised my wrist and jiggled the adinkra bracelet, hoping she would notice the sky god's charm and not kick me all the way to MidPass. I'd seen her punt before, and let me tell you, NFL teams would be begging her to play for them if they knew.

To my profound relief, Kumi didn't follow me. She nodded, then turned and resumed guarding the plaza. A thought wriggled to the front of my mind—what exactly was she watching for? My thoughts were interrupted when Junior let out a shout of joy as he ran through Nyame's gate. I growled and barreled forward.

Once he was past the gate, Junior slowed a bit to marvel at the palace orchards on either side of the path, whistling as he jogged. A sly grin spread across my face. He didn't know I was right on his heels. He looked back, startled when he saw me, and the whistle died on his lips as he began to run again.

The paved road flew under our feet. Inch by inch, breath by ragged breath, I began to pull even with him. We were shoulder to shoulder. Then slowly, by the slimmest of margins, I pulled ahead! Junior was sweating now, and the plaits had come loose from his ponytail and were fluttering behind him as we flew up one rolling hill and down another. My sides began to cramp, but I didn't dare slow down to massage them out. Nyame's palace was just ahead, and I was going to *win*.

Two black shadows rippled across the path. I didn't have time to look up, though I noticed they seemed pretty large. The only thing I was focused on was the huge entrance at the base of Nyame's palace with a curtain of water falling down in front of it. Almost . . . there . . .

I slapped the stone wall next to the waterfall just before Junior did, and I threw up both my hands and stood victorious. "Ha!" I said, grinning as Junior sulked. "Take that! Now show me your secret way inside so I can talk to John Henry."

Junior wiped the sweat from his forehead and calmly tied his plaits back. Then he shrugged. "All right, all right. You beat me. Thought I had you there back at the gate. That old lady never lets me through, but she was distracted by you this time."

"Yeah, yeah. Quit stalling and get me inside."

Junior rolled his neck, then flashed a wide, dimpled smile. "Haven't you figured it out yet? I already did." He pointed up to the sky. "Personal escorts."

The huge black shadows from the orchards slid across the ground toward us, and I finally looked up to see who they belonged to. What I saw sent all the air in my lungs rushing out in a giant *whoosh*.

Huge black wings spread wide.

Ivory white robes trimmed in black-and-gold braid.

Miss Sarah and Miss Rose, goddesses of MidPass, dropped to the ground, stern expressions on their faces.

"Tristan Strong—" Miss Sarah said, staring at me over the top of her glasses.

"—you are in big trouble," her sister finished.

Junior knew this was gonna happen. He was almost as tricky as Anansi.

The two winged goddesses marched us down marble-and-gold hallways in complete silence. Well . . . Junior and I were silent. Our guardians kept up a steady stream of commentary. You know the kind—the thing adults do when they're talking to you and asking you questions, but *you don't dare answer them*. It's a trap! They're just trying to get you to say something so they can lecture you even more. I call them mom-ologues.

"Honestly, you two—" Miss Sarah said.

"—should know better," Miss Rose finished.

"Everyone's very busy, and—"

"—you shouldn't be disturbing them."

"In fact—"

"—you should be helping—"

"—instead of playing silly games with this one—" Miss Sarah added.

"—who knows better—"

"—and should be keeping a low profile."

Junior frowned but didn't look up. He'd been quiet since we entered the palace, and I could tell he'd gotten in trouble with the Flying Ladies before. The expression on his face reminded me of mine the time my mother caught me trying to do a handstand and eat a stack of Oreos at the same time. Yes, I knew better, but think of how cool it would've been if I'd succeeded! Also, yes, I'd fallen and crunched a million Oreo crumbs into the carpet, but you can't make an omelet without cracking a few eggs.

"And another thing..." Miss Sarah continued, and I groaned under my breath.

Back and forth they went, their large raven-black wings draped over them like cloaks. Miss Sarah, tall and slim with a fade that would've made any barber back home proud, wore copper-braid glasses perched on the tip of her nose, while Miss Rose was short and wore a black-and-gold headwrap high atop her head. Both moved quickly, and both looked extremely tired.

We walked through an arched passage and entered an open-ceilinged room filled with soft rosy light. The carpet was grass, strewn with feathery white petals that smelled like vanilla and mint, and a gentle breeze blew through the space. It would've been very peaceful and inviting if not for the huge pile of stone, lumber, and tools stacked in the middle. The next room we entered was similar. As was the next. Every one of them was filled with the supplies needed to rebuild the damaged parts of the Golden Crescent. A big reminder that the work wasn't done yet. But as much as I wanted to help rebuild the second-greatest city I'd ever seen (Chicago over everything, baby), I had another urgent task.

"Um, Miss Sarah, Miss Rose?" I said. "Where are you taking us? I actually came here because I need your help. All of you. Well, I know John Henry is injured, but..." My voice trailed off as the two goddesses came to an abrupt halt and spun around. All the sunlight in the open-air hallway seemed to drain away as the two women loomed over us, their wings stretching around us to prevent our escape.

"What do you know of this?" Miss Rose hissed. Her eyes darted right and left. "Who told you?"

Miss Sarah's wings flapped once, a single powerful move that lifted her several feet into the air so she could scan the area for eavesdroppers. After a few seconds she landed, nodded at Miss Rose—who sent a bewildered Junior to the far end of the corridor to wait, protesting loudly the whole time—then folded her arms across her chest. "Speak," she said.

I didn't have a choice. So, keeping my voice low, I told the goddesses about the events Anansi and I had seen unfold through the SBP. My voice faltered a bit when I came to the part where the Shamble Man attacked John Henry. It was still a shock to me—the man I'd thought was unbeatable, the strongest person ever, had been bested! When I finished, I fell silent and stared hopefully.

Miss Sarah and Miss Rose looked at each other uneasily.

"So it *was*—" Miss Rose muttered.

"—who we suspected," Miss Sarah finished.

"Who?" I asked, unable to control myself. "I have to find him. If you know who it is..."

"If you knew who it is, and what he is capable of, you would not be here, Tristan. You have to leave this to us."

"Are you going to go find him, whoever the Shamble Man is?"

They shook their heads at the same time. "The Golden Crescent still hasn't recovered from fighting the iron monsters," Miss Rose said. "With Brer Rabbit still not one hundred percent, and John Henry...well, it's just us and Nyame until High John gets back, and it will take more than that to stop...to stop the Shamble Man."

Before I could protest again and tell them about Nana, a young Alkean girl in pigtails ran up behind us to speak to the goddesses. The girl was out of breath, and the Flying Ladies had to bend over to make out her whispers.

Miss Rose listened for a moment, then scowled. "Again?"

The little girl nodded.

Miss Sarah sighed. "We'll deal with it. Run along and find your parents."

The girl skipped away, and the flying goddesses turned as one to face me.

"We'll have to continue this conversation later," said Miss Rose. "For now, you two come with us." We walked over to Junior, who was standing at the end of the hall with a confused look on his face. The goddesses led us into a sitting area surrounding a tiny fountain. In the center of the fountain was a statue of a tiny dancing child. A spout of water shot out of its mouth and landed in the circular marble pool. The oval room's walls were glossy white and once again there was no ceiling, so the gray light of the overcast sky filled the room. The goddesses stared at the clouds uneasily, murmured to each other, then turned to us.

"You will wait here—" Miss Sarah said.

"—until Nyame returns," Miss Rose said.

"And don't speak another word about John Henry."

"But—" I tried again, and once more they ignored me.

Just then, a booming voice rang from outside. "KUMI, WHERE ARE ROSE AND SARAH?"

"Oh no," I said under my breath. The sky god did not sound like he was in a great mood. Perfect. Just what I needed. At this rate I was collecting lectures like me and Eddie used to collect Pokémon. Nyame was probably an air type. A hot-air type. The first time I met him, I'd just freed him from the clutches of giant iron monsters who'd been slowly poisoning him to drain him of his powers. Suspicious of all outsiders, he'd instructed Kumi, the warrior statue outside, to escort me and my gang of adventurers to his throne, where he interrogated us mercilessly.

It looked like it was déjà vu.

"Wonderful," I muttered. "We're in a perfect place to get yelled at."

Miss Rose sighed, then pointed a finger at me and Junior. "You two . . . behave. Understood?"

We both nodded, and the winged goddess pursed her lips in suspicion. Then she and Miss Sarah flapped their wings and soared into the gray sky above. Within seconds it was just me and Junior in the sky god's sitting room. I stared around with glum resignation. Forget my adinkra bracelet and my now-unresponsive talents as an Anansesem. My superpower was getting lectured. Any moment now Nyame would step out and—

Plunk

Something flew through the air and beaned me in the back of the head. "Hey!" I said, turning and glaring at Junior as I rubbed the sore spot. "What is your problem?"

He squinted at me. "What?"

"Don't act innocent. Quit messing around before we get in even more trouble."

He shook his head and turned and walked away. I stared daggers at his back, then moved in the opposite direction. But I hadn't gone more than a few steps when Junior yelped.

"Ouch!"

When I turned around, he was rubbing his arm and scowling. "Is that how it is?" He picked up a rock and threw it at me. I managed to duck just in time and it whistled past my ear, barely missing.

"Are you serious?" I shouted. This kid was working my last nerve! (I don't know where that expression comes from, but Dad uses it all the time when I'm bugging him. Can you lose your nerves? Do they disappear as you get older? Where's the last one? Grown-ups are weird, I tell you.)

"You threw one first!" Junior shouted.

"No, I didn't. What's with you? Ever since I got here you've been acting like a spoiled brat!"

"I'm not the one with the hero complex," the boy said through gritted teeth. "I'm sick of hearing about you. 'Tristan did this. Tristan saved that. Tristan, Tristan, Tristan.' But when it's time for the real work, to rebuild what we lost, suddenly the great hero is nowhere to be found."

My jaw dropped. Was he for real? "Who do you think you're talking to?"

"You—" He stopped suddenly, looking around. "Wait. Something's wrong."

I took a step forward, shaking my head as my temper flared. "Oh no you don't. Ever since I came here you've been messing with me. Talking slick like nothing was gonna happen. Well, now it's time to put up or shut up."

"No, I'm serious." He looked around nervously.

"Yeah, me, too." I stalked toward him, fully ready to start a fight. I knew good and well it would get me into even more trouble, but at that moment I didn't care. The Shamble Man had Nana, everyone in Alke was keeping secrets, and this new boy—Mr. Popular—was accusing me of being a fake. I couldn't take any more. I was a foot away from him when he froze, then looked past me.

"Hey," he said very carefully, "wasn't there a fountain in here?"

I stopped, confused. But when I looked around, he was right. The statue of the child was missing, and the room had gone silent. Only the pool remained. All my senses screamed danger, but before I could turn and run, or put up my fists, or even let out a high-pitched scream, a dark shape rose from the top of the wall overhead and hurled itself at me like a missile.

15
WHEN THE GODS FADE

THE DARK SHAPE COLLIDED INTO ME LIKE A RIGHT HOOK. I WENT
sprawling to the ground, knocking Junior over in the process.
He shouted in surprise; I was hollering up a storm as I tried
to defend against the sneak attack, and the small assailant
was singing at the top of their lungs.

The attacker peeled off of me—taking some of my arm
hairs with them—and skipped, yes, skipped, around the
room. I squinted from where I sat on the floor. They were
the right size. And yet...

A short, deep-brown creature with a giant head stood a
few feet away. Big hollow eyes stared at me, and its oversize
hands dangled almost all the way to the floor.

"Oh, you don't know nobody now."

Its high-pitched voice made me wince. Junior—our argument forgotten—leaned toward me with a carefully neutral
expression and whispered, "You know this... thing?"

I shook my head.

Wrong move.

The creature put its hands on its hips, or tried to, before giving up and stomping to where we sat. "Don't you know it's rude to whisper! After everything we've been through, you don't know nobody. You too famous. Got too big for your switches."

I started to scoot backward, unsure of what was happening. "I . . . You mean *britches*? Gum Baby, is that you?"

"There you go again. Always trying to correct somebody. Of course it's Gum Baby! Who else it gonna be? Bum Gaby? Gum Baby swears you're the stupidest smart person she knows."

As the creature stomped forward, something amazing happened. A seam appeared at the top of its giant head, and like a zipper, it began to travel down and peel apart. Wisps of steam escaped as the two halves separated, and out popped a tiny brown doll wearing what looked to be a black-and-gold onesie and box braids.

Gum Baby stood in front of me with her hands on her hips and glared. "After Gum Baby saved your behind, you gonna act brand-new. And here she was, ready to invite you to join her next secret mission."

I stood up, and Junior did as well. "What mission?" I asked. "And . . . wait, what's with the disguise?"

Gum Baby stopped glaring and smiled proudly. "It's a sap

suit! Gum Baby designed it herself. Well, sort of. Gum Baby got the idea from Anansi. See, he pretended to be Brer Rabbit, but it was really a disguise. So Gum Baby figured she'd create her own disguise. Nobody will ever know it's her!"

I looked at the suit, which was slowly collapsing under its own weight, then at the fountain. "And...you pretended to be a fountain? How did you get the water to flow out of the sap suit?"

Gum Baby shook a hand at me, sending sap everywhere, and begin to fold up the suit until it was the size of a sticky handkerchief. Then she tied the corners around her neck and draped it over her shoulders like a cloak. "Flow? Gum Baby just spat out a stream of water. Tasted nasty, too."

I looked at the pool, remembered trailing my fingers through what I thought was fountain water, and grew nauseated.

"Anyway," Gum Baby continued. "There's a new mission. And should you choose to accept it—which you will, because Gum Baby didn't spit out a gallon of dirty water for you to get a case of the shiver knees—we need to go now. You can even bring your friend."

Junior and I glanced at each other. "He's not my friend," we both said at the same time.

"Jinx. Now you two can't talk until Gum Baby says so. Let's go. John Henry's waiting."

And with that, the tiny loudmouth stomped while—get this—muttering stomping sounds.

"Is she always like this?" Junior asked.

I sighed, nodded, then followed her. What choice did I have? She, apparently, knew where John Henry was, and if I was going to find out who the Shamble Man was, where he was keeping my grandmother, and why he apparently hated me, well (and I really hated to admit this) . . . I had to listen to Gum Baby.

Nyame's palace reminded me of a shopping mall built out of sunsets and dreams. Golden walls rose out of polished stone floors so shiny I could see my reflection in them. More waterfalls spilled over doorways that led to rooms of all sizes. Bedrooms, chambers, halls, auditoriums, alcoves, atriums, and—more than I could count—sunrooms. Of course the sky god would have a bajillion sunrooms. I pictured Nyame sitting in a golden rocking chair while reading the paper and I snorted.

"Gum Baby knows you ain't laughing."

I looked up to find her sitting on Junior's shoulder, the two of them apparently in mid-conversation. Something about seeing the two of them cutting up like old friends sent a hot spike through my chest. And thinking about that made me angry. Let her sit on his shoulder for a change. We'd see how he liked shampooing *his* hair seven times in a row to get all the sap out.

Gum Baby leaned next to Junior's ear and started to whisper, looking back at me several times to make sure I was watching. "And then we were flying, and *somebody* was screaming his head off...." I rolled my eyes and kept walking.

We reached a large chamber with a huge doorway. I mean enormous. Another waterfall splashed down in front of it, and it was so large the noise was deafening. This room—it stood out like a pimple in the middle of a forehead. Black stone columns covered with intricate engravings framed the entrance that stretched all the way to the ceiling.

"Gee, I wonder who's inside," I said.

Gum Baby shook her head, her box braids flinging sap everywhere. "Some people just don't listen. Gum Baby told you already. Three times!"

"No, it was just a...Never mind."

Junior bit back a smile and I narrowed my eyes at him as I walked up to the waterfall door. I took a step forward—

And got knocked on my butt by a thousand buckets of water. Gum Baby shook her head at me, then hopped down, walked to the left side of the door while staring at me, and pressed a button I hadn't seen. Silently, but still shaking her head and maintaining eye contact, she marched back over to Junior, scrambled up onto his shoulder, and pointed. A giant seam seemed to split the wall of water in half as it slowly stopped falling.

"Now," she said, slowly, "do you want to try again?"

Just once I'd love to visit Alke and not get soaking wet.

We moved inside, and the first thing I noticed was how dark it was. It surprised me, because, well, Nyame was the sky god. I associated the light of the sun with him, from the clothes he wore to his golden eyes. But in here it was as if night had fallen and was here to stay. I could barely see a few feet in front of me, and we moved cautiously forward until—

"I'd say that's far enough."

The voice rumbled low from the far corner, shaking my bones and rattling my teeth. My heart swelled at its familiarity, even as the beginnings of unease tickled the back of my neck.

"John Henry?" I called. "It's me, Tristan."

A deep sigh sounded. "I reckoned as much. Knew when I saw you in the wall you'd find yourself here, some way, somehow."

I took another step forward. "I saw what happened, what the"—I looked around, then inched closer—"what the Shamble Man did to you. I need to find him."

A rumbling sound filled the room. It took me several seconds to realize that John Henry was chuckling. I could feel the vibrations in my feet! The tiny doll looked concerned, and Junior's eyes were wide as he moved behind me. Good. Not so tough now.

"Listen to you. I knew you'd find your strength, Tristan. Reckoned it'd take you a bit longer, but you're a leader. People look up to you. Might go so far as to say they depend on you." There was a creak in the darkness, like someone was shifting in their seat, and I frowned. But John Henry kept talking. "So I need you to hear me very carefully. Are you listening?"

"Yes. Yes, I'm listening."

"And who else is in here? Gum Baby? That you?"

"Gum Baby's right here." Her voice was so soft and full of worry that I looked at her. What did she know that I didn't? Was it the reason John Henry was staying here in the dark? How badly injured was he?

"I am here as well," Junior said. He cleared his throat. "If that is all right, sir."

John Henry grunted. "Told you about all that *sir* business. Nyame still ain't letting you roam around?"

Junior kicked at the floor. "No."

Now what did *that* mean? Why would Nyame want to keep an annoying know-it-all like Junior inside the palace? Was he grounded? Everyone seemed to know something about the skinny boy but me, and it was starting to get irritating.

"That's just fine," said John Henry. "You need to hear this, too, and all of you better listen." He paused, and I felt the room go silent, like the calm before the storm, or the disappearing ocean before a tidal wave. Again I heard furniture creak.

"Don't. Go. Looking. For. The Shamble Man."

The words landed like hammer blows. I stared at the darkness in disbelief. How could he say that? Why wouldn't John Henry want to find his attacker? What could scare John Henry? Was the Shamble Man in league with the Maafa and the iron monsters? I had so many questions and no answers, and my patience had worn thin.

"You don't understand. He took my—" I began, but John Henry cut me off.

"Oh, but I do. Now's not the time to be a hero, Tristan. It's the time to be a leader. Sometimes them things ain't the same."

"But—"

"NO!" The shout rattled the stone walls, and dust fell on us. Heavy, labored breathing followed, then the creaking sound you hear when someone reclines on a bed. A long, drawn-out exhale came next.

"He's dangerous, Tristan," John Henry said. "You don't know him like I do. He's angry. At all of us, but you especially. Leave him alone in the Storm Lands. Right now he has my hammer, and I just . . ." His voice faded for a moment. When he spoke again, it was with the weariness of someone ready to accept defeat. "I asked Gum Baby to bring you here so I could tell you this, face-to-face. Leave this to the other gods. They'll handle it."

He has my grandmother! I wanted to scream, but before I could, the words John Henry had just spoken registered in my mind. What did he mean *They'll handle it*? He wasn't going to help? The only thing that could keep John Henry from standing up and doing what was right was if…

I squeezed the Gye Nyame charm on my adinkra bracelet and activated the powers of the sky god. When I opened my eyes, the entire room was revealed like a picture drawn in invisible ink. Gold-and-silver words outlined everything, from the floor to the walls to the ceiling. They wove together to give shape to the room, and I shook my head in disbelief. No matter how many times I used this power, I was amazed. Alke was really a giant story, and it was no wonder Anansesems were so revered here.

Then I saw the bed.

And the figure sprawled on top.

John Henry lay on his back, his head propped up by a pillow the size of an armchair. The massive god had his hands folded across his chest. From the waist up he looked fine. His story swirled about him, fragments of folktales collected into a legend so powerful it had inspired millions in this realm and in my own.

But his feet—especially his right one—were slowly disappearing.

His story, which framed his body and made John Henry himself, was slowly unraveling and disappearing off into the darkness.

At first I thought something was wrong with my eyes. Or with the adinkra. Whatever this was, it had to be impossible, and I didn't want to believe. But as I watched, the god lying in the bed lifted his head and stared at me. In that moment I knew, and he understood that I knew. No wonder he was being kept in a dark room. No wonder everyone wanted to keep it hush-hush, so as not to start a panic. If it could happen to the leader of MidPass and one of the strongest gods in Alke, it could happen to any of them.

John Henry was starting to fade away.

16
BUMBLETONGUE OVERBOARD

MY FINGERS CLENCHED AND UNCLENCHED ON THEIR OWN.

Gum Baby and Junior let me be as we hurried down the hallway. They shot me glances every so often, but nobody spoke. The magnitude of what I'd seen tore through my mind, leaving me no chance to even think about forming words, let alone sentences. John Henry. Fading.

How had the Shamble Man's attack led to the unraveling of his story?

Before we left the giant folk hero, I'd promised him I was going to make things right, no matter what anyone said. "Would you just sit by if it was your grandmother?" I'd asked.

John Henry had only sighed and said, "I reckon I wouldn't. But that's what friends are for, Tristan. To help you see things you might've missed 'cause you're so fired up. Don't let your anger get ahold of you. Or else you might find yourself standing right alongside the Shamble Man. But I can't stop you. Just know, if you're not careful, you could make things worse."

I wasn't sure how things could get any worse. John Henry was down for the count. The Shamble Man had Nana. Had he hurt her, too?

Dozens of frightening answers to that question rattled around in my brain, leaving no room for anything else. I could barely manage to place one foot in front of the other, so it was a big surprise when a hand suddenly grabbed my shoulder and stopped me in my tracks.

"Hey, are you okay?"

I looked up in confusion at the sound of Junior's voice. We'd returned to the sitting room where Miss Sarah and Miss Rose had left us. Gum Baby had scampered off somewhere, leaving me and the new boy to make idle small talk. Great.

"I'm fine," I said. "Where'd Gum Baby go?"

"She said something about getting the gang back together. I don't know. But stop trying to change the subject. You're not fine." His hand dropped away and returned to cradling the satchel he'd had slung over his back. "I can tell."

"Oh yeah?" I challenged. "And just how do you think you can tell?"

He shrugged. "Because I've seen that expression before.

The one you're wearing right now. It's the expression you have when you realize someone you've looked up to isn't invincible. They aren't perfect. I've worn that expression. And I was in the room back there with you. Everyone knows the stories about you, Tristan. The boy with all the gifts from the gods. Your eyes went golden in the room with the big guy. That's Nyame's power—seeing the stories, right? So you know what I think?"

"What?"

"I think you saw something terrible in there. Something all the gods around here know and won't share. They won't tell me, and I'm guessing they didn't tell you, either. But you saw it. You *saw* it."

There was something in Junior's tone. Something raw. Jealousy? No, it was more subtle than that. He was envious. Of me. The realization jarred me out of the funk John Henry's state had put me in. I would give up all my powers if it meant I could have my grandmother back. I wanted nothing more than to walk with Nana back to our farm in Alabama and have everything return to normal.

"You wanna know what I saw?" I asked.

Junior nodded, a desperate hunger in his eyes. "I do."

I opened my mouth to tell him, then paused. The look on his face was something between fear and horrified anticipation. That's when I understood. The knowledge could hurt him. If the gods could fade, the people of Alke could fade.

Weren't they stories, too? Granddad had said that people did funny things when faced with their own mortality. I didn't want to start a panic. *It's the time to be a leader.* The words of John Henry echoed in my ears. So I didn't tell the complete truth.

"John Henry is . . . sick," I finally said.

"Sick?" Junior searched my face. "Is it bad?"

I hesitated, then sighed. "Maybe. I don't know. What I do know is that if I don't find the Shamble Man, John Henry won't be the only one suffering. That's the number one priority right now."

He nodded, then stopped and looked at my hands. "Hey, weren't you wearing gloves before?"

I winced. This dude was sharp. I was hoping no one would notice I'd taken them off back in the room. "Yeah, I . . . Well, they were John Henry's, and I wanted him to have them back." What I didn't tell him was that the gloves were imbued with the steel-driving man's strength, and I thought they might restore a little bit of his power. It was a long shot, but I could hope.

Luckily, I was saved from having to explain anything more, because Gum Baby returned, this time on the shoulders of Ayanna, who was carrying a familiar rectangular piece of wood on her back. Unfortunately, it wasn't in great shape.

"Your raft!" I said. "What happened to it?"

A thick crack wound its way through the magical craft.

It had been smeared with pitch, and thin ropes were tied around it, trying to keep it from splitting any further.

Ayanna shot a stern look at Gum Baby, who was doing her best to avoid eye contact. "Someone was supposed to borrow it for an hour and ferry supplies to the workers rebuilding the market, but *somehow* that certain someone crashed into a minaret and nearly brought the whole tower down."

"Gum Baby thought she saw a rainbow," the little rascal said with a pout.

"Whatever happened, we have to go. Now," I said. "Before someone comes along and tells us we're being foolish." I quickly summarized my exchange with John Henry, once more leaving out the details of his affliction. I didn't know exactly how much Ayanna and Gum Baby knew, and a problem shared was a problem doubled. It was up to me alone to fix this.

"'The Shamble Man is in the Storm Lands?" Ayanna said. "That doesn't sound good. If he went where I think he did, we all might be in trouble."

"What do you mean?"

"The Storm Lands is a nickname for Nyanza, the City of Lakes in the Grasslands. According to Annie, a powerful goddess lives there. If the Shamble Man attacks her..."

Ayanna didn't finish the thought, but she didn't have to. The image of John Henry fading away was seared into my mind. "I have to make sure that doesn't happen," I said grimly.

"*We* do," Ayanna corrected.

"Yeah, stop hogging all the glory, Bumbletongue." Gum Baby was unfolding her sap suit and preparing to climb inside it again. We all stared at her, and she looked around. "What? Not yet? Oh, excuse Gum Baby, she thought it was business time. Y'all still lollygagging. Gum Baby's sorry, go ahead and waste a few more seconds. She'll wait."

I shook my head, but she was right. It was time to go. Before I took a step, Junior cleared his throat. "I can't go with you."

Ayanna frowned. "Why not?"

Personally, I didn't care. No one had invited him anyway. But I kept my mouth shut and tried to seem shocked. "Oh no, why not?"

He rolled his eyes at me. "Nyame wants me to stay where he can see me."

"Why does he care so much?" I asked. It was like Junior was on house arrest, which didn't exactly make me want to trust him.

Junior shrugged. "All I know is, if I stray more than a few yards away from the palace, our favorite sentry statues stomp around the Golden Crescent trying to find me, or Miss Sarah and Miss Rose swoop down out of nowhere and yell at me.

But I can at least distract them for you. Give you a chance to get a head start."

"Oh," I said, surprised at his offer. "That's ... actually pretty cool. Thanks."

Junior raised an eyebrow. "I'm not doing it for you." He turned and flashed his wide smile at Ayanna. "I'm doing it for *her*."

Ayanna had the nerve to blush.

Aaaaand just like that, it was time to go.

We found Keelboat Annie at the marina, on the deck of her boat, yelling at the water.

"I don't care if the waves itch! You better start actin' right or Imma give you more than an itch to worry about." The goddess looked up as I walked over with my eyebrows raised, Ayanna, Gum Baby, and Junior a few yards behind me. She'd changed into a long floral dress, and her hair was smoothed into a long braided ponytail that draped over her right shoulder. When she shook her head, it twirled circles in the wind. "'Scuse all the yelling. Some rivers are just always complaining."

Behind me, Junior shuffled his feet. "Is she ... arguing with the water?" I heard the boy whisper. "Orrrr ..."

Gum Baby patted his ankle. She'd hitched a ride in the cuff of Junior's pants. Good luck to him getting out those stains later. The morning I returned from Alke, Granddad had looked at me for a solid five minutes when he'd caught me trying to wash the sheets from my first encounter with Gum Baby. You know the look. The *Boy, if you don't...* look. Then he walked off grumbling and shaking his head, and the next day I found two bars of soap and a brand-new washcloth stacked on the dresser in my room.

Ayanna held back a laugh as Gum Baby started lecturing Junior in a very serious tone. "Sometimes when a goddess and the magical body of water that carries her everywhere love each other, they argue. Gum Baby's seen it all the time. So no, it's not about you. Take a seat."

I jogged up to the boat. "Hey, Annie, do you think you can give us a lift? We have to get to the Grasslands region, and fast. To, uh..." I looked to Ayanna for help.

She snorted. "Nyanza."

"Right," I said. "Nyanza."

Keelboat Annie whistled. "Nyanza, huh? That's no pleasure jaunt. Especially with ole Frothy Bottom down there grumbling."

"Please," I said. "It's an emergency!"

"What, the big shots in the palace couldn't help you? You had to come back here to beg a ride from me?"

"No, no, nothing like that," I said, stumbling over my words as I tried to think of a way to placate a ticked-off goddess. "It's just—"

"BWA-HA-HA-HA-HAAA!" Keelboat Annie's laugh

exploded out of her, and the whole boat shook as she threw back her head and slapped the hull. "Hoo-whee! The look on your face. Get on in here, y'all, it ain't no problem. Giving folks rides is what I do. Never let it be said Keelboat Annie is petty. Powerful, yes. Punctual, you betcha. But petty? I'll leave that to high-and-mighties in the palace."

Everyone climbed the ladder. As Ayanna stepped aboard, Keelboat Annie jerked her chin back at the tiller. "Don't get comfortable, Miss Thang—it's time for you to get some practice in."

"Me?" Ayanna said, her eyes wide.

"It's what you're here for, ain't it? Besides, I'm not messing up my favorite dress."

The pilot gulped, but she nodded and unstrapped her golden-tipped staff, whispered to the face on the end of it, then marched with grim determination to the tiller. She wasn't planning on using that little thing as the keel pole, was she? I grinned, then stepped closer to Keelboat Annie. "Where's . . . the SBP?" I asked in a low voice. No need telling everybody I let the Story Box and Anansi out of my sight.

Keelboat Annie made a face. "I left that thing beneath one of my old boots in a storage locker. Don't need Mr. Web Butt doing something he ain't supposed to. Go on and fetch him if you like. Good riddance."

I quickly walked over to the locker that Annie had indicated, found the beat-up, funky boots she'd mentioned, gingerly pulled out the SBP, and let a sigh of relief escape my lungs. Anansi was still snoring in his web hammock, a strand of drool dangling from his mouth as his hat covered his eyes. Thank goodness. Everybody was where they were supposed to be.

Well, almost everyone.

When I returned to the railing, Junior continued to shuffle his feet on the dock, his toe tracing one of the worn carvings. From here he didn't look as sure of himself as when he was talking junk on the beach. In fact, he looked . . . well, like a boy whose friends (AND I USE THAT TERM LOOSELY) were about to leave him behind. So while the others prepared for the trip, I called down to him, "You still worried about Miss Sarah or Miss Rose finding you?"

He scowled. "I'm not afraid." Then the scowl disappeared and he said, "And they're not that bad, really. They just worry. It's really Nyame who's always after me. I'm trying to avoid hearing any more lectures about my future, how I could be better than my father, blah-blah-blah."

Now *that* I could understand. Grown-ups are always going on and on about the future, but it's the *now* we have to suffer through. It's hard thinking about next week when today is punching you in the face. Guess you get better at it the older you get.

I felt sorry for Junior. He was a bit of a jerk sometimes (a lot of times), but . . . I don't know, sometimes when people are going through things, they act out. I'd gotten a lot of detention slips for fighting in school the weeks after Eddie died. I'd picked up on every insult, real or imagined. If Junior's trouble with his father, whoever he was, was impacting him the same way, maybe I had to give him another chance. What was it Keelboat Annie had muttered to herself? *Sometimes it's something deep in the water that's stirring things up on the surface.* That sounded like it could apply to humans, too.

"Okay," Ayanna called out. "We're ready! Wait, that isn't supposed to do that.... Oh, we're good!"

I made a snap decision. As Keelboat Annie moved around the deck loosening lines and doing her best to ignore Gum Baby stomping behind her and shouting out fake sailing orders, I gestured to the ladder.

"Come with us," I said to Junior. "Worst thing that can happen is they yell at you. Again."

Junior squinted at me suspiciously. When he realized I wasn't joking, he grabbed his hair with both hands. "Are you serious?"

I nodded.

"Ha! You aren't as stuck-up as they say you are." He scrambled up the ladder and then vaulted over the deck railing with one hand, the other firmly grasping his satchel. He punched me in the shoulder and jogged over to where Ayanna was gripping the tiller. He said something and she laughed, the tension slipping out of her shoulders.

"Smooth, ain't he?" Gum Baby appeared on the railing, walking it with both tiny arms outstretched like she was on a tightrope. "Gum Baby would hang with him any day."

"Yeah, yeah," I muttered, rubbing my shoulder and turning away. "Real smooth."

"Aw, don't be jealous, Bumbletongue. Gum Baby would hang with you any day, too. Well, no, it'd have to be a specific day. In the afternoon. Gum Baby can't deal with you first thing in the morning. So... let's say on Tuesday afternoons. That's when you can come hang out." She stared at me for a second and shook her head. "On second thought, make it *every other* Tuesday."

The boat rocked from side to side, and Keelboat Annie glared down at the clear blue water of the bay. "Don't you start with me," she warned.

I frowned. This was the second or third time she'd gotten upset with Old Man River, and the situation was beginning to set off warning bells in my head. I pinched the Anansi adinkra on my bracelet. It was warm. Not hot to the touch— just warm. What did that mean? Half an iron monster was nearby? Somewhere a hullbeast was calling me names? What was I supposed to do with that?

Ayanna held out her staff behind her, whispering beneath her breath, and my eyes grew wide as Keelboat Annie's giant pole mimicked her actions. When Ayanna lifted her staff, the keel pole went up, too, and when she brought it down, the boat shifted beneath us, lurching awkwardly out of its slip in the marina. It moved in fits and spurts toward one of several river mouths that emptied into the bay, this one guarded by large boulders with deep shadows.

The boat tilted. "Sorry!" Ayanna called. Her face was creased with determination. "I thought that would be smoother."

I bit my tongue.

Gum Baby, however, did not. "Don't you get Gum Baby's hair wet! It ain't a wash day."

The staff lifted and descended carefully, and so did the keel pole. The boat jerked forward abruptly, then shook, and as we passed between the giant boulders, it began to pick up speed.

"Um . . ." I said as I grabbed the railing for dear life. Junior stumbled back over to where I stood, his jaw clenched as he stubbornly held on to his satchel instead of the hull. That boy needed to prioritize better.

"It's not me!" Ayanna said, her voice filled with panic. "Look, I'm not moving it!"

Sure enough, she held the staff up in the air, and the giant keel pole had risen out of the water, too. And yet the boat was steadily racing along the river, sloshing around curves and scraping across shallow bends.

The SBP vibrated as Anansi woke up. "What in the seven webs is going on? Boy, what have you done now?"

Beside me, Junior stiffened. I glanced at him, then showed him the phone screen. "Ignore him. He's just—"

But while I tried explaining how rude the trickster god could be, Junior dashed to the other side of the boat, slipping and sliding as he went. I stared in disbelief. What had I said?

Keelboat Annie shook her head, her eyes narrowed. "Something ain't right," she said quietly. "Let me take over, maybe Old Man River wasn't just hollerin' to holler earlier. Maybe if I—"

She didn't even have a chance to unbind the pole before the boat shot forward as if out of a cannon, throwing everyone to the deck. A huge wave slammed over the railing, dousing everyone with ice-cold water, and the taste of something metallic got into my mouth. I spat it out, disgusted, then froze.

Metallic.

Iron.

"Wait a—" I began to shout, just as another wave washed over the railing, picked me up, and slammed my head into the deck. The world blurred. I felt the boat list to one side, and the last thing I heard was someone screaming as we all tumbled into the freezing river.

17
KULTURE VULTURE

BACK IN CHICAGO, OCCASIONALLY IN THE SUMMER WHEN IT GOT really hot, one of the fire hydrants in the middle of my block would be opened. Sometimes the fire department would do it, swooping into the hood with their truck sirens off but the lights flashing, and one firefighter would toss out candy while another wrenched open the hydrant and let out a jet of water for us to cool off in. Other times, somebody from the block would do it. Kids would laugh and play in the spray, and even a few adults would dip their toes in.

Once, when I was very young and feeling brave, I stepped into the blast of water and it hit me in the chest like a freight train, knocking me over and sending me head over heels down the street until I crashed into a lamppost. Every now and again I remember that scary feeling of suddenly being out of control as some incredible force carried me away and I was powerless to do anything about it.

That's how I felt as the river swept me along.

My head was just barely breaking the surface, allowing me the chance to breathe. But I couldn't see anything but gray water, and a constant roar filled my ears. Old Man River was in pain—I could hear the cries of someone being forced to go to a place against their will. More water got into my mouth as I was propelled forward, and I just hoped it didn't have anything nasty in it. Like blood. Or flat soda. Bleeeeech.

"Oomph!" I gasped as I crashed into something round and solid. It felt like a light pole, and I grabbed it before I was carried away again. My legs flailed behind me as the rushing current tried to pull me along, and my arms grew tired as I hugged that pole like it was my favorite teddy bear.

I mean...the stuffed animal I lost.

A long time ago.

And definitely wasn't still sitting on my bed back in Chicago.

ANYWAY...

Just when I felt my grip begin to give way, the water receded all at once, like someone had shut off the magical-river faucet, and I crumpled on the ground in exhaustion. It felt like the earth trembled beneath me when I landed, and I groaned.

"There's gotta be a better way to get around Alke," I said, wincing as I sat up, pausing as the ground shook again, just a little. What was going on? "First a fiery sinkhole, and now rivers with attitudes. What's next, blizzards that make fun of your haircut when you cross the mountain?"

No one laughed. Or said anything. I was alone. The mist slowly began to fade, and I saw that I was sitting on a patch of grass so green it looked fake.

"Hey!" I shouted. "Ayanna. Annie? Junior?"

No answer. Where had everyone gone? It's pretty hard to hide a twenty-foot magical riverboat. My backpack hung limply off my shoulders and I panicked, peeked inside, then let out a sigh of relief. The inner lining was waterproof. Nana's quilt, even though it was in tatters, was safe.

"Phew. Got scared there for a second." I patted my pocket and pulled out the SBP. "Anansi, where—"

I stopped mid-sentence and stared in horror at the phone. "No."

It couldn't be.

"Ohhh no."

There, right down the middle of the screen, was a giant crack that ran from top to bottom. The phone was off, the screen dark and unresponsive. Worst of all, Anansi was nowhere to be seen.

"Oh no. Oh no, no, no, no, no."

When I flipped over the SBP, water dripped from between the edges of the screen and the back cover. Somehow the insides had gotten wet! But Anansi had said the SBP was waterproof. Had he been mistaken? Or lying? I couldn't put anything past him, but right then I'd have given my left arm to hear his advice about what to do next.

I had to dry out the phone, and fast.

As I sat there and worried (just a little) and panicked (okay, a lot) and tried to regain my breath, I looked around. The mist had disappeared completely.

"Sweet peaches."

The object I'd crashed into wasn't a light pole. It was the strangest tree I'd ever seen, with a straight, turquoise-colored trunk that seemed to ripple as winds gusted against it. The branches curved in the air like outstretched arms, and the leaves alternated between coral blue and emerald green depending on which way I turned my head. Other trees just like it grew nearby. Tiny ornamental shrubs and bunches of multicolored flowers grew between the trees, and tall, stiff stalks of grass covered the landscape everywhere else. It was a garden, a small and beautiful one, and for a moment I thought I was back above Nyame's palace in the Golden Crescent.

But there were no waterfalls, no view of the Ridge to the north, nor the bay and the Burning Sea to the south and west. Instead, there was a massive cloud system that covered the land, turning everything charcoal gray like a thick, drab curtain. Was this the storm we'd seen on the horizon?

"Enough sightseeing," I muttered to myself. I had things to do. Fix the SBP. Go to Nyanza and find the Shamble Man.

Finally, I had to get my nana back. I got up filled with determination and marched through the garden to the ... edge of the ground?

Wait a minute.

Nothing but gray sky surrounded me and the garden. Another gust of wind blew through the trees and I felt the earth tremble. I held my breath and gripped the tree nearest me as I leaned past it to look over the ledge.

"Ohhh," I said.

I hadn't landed on the ground—I'd landed on a roof.

A very-high-off-the-ground, wind-yanking-at-my-clothes sort of roof.

"Ohhh nooo."

Far below, a nearly dry lakebed stretched as far as the eye could see. Brown mud and sand surrounded the few remaining pools of water, but the most amazing part? There was a city growing out of the middle of the lake.

You heard me right.

An honest-to-goodness city.

Single-story homes and tall skyscrapers rested on giant lily pads currently nestled in the mud, and enormous plants on the shoreline provided shade. Tall grass grew between the lily pads, while miniature forests topped the skyscrapers, like the one I'd apparently landed on. I was very thankful the tree had been there to keep me from falling off.

In the middle of it all, like a jewel set in a ring of amber and jade, was a large turquoise dome the size of a football stadium, sectioned and patterned like a tortoise shell. It looked like an upside-down bowl made out of a stained-glass window, bright and semitransparent, and even from this distance I could see more homes and buildings inside it.

Inverted emerald arches floated in the air above the dome, as if someone had drawn smiles in midair. They hovered in a circle like the tips of a crown. Every so often the ground would rumble, and a surge of water would come from a hole in the top of the dome. Very little of it landed in the lake. Instead, it went into the U shapes, where geysers shot the water into the clouds above the city. Not the huge thunderhead on the horizon, but smaller rain clouds that could feed the plains below.

All in all, this place was actually pretty cool.

Except for me having to cling to the tippy-top of a narrow roof.

"Deep breaths," I said. "Deep breaths. You're fine. You are absolutely fine. You're talking to yourself while in a magical land with blue trees, but you're fine. Just . . . find a way down." I still clutched the damp SBP in my right hand, and I had the irrational urge to find a bowl of rice to drop it in. That's what fixed a wet phone, right? Rice? Or was it oats?

I was imagining the SBP sticking out of a bowl of oatmeal, with Anansi begging me to save him from his wholesome, cinnamon-flavored demise, when a shadow swept across the rooftop. A gust of wind carried a foul scent and something brushed my ear. I recoiled.

"Easy there, li'l fella," said a drawling voice behind me. "Easy there. Another half-drowned fish floppin' about. Stuck in the mud, huh? Just you lie still and don't wriggle around so much, and this won't hurt a bit."

I turned and froze.

A six-foot-tall bird with a wicked hooked beak and wings was perched on the tree above me, and it stared at me hungrily as it reached out with talons as sharp as knives.

This bird . . . this bird was enormous. Gigantic. Half dinosaur, maybe, I don't know. The weird monster had a bare head and wings the length of couches. It was covered in matted and droopy grayish-brown feathers and . . .

Wow.

Okay.

The bird wore tattered blue jeans that had been ripped into uneven shorts. But the weirdest and scariest thing (if that last sentence didn't terrify you enough) was that the creature wore a necklace of what looked to be trinket-covered bones.

A sickening odor drifted from the bird as it fluttered down to stand over me. It turned its head sideways so one large eye could swivel to examine me, and then it spoke, its huge hooked beak clacking with each word.

"Ahhh, *rehk,* what do we have, what do we have here? A

flying worm? A floating deer? A meandering morsel on my side of town? Hoo-whee, *rehk rehk,* it's about to go down!" The bird did a little hop-step and flapped its wings. I gagged. That odor was *nasty*! And...was it rapping to me?

Just then I realized it wasn't alone.

A group of smaller birds—magpies, hawks, even a trio of chickadees—circled above, shouting out encouragement to what was apparently their leader.

"Get him, boss!"

"Tell him what the deal is!"

"Break it down for him on the one and three!"

Great. Hype men. Hype birds? Whatever.

The giant bird strutted forward and shook out its feathers. "What's the matter, dinner number two? You come to my home and think I wouldn't notice you? I run the Nyanza, baby, this my turf. Now just hold still, or this'll hurt much worse."

Nyanza. So I had made it to the City of Lakes. But... that was in the Grasslands. How had I ended up so far away from the Golden Crescent? What had Old Man River been thinking? And where was everybody else?

"I'm talking to you, little grub."

I didn't think it was wise to insult a creature that looked like it could rip me to shreds in any number of ways, so I just shook my head and covered my nose and mouth with the crook of my elbow.

"Who are you?" I asked in a muffled voice.

"Me?" The bird hop-stepped again. "Me? *Rehk rehk,* I'm the bird with the word! The deacon of speakin', the chaplain of what's happenin'. You can't get flyer than me, my little snack, and it's not just because of these wings. I coast on the rhythm and soar on melodies. You can call me DJ Kulture, with a *K.* Throw a 'sir' at the end to put some respect on my name."

Okay, first of all, I didn't like the way the bird—DJ Kulture, or whatever— kept referring to me as some sort of meal. Second, I *definitely* didn't like the way his talons clicked closer with every little hop. I needed to get off this roof and down to solid ground, but there was no way I was jumping from this high up. Where was Ayanna's raft, or even Thandiwe with her forebear when I needed it? I would've given anything, even some of their good-natured ribbing, to have their help right now.

The bird flapped again. Those wings dwarfed me—he could probably carry me to his nest or wherever he lived and eat me there if he chose.

Wait.

Carry me.

A plan began to form in my mind. A stupid plan. Possibility of dying: 85 percent. But it was the only thing I could think of. I scooted backward until I rested against a tree and then slowly stood up to my full height. The bird hopped, twisting his head to the left and to the right, switching which large eye studied me. "Okay," I said, peeking behind me quickly and grimacing at the long drop to the muddy ground below. "Okay, Mr. Deacon of Speaking, you think maybe you could help me get down from here? I landed—"

The bird threw his head back and let out a screech. It wasn't until I saw his feathers quivering and his head bobbing up and down that I realized he was laughing. At me.

Anger bubbled up in my chest and I folded my arms. "What's so funny?"

The bird clacked his beak and cocked his head at me. "You, my little smug smorgasbord. Only way down for you is through my beak and into my stomach."

Remember the plan. I pressed my back against the tree as the bird flapped his wings. "I didn't think crows ate people," I shouted over the gusts of foul air.

"Crows?! Crows?!" The flapping stopped and DJ Kulture hopped angrily from foot to foot. "Do I look like a *rehk rehk* featherbrained marble chaser? I'm a flesh-rippin' raptor! A buzzard ballin' from the egg to the nest, you understand me? A crow? Why, little boy, I oughta—"

I couldn't help it. Really, I couldn't. I started to laugh. "Wait. Wait. A buzzard? As in a vulture? DJ Kulture Vulture? With a *K*?" I started laughing again as the stinky monster flapped and squawked in rage.

The bird's cocky attitude and manner of speaking began to change as he got angrier and angrier. "I am not *a* vulture.

I am *the* vulture. An avian aeronaut who rules the skies. Perhaps you've heard of me? I'm the one who chased those metal beasts back to the sea from whence they came. I'm the savior of the skies, the one who extinguished the burning seam in the sky with a flap of my wings."

Hold up.

This bird was taking credit for things my friends and I did! And, to make matters even worse, the necklace looked familiar. *Reeeally* familiar. I recognized some items around his neck. A few of them, at least. Kulture Vulture had taken trophies from around Alke—as far as I could tell—and collected them in a necklace. There was a lifeless brand fly and a small fetterling. There was a kierie from the Ridge and strands of the Thicket, all of them twisted and shaped around bleached-white tiny skulls and finger bones.

"If it wasn't for *me*," Kulture Vulture continued, "the web-spinner would never have been found."

That did it. I whipped out the SBP, intending to show Anansi how this...this thief was taking our exploits—no, *my* exploits—and twisting the narrative so he was the hero. Unbelievable! But when I looked at the screen, my shoulders slumped. I'd forgotten it wasn't working.

"My, my, my," Kulture Vulture said, suddenly so close I could see each dirty, dingy feather on his chest quiver as he spoke. "What is that? Hoo-whee, you're full of surprises, little morsel. Maybe I'll— Oh, no you don't!"

Before I could slip the SBP back in my pocket, Kulture Vulture lunged forward, snagging the phone with his beak and retreating with a flapping hop-step backward.

"Hey!" I shouted.

The bird let out a harsh *rehk rehk* and turned to flap away with his prize.

I threw caution to the winds...I had no other choice. I dashed forward, lowering my head, and leaped at the bird. I grabbed Kulture Vulture around the neck and we tumbled off the roof.

I'd ridden on the back of a shadow crow the size of a bus. I'd ridden on a magical flying raft and a metal shield that converted into a hoverboard. I'd ridden the L train in Chicago—red, blue, orange, you name it, I'd ridden in cars you wouldn't be caught dead in.

This—and I cannot stress this enough—was the worst of them all.

Riding on the back of a screeching, grown-man-size vulture that smelled like he had rolled around in spoiled meat (right before he ate it) was enough to make me wanna puke. And I would have, if not for the fact we were hurtling to the ground at a kajillion miles per hour. Anything I unleashed would just splatter right back into my face.

How's that for a mental image?

"*Reeeekh!* Get off, get off!"

Kulture Vulture's words whipped by my ears, barely audible as the wind rushed past us. At least the bird wasn't trying to rap anymore. His wings flapped wildly as he attempted to steer himself. An emerald U went whizzing by, nearly clipping a wing. Another roof zoomed up at us, heavily carpeted in a green tangle of vines, but we shot past that, too. If I ignored the gorgeous rooftop gardens, the kaleidoscopic jeweled windows, and the crystal balconies that jutted out every so often—invisible if you didn't look at them at a precise angle—it would have looked like I was dive-bombing downtown Chicago. That's how many skyscrapers were bunched together, plants growing out of every surface.

"Give me back my phone!" I shouted.

"Rehk rehk!"

The ground was approaching fast. Old Stinky Beak spread his wings wide, trying to slow down, and at the last second, just as we reached the blue-green surface of the pond, I leaped to my feet and kicked off of the giant feathery back. The bird squawked in outrage before he plunged into the water, while I landed heavily on the shore. Pain shot through my right wrist, and I winced as I got to my feet. I could still move it, but it definitely felt sprained and throbbed every time I took a step.

I groaned as my sneakers squelched in thick mud. "Every. Single. Time. Next time I'm wearing sandals. Or swim shoes. Apparently you can't be fly and save the world."

The back of my neck prickled, and I stopped talking. It felt like someone was watching me. I looked around, cupping my hand over my eyes to block the glare from the jewellike windows of the dome. Nothing. Not a trace of anyone.

Except Kulture Vulture. He spluttered in the water and flapped his way out, until he stood dripping wet in front of me with a furious expression on his face.

I dropped into a fighting crouch with both fists up. "Give me back the phone," I growled. "Now."

I seriously needed the SBP. I had to figure out a way to fix it. If not, I was stuck out here with no way to get help, no way to find Nana, no way for anyone to find me, and no way to get back to my world, leaving me with nothing to do but wait around and hope that eventually I'd be rescued.

"*Rehk!* A phone?! A phone?! You could've killed the both of us, and you're worried about that trinket?" The vulture shook his feathers, sending droplets everywhere. "I ought to rip you apart and slurp the marrow from your bones. Do you know who I am? I ..."

The musty buzzard continued to shout threats as he shook his wings dry. The sensation of being watched came over me again. From every direction. There *were* people around, I knew it. Why didn't they come help me? What were they waiting for?

I didn't have a chance to shout for help. Kulture Vulture flapped closer, and I noticed something peculiar about the necklace around his neck. It was shimmering like heat rising from asphalt. I closed my eyes, then reopened them while holding Nyame's adinkra.

The vulture had stopped shouting and was staring at me, his head cocked to the side again. "What's wrong with you?" he asked. "Why's your eyes glowing?"

I ignored him and studied the necklace with growing horror. What I'd thought were simple knickknacks, little charms and trinkets, were actually pieces of people's stories. Dull gold words twisted around them, fragments of sentences and phrases linked by the chain of bones. MY LOVE, MY HEART WILL ALWAYS BE snaked around a dark metal heart-shaped bangle. TO MY BEST FRIEND IN THE WHOLE curled around a locket. Something told me none of these items had been given to the buzzard willingly.

"I'm through playing around with you!" the vulture said. "Just who do you think you are, coming into my territory and messing with me? With me! Don't you know who I am? I rule this miserable mud puddle, little worm. Me! And you think you can muscle me out?"

The necklace wiggled as the bird-monster flapped in anger. Part of it was hidden, stuck beneath a clump of matted and muddy feathers. It captivated me. I found myself fixated on learning what that last trinket was. The vulture spread his wings wide in preparation to fly at me, and the necklace jostled into view.

There it was.

The gold-and-black trim, the sleek and reflective case.

The SBP.

But what I didn't expect to see, what forced a strangled cry to escape, formed from frustrated anger and fear and desperation all at once, was a familiar, slightly bent golden quilting needle twisted around a small bleached-white bone.

18

BIRDS OF A FEATHER

NANA.

Kulture Vulture had seen Nana! I was sure of it. At some point the mangy-feathered bird must've run (or flown) into the Shamble Man—recently! I had to figure out where she'd been taken. Was she okay? The image of John Henry fading, fragments of his story drifting off him like ash from a burned house, gripped my heart and squeezed.

My fists clenched even tighter at the thought of that foul-mouthed birdbrain touching *anything* of Nana's. The water of the very shallow lake sloshed around my ankles as I widened my stance. Kulture Vulture screeched a challenge, flapped his mud-spattered wings, and launched himself at me in a rush of feathers and lake water.

"I'm going to tear you apart, little worm! Your fingers will be my appetizers. Your kneecaps will be my dessert! Your—bluurrgggh." He spluttered as I kicked a glob of sand

and mud into his face. Ain't no rules in street-fighting. Or . . .
lake-fighting, I guess. The large bird fell with a splash, flailing his giant dirty wings in an attempt to clear the dirt from
his eyes and beak.

"Where's my grandmother?" I shouted.

Kulture glared at me with eyes that streamed tears. "What
are you sniveling about?"

"My grandmother. That needle on your necklace—that
was hers."

"Everything around my neck is mine, worm. *Rehk rehk,*
whatever claim you think you have on it is gone. No more.
Finished, you hear? You're looking at the baddest, flyest, most
talented bird with the word. Whoever you're looking for I
can't help you with, but I can promise you one thing—you
found a world of hurt."

He flapped his wings as if getting ready to take off. I
wasn't going to give him the chance.

I dashed forward, lifting my knees high to clear the water
in chopping steps. I guess there was a benefit to Granddad's
training on the shores of Lake Michigan. I covered the
ground between me and my feathery foe in a couple seconds
and squeezed my fists to make the akofena shadow gloves
appear, ready to launch an attack.

A sharp pain stabbed my right wrist. I'd forgotten I'd
injured it during the fall.

"Ah!" I shouted, grimacing in agony. The gloves pulsed

briefly before they began fading from view. Their power wasn't working! But it was too late to pull them back now, so I made the best fist I could make and threw a flurry of punches. Several connected. Kulture Vulture's bald pink head snapped back, and flecks of mud went flying. But the giant bird remained on his feet and snapped at me. I shifted my weight, turned my hips, and fired a straight left. Again the punch connected . . . but the bird wasn't going down. He tried to rake me with a talon. My backpack, with my provisions and Nana's quilt pieces inside, threw off my accuracy, and the blows weren't connecting like they should have. I was just about to launch a third attack when Kulture Vulture leaped high in the air; with two massive flaps he flew awkwardly into the sky, sending water and mud everywhere.

"*Rehk,* you miserable maggot! Who do you think you are?" The vulture flew in a wide circle, his shadow sliding over the surface of the lake like an oil slick. Above him, the storm lurked in the distance, promising to deliver punishment to whoever remained standing. "I will strip the flesh from your bones and use you as a puppet!"

The smaller birds, who until this point had given their boss a wide berth, now flapped around me, preventing me from escaping. I shielded my head from their onslaught as they shouted insults and encouraged their leader.

"That's right, make a puppet outta him, Kulture!"

"Don't let the groundworm getcha, boss!"

"Ooh, you gonna let him rough you up like that?"

With one more powerful flap, Kulture Vulture dove out of the sky, wings folded against his back and talons outstretched. I tried to dodge, but when I moved my head to the left, my feet went to the right, slipping on the muddy lake bottom. Luckily the talons missed my face, but they snagged on my hoodie and yanked me farther off-balance.

SPLASH!

I toppled into the lake face-first and swallowed a mouthful of mud.

You heard me.

Swallowed. Mud.

"Bleeeech!" I spat out a couple of pebbles and a wriggling something I didn't want to think too hard about. My clothes were completely soaked again. I wiped sand from my eyes and looked around. Kulture Vulture was nowhere to be seen, and his bird brigade was hooting and chirping. My legs wobbled as I got to my feet. I was so tired, it felt like I was wading through cement. This couldn't go on much longer. I had to find Nana. I had to stop the Shamble Man, and... and... and...

Exhaustion dragged me down to one knee in the water.

And that's when Kulture Vulture struck.

Whumph!

It felt like one of Reggie's punches hammering into my ribs. The buzzard's talons gripped me around the chest, backpack and all, and yanked me into the air. Giant dusty-black wings flapped on either side of me as a loud screech rang in my ear.

"*REHK!* Where's all the big words now, little worm? You're not so tough up here, though you squirm!"

Oh, for the love of— The rapping was back.

As Kulture Vulture failed all of hip-hop in this realm and mine, the ground dropped farther and farther away, until I could see a series of nearly dry lakes stretching to the horizon, the emerald city rising in the middle with the U-shapes floating above it. Every so often a thundering surge of water would come from the octagonal dome, filling the half rings on their way into the clouds.

It was beautiful.

I would've loved to watch them a little longer, but, you know, I was trying not to get eaten.

"You like falling out of the sky so much, why don't you try it some more?" With that, the talons let go, and I started plummeting to the ground. The lakes tumbled wildly as I flipped head over heels and back again. I tried to scream, but the wind ripped the sound from my mouth. The muddy surface of the water raced toward me, and at the last moment I closed my eyes and braced for impact.

Sharp talons snagged me once again, and I grunted in pain.

"No, little worm, I'm not done with you yet. I like to play with my food a little before I start to nibble." This time

Kulture Vulture had me facing upward, my back to the ground, so I could see him leering at me. A purple snake-like tongue ran over his beak, and I shuddered. Out of the corner of my eye I saw the bird brigade returning, and they squawked and hooted as they followed us.

"What's the matter, little grub? Catbird got your tongue? That's a shame—I was planning on eating that delicacy last. Well, if you don't have anything more to say, I guess the party's over, hmm? Unless it's a dinner party...In that case, you're cordially invited!" His yellow eyes narrowed in antici-pation. "I insist."

I wriggled left and right, struggling to free myself, but Kulture Vulture's grip was like iron. His beak snapped inches from my face as he leered down at me. I couldn't escape. This was it. The end of Tristan Strong, one-time hero and a failure of a grandson. Cause of death: digestion.

Kulture Vulture's feathery friends laughed and jeered at my efforts, calling out helpful tips to mock me.

"Wriggle around some more, little worm, you almost got it!"

"Ooh, that was close!"

"I can't wait for Kulture to tell this story."

I spotted something in the distance. A dark spot racing beneath the clouds. It was going to be the last thing I saw before a giant beak devoured me whole.

Kulture lowered his head, his fowl breath (Get it? No? Not

the time? Oh, okay.) making me gag... when a rock whizzed through the air and clacked off the bird's giant beak. He squawked and lost his momentum. Another rock hit him, and another, and soon a hailstorm of smooth stones the size of my fist began to pelt Kulture Vulture. With wings flapping awkwardly, he dropped out of the sky, and we splashed into a giant mud puddle. I scrambled away, kicking and swinging as the bird brigade began to dive and swoop to harass me.

Then the rocks started hitting them, too.

Bink

Bink

Bink

Three rocks thrown, three birds from Kulture's goon squad sent flapping in outrage to the mud below. It was unbelievable. I'd never seen anyone aim so well. I could barely get my trash into the trash can. The rest of the birds stopped attacking me and started to retreat. One by one they changed course, flying away as more rocks chased them off.

"Hey!" Kulture Vulture shouted after his winged goons. He stood wobbly on his legs and shook his feathers. "Get back here, you cowards! They're just three little morsels!"

Three?

Just then, a familiar voice rang out. "Tristan!"

I turned to see Ayanna, staff gripped in her hand like a baseball bat, running through the mud toward me. And, to my extreme surprise, Junior was following. The boy had his satchel slung around in front of him, one hand inside it, the other holding a stone like the ones that had just whizzed through the air.

Kulture Vulture let out a deafening squawk, and his gang of feathered flunkies wheeled around and flew sheepishly back toward us. Soon we'd be outnumbered again. Kulture Vulture turned to us and clacked his beak.

"That's it!" the buzzard shouted. "I played with you for too long and you got a couple more morsels to join you. Between the three of you I might get a decent meal." With that, the giant monster bird bent over, wings low to the ground, wicked hooked beak aimed directly at my face. But behind him, over his head, I saw that weird silhouette in the sky again, and this time it was closer. It moved in an odd fashion, jerking to the left and right.

It couldn't be...

"Tristan! What are you doing?" Ayanna shouted.

I rolled my head. "Follow my lead," I said. "When I give the signal, attack."

"You have an idea?"

"Something like that."

"That's inspiring," Junior muttered. "Are all your heroic speeches like that?"

I ignored him. At the moment, I needed his aim. Ayanna brandished her staff and Junior hefted his stone. Me? I couldn't make a proper fist with my right hand to engage the akofena, but that didn't mean I was helpless. As Kulture raced forward, I leaped into action, sprinting to meet him. Knees high, just like Granddad taught me. The timing had to be perfect. If I arrived too soon, my plan would fall apart. Too late, and I'd be eaten. I guess that counts as my plan falling apart, too.

Luckily, I was right on time.

I skidded to a stop, spread the fingers of my left hand, twisted around, and slapped the giant bird.

Everyone stopped.

"Did you just—" Ayanna began to ask.

"Did you just smack him?" Junior interrupted.

The smaller birds flapped overhead, stunned into silence. Kulture Vulture brought one wing to his head, then looked at me, confused. "You slapped me!" he said in an accusatory tone.

"I did." I folded my arms across my chest and shook my head in exaggerated disappointment. "You left me no choice."

"But—"

"Honestly, you ought to be ashamed of yourself. Coming out here and terrorizing everyone and you haven't even brushed your teeth. The nerve."

Kulture Vulture's eyes looked like they were going to pop out of his head. "I don't have teeth!"

"That's what happens when you don't brush. Just like my grandmother always said."

One of the bird flunkies snickered, and the giant vulture let out a screech of frustration. "*REHK REHK!* That's it! I've had it. I'm not playing with my food anymore. First the old woman talked my beak off before the Shamble Man came back for her from that ole shining city over there, and now you. Birds of a feather. Well, now it's time to get plucked. Get over here!"

I inhaled sharply. So Kulture *had* seen Nana. And the Shamble Man. "You tried to eat my grandmother?"

The vulture shuddered, his muddy feathers flinging dirt everywhere. "Naw, little worm, not to my taste. Besides, that masked giant said she was off limits. You, on the other hand..." With a huge flap of his massive wings, Kulture lunged for me. But he'd waited too long. Just behind him, swooping down from the clouds, came our savior.

"Now!" I shouted.

Junior tossed a stone in the air and Ayanna batted it like a designated hitter. It smacked Kulture Vulture right in the eye and the bird reared back. Junior's hands were already pulling more stones from the satchel. He whipped them through the air so fast, they hummed as they passed me. The buzzard stumbled and fell, and I dashed forward, snatched his necklace, and dove away. I stashed the goods in my backpack for safekeeping.

Kulture Vulture squawked in outrage and tried to get up, but he couldn't while the rocks were still raining down.

Finally he staggered to his feet and took to the air, spiraling up to get out of range—

Right into the path of Gum Baby on Ayanna's flying raft.

"PRECOFFINARY MEASURES!" the tiny doll yelled. The raft was covered, and I mean covered, in sap. Mounds of it. Gooey strands trailed from it like tentacles on a jellyfish. The vessel jerked left and right, snaring Kulture Vulture and his crew in one giant sticky knot. They flapped and struggled in vain. I winced, knowing from firsthand experience just how secure that sap was.

When she got close to us, Gum Baby backflipped off the raft as it shot into the sky. I was so busy waving cheekily at the birdbrains that I failed to notice where she planned on landing until it was too late. Big mistake.

"Oomph!"

Ayanna and Junior snickered as Gum Baby peeled herself off my head—ripping out a patch of hair as she went—and slid down into my hood. She patted my cheek, smearing sap on my face in the process. "Did you miss me?"

"No," I said, groaning as I scrubbed at my skin. "And what about the raft? How are we supposed to get around?"

"'How are we supposed to get around?'" Gum Baby mimicked in a whiny voice. "Gum Baby just saved your muddy behind and this is the thanks she gets? Rude."

Ayanna intervened before the argument could continue. "Thank you, Gum Baby, you were wonderful."

"Yeah," Junior said, offering the little loudmouth a short bow. "At least you did something."

"Hey, all this was my plan!" I said.

Junior whistled. "Some plan. Let everyone else do the work after you make the monster mad. Good job with that."

"Anyway," Ayanna said, glaring at us both, "the raft will return in a little bit. Not that it'll be good for much."

I hoped Gum Baby looked sheepish, but I couldn't see her.

"In the meantime, we walk," Ayanna finished. She set off, skirting the muddy water, and headed to where the emerald city of Nyanza sparkled in the distance. Junior followed, and Gum Baby snuggled down into my hoodie and yawned.

"Be a good Bumbletongue and carry Gum Baby. It ain't like you're carrying your own weight around here anyway." And before I could think up a response, she started snoring, leaving me gritting my teeth as we trekked off to find my grandmother.

19
THE CITY OF LAKES

"LOOK, GUM BABY SAID SHE WAS SORRY!"

After we'd slogged for nearly an hour through the receding lakes of Nyanza, with the emerald city barely getting any closer, Ayanna's floating raft finally returned to her. Dingy feathers covered it from front to back, stuck in sap. I didn't know what had happened to Kulture Vulture and his gang, but they'd sure left a mess. It looked like a turkey had exploded in an oven filled with hamburger grease.

Yep. Think about it.

Ayanna touched her golden staff to the vessel and whispered. Slowly the sap melted and most of it slid off, taking the feathers with it.

"Come on," she said, and we all climbed aboard. "Gum Baby, you steer while I get the rest of this cleaned up."

Junior took up a position near the front of the raft, out

of the way. I watched him get settled. Something was still bothering me about him, but between Gum Baby's terrible flying skills and my desperate efforts to avoid sitting in sap, I couldn't focus on one moody boy at the moment. And, as if those discomforts weren't enough, a giant thunderstorm lurked low and menacing on the horizon, back to the west. Thick, ugly gray clouds. We cruised (if you could call it that) closer and closer to the domed city. I had time to actually examine it and the surrounding area—you know, without being attacked by flying appropriators.

The dome wasn't completely sealed like I'd originally thought. I could vaguely make out the shapes of houses inside through seams in the glass, and smoke escaped from cleverly designed chimneys that were invisible from above. Plants grew out of cracks in the giant jade tortoise shell and snaked their way to the lake below, where huge lily pads with flowers the size of canoes awaited. In fact ... I narrowed my eyes ... they *were* canoes—giant flower canoes with big leaves that doubled as paddles. It looked like the lily pads were actually docks. Floating driveways for a city built on a lake.

If only the lakes weren't drying up.

"Who lives there?" I asked Ayanna in a low voice.

She poked at a stubborn clump of stuck feathers with a grimace, then sighed. "This is going to take forever. Maybe I should— What did you say? Who lives where? Oh ... Well, rumor has it another goddess is inside. Like Keelboat Annie in a way, she managed to keep her people safe from the iron monsters by drastic means."

I frowned. "But Annie went on the run—her and Old Man River."

"Yes, and—you didn't hear this from me—I heard this goddess shut down the whole City of Lakes."

I'd just opened my mouth to ask what that meant when the raft shuddered again.

"Can you fly straight?" Junior's comment grabbed my attention. Gum Baby's as well.

"Gum Baby is a pilot. Put some respect on her name."

The exchange brought my attention back to our current sticky situation. I turned to watch Gum Baby struggle with the rudder at the rear of the raft, racing from one side to the other to keep it in line, sometimes going so far as to jump on top of it and wrestle it into position. I didn't let out a single chortle, though. Not a one.

Gum Baby looked up at me anyway. "You laughing at Gum Baby, Bumbletongue? Better not be. Gum Baby'll snatch that smile of yours and use it as floss."

I raised my hands in the universal gesture of *Couldn't be me* and fought to keep a straight face.

Junior looked back and forth between us, his eyebrows raised. "Why *did* they make you a pilot?" he asked her.

Gum Baby let go of the rudder and stood proudly with

her hands on her hips, only to yelp and leap for the raft's controls when we started to nosedive. "'Cause Gum Baby deserves! Took them long enough. Gum Baby had to do two more missions before they'd give her a chance, and then old Shovel Hands Henry said it was only temporary, that Gum Baby needed to prove herself some more. As if Gum Baby ain't the best at whatever she chooses to do." She sniffed, then squinted at the edge of the raft, eyed the rudder, dashed to peek over the side to see where we were headed, then raced back to the rudder before we crashed. "Gum Baby's a pro."

I snorted, then went back to scanning the area for signs of the Shamble Man or Nana, or anything that would give me a clue as to what to do next. It pained me to say it, but without Anansi I was lost.

I couldn't help it. I pulled out the phone one more time, just to check.

Nothing.

"Ooh, Gum Baby's gonna teeell." The raft dipped suddenly as the tiny terror abandoned the rudder and scrambled up to my shoulder to examine the broken phone. "You didn't have a scream protector? Wow, Bumbletongue, you must be rich-rich. Guess you're just gonna buy another one of those magical phones made from the precious treasure and heirloom of the gods. Oh, wait..."

The glare I bestowed upon the sticky nuisance could've curdled milk, even if she was right.

"I have a *screen* protector," I said, "but—"

"Whoa, you broke the Story Box?" Ayanna asked, interrupting me. She stepped over to look, and Junior peeked as well. "What is Nyame going to say?"

"Nothing," I said, "because I'm going to get it fixed before he finds out."

"Boy, whatever," Gum Baby said. She hopped down, returned to the rudder, and pointed at a shiny button on the left strap of her overalls. "People can't trust you with nothing. That's why you don't even have a badge! When Gum Baby became a pilot, she got one. You're looking at Pilot Gum N. B. Baby."

I frowned. "What does the *N. B.* stand for?"

"Nunya Business, that's what. Always nosy. This why people don't invite you anywhere. Always—"

Thump

The impact threw us to the floor of the raft in a tumbled heap. I groaned, a weight on my head pushing my face into the rough and sticky wooden planks. It took me a second to realize that Gum Baby had landed on me.

"Gerroff!" I said in a muffled shout.

"Hush, boy. Your big ole head is like a couch. Gum Baby could put her feet up and stretch out." But the tiny terror hopped off with a sticky *plop*, and I winced. You ever have a bandage yanked off? That's what it felt like. Pretty sure another patch of hair was missing thanks to her. Gum Baby peered around, then dusted her hands, her coal eyebrows bunching into a frown when they got stuck together. "Perfect landing," she said. "Ten out of ten."

We'd crashed into one of the giant lily pads resting on the shallow lake that held the emerald dome. Ayanna and Junior jumped off the raft and I followed. We climbed the bank to find a dry creek bed as wide as a street. It led to the city.

"Why is all the water gone?" I muttered. "And where are the people?"

No one answered. Gum Baby scrambled up to my shoulder, and Ayanna readied her staff, while Junior pulled a stone from his satchel. (How many did he have in there, anyway?) We crept forward. The silence was unnerving. No chatter, no animals, no sound from the city whatsoever.

It was as if Nyanza had been abandoned.

We crested a small hill, still inside the creek bed, to find a solid green metal gate blocking our path. Beyond it, a waterfall splashed down, rainbow-colored and as loud as thunder. It shrouded the area in a fine mist we couldn't see past.

"A sluice gate," Ayanna said, her eyes wide. "Keelboat Annie told me about them. They control the flow of water, and not even Old Man River can get through one that's lowered. Looks like these people really want to keep everyone else out."

I thought about that as we walked closer to examine the gate. What would make folk want to guard against a magical river? Did this have something to do with all the dried-up lakes and streams in Nyanza? Or with the Shamble Man?

Just as we reached the gate and the clumps of wild grass growing on either side of it, a bright blur streaked past my face.

Thunk!

"That's far enough!"

The shout surprised me, but not as much as the blue-green spear that now quivered in the ground in front of us. A rope attached to the end of the spear's shaft trailed up the river-bank and disappeared behind the high grass. I looked for the thrower but didn't see anyone. I'd started to step forward to investigate when another spear whizzed through the air and landed near us. I scuttled backward, and a third *thunk*ed into the ground behind me, cutting off my retreat.

We clustered together, staring around. No attackers revealed themselves. Had Kulture Vulture returned with reinforcements?

"Into the canal, all of you," a second voice said, just as the giant sluice gate groaned open, clear blue water splashing through to fill the creek bed up to our ankles. "Now!"

I gulped, a sinking *Here we go again* feeling in my stomach, and waded through.

Gorgeous.

Incredible.

Breathtaking.

Those were just a few of the words rattling in my head as we walked into Nyanza. Not right away, mind you. At first, the City of Lakes wasn't nearly as awe-inspiring as Isihlangu or the Golden Crescent. We sloshed through a dim tunnel until we reached a scuffed gray door without a handle. I eyed it with dread as we approached, hoping it wasn't an entrance to a prison. It opened automatically when we got near, and we stepped through to enter the world within the dome. My jaw dropped and my breath caught in my throat.

Sunlight drifted down in different shades of green to bathe everything in a soft glow. Small trees grew in a field on my left—an orchard of some sort. I didn't recognize the fruit, but the fragrance of something light and sweet reminded me that I hadn't eaten in a while. In front of us, a wide avenue lined with gently bending stalks of giant wildflowers led over a hill and into the middle of town, where structures that were half-building, half-plant grew toward the light. I raised my eyes to the dome high above, inhaling the scents of this incredible oasis.

It was so peaceful.

At least, it would have been if not for the tension lurking just beneath the beauty. We marched with our invisible guards calling out instructions every few steps.

"Take this footbridge."

"Step lively now."

But the voices floated to us without a glimpse of their speakers. Every so often I heard a rustling just to the side of the road we walked on, and I thought I caught a glimpse of more of those sharp spears, but every time I squinted into the brush, I couldn't see anything except waist-high grass waving in the steady warm breeze that carried traces of citrus and honey.

Were we being taken captive? I wondered. I didn't have time for that—I needed to find Nana.

Just when I thought I couldn't walk any longer, we reached the top of the hill and my complaints were forgotten. The city sprawled below like one of Nana's quilts, a sparkling weave of sapphire-blue streams, multilevel rows of plant-houses, and dozens of colorful orchards filled with fruit-laden trees.

And, in the middle of it all, resting on a huge gilded lily pad that floated in the air, defying gravity, was a dazzling palace the same shade of emerald green as the dome high above us. Water that sparkled like diamonds cascaded over the edges of the lily pad and collected in dozens of lakes and ponds at the bottom of the dome. It had to be the source for all the streams in the city.

The City of Lakes indeed.

But with all this water inside, why was the land outside so dry? Was Nyanza hoarding water? As the questions floated around my head, I wanted to stay and drink (ha!) in the sight forever, but I was still wondering about something.

"Hey," I said. "Where is everyone?"

Our invisible guards didn't answer me. Not that I was expecting them to. Ayanna looked around at the darkened homes and empty orchards and pursed her lips. Junior's eyes had a hard edge, and I could see the tension in each careful step he took. He was still clutching a stone.

Gum Baby patted my head and pointed at the palace. "Move it, Bumbly. Stop lollygagging. Straight ahead to the giant floating building."

I sighed and started walking down the hill. Some things never changed.

"Stop here."

The voice came from a shadowy hole next to a small pond. A waterfall spilled down from the palace high above, so smooth and uninterrupted it looked like a glass sculpture. A lily pad the size of a twin bed floated nearby, but I didn't see any flower canoes. We all looked around, awaiting further instructions.

"Get on," the voice commanded.

"Get on what?" I asked.

"I think he means the lily pad," said Ayanna.

My eyes widened. "We're supposed to ride this?"

"How else are we gonna get to the palace?" Gum Baby shook her head, climbed down off my shoulder, and hopped onto the pad, jumping up and down and splashing the rest of us. "Gum Baby is *so* glad you're not the brains of this

205

operation. Good help is hard to find these days, otherwise Gum Baby would be looking for a new sidekick."

Ayanna snickered and Junior snorted as they climbed aboard. I glared at them all as I carefully stepped onto the lily pad. Much to my surprise, it was rigid and pretty stable. "I am definitely *not* your sidekick. Ever."

She sniffed. "Not with that attitude. Gum Baby's gonna demote you to minion soon."

"I—"

But before I could tell her how I really felt, the lily pad moved, with a lurch that sent me stumbling to the waxy floor. It began to rise in the air like an elevator, ferrying us *up* a waterfall to the palace in the sky.

"Sweet peaches," I mumbled, flattening myself and staring into the sky as a fine mist sprinkled over us.

"Same old Tristan," Ayanna said. "Hey, would you stop that!" she shouted to Gum Baby, who was dangling off the side and kicking her feet into the waterfall. I swallowed a nervous lump and counted to fifty. But, for all my discomfort, the ride was relatively smooth.

We came to a stop in front of an arched entrance to the palace. It was flanked by small ornamental trees growing out of crystal-clear pools, and birds trilled in the branches. Tiny silver, ruby, and sapphire fish with neon fins circled us, darting through the air so fast they looked like a rainbow.

"Get off," came the disembodied voice. I looked around, confused. A shadow was flitting away in the distance. Was that our captor? Was the mysterious goddess waiting for us inside the palace? We were going to have to proceed cautiously and take our first opportunity to escape. Nana was waiting for me, and our getting thrown into an emerald dungeon wouldn't help anyone.

But of course Gum Baby was the opposite of cautious. "Hurry up! Gum Baby hates suspense," she called as she scuttled into the emerald-green palace.

"Hey!" I shouted. Ayanna and Junior took off after her, leaving me alone. I muttered something I shouldn't have and ran to catch up. I slipped in between the trees, their flowers giving off a minty smell, and plunged through the two green pillars at the entrance.

"No. Way," I whispered, skidding to a stop.

Inside was a giant open-air atrium filled with miniature fruit trees growing on pedestals, marble-lined ponds filled with fish so colorful I thought they were flower petals at first, and in the middle of it all, a deep pool so blue I mistook it for a painting. A throne floated on top—a living ornamental tree whose branches had been woven into a chair shape and covered in wildflowers of all different colors.

And at the foot of the chair, surrounded by colored pencils and scattered papers covered with drawings, sat a tiny bunny so familiar I thought my face would crack from smiling. She looked up as we all approached and let out a squeak of happiness.

"Tristan!"

"Chestnutt!" I said with a laugh, and scooped her into my arms. "What are you doing here?"

We all sat around a small pond filled with more of the tiny fish that Chestnutt called cichlids. These particular ones appeared to be neon purple with bright-blue fins. Every so often they leaped out of the water, dazzling us with aerial displays. It would've been amazing if Gum Baby hadn't been trying to hit them with sap balls.

Some people, I swear.

"It's so good to see you," Chestnutt said. "But you shouldn't have come. It's dangerous here these days, what with the Shamble Man's random attacks and that giant vulture trying to eat everybody. How did you get here? Did Anansi bring you?" The tiny brown-and-white bunny nibbled a piece of fruit from one of the many trees, and I had one of my own, a horned melon called a kiwano that tasted like a cross between a cucumber and a kiwi.

I popped another piece in my mouth, chewed and swallowed, then leaned forward. "No, Annie did. Keelboat Annie."

Chestnutt grinned. "Of course she did. Where is she?"

I shook my head, wincing. "We got separated." I ran down everything that had happened since the fight with Reggie. Had that only been yesterday afternoon? It felt like years ago. I hesitated when I got to the part about John Henry. I could feel Junior's stare burning a hole in the side of my face, but once again I skipped the fact that the folk hero was slowly fading.

The bunny shuddered. "Everything is falling apart," she muttered.

"What do you mean?" Ayanna asked.

Chestnutt hopped to her pile of sketches and rummaged around, finally pulling out three and dragging them in front of us. "You see this?" she asked, tapping the first picture. It was a giant storm cloud, gray and black with bolts of green lightning streaking through it.

"Yeah, that's the storm outside, right?" I stared at it. "I forgot how good your sketches are." The way Chestnutt had drawn it so close to the ground and with sharp lines, it looked ominous. Deadly, even.

"Thanks! But that storm has been hovering over the same spot for weeks now," Chestnutt said, her voice growing grim. "And it's growing larger. That alone is worrisome, but when you add these next two things to the mix..."

She pulled the second and third pictures forward. One was of a face I knew all too well—the masked figure of the Shamble Man. Red eyes that glowed like coals stared out from the paper, and I could feel the hatred in his gaze. I quickly moved on to the next portrait and paused. The person in it seemed familiar, but I couldn't quite place her.

It was a beautiful brown woman, her hair braided into a single twist that curled down her back. Her eyes were like opals and her skin seemed to shimmer. I leaned closer. She almost looked like the spirit girl from the barn, Ninah.

He's taken my mother.

With Ninah's words echoing in my ears, I sat up straight. "Is this...?"

"You're looking at Mami Wata, the goddess of Nyanza, the source of the City of Lakes," said Chestnutt. "And, as of two days ago, missing."

20
WHERE'S MAMI WATA?

MISSING.

All the lakes and waterfalls in the palace froze for a fraction of a second as that word echoed around the palace, a pause so brief I thought I was imagining it until I saw Junior scanning the area as well. Our eyes met, and for once he didn't glare at me. I guess we were both worried.

I leaned closer to Chestnutt, recalling Ninah's words. "Was she . . . taken?"

The little bunny nodded. "We think so. That's why I'm here. I'm on a mission for the Warren. They wanted someone here to investigate Wata's disappearance."

I didn't need a network of cute and fuzzy spies to figure out what had happened. "It was the Shamble Man, wasn't it?"

She nodded again. "Most likely. And it couldn't have happened at a worse time."

"What do you mean?" Junior asked.

Her ears drooped. "There was supposed to be a big summit. All the gods were supposed to attend. From the Sands, the Horn, the Grasslands, and MidPass. Nyame was planning on hosting it in the Golden Crescent. 'The Future of Alke,' he called it. But then Mami Wata disappeared and that giant vulture showed up. I was sent here to find clues about where the goddess could be."

"And?" I asked. "Did you find any?"

"Yup, yup!" Then Chestnutt hesitated. "Well, a few. But I need to confirm them."

I shook my head and a wry smile crossed my face. "Look at you. Keeping secrets. You're a regular spymaster. Brer Rabbit would be proud. The *real* Brer Rabbit, not the impostor in the SBP."

She wrinkled her nose. "SBP?"

Gum Baby, still trying to hurl sap balls at the leaping fish, missed and stomped her foot. "Story Box Phone. Bumbletongue's trying to be less bumbly, so he's making up words now."

I ignored her. "Chestnutt, that monster—the Shamble Man—he has my grandmother. He came to my world! Stomping around and destroying my grandparents' house. And he took her. I have to find him. I *have* to save her."

A giant sigh that felt way too big for such a tiny bunny escaped from between her whiskers. "I haven't pinpointed his exact location yet. I've been trying for days."

I sat back, frustrated. The others remained silent, Ayanna staring at her staff and Junior tossing a few stones in the air. Too many pieces of the puzzle were still missing. Why kidnap Mami Wata? What could the goddess have that the Shamble Man needed? Why take Nana? Trying to come up with answers felt like trying to grab greasy ice with my toes. *Im-poss-i-ble.*

I blew out a puff of air. "If only I'd listened to Ninah when she first tried to warn me. Instead, I acted like a blockhead."

Chestnutt sat up straight. "Wait, you saw Ninah? Everyone thought she'd gone missing along with Mami Wata, since she was one of her favorite daughters. Where is she? If anyone can fill the lakes again until Mami Wata gets back, it's her."

I winced. "I don't know where she went. Everything got confusing after the Shamble Man arrived. And why aren't the lakes working? It's so dry out there."

"More like City of Fakes," Gum Baby said. She flipped a sap ball and it knocked down a fish. "Got it! Wait. Oh no, fishy! What did Gum Baby do?"

Chestnutt hopped around in agitation. "It has something to do with Mami Wata and her power. Do you know her story? Maybe if I heard it, or saw it, we could figure out what to do next."

I felt my cheeks grow hot as Ayanna and Junior looked expectantly at me. I mumbled a response. "I . . . can't remember any stories. It's Nana. I don't know, ever since she was taken, whenever I try to think of one of her tales, I get ... I just can't do it. I know I have to try and work through it...."

"And have you tried?"

I glanced at Ayanna. "No."

Silence filled the space, broken only by Gum Baby's sobs as she cradled the fish she'd knocked out of the water. After a moment, Chestnutt brightened and hopped in a circle, thinking hard. "Wait. You have Anansi, right? He could probably tell you the story. It was his Story Box for a while. Why don't we ask him?"

I flinched, but before I could say anything, Junior beat me to it. "He can't. It's *broken*." He crossed his arms over his chest and nodded at me. "Go ahead, then. Show her."

I had no choice. I pulled the broken SBP out of my pocket and laid it in front of us. Chestnutt's ears drooped so low I thought she'd trip on them.

"I'm sorry," I said. "I think I broke it when I landed. Plus, it got wet and now it won't turn on."

Chestnutt studied it. "Did you put it in rice?"

Something hit me in the back of the head. "Ouch!" I said. My hands came away sticky, and I looked up to see Gum Baby pointing at me, her face covered in sappy tearstains.

"Th-that's what Gum Baby told that fool, but he didn't wanna l-l-listen. Big head and hardheaded, too. I should've hit *him* with the sap balls and not the f-f-fishyyyyyy!" She collapsed into wails, blowing snot sap everywhere as she sniffled.

I threw up my hands, stood, and stomped over to Gum Baby. I knocked the fish out of her hand and back into the water. After a few seconds the fish wriggled, then swam away. "There, see? It's fine. And enough about rice—it isn't going to fix a cracked phone!"

"Depends on what kind of rice you put it in. And..." Chestnutt's voice trailed off, and she froze. Then, she exploded into motion, diving into a pile of papers. Gum Baby and I watched her, confused, as the pile shook and then exploded. The bunny emerged, quivering with excitement, a rolled-up note in her mouth. I unfurled it.

"Look!" said Chestnutt. "Lady Night! She can help you."

"Who?" I asked.

"I've heard of her," Ayanna said slowly. "Bits and pieces. She's a boo hag, right?"

Chestnutt nodded. "Yup, yup! She can help you."

I froze. "A boo hag?"

"Yup, yup! She lives on the outskirts of the Golden Crescent, in the area the folks from MidPass moved into. According to the Warren's notes, she fixes up magical items and even enchants a few of her own. If you can get her to repair the Story Box—I mean, the *SBP*—you and Anansi can use it to figure out where the Shamble Man has gone and rescue Mami Wata and your grandmother."

"Wait, wait," I said, holding up a hand. "How can the SBP do that?"

"Because the Story Box is attracted to stories. Do you have something of your grandmother's?"

I started to say no, then paused and slapped my forehead. "I do! Nana's quilt!"

"Great!" Chestnutt said. "The Story Box is drawn to that sort of thing. It can collect stories from objects like a wolf tracking a bunny." She shivered a little at her own analogy. "So maybe you can track your grandmother that way. And if that doesn't work, you could always get Anansi to tell you a story about the gods. Then the Story Box will be attracted to him like a magnet."

I was getting lost. "Who's 'him'? Anansi? What are you talking about?"

"No . . . Never mind. It's just a theory. The Warren doesn't want me spreading rumors."

"Please, Chestnutt, if you have information that can help, I want to know it. I have to find Nana. Who knows how she's holding up. Please, tell me," I begged.

Chestnutt's ears drooped lower than I'd ever seen them go. She sank into a tiny furry ball, and her voice was a whispered squeak so faint I had to lean close to hear her. "I think the Shamble Man is a god of MidPass."

21
BOO HAG BLUES

THE RAFT SOARED THROUGH SKY, HEADING WEST TOWARD THE looming thunderclouds. We'd left immediately for Lady Night's home with one of Chestnutt's famous hand-drawn (paw-drawn?) maps, leaving the fuzzy little spy behind. She'd wanted to come with us but couldn't leave her post. The sun was low on the horizon, and the City of Lakes acted like a prism behind us, sending brilliant multicolored rays into the sky, a rainbow guide to Alke. It was a beautiful sight that would soon be gone forever if the water goddess wasn't found.

The storm lurked ahead, an ugly bruise threatening to roll over us all, a final finishing punch that would cap off a brutal round for Alke. Mami Wata gone. Nana gone. John Henry slowly disappearing from this world.

And the person responsible . . . was a god from MidPass?

I mean, I trusted Chestnutt, you get me? Anyone who didn't listen to her was a fool. And yet I understood why the Warren didn't want her spreading that information. If everyone started blaming MidPass for the current troubles, would they ever trust them again? Would they even allow the refugees from the burned-out island to stay?

A god from MidPass. Who could it be?

Images flashed in my mind, and I recoiled from each, refusing to believe that any of the gods I knew could've turned into such a monster. Could've unleashed plat-eyes and forced them to harass spirits and the living. Could be working with Kulture Vulture and his band of scavengers.

Miss Sarah and Miss Rose?

Brer Rabbit?

High John?

Impossible. Right?

I shook my head and collapsed onto the raft. I didn't want to think about it anymore. I just had to find this Lady Night and see if she could fix the SBP. We could take things from there.

But one picture kept worming its way back into my brain, poisoning my thoughts and turning my stomach:

The Shamble Man holding John Henry's hammer. Where would he strike next?

"We're here!" Gum Baby shouted an hour or so later, her tiny voice barely carrying over the wind blowing around the raft. She struggled to hold the vessel steady, even with the step stool she'd made out of sap to anchor herself. The sun had just set, leaving Alke to deal with the gathering storm, and a new horror: the dark clouds now had a faint tinge of green around the edges.

I gripped Anansi's adinkra nervously, but it was cool to the touch. For now. Maybe I was just imagining things.

The raft shuddered. It felt like all of a sudden we began to drop, slowly at first, but then quickly picking up speed.

"Gum Baby?" I asked, my voice filled with uncertainty. The ground couldn't be that far away. A gleam flashed in the distance, then another. That had to be the palaces of the Golden Crescent in the distance. A dark smear rose to meet the stars to the northeast, a high wall that obscured the silvery clouds. Isihlangu, the mountain fortress.

That meant we were somewhere between the two regions of Alke. From the looks of it, I was about to learn exactly where very soon.

"Gum Baby!" Ayanna called out. She seemed a bit worried as well.

A group of hills rolled beneath us; on top of the highest one, a collection of lights twinkled around a sprawling ranch-style compound containing a large, flat building and several small log cabins. The faint sound of jazz music drifted up to my ears.

Sounded like we were about to crash Lady Night's party. Literally!

"Gum Baaabyyy!" Junior screamed.

The raft landed, skidding down a grassy hill straight toward the wooden fence around the compound. I braced myself and squeezed my eyes shut.

WHOMP!

The impact threw us forward, and for the second time that day I found myself facedown with a sticky demon on my head. I groaned, unable to form words because the breath had been driven from my lungs.

Gum Baby scrambled off the raft and brushed grass from her clothes. "Gum Baby's getting good at this pilot job. Landing in the dark with no gumming lights? Ten out of ten, thank you for flying Sap Attack Air, take all your Bumbletongues with you."

"Sap Attack Air is a horrible—"

A ball of sap struck the side of my head and I shut my mouth, contenting myself with thinking of all the ways a diminutive folktale character could be disposed of discreetly.

Just then I realized the jazz had stopped. A door in the main building opened, and light spilled out of it. Before I could move, six or seven large men and women with axes and pitchforks surrounded us, suspicion in their eyes. As quick as oily lightning, Gum Baby slipped out of sight in a tall clump of grass, leaving me, Ayanna, and Junior to face the music. I glared after her, ready to let loose a few insults, when all of a sudden several sharp pointy objects were shoved into my face. I bit back what I was about to say and tried my best to look innocent as I righted myself and stood up slowly and carefully with my hands raised.

"Just a few kids," one of the women muttered. "Maybe we should let them go."

A couple of the others nodded, pulling back their make-shift weapons and letting the tension drain from their postures. That made me feel a little bit better, and I took one step forward.

"Hi," I said. "We're here to see—"

"WHO'S INTERRUPTING MY PARTY?" a ground-shaking voice bellowed into the night. To my surprise, the group of adults seemed to hesitate, looking at one another to see who would move first. Then a second shout rang out. "BRING THEM INSIDE SO I CAN USE THEIR BONES FOR CUP HOLDERS!"

That seemed to settle it. I watched in confusion as the men and women seemed to shrink into themselves. They looked old enough to hang out with my father and mother and do whatever grown-ups do for fun. (Harmonica practice? Macaroni portraits? Who knew?) Rough hands gripped my arms and marched me inside. A sign stretched across the lintel, reading HAPPY BIRTHDAY, BIG BIG! in bold letters. It took a few seconds for my eyes to adjust to the bright lights inside, but when they did, I gasped.

We stood in a large hall that resembled my school cafeteria

back in Chicago. But instead of the walls being covered in murals of the school mascot doing backflips, an odd array of items hung on display. A giant shield. An old banjo. Three sets of throwing knives that still looked sharp. An entire row of book covers. I mean, the place was really strange, you get me?

A group of people and one large boar (yes, I said a boar, as in a wild pig with tusks) were milling about on an elevated stage on the right side of the room holding musical instruments of all sorts. (Yes, even the boar, I'm not making this up.) More instruments stood next to them.

No.

Wait.

Floated next to them.

"Sweet peaches," I mumbled.

A dance floor occupied the middle of the room, and the walls were lined with tables and chairs. Partygoers sat around, or stood on the dance floor, or leaned against the walls. Men, women, children, and animals—I even saw a pair of giant oxen sitting near the back, wearing weird oversize sunglasses like they were trying to stay incognito. A nervous tension filled the space as everyone stared at us, and I gulped.

The crowd on the dance floor shifted, and from behind it stepped the widest man I'd ever seen. Not tall, just wide. His shoulders seemed to stretch from one side of the room to the other, and his legs could've been two barrels stuffed into a pair of pants. John Henry was the largest man I'd met to date, but whereas he was tall, this dude looked like two linebackers side by side in a trench coat.

He was also super ashy, like his skin had never seen a bottle of lotion, a jar of cocoa butter, or even a dab of old bacon grease.

He wore rough gray trousers, no shoes or socks (toes looking like ten dirty marshmallows), and a white T-shirt soaked with sweat. A curious garment hung around his neck— it looked like a black silk scarf at first, but when the man walked forward to stand in front of me, it seemed to shimmer and appeared milk-chocolate brown. And it fluttered. There was no breeze inside as far as I could tell, and my captors had shut the door on the way in. I tried to get a closer look at it with Nyame's adinkra, but a strong hand gripped me.

"So what do we have here?" The man's hand encircled my injured wrist easily, preventing me from touching the sky god's charm and causing me to wince. He lifted my arm to examine my bracelet. "Well?" he asked one of my captors.

"Found them in a heap by the door, Big Big," a woman said. She sounded apologetic, and she looked at us sadly. "Like they'd been tossed from the sky."

The man—Big Big—continued to stare at the adinkra charms. Then he considered me thoughtfully. "Anybody else with them? Any adults?"

"Well, we didn't really check, but—"

"Then go check! There may be more of these freeloaders outside." Big Big spat on the floor in disgust and then, keeping an eye on my face, yanked the bracelet off my wrist before I knew what was happening.

"Hey, that's mine!"

"Hmm, that's not the way I see it," Big Big said with a conniving grin. He gestured to the walls with a sweep of his hand. "In case you couldn't tell, I'm a collector. Antiques. One-of-a kind items. Trinkets." He held up the bracelet and his grin widened as my eyes followed it. Then he motioned to Ayanna, who reluctantly handed over her staff. Junior clutched his satchel of stones like it was the most valuable thing on earth, but after Big Big scowled and formed a massive fist, the boy handed over the bag.

"But most importantly," Big Big continued, "I collect secrets. Rumors. Shifts in the tide of Alke's whims. So when a little birdie tells me there's a kid running around with the powers of the gods, maybe I listen. Maybe I figure, if I can get my hands on those powers, interested parties might pay me a fortune."

I struggled, but the man's hand was still tightly clamped around my wrist.

"COOKIE!" he shouted. "Where is that—? COOKIE! Where are you?"

There was movement in the crowd, and then a person draped from head to toe in a hooded cloak appeared next to us. Whoever it was, they were slightly smaller than me, and I briefly got a glimpse of red-rimmed eyes, though whether that was from crying or that was their natural color, I couldn't tell.

"About time," Big Big said in annoyance. He shoved me toward the newcomer, and for a brief instant I thought about fighting back. I could have unleashed a combination that would've made Granddad proud.

A soft touch on my shoulder stopped me. It was the cloaked person. They gave me the tiniest of head shakes. *Not now*, it seemed to mean.

"Cookie, take these kids and lock 'em in the back. Then get one of your pots going—I'm starving again. And not that same rice dish you always make. Give me something different."

The hooded figure shifted. "The rice dish is all we have, since you won't allow the farmers to farm."

Big Big reddened, gripping the scarf-like garment around his neck in frustration. "None of that sass, now, Cookie. Or do I need to . . . ?"

The cloaked figure seemed to deflate. "No. I'll . . . see what I can do."

"Better."

I watched this exchange, baffled, and then checked the crowd. Everyone seemed nervous and on edge. Big Big realized this and waved his hands. "All right, enough! Get some music going. It's my birthday! And I just got the best present of all." He held up my bracelet—*my bracelet*—and laughed. I followed him with my eyes as he turned and headed back through the crowd to a table at the front edge of the dance floor. Burning rage collected in my stomach, bubbled, then spread through my limbs until it felt like my entire body would explode if I didn't get that bracelet back.

The band started up again (that boar could play a mean saxophone), including the instruments floating in midair. Two drumsticks—with no one holding them—began to tap out a snazzy rhythm, and people started shuffling on the dance floor under Big Big's watchful eye. Something weird was going on here, but I couldn't see it while my adinkra bracelet was in that giant bully's hands.

Someone tugged me gently. It was the cloaked person. With a slim gloved hand, they pulled me forward, and Ayanna and Junior followed as we skirted the edge of the crowd and headed toward a dark storage room in the back. People and animals alike stepped aside for us, inclining their heads as we walked by. I didn't get it.

"Quickly," the person called Cookie said in a low murmur. It sounded like a woman's voice. "I'll explain it all later." She led us into the storage room and closed the door. I stood still, unable to see a thing in the dark. Something scraped on the floor. A spark winked not too far away, and then another, and then a torch was lit. The flickering orange glow cast dancing shadows across Cookie's hooded cloak as she came closer.

Beneath the hood, deep in the shadows, her red-rimmed eyes stared out at me.

"I need your help," Cookie said. "In exchange, I'll help you get the adinkras back."

Ayanna narrowed her eyes. "You know what they are?"

"I do. And yes, I will also get back your staff and your father's stones." This last bit she directed at Junior.

His father's stones?

But before I could puzzle that out, the cloaked person continued. "I know what you are, Tristan, and that you can help me. Please. We don't have much time. Big Big sent off a message. Any moment now the Shamble Man might show up through that door, and then we're all in trouble."

The Shamble Man! I hesitated, but I didn't see how I had a choice. There was no telling where Gum Baby had gone. Maybe she went to get help. More likely, she was lost. No, this looked like the only chance we had to escape the Shamble Man's clutches. I needed to approach him on my terms, not his.

"Fine," I said. "What do you want from us?"

I heard a deep inhale, and in a shaky voice, Cookie spoke.

"I want you to help me steal back my skin."

22
JUKE JOINT JAMBOREE

ONE TIME WHEN I WAS LITTLE, WHILE DAD WAS OFF TRAINING
with Granddad, Nana came up to our apartment in Chicago
to help Mom and give her a little break. (Side note: Did you
know adults take naps? I didn't at the time. And they do it
willingly! Mind-blowing. Anyway...) I woke up screaming
one night, terrified that something was coming to get me.
Maybe through the window, maybe from under the bed...
Wherever it was from, it wanted to take me away. Nana burst
into my room to find me shivering in my blankets.

"A witch is gonna get me," I said, scanning every corner.

She calmed me down, then brought me to the kitchen to
help her clean up from dinner. While I dried dishes, Nana
started telling one of her stories. It was more a history lesson
than a folktale. You know Nana, though. Every story she told
felt like an award-winning production.

"Have I ever told you about the island folk?" she asked,

handing me a plate. We were standing in front of the sink, she in her stocking feet and me barefoot on a step stool.

I shook my head solemnly.

"'Bout time you learned. Shame you don't get this in your school, but that's neither here nor there. I'm called to teach, and you about to learn. Dry this pot, baby." She cleared her throat, thought for a few seconds, then began.

"The island folk have different names, depending on who you ask. Gullah, Geechee. No matter what you use, do it with respect. But they keep their own business. Rituals, language...they passed them down and kept their traditions local. Same thing with their stories. Well, one story I've heard told is about what they call boo hags. Creatures that slip their skin off at night. They creep into your home while you're asleep, sit on your chest, and suck the air from your lungs. You wake up tired and drained, as if sleeping had been a struggle. By then the boo hag is long gone, back in her lair, reunited with her skin. According to those stories, one way to defeat a boo hag is to take her skin before she can retrieve it—then you hold power over her. Some people went to conjure women—root witches—to get wards to keep boo hags away."

I'd stared at her in horror. "Witches? Aren't they evil?"

She didn't answer me right away. Finally she sighed and gave me a half smile.

"Yes and no, baby. Yes and no. See, there's some powerful

folk out there. Powerful folk, with magic straight out of legend. And, just like everybody, you got your good ones and your bad ones. The thing is, some people don't like when others have power. Even if it's being used for good, they don't care. They've got to control it, to own it, and if they can't own it, they want to destroy it. They might call you a boo hag even if you're only helping people as a conjure witch. Especially when those people are writing the stories about you. At the end of the day, the only thing you can control is how the power you got is used."

Nana had paused while washing a pan and stared at me with a serious expression. "So, that nightmare you had? That creature coming for you ain't got no power over you. *You* got the power. Let 'em know you got a conjure witch looking out for you. I know a couple, matter fact."

"But how will I know if a witch is good or evil?"

She resumed her scrubbing. "You just gonna have to decide who to believe—the witch, or the one writing the witch's story."

Now I was facing a boo hag in person. I stared at Cookie in disbelief, positive I'd heard her wrong. "You want me to do what now?"

"You're her!" Ayanna said. "You're Lady Night."

The cloaked head rose defiantly, even though I couldn't see what was underneath. "I am. And I'm the rightful owner of this juke joint. I want you to help me steal my skin back from that giant lumbering oaf out there. Before he took over, this was a place of refuge. Of shelter. Somewhere the tired and weary and downtrodden could come and relax safely, in the company of others like them."

"Juke joint..." Junior said thoughtfully. "My father used to say they were oases for our people."

Lady Night cocked her head, like she wanted to ask a question. From beneath her hood, her glowing eyes stared at Junior, then she nodded as if realizing something. "Indeed. Well, in exchange for your aid, I will help you get your items of power back. The bracelet, the staff... and those peculiar stones."

I opened my mouth, then closed it. She knew something about Junior, and again, that niggling feeling that I was missing something tickled my mind. But I didn't have time to think about that. This was the wildest bargain I'd ever heard of. What were you supposed to say to a deal like that? *Okay, I'll get you some skin.* Like I was running to the corner store for a bag of Doritos. Skin wasn't supposed to be misplaced like keys. But then again, the fact that she'd lost it gave me an advantage....

"As it turns out, I need your help, too," I said.

"With the bracelet? Yes, I—"

"No. I mean, yes, with that, but also with something else. I broke it by accident when I came here, and without it I won't be able to find my grandmother. Chest—uh, a friend told me you can fix magical items. Like, even badly damaged things. Can you?" I hated how desperate I sounded, but . . . well, I was desperate. Slowly I pulled out the SBP from my shorts pocket. It took every ounce of effort I could spare to part with it, but I didn't have a choice. I needed it fixed, and fast.

Lady Night took it from me and studied it. "Is this what I think it is?"

I nodded.

"Did you put it in rice?"

I bit my lip and tried not to scream. She noticed, and her shoulders shook. It took me a second to realize she was laughing.

"Easy, Anansesem," she said. "I'll tell you what. I will fix your phone for you—"

I started to grin.

"—after you get my skin back."

The grin froze on my face. She shrugged. "If you don't, I can't help you. Literally. Without my skin I'm powerless. It's why that giant thief out there keeps it on his person at all times. When I get it back I'm gonna make him sorry he ever set foot in my joint."

I closed my eyes, took a deep breath, and tried to think of a plan. Something that would trick Big Big into taking off Lady Night's skin for a fraction of a second. From the way he clutched it, and the way everyone in the place jumped to do what he said, he didn't seem like someone who would listen to reason. We would have to be clever. This wasn't the time for wild heroics and fisticuffs. We needed to—

WHAM!

A thundering crash shook the walls, and my head jerked up in surprise. The sound had come from the main room. Had Big Big tripped and fallen or something? Lady Night and I glanced at each other when a loud, squeaky, familiar voice cut through the chaos.

"HEY, BUG BUG! GUM BABY'S FISTS GOT SOME QUESTIONS YOUR FACE NEEDS TO ANSWER!"

"Oh no," I whispered, my hands covering my face.

Lady Night slipped past me and opened the door a crack. "What is it? Who's that? Do you know them? It sounds like your reinforcements have arrived."

"No," Junior answered for me, trying to see through the opening. "She's just loud."

We all peeked out. And...look, everybody has that one person in their life who gets labeled "extra." You know what I mean. They're extra loud, extra energetic, and their whole personality revolves around doing everything just a bit too much. That was Gum Baby.

"Oh no," Ayanna said. "I *just* cleaned it."

Lady Night's eyes—the only part of her that was visible—were wide in astonishment.

Junior was actually laughing. At a time like this!

And me? I just sighed.

Gum Baby, the tiny terror, had rammed through the juke joint's entrance while *riding Ayanna's raft* and was zipping around the room like she was surfing in a whirlpool. A scrap of dirty white cloth was tied around the lower half of her face so all we could see were her eyes and her angry eyebrows. She was pointing at Big Big as she circled the room. Band members, floating instruments, and people in the audience dove to the floor as she dipped toward them. The boar let out a cry of surprise and flung himself flat to avoid getting clipped by the raft.

"Enough!" shouted Big Big. He slammed a hand on his table and stood up, the chair shooting backward. He shoved the furniture out of his way and stomped to the middle of the dance floor, one hand clutching Lady Night's skin. He'd taken it from around his neck and tied it around his fist, the way Granddad would wrap my knuckles before boxing practice. "Who do you think you are, interrupting my party? Do you know who I am? I've picked crumbs out of my teeth bigger than you!"

"Sounds like you need to brush better!" Gum Baby called down. Her arm moved in a blur and a small sap ball bounced off of Big Big's head. "Does poor little Bug Bug need help flossing, too?"

"It's *Big Big*!" the man shouted. He jumped and tried to

swat her out of the air, but Gum Baby swerved aside and laughed.

"Too slow, Bugaboo. What's the matter?"

Big Big growled something I can't repeat and swiped at her again. He tried to run after her, but Gum Baby stayed just out of reach, sitting down on the raft and dangling her legs off the edge. She kicked them back and forth, looking like she didn't have a care in the world. She lazily tossed sap balls at her pursuer like she was skipping stones on a warm summer day, all the while keeping up a steady stream of insults:

"Sap attack! Wow, it's like your big ole head just leaped in the way."

"Are you trying to show your friends how *not* to act?"

"Sap attack. Two sap attacks. Gum Baby can do this forever, you know. Let Gum Baby know if you need to take a break for a snack. You want a sappy cup, Boom Boom?"

Beside me, Lady Night started to go through the door, but I raised a hand to stop her. "Wait . . . I think I know what she's doing. And, I can't believe I'm saying this, but it's actually working."

"What, making him mad?" Lady Night asked.

"Actually . . . yes. Trust me, she's reeeally good at that."

As if she'd heard me, Gum Baby tossed one more sap ball before collapsing dramatically to the floor of the raft, her hands behind her head. "Gum Baby is booored. Thought there would be more action than this. Gum Baby should've brought her knitting along. At least that way she could've made a little blanket for Bobo."

Big Big's face was turning an odd shade of purple and his mouth was wrinkling into a twisted frown. I knew that expression—I made the same one every second I spent around the little loudmouth. I pulled the door open a little bit wider and whispered, "Get ready. When the time comes, grab your skin."

"The time?" Lady Night asked in alarm. "What time? What are you about to do?"

Ayanna sat down on the floor and motioned for Junior to do the same. "Might as well take a seat and watch. He's gonna go be a hero. He acts like he hates her, but Tristan and Gum Baby make a really good team."

I made a horrified expression. "Us? A team? Please don't speak that into existence."

Just then, Big Big let out a violent scream and leaped into the air, grabbing the raft with both hands. "MY. NAME. IS. BIG BIG!!!" The raft actually dragged him forward a few paces before he dug in his heels and slowly pulled the magical vessel down to the floor. Gum Baby had jumped to the other end and was flinging sap ball after sap ball at the giant's bald head—so much that it looked like he was growing a sticky afro.

"Be ready," I whispered urgently to Lady Night, then yanked the door open and dashed out.

No one was paying me any attention. They were too focused on the battle between the pint-size pirate and the troll. So when I scampered up onto the stage, got a running head start, and sprang through the air onto Big Big's back, everybody was surprised. I mean, *I* was surprised. I recovered quickly, though, and patted the man's new sticky hair.

"Nice look on you, Butt Butt," I said, before yanking the boo hag's skin off his hand and flinging it into the crowd. "Lady Night—now!"

Big Big's eyes grew wide and he let go of the raft so fast it shot forward. Gum Baby yelped as she skidded across the dance floor and into the back room I'd just left. Big Big turned, grasping for his neck, but the skin was gone. "No!" he shouted. "Nooo!" His hands found my arm and he yanked me over his shoulder and then threw me down on the dance floor.

"*Oomph.*" The air left my lungs again for the second time that night, and before I could recover, Big Big's massive hands dragged me upright to face him. A look of unbridled fury turned his features into those of a jungle cat.

"You!" he snarled. "I should've disposed of you when I first saw you. The Shamble Man ain't gonna get a chance to bury you, because I'm gonna dig a hole for you so deep no one will ever find your bones. You hear me? I—"

"Clifford!" a sharp voice called out from across the room.

Big Big flinched. He turned, still gripping me by the collar, and my eyes grew wide.

Lady Night stood alone on the stage, still cloaked, her skin in her hands.

No. *On* her hands. The glimmering garment seemed to pour itself like honey, slowly slipping up her arms and into her cloak. Her stance grew straighter, and she gripped the edges of her hood and pulled it back.

A beautiful woman with skin dark like twilight and eyes glittering like diamonds stood in front of us. Her hair was twisted into a curly faux-hawk that sat atop her head like a crown, and the cloak fell away to reveal a long dress that shimmered like moonlight on ink, and silver heels that threatened to pull you inside if you stared at them for too long.

Lady Night's gaze swept around the room before her eyes returned to pin Big Big in place. She stepped deliberately, emphatically, to the edge of the stage, and a few people in the crowd rushed to offer their hand to help her down. She accepted one regally, and then walked across the floor to where Big Big and I stood. Movement rippled in the corner of my eye and I craned my neck to see Gum Baby trotting across the floor. To my surprise, she climbed up to Lady Night's shoulder and sat there as if she were the queen's right hand. Lady Night spared her a warm smile before turning back to Big Big.

"Clifford, let him go." Her tone was low but intimidating.

Big Big gulped, then lowered me to the floor, unclenching his sausage-like fingers from my collar and patting my shoulders gently.

"There, I didn't mean no harm, right, kid? Just foolin' with you."

I glared at him and shook my head. "Clifford?"

He flinched. "S'why I go by Big Big."

"You think that's better? Honestly, I'm disappointed in you."

"Yes," Lady Night said, though her words held more of an implied threat. "We all are."

Big Big—I mean Clifford—swallowed nervously and took a couple steps back. Two giant steps back. Honestly, seeing the expression on Lady Night's face, I was tempted to step back, too, but I didn't want to call attention to myself.

But of course Gum Baby was nodding her head and cosigning everything. "Nah, don't back up now, Bing Bong, you done messed up. You know you done messed up, right? Yeah, you do."

Big Big raised both hands in a pleading gesture, his rumbling voice suddenly very nervous. "Look, ma'am, I wasn't gonna keep your skin forever. I was gonna give it back, honest. I was just tired of you bossing me around."

"I gave you a *job*!" Lady Night's voice cracked like a whip. "When your home burned on MidPass, I took you in and sheltered you. Fed you. And you didn't like taking orders from me, so as soon as that masked Shamble Man dangled his offer, you betrayed me?"

"I was only—"

"Enough!" Lady Night looked at me, then back at Big Big. "Give them back what you stole."

He hesitated, then when her eyes narrowed, slipped his hand into his pocket and pulled out the adinkra bracelet. Reluctantly, he tossed it to me. Ayanna and Junior came out of the back to reclaim the staff and satchel of stones. I slipped on the bracelet and briefly contemplated using the akofena charm to go upside his head. I didn't, though. One, my right wrist still throbbed, and two, Lady Night had everything well in hand.

"Now, then," she said. "What is an appropriate punishment for a thief and a bully?" She tapped a long, manicured nail with black fingernail polish against her chin. "How should I teach you a lesson?"

Gum Baby, juggling sap balls now, chimed in. "Maybe take his skin?"

"I don't think it works like that," I said with a grimace.

"Who asked you, Bumbletongue?"

Lady Night let a ghost of a smile cross her lips. "I cannot take his skin, little one, but I can make him uncomfortable in his own." She flicked her fingers down toward the floor and her cloak zipped into her hands. She held it to her face and whispered into it, letting her words fill the garment with power.

I couldn't resist—I had to see the magic. I grasped Nyame's charm and closed my eyes. When I opened them, I inhaled sharply. Fragments of a fable swirled around the cloak, stretching it sideways and elongating the hood. Lady Night tossed it into the air, and like a magnet it flew straight to Big Big, swallowing him whole. His muffled shouts filled the air, but the enchanted cloth swaddled him like an infant, entangling his arms and legs and sending him crashing to the floor. He wriggled and writhed for a few more seconds, then grew still.

I blinked, letting the magic fade from my eyes. "Is he . . . ?" I couldn't finish.

"No," Lady Night said with a chuckle. "Just . . . wearing a more appropriate skin, since he wanted one that wasn't his own."

Gum Baby dropped to the floor and kicked the cloak aside, revealing a large wrinkly-skinned weasel. She squealed in delight and hopped on top of it, then pointed toward the door. "Giddyup, Bam Bam, awaaaaaay!"

Big Big the weasel took a step, then paused before taking another. He inched forward like that, slowly and cautiously. Gum Baby kept her hand raised. Another step. A frown crossed her face. "Is this the fastest you can go? Gum

Baby has seen hair grow faster than this. Gum Baby wants a refund."

The people and animals in the juke joint cheered and crowded around Lady Night. She acknowledged them all, expert hostess that she was. Everyone got a smile, and she knew everyone's name. The band hopped back onstage and the boar ("Benny the Boar," he said by way of introduction) led them in a snappy little melody with a drum pattern that had my head nodding. Someone passed around cups of chilled mint tea, and in the back, cooking pots started bubbling.

"Where did all this come from?" I said in amazement.

Lady Night laughed and linked my arm with hers. "I'm a witch, remember? Now come, let's see if we can find a pot of rice for your phone."

23
JOLLOF RICE

ENCHANTED DRUMS BEAT A SLOW RHYTHM AS WE MOVED TO THE
back of the juke joint.

There was a booth in the corner, a C-shaped seat curved around a heavily stained and scratched table. In the middle of the surface was a large black cook pot resting on top of three silver stones the size of grapefruits. I stared at the pot suspiciously. It looked mighty close to something I'd call a cauldron.

Lady Night slid into the booth with a sigh and motioned for us to join her. Ayanna, Junior, and I squeezed into the other side, the three of us nervously huddled together.

The older woman chuckled softly. "Relax, children. Be like your friend. She seems at ease." She pointed to the middle of the club, where Gum Baby had stayed with the crowd, shouting and dancing and leaving sticky little footprints all over the floor.

"So," Lady Night said, turning to me, "I believe I promised to fix your magical phone."

I pulled out the SBP and, glancing around to make sure no one else was watching, slid it over to her.

Ayanna shook her head sadly.

Junior leaned forward. "It *can* be fixed, right?"

I rolled my eyes. "C'mon, man, give it a rest."

"I'm just making sure. *Some* of us actually care about the things we're put in charge of."

"Listen," I said, turning to him, "you've got one more time to—"

"Children!" Ayanna said loudly. She looked at Lady Night and made a face. "Excuse them. Please continue."

The woman eyed the three of us, picked up the SBP, and sighed. "Such a little thing. And yet . . . the power it holds. If I fix this, young man, you have to promise to be more careful with it."

My face grew red at her stern tone, and I tried to ignore Junior's smug look. "I will," I mumbled.

"Good. Because if this fell into the wrong hands, we'd all be in mortal trouble. You know that, right? With this, someone could do inconceivable damage and hurt a lot of people."

"Someone. You mean the Shamble Man?"

"I don't know what his ultimate goal is, but theoretically, yes."

I fiddled with my thumbs as I thought about that, and the question I wanted to ask next. At last I took a deep breath and blurted it out. "The same person—well, bunny—who told me to come find you also suspects the Shamble Man is from MidPass. A god. Is that true? That can't be true, right?"

Lady Night didn't answer. She drummed her fingers on the tabletop and surveyed the crowd. Gum Baby had clambered onto the stage and was now banging on a pair of drums, and surprisingly, not doing too bad a job. The crowd loved her, but I wasn't sure how the enchanted sticks felt about getting all gummed up.

"I think," Lady Night began, "that I don't want to jump to any conclusions. We all saw what happened with Anansi and Brer Rabbit."

I nodded. The division between MidPass and the rest of Alke had been so distracting that the trickster god was able to impersonate Brer Rabbit without anyone noticing until it was almost too late.

And yet, I saw a fleeting expression on her face. That little hesitation adults have when they don't want to lie. She hadn't answered the question because she wasn't sure, either.

And that scared me.

"Speaking of Anansi..." She picked up the phone and tossed it into the pot.

We all gawked at her.

"What are you—?" I began.

"Hey!" Junior said, partially standing.

"Relax," Lady Night said. "I'm just putting it in rice."

My jaw dropped to the tabletop, and then I stood and peeked into the pot. Sure enough, the SBP rested on top of a pile of rice. But it wasn't the white rice I'd expected. It was slightly orange in color, with peas and chopped up carrots mixed in. Bits of red pepper had been shaken on top, and the dish smelled spicy.

"What sort of rice is this?" I asked, worried about it doing even more damage. When they said *Put your phone in rice*, this wasn't what I'd had in mind.

Lady Night frowned. "Jollof rice, of course. Jollof fixes everything."

"Of course," I mumbled, slightly—no, incredibly flabbergasted. I watched as she touched all three of the heating stones, whispering under her breath as she'd done earlier with her cloak. The stones started to glow, and wisps of steam curled out of the pot. The aroma that began to fill the air made my mouth water and my heart swell. It smelled like...well, it smelled like comfort. Like Sunday dinner, or a new book, or fresh rain on a spring morning. It was hard to explain, and yet when I looked around the table, Ayanna and Junior looked just as surprised.

"What do you smell?" I asked them.

Ayanna smiled dreamily. "A fresh crisp breeze as I'm soaring through the air."

Junior kept his eyes glued on the phone and didn't answer right away. Finally, he shifted uncomfortably in his seat. "Plantains," he said softly. "Fried to a slight crisp and cooling on the windowsill."

After a second, I spoke up. "A new book, when you first open it and the pages are stiff."

Lady Night nodded. "It is the smell of the stories that call to you, and the times in which you heard them. But it appears I will need your help, young Anansesem. This . . . Story Box is active, but just barely, and it isn't responding to me fully. There is a trace of power rippling through it, but it will not return to form without you, for some reason."

When I looked away from her and into the pot, the crack across the screen had disappeared. The power was still off, however, and I bit my lip, worry gathering in my stomach. How was I supposed to help? Fingerprint unlocking? Eye scan? A secret password? Oh man, I hoped it wasn't a password. I only had one that I used for everything (I know, I know, but it's a good one, trust me) and there was no way I was saying that out loud. Nuh-uh. Not happening.

Gum Baby had finally finished her drum solo and skipped over to our booth. Just in time to hear Lady Night lean over and say, "You're an Anansesem. So . . ."

"So it needs a story," I finished. I looked around the room, unsure. It made sense. I'd been neglecting the Story Box, what with everything that had been going on. I hadn't been collecting stories like I was supposed to. I had to face it—I was a failure as an Anansesem.

Lady Night nodded. "It will need a *lot* of stories, powerful ones. But there is a risk to this. He who has your grandmother wears armor made out of iron monsters. The same creatures who were—"

"Attracted to stories," I finished grimly. Great. I needed Anansi and the SBP to find Nana, but fixing it might draw the attention of the Shamble Man. Of course there was the chance he might bring Nana with him, but I couldn't count on that. What if I couldn't think of a powerful story to tell? And if I tried and failed yet again, what would everybody say? They might not think I was even worthy of carrying the title of Anansesem and wielding the SBP. . . . Maybe Junior was right.

Lady Night saw the look of despair on my face, but before she could say anything, Gum Baby hopped onto the table and took a whiff of the pot's contents. "Hoo-whee!" she said. "Whatever is cooking in there, Gum Baby wants a plate. Smells like it'll clear the Simon Says."

"The what?" Lady Night asked with a frown.

"The Simon Says."

Ayanna cleared her throat. "*Sinuses*, Gum Baby. It'll clear your sinuses."

"If you even have any," I added.

Gum Baby shot me an evil look as she snuck her hand into the pot, only to pause, then peer closer inside. "Ew, Bumbletongue, is this your phone? You put your phone in the food? That's just... Is Gum Baby the only one around here with any home training?" She stomped across the table to stand in front of me, one hand on her hip and the other pointing at the pot. "Gum Baby tries and tries to teach you some manners, and they just go in one ear and out the other. Gum Baby's gonna talk to your grandmother when we find her. What would your nana say?"

I rolled my eyes, then froze.

Nana.

"That's it," I whispered. "What would Nana say?"

"What? Speak up, boy."

"Gum Baby, you're a genius."

The little loudmouth sniffed. "About time you recognized."

I looked at Lady Night, excitement replacing my previous despair. "I know how to power the Story Box. I don't always have to be the one to tell the story. Nana, my grandmother, she told me that. I just have to be the one to *listen*."

A confused look crossed her face, but I squeezed past a baffled Junior, grinned at Ayanna, and slid out of the booth. "Lady Night, would it be okay if I moved the pot and stones to the stage?"

"I suppose..." she said. "Let me cool them down so you

don't burn yourself." She blew once on the outside of the pot. "There, that should do it."

I poked the pot with one tentative finger. Cool to the touch. "Thank you." I put on the lid, grabbed the pot. "Gum Baby," I called back over my shoulder, "grab the stones and meet me on the stage."

"Why?"

"We're gonna crowdsource a story."

While I carried the pot, Gum Baby sat on my shoe, juggling the cooking stones and calling out directions.

"A little to the left!"

"No, your *other* left!"

"Watch out for that—"

I stubbed my toe against the bottom edge of the stage and toppled forward. I managed to keep the jollof rice from spilling out, but I banged my knee and collapsed into a heap. Gum Baby executed a perfect somersault and landed in the center of the stage, bowing to a smattering of applause from the crowd.

I glared at her as I picked up the cook pot and sat it on the stones, which Lady Night had set to glowing again from the back of the room. "Some guide you are."

"It ain't Gum Baby's fault you're clumsy," she said.

You know that look grown-ups give you when you just did something wrong and they're ready to unleash a blistering lecture that would strip paint from the walls, but they can't because they're in public? That's the look I turned on Gum Baby. People were starting to gather around the stage, so I gritted my teeth and gave her my best *You're gonna get it later* glare, which she ignored. I turned to watch everyone approach and got a good gander at the juke joint's patrons.

They were a mix of folk. Farmers in boots caked with mud and couples in fine outfits and expensive jewelry. The boar who'd led the band cradled his saxophone in one hand and smoothed down the bristles atop his head with the other. A trio of badgers the size of golden retrievers huddled close together near the edge of the crowd. The strange pair of oxen from before, still wearing the weird sunglasses. And still more Alkeans flooded through the door, filling the room to capacity and then some.

There was a pocket of space surrounding an empty table on the edge of the dance floor, and on a hunch I held the Amagqirha's bead from Isihlangu.

Sure enough, the table I'd thought was empty actually seated five or six spirits. Their golden eyes were turned to me, curious and expectant.

Lady Night had said that before Big Big took over, the juke joint was a place of refuge, a place to forget troubles, if only for a couple of hours. Entertainment and stories and good times were had. I guess word of Big Big's downfall had spread quickly throughout the area.

And now they're all looking at me, I thought. *No pressure.*

I clapped my hands once, twice, three times. "Alkeans," I said loudly. "People. Animals. Spirits. My name is Tristan Strong."

"I know you," someone said. The boar. He pointed at me with the saxophone. "You're that storyteller. The one who battled them iron monsters."

The crowd murmured and I nodded. "Yes. That's me."

"You gonna tell a story? One of them magic ones?" Everyone seemed to lean forward at the question, and I swallowed a lump in my throat and shook my head. I wasn't even going to attempt it.

"No. Not today." The disappointment was audible as everyone in the room seemed to deflate. "Today, I need *your* stories."

Silence.

"Alke's in trouble," I said. I forced my voice to project to the far corners of the room. "There's a menace stalking the land, taking our joy and leaving behind fear."

"There's always a menace!" someone else shouted.

"That's true. There will always be some new evil on the horizon looking to sneak into our lives when we aren't looking and take what isn't theirs. We will have to be on guard constantly."

Lady Night moved through the crowd, slipping between her patrons with ease, until she stood just to the left of me, off the stage. She nodded at me to continue, Big Big the weasel now in her arms like a rich person's Chihuahua. Ayanna and Junior joined her. Having friendly faces to focus on when I got nervous helped. I took a deep breath and spread my arms wide.

"I ... need your help." Saying those four words felt like pulling nails from my heart, but it got easier after that. "Someone—the Shamble Man—took something from me." When I spoke the villain's name, the murmuring crowd fell silent. "Not something, but *someone*. Someone special. And I'm going to get her back."

I paused, then spoke those words again, slowly. "I'm going to get her back. Whatever it takes. However long it takes. I know I'm asking a lot, and we risk drawing the attention of the Shamble Man. You don't have to help me. But ... I would appreciate it greatly if you did."

I stopped speaking abruptly. It was like my words had just run out and all that was left were the indescribable emotions rattling around inside me. The crowd shuffled, and murmurs traveled throughout the room. For once Gum Baby didn't have anything to say.

Because she was sleeping.

She was lying on her back on stage left, one arm thrown over her eyes and a sap bubble slowly inflating and deflating as she snored softly.

Some people, I swear.

Just when it felt like I was completely on my own and

nobody was going to put their life on the line to help me, some movement caught my eye. A mother and daughter who'd been keeping to themselves in the back now made their way to the stage. The little girl couldn't have been more than four. She wore a simple gray dress and black shoes with silver buckles. Her hair was braided into two pigtails, each with a white ribbon tied in a bow at the end.

Her mother, with tired eyes but a gentle smile, nodded at me. "How can we help?" she asked.

I smiled back gratefully and dropped into a squat. "I am an Anansesem. I tell stories, and I collect them to share with others. Right now, I need your stories." Standing up, I looked around the room and raised my voice. "I need stories about those people in your lives who helped you when no one else would or could. You know the ones I'm talking about. The people who, at a time in your life when you were struggling to keep your head above water, threw you a rope and pulled you to shore. Tell me about them, so I can find the person who helped me like that."

No one spoke for a moment, and then the little girl raised her hand. I smiled and pointed at her. "Yes? Who's your story about?"

She dropped her head shyly, fiddling with her hands as she spoke. "My grandfather. When my mommy was trapped inside the mean ship, he took care of me. When I cried or was afraid, he'd make silly shadow puppets by candlelight and tell me stories."

Her mother's hands held her close, and I met her eyes in shock. She'd been inside the Maafa, the slave ship that had sent forth the iron monsters. That experience, the trauma—it was something you never forgot.

I knew.

I nodded at the little girl. "Your grandfather is a wonderful man." That made her smile, and she hugged her mother, happy to have contributed.

"My sister," another man called from across the room. A farmer leaning against a wall. "When my home burned in the MidPass fire, she opened up hers to me and a few others until we got back on our feet."

Lady Night caught my eye and nodded at the cook pot. It was glowing. The stories were working!

"Anyone else?" I asked. "Who stepped up for you when no one else would?"

The badgers stood as one. "The raven who lived in the tree above our den! He helped us escape the fires."

"My aunt."

"My brother."

"Mami Wata from Nyanza."

More people began to call out the names of those who had left an impression on their lives.

Like my nana.

The juke joint was filled with laughter as people swapped stories about their heroes. At my feet, the cook pot began to pulse with a silver-blue glow. I crouched just as Gum Baby yawned and stretched.

"How'd we do?" she asked.

"*I* did okay." I lifted the lid of the cook pot and was hit with steam and spices that made my eyes water and my stomach growl. But I hungered more for the sleek black-and-gold phone resting on top of that mound of savory jollof rice.

It blinked to life, and the splash screen appeared: a tiny spider crawling across the display. That disappeared, and the home screen I'd been used to seeing dissolved into view. And there, in the top corner, Anansi lay sleeping in his web hammock.

I'd never been happier to see someone I didn't actually trust.

I wiped the phone clean with a handkerchief the boar handed me. (Yes, I know, just roll with it.) For the first time in a long while, I felt like I had my feet under me and I just might have a chance of finding the Shamble Man, rescuing Nana and Mami Wata, and returning to my world safely.

And that's when the plat-eyes returned.

24
THE PLAT-EYES' TALE

I WAS IN THE MIDDLE OF CELEBRATING.

I stood on the stage holding the SBP, grinning down at
Anansi as he slept through all the chaos and turmoil. I raised
the lit-up phone, and the crowd cheered. Ayanna and Lady
Night high-fived. Everyone smiled and continued to call out
the people who helped them, and the mood in the juke joint
was incredible.

Except for Junior. He stared at me with a baleful glare.
What was up with him now?

Meanwhile, Gum Baby was running back and forth across
the stage, encouraging the crowd to tell their stories. "What
about you? Somebody helped you with that outfit, 'cause
Gum Baby saw you last week, and you were a mess. Shout
them out!"

Everyone laughed, and I got an idea. I tapped the Listen
Chile icon, the app that recorded stories and translated them

for me so I could retell them on my travels. A blinking red light appeared in the corner of the screen, severing one of the anchor strands of Anansi's hammock and sending the trickster god tumbling to the bottom of the phone.

"Hey!" he shouted, but I ignored him and held the SBP's camera steady as I videoed the crowd, watching in awe as the names being mentioned appeared as golden text bubbles above each speaker, before bursting into dazzling confetti that floated to the top of the screen and filled the battery meter.

"Their stories are charging the Story Box," I said in wonder. Lady Night stepped up onto the stage next to me and peeked over my shoulder.

"Of course they are," Anansi grumbled. He climbed to his feet and dusted off his pants. "I could've told you that if you had— Oh, excuse me." His gaze fell on the boo hag and his manner switched completely. "Pardon me, ma'am, I don't believe we've met. My name is—"

"Anansi," she interrupted. "The Weaver. Trickster god. Spinner of tales and tangled lies. I know who you are."

I fought back a grin as Anansi hemmed and hawed, unused to being labeled so accurately. Lady Night winked at me and I shook my head, continuing to sweep the crowd, when a sound reached my ears.

He's coming.

Those weird whispers again. Like when I'd seen the spirits in my grandparents' barn. Right before . . .

A chill ran down my spine. Right before the plat-eyes had arrived.

I scanned the crowd. There, near the back of the club, was one of the creatures I'd thought was an ox, with the weird sunglasses.

You might think it strange that I said *one of the creatures I'd thought was an ox*, and you'd be perfectly justified in thinking that. However, one thing I need to make perfectly clear is THAT WASN'T AN OX!!!

"Anansi," I whispered, "there's a plat-eye in here."

He glared at me. "Don't you start..." His voice trailed off when he saw where the SBP's camera was pointed. I pretended to move the phone around, but I kept it mostly on the plat-eye. Now that I studied the spirit, I didn't see how I ever could've been fooled.

The sunglasses barely covered the creature's giant white eyes. One horn was broken and dangling off the side of its head. Its fur was gray and matted, and clouds of steam trailed from its nostrils. The SBP outlined the creature in faint green, the same color Anansi's adinkra glowed when there were iron monsters nearby, but I hesitated to jump to that conclusion. This wasn't an iron monster...it was a creature from folktales. Now, what was it Nana had said about them? They could change shape and grow....

Before I could remember all the way back to...yesterday (wow, time flies when you're saving the world), someone screamed.

I whipped around to find the second ox—no, of course, it was a plat-eye, too—standing next to the little brown girl with the pigtails. Her mother shielded her as the spirit stood on its hind legs and snorted. This one had three horns, the third peeking out from under its top hat. I really needed to work on my ability to see through shoddy disguises. If these were the same two that had attacked me in the barn, they'd looked a lot better as rottweiler cats.

"Is anyone here *not* a plat-eye?" I shouted, hopping off the stage before shouting directions. "Gum Baby, you're with me! Ayanna, Junior, Lady Night, crowd control, please!"

The three of them nodded and spread out, directing people to a side exit. Lady Night spoke in a clear calm voice as Ayanna and Junior helped those who couldn't move fast. The patrons listened to them, thankfully, which left me, a ten-inch sap doll, and a god trapped in a smartphone to face two plat-eye monsters.

Light work.

"All right then, y'all wanted to crash the party," I told them. "Let's go!"

Gum Baby ran up my side and flipped onto my shoulder, sap balls in hand as she waited for one of the spirits to make the first move. I slipped the SBP into my shorts pocket, vowing not to let it get damaged again. Then, favoring my uninjured wrist, I raised my hands and dropped into a boxer's crouch. "C'mon, then!"

Several tense seconds passed. Then a minute. Still no one moved. The plat-eye duo shuffled their feet (hooves?) and kept glancing at each other. It was almost as if they were stalling. I jabbed a foot forward, feinting an attack, and they retreated. By this time the juke joint was empty, the enchanted drums tapping out a medium-tempo rhythm with the booming thump of the kick drum interrupting every so often. Ayanna and Junior returned and divided to take up stations on opposite sides of the room. We now had the plat-eyes surrounded.

Gum Baby shifted on my shoulder. "Are these cowboys gonna fight or what? HEY! ARE Y'ALL GONNA FIGHT?"

But it didn't seem like the monsters wanted to. In fact, the way they snorted and tossed their heads at each other, it was almost as if each was trying to convince the other to make the first move. Like a dare. Or they were trying to work up the courage to . . .

"They've got something to say," I said slowly.

"What?" Gum Baby accidentally smooshed a sap ball in my face as she turned to look at me. "Say something? What're they gonna say? Moo? Speak up, Bumbletongue. You can't just start talking to Gum Baby and not finish your sentence."

I wiped sap from my lips and glared at her. "I *said*, I think they've got something to say, but I can't understand it. We need a translator, something that can help me with . . ."

The SBP vibrated in my pocket at the same time that

I realized the answer to my problem. When I took it out, Anansi was leaning against the edge of the screen eating an apple he'd pulled from... Actually, I had no idea where he'd pulled that apple from. He tossed the core away and it disintegrated into pixels as he brushed his hands on his pants. "So... are you ready to listen?"

"Yes," I said, straightening. "Yes, I'm ready."

"Good. I seem to remember your grandmother telling you about the plat-eyes, and what they represented. Do you?"

I wrinkled my forehead as I tried to think. "They're spirits that can't move on. There's something they need to get done, and they haunt the person they think can help them."

Anansi nodded, then reached into his pocket and pulled out a giant wallet. He opened it and flipped through the billfold like a rich person searching for a bill smaller than a hundred. But it wasn't money he pulled out.

"Ah, there it is." He stuck in his fingers, then his whole arm, until his shoulder had nearly disappeared into the wallet, and emerged with a rounded rectangular app clutched in his hand. The icon had a glittering black background with a single uppercase letter *D* in the center that flickered from red to green. Anansi tossed it into the air, where it began to spin slowly in the middle of the screen.

"What is that?" I asked, keeping an eye on the milling plat-eyes at the same time.

"That, my boy, is the Diaspor-app."

"It's bigger than the others."

"It better be. All those permissions you were so kind as to grant me? They went into the construction of this beauty. It's your one-stop shop for everything dealing with the Diaspora. Those stories you collected? They will be sorted and categorized, and you will be able to trace their origins and also the relationships between them. Ever wonder why Brer Rabbit's stories are so similar to my own? Find the roots. Mine are the originals, of course, but that's a lesson for another day. Right now, you need a translator. Well, pop open this one-of-a-kind web app and watch the language barrier disappear."

I raised an eyebrow.

"Go ahead," Anansi said. "Give it a whirl. Sure beats standing around doing a whole lotta nothing."

"Tristan?" Ayanna called. "Is everything all right?"

Gum Baby tossed sap balls menacingly. "No, it ain't all right! He's gonna try and talk it out! Can you believe that? Gum Baby came with two tickets to the gum show, and she ain't handing out rain checks."

I ignored them all and tapped the icon. The SBP vibrated twice, and then the screen went black. After a few seconds, a pulsating amber globe appeared and started to rotate. I waited for something else to happen, but nothing did.

"Sooo," I started to say, but I stopped when the globe pulsed sharply. It was reacting to my voice. I looked at it, then up at the plat-eyes, then back at the orb. "No way," I muttered. The sphere transformed into Anansi's face, and he winked at me before it immediately reverted to the globe. "Fine."

I took a long, deep breath and stepped off the stage and down to the dance floor. Slowly, and I mean very, *very* slowly, I walked over to the two plat-eyes. They stamped their hooves nervously and snorted giant spouts of steam, but they didn't attack. I edged closer and held out the phone.

"Okay," I said, looking between the two of them. "I'm here. I'm listening. What are you trying to tell me?"

The golden sphere contorted and expanded as the plat-eyes in oxen form began to snort and stamp and bellow. The icon stretched and unfolded, and shapes appeared from the tangled mess. The shapes became houses and trees, people and creatures, and I watched as MidPass came to life on the screen. This is the story the plat-eyes told:

Once a brother and sister lived with their father on a small farm. When their father traveled for work, they did as most children are wont to do when their parents are away—they played games, sang songs, and tried not to make *too* big of a mess. Every day, the father would come home and sweep them into his giant arms and march around the farm telling them stories and tickling them until they thought their sides would split. It was a wonderful time, but such times must always come to an end.

The brother and sister had an uncle—a close friend of their

father's, really, but he was always around, so that's what they called him. He and their father were pals from way back, the kind of friends who knew what the other was thinking without it ever being said. The two friends would sit on the front porch of the farmhouse long after the brother and sister were supposed to be in bed, and talk in low voices about the state of the world and the trouble on the horizon. They would make plans, emergency steps they hoped would never be necessary, and sit quietly afterward until Uncle flashed a gentle smile, clapped their father on the back, and headed off into the forest.

Brother and Sister thought nothing of it. They played games beneath the forest canopy, sang songs by the stream, and tried not to make *too* big of a mess.

One afternoon Brother thought he heard screams coming from deep in the forest.

One morning Sister thought she smelled smoke drifting through the trees.

They never told their father about these things, because they didn't want to worry him. They wanted his stories and his laugh and his threats of tickles, not his fear and sorrow. So they ignored the growing unease in the forest and did what children do.

They played games.

They sang songs.

They tried not to make *too* big of a mess.

Then Uncle stopped coming around. Brother and Sister missed his easy smile, the way he let them ride his reddish-gray tail as he marched around pretending to look for them. Their father missed him, too. He grew moody and distant, and at night he would stand on the porch and stare into the darkness. Brother and Sister tried to cheer him up by playing and singing, but each day it took more and more to pull their father out of his depression.

He left one morning as he always did, off to search for something. He never found it, but he was always looking. Brother and Sister didn't know what *it* was exactly, only that it was special, precious, and something a lot of people were after.

The fires swept through the forest that afternoon.

And with them came the monsters.

When the smoke cleared, Brother and Sister waited and waited for their father to come home. They wanted him to sweep them up in his giant furry arms and tickle them with his massive paws. They wanted to play and to sing, but for some reason they couldn't.

Father finally came home, tired and hoarse from shouting, his shaggy fur smoking and his eyes watering. Brother and Sister tried to talk to him, but he couldn't see them. His eyes passed right over them. He couldn't hear them, either, no matter how loud they shouted. His paws brushed right through them. What was the matter? Why couldn't he find them?

They watched him sit and shed tear after tear, and Brother and Sister cried with him, though he couldn't hear their sniffles. They watched day after day as he searched for them, calling their names, even though they were right there.

Father started talking to himself. Muttering about a boy who could talk to spirits, a boy who saw the living and the dead. A boy who ripped a hole in the sky, who made friends with gods and enemies of evil. A boy who brought the monsters to the forest, and who'd taken everything. He wanted to find that boy, to shout and scream and ask him why, why couldn't he find his children.

Brother and Sister wanted to find the boy, too.

He could help them talk to their father.

I let the arm holding the SBP drop to my side and stared at the plat-eyes. They were . . . they had to be the brother and sister in the story. They'd suffered so much. Lost so much. And they'd been trying so long just to get their father to see them, to understand that though they were spirits, they were still here. That was their mission, their reason for hanging around.

And I could help them accomplish it.

There were just two big problems standing in my way. First, their father blamed me for their loss. To be honest, I could understand why. I did punch a hole in the sky, letting a haint into Alke, and riling up the iron monsters and the

Maafa that controlled them. Yes, I had fixed my mistake (with help from others), but it had cost a lot of people dearly.

The second problem was I knew who their father was—the Shamble Man. But you saw that coming. What you probably didn't see coming is that I knew who was underneath the mask. And from the way Anansi's adinkra was burning my wrist, he was on his way. In fact, any second now—

BOOM!

The back of the juke joint shook as something massive landed on the roof. The plat-eyes vanished, the frightened expressions on their faces the last thing I saw. Giant footsteps shook the foundation as they marched toward the front of the building. A heavy thump sounded just outside the door. I took a step forward and tried to calm my nerves in preparation to meet my nemesis.

See, I'd recognized someone in the plat-eye siblings' story. I'd know that reddish-silver tail anywhere. It was Brer Fox, though when I'd met him he just went by Fox. Which meant the Shamble Man was . . .

WHAM!

The double doors exploded inward as a huge foot kicked them in. Junior yelped and hurled a stone, only to fling himself to the ground when a paw batted it back at him. The Shamble Man stepped through the dust. His iron-monster armor had the fading glow of cooling coals. I barely noticed. Instead, I studied the profile of the villain who'd kidnapped

Nana, kidnapped Mami Wata, and stolen the weapons of the gods to do who knows what. How could I not have recognized him before? His hood had been pulled low, sure, and his fur was missing in patches. The armor covered up a lot, but now that I had seen the story, his demeanor seemed unmistakable.

"Little hero, *grum grum*. We meet again."

I squared my shoulders and looked straight into the twisted amber mask, and the bloodshot eyes behind it.

"Hello, Brer Bear."

25
I DON'T WANT TO FIGHT

IN NANA'S STORIES, BRER BEAR WAS A HULKING ANTAGONIST TO
Brer Rabbit. He was the muscle for Fox's conniving plans, the
one who stood in the background and growled or gnashed his
teeth as needed. He never really acted of his own free will.
An enforcer, that's what he was. And, like all the larger foes
that Brer Rabbit faced, Bear often ended up on the wrong
side of the story.

Most of the time Nana would end the stories with Brer
Rabbit escaping, Fox and Bear made to look like fools once
again. But sometimes—and I loved when this happened—she
would raise her hand before I could move from my seat at the
foot of her rocking chair. My parents had bought that chair
just for her visits, and the *creak, creak, creak* of the wood as
she rocked to and fro was like music to my ears. She'd lean
forward, hand raised, and a look would cross her face.

"Just a minute now, boy," she'd say. "I ain't finished just yet. There's more to this here tale."

And so I'd stay, and Nana would stare off at nothing and gather her thoughts, pulling them together just as her knitting needles pulled yarn into a growing blanket.

After one tale about Brer Rabbit, Fox, and Bear, she said, "You ain't always gonna be able to outwit everyone who wants to take you down a peg. Can't talk your way out of everything, can't outsmart everybody. One day, someone bigger, stronger, and faster is gonna test your limits. You hear me, child?"

"Yes, ma'am."

Her needles clicked and her rocking chair creaked. "You'd better. Because right or wrong, you gonna be tried and tried again, and the Brer Bears of the world will hound you from one corner of the earth to the other. They have the power and the strength and the stamina to do it. Whether it's with laws or water hoses, *they will do it*. Never forget that."

I remember watching Nana, her eyes trained on something long past, before she turned to me and said fiercely, "Do you know how to fight against somethin' like that, somethin' that knocks you down and tells you to stay down if you know what's good for you? Do you know how to beat that?"

I shook my head, silent.

Her golden quilting needle pointed at me, and Nana leaned forward.

"You get. Back. Up."

Boom tiss boom tiss rat-a-tat-tat
Boom tiss boom tiss rat-a-tat-tat

The enchanted drumsticks tapped out a soft rhythm as the confrontation unfolded. Background music to a showdown that scared the living daylights out of me. Dust still drifted in slow swirls from the destroyed doorway, and the lights flickered every couple of seconds. I stood on one side of the dance floor, Ayanna and Junior on either side of me, and Bear loomed over us even from across the room. Moonlight spilled around his frame to give him an otherworldly glow. At least he hadn't brought John Henry's hammer.

He took a step forward out of the light, and his lopsided amber mask shifted.

Bear was smiling.

"Clever little hero. Thinks he figured it all out. Give him a medal, *grum grum.*" He brought his massive paws together twice in feigned applause, and I swallowed as light glinted off his claws. Each was the size of one of my fingers and looked frighteningly sharp.

"I don't want to fight you," I said slowly. I was proud of the way my voice didn't quaver. "I know what you're looking for.

Let me help you. You don't have to do whatever it is you're thinking about. We can work together and—"

Bear's laugh boomed around the room, nearly shaking the floor. His fetterling armor rattled and clanked as he grabbed his stomach and threw back his head. I gritted my teeth and clenched my fists.

"Just stop this!" I shouted. "I know you're looking for your two chil—"

"Move, fool!" yelled Gum Baby.

If she hadn't warned me, I would've been pulverized. Bear's movements were lightning fast, unfair for a creature of his size. With a lunge I only saw in a blur, he crossed the dance floor with a loud snarl. A single shaggy paw, with hullbeast armor fitted around his arm, crashed into the floor where I'd been standing moments ago. I guess he didn't need the hammer. I dove to the right, rolling over several times and knocking over chairs in the process, my heart in my throat.

Gum Baby flipped into the air, hurling sap ball after sap ball at the mask, but Bear batted them away easily with the backs of his paws, where the fetterling armor was thickest. She tried to scamper away, but she'd gotten too close to him. Bear kicked her across the room and she bounced twice and skidded out through the broken doorway. Then, with both front paws, he slapped the floor again in rage.

"YOU WILL NOT SPEAK OF THEM!" Bear roared.

My chest pounded as I rolled to my feet, my fingers itching to curl and bring forth the akofena shadow gloves. But he didn't press the attack. The hulking giant slowly stood on his hind paws again, bits of the splintered wooden floor sprinkling the ground as he did. His mask rippled as a black shadow swam across it, catching my eye and making me pause. There was something familiar. . . .

"Do not," he said slowly, wresting my attention away from the mask, "speak of them. You do not have that right. You may have deceived the others, *grum grum,* but I know what you truly are."

"Oh yeah? What's that?"

"Tristan . . ." Junior said in warning. I looked at him, and he made a *Calm down* motion. But I wasn't the one attacking people! I began to tell him that, but Bear cut me off.

"You're a coward," Bear sneered. "A traitor. A betrayer."

I shook my head, anger pushing its way past the fear in my chest. "Says a god of MidPass. I'm not the one who attacked his friends and is kidnapping others in this world and outside of it! You're the traitor. Do you know what you did to John Henry? He is *dying!*"

A small sob sounded. Ayanna had both hands covering her mouth as she stared at me in disbelief. She turned to Junior, who nodded slowly. "What do you mean, dying?" She looked at Bear, tears welling up in her eyes. "You attacked your *friend*?"

"Everything I do is for the good of Alke." There was a note of sadness in Bear's voice, but it was soon drowned out as he thumped the hullbeast chest plate, the echo of it syncing eerily with the enchanted drums. "I carry her enemies so she doesn't have to shoulder the burden."

"I defeated those enemies!"

"You cowered in fear as your friends were attacked mercilessly," Bear said. He leaned forward. "Was it you who defeated this creature, or was it a magical ax? When flames devoured MidPass, did you carry the weak and the sick across the Burning Sea? Who enraged the monsters in the first place? Where were you when MidPass needed you most? Hmm? WHERE?"

His questions ate away at my core, robbing me of my anger and leaving me shaken. "I tried—"

"You failed." Bear spat the words out like poison. "And we all suffered as a result."

A soft groan floated in from outside. Gum Baby? I wanted to check on her, but I couldn't see a way to get around the armored god. And neither Anansi nor the SBP were going to be of any help now. Unless...

An idea sprang into my head. The SBP was in the pocket of my shorts, and I let my left hand drop to tap the phone through the fabric. In response, I heard a couple of muffled words I probably shouldn't repeat.

"When the other gods catch you," I said loudly, raising my fists, "you'll suffer some more. It's only a matter of time."

Bear scoffed. "Those fools are too busy holding a pointless summit, squabbling over who is in charge of what, like mice over crumbs. Without his hammer John Henry is toothless and dying the slow death of the forgotten. Your crow-loving bumpkin High John has disappeared again, and even if he were here, he wouldn't lift a finger to help an Alkean—he and Nyame argue all day long. And I will pluck your winged goddesses clean if they so much as flap a feather in my direction. No, little hero, you're on your own, *grum grum*."

"He's not alone," Ayanna said, raising her staff.

Junior groaned and muttered, "Here we go again," but still he withdrew two stones from his satchel, one in each hand. They stood shoulder to shoulder with me. At that moment it didn't matter if my wrist was injured, if I couldn't use all the adinkra charms, or even if the odds were against us. They had my back and I had theirs. That's what mattered.

Then Bear turned to look at Junior.

The boy wouldn't meet his eyes. Junior held his stones at the ready, but he kept shifting his weight, bouncing first on one foot and then the other, as if he were nervous. As if he didn't want to look at Bear full-on out of fear. Fear that—

"I know you," Bear rumbled. The mask tilted as Bear studied Junior. "Yesss, I believe I do."

I took a step forward. "Leave him alone. You're dealing with me right now."

The mask turned to me, then back to Junior, and—to my surprise—Bear started to laugh. "He doesn't know. The little hero, *grum grum,* the know-it-all, has no idea. Even with the eyes of the gods, he can't see what's plain in front of his face. Oh, well. Soon it won't matter at all."

What was he talking about? I looked at Junior for a clue, but he avoided my gaze, too.

Frustration and anger spiked through me, and I pointed at the hulking god-turned-traitor. "We've stopped all your flunkies. Kulture Vulture. Big Big. We can stop you, too."

Instead of shouting like I thought he would, Bear sighed. "I came here hoping you would. Your grandmother said as much to me."

I froze.

Nana.

"She had such high hopes for you. But if you cannot discern enemies from friends, I see she was mistaken. We all were. You are a boy pretending to be a man, waving around the powers of the gods with no idea of what to do next. So it is. So it shall remain." Bear started to pivot to exit the juke joint.

Stung, I clenched both fists, not caring about the pain

in my wrist. "That's it? You're just going to turn your back on all the damage you did, just like before? You don't care about anyone but yourself! Did you even mourn Fox? Or Brer Rabbit?"

He stopped in his tracks.

The SBP vibrated against my thigh. Anansi understood what I was trying to do. Now all I had to do was stall. If I could keep Bear talking, maybe, just maybe, the other gods would come and help take down one of their own. From the look Bear turned on me, a baleful scowl practically glowing from behind the mask he wore, stalling might be my last resort.

"What did you say?" His voice, though soft, rumbled like a muscle car getting ready to accelerate. "What . . . did you just say?"

"I said, what about Brer Rabbit and Fox? Your friends. You all used to—"

The giant grizzly exploded across the dance floor, one massive paw lifting me off the ground by the throat and slamming me against the wall behind me, driving the breath out of my lungs and causing pain to shoot through the back of my skull. Ayanna screamed, and Junior was knocked aside by Bear's other paw. The enchanted drum set toppled over at the impact and the furniture shuddered, as if unwilling to witness what was about to happen next.

Bear leaned in close, so I could see every putrid lump and bubbling pustule in the shifting amber mask. Beneath the surface the oily shadow I'd seen before shifted back and forth. I narrowed my eyes at it, which didn't help my headache, but I didn't get a chance to investigate, because Bear opened his mouth and a harsh snarl slipped through teeth the size of knives.

"You don't get to say those names," he said softly, inches from my face. "Your very existence is a betrayal of their lives. Fox is dead thanks to you. Brer Rabbit was kidnapped and held captive, and now he clings to life because of that little bug you're so buddy-buddy with, whose offspring plots under your very nose. You . . . sicken me."

I stopped struggling for a moment, stunned. I looked at Junior.

He opened his mouth, paused, then looked away.

"Yesss," Bear hissed. "You see it now. Too little, too late, *grum grum*." Still gripping me tightly with one paw, Bear used the other to pull up my left wrist. I was terrified he was going to take my adinkra bracelet, but instead, he outlined my hand with a wicked sharp claw. "Where are those blessed gloves of yours, hmm? Did you lose them like the little boy you are?"

I squirmed and gasped for air.

"Tristan Strong punched a hole in the sky," Bear said in a whisper. "And brought the evil in."

A chill slid down my spine. "No," I said.

"Cities burned, now what did we learn?" He bared his teeth at me. "Don't let him do it again."

He let go of my throat and I slid to the floor with a jarring *thump*. I coughed and rubbed at where his claws had pricked my neck. "Where is my nana?" I said with a rasp. "What have you done with her?"

Bear winced for the first time. "That yammering old lady is safe. For now. But she won't be for long...not if I don't get what I want."

"What do you want? The Story Box?"

He laughed, then scooped me off the floor and flung me across the room. I landed hard on my shoulder, and lightning shot down my whole right arm. "Keep your stories, little hero. You can use them to entertain your friends when I bring your world down on your head."

"Then what?" I shouted in pain. "Just give me back my grandmother!"

"YOU CAN'T HAVE HER BACK!" Bear roared. "I want you to suffer! You hear me? Suffer! I'm taking from you what you took from me. Someone you care about, *grum grum,* and they will die, just like you will, knowing that you failed to save them. Just like you failed to save MidPass."

"Your children—"

An earsplitting growl shook the juke joint as Bear launched himself forward, his hind paw crashing into my chest and pinning me down. Stars bloomed in front of my eyes. My fingers feebly struggled for the pocket where the SBP was.

Bear laughed and shook his head. "What, you think I don't know about your plan?"

He lifted his paw off me and I froze.

"Go on. Call your gods. They won't come even if you beg them to save you. They are leaderless, divided, squabbling like children forced to share. You are alone, Tristan Strong, champion of MidPass, warrior from the Battle of the Bay. Scream for your gods. I would rip them to pieces in front of you if they dared to show their faces. CALL THEM!"

My fingers hovered over my pocket, eyes prickling with tears as my lungs wheezed. Was he right? Had the loss of John Henry thrown everyone into disarray? Were they afraid? Fear gripped me tight, a block of ice around my chest, and Bear began to cackle.

Not laugh, cackle.

I dropped my hand.

"Pathetic," Bear said. "I'd planned to let you live to see the destruction you will be blamed for. But now your presence is a stain on everything that all *except for you* have sacrificed. Better to crush you like the bug you shelter in your pocket, *grum grum*."

He stepped outside for a moment, and I heard a woman's cry of surprise and pain. Bear came back in with John Henry's hammer. The massive symbol of MidPass's strongest god looked warped in Bear's claws, and as he gripped the handle, the iron head began to glow with a pale-green fire. "Your world will burn, little hero. And everyone will think you did it. Again."

Bear raised the hammer over me with both paws, his face twisted into a snarl. I closed my eyes.

Thok, thok, thok

Stones hammered Bear's mask, knocking it askew and sending him reeling backward in outrage. Junior stood on the stage, his hands a blur as he threw with painful accuracy. Fear was written all over his face, but his mouth was pressed thin and he didn't flinch as Bear roared with each blow.

I scrambled away and took refuge under a table in the back.

CRASH!

Bear stumbled as the drum set from the stage launched itself at him, the snare and the hi-hat cymbals colliding with his mask. The kick drum flew across the room and knocked into his legs, sending him crashing to the floor. The drumsticks battered his head and poked at his eyes through the holes in the mask.

I gawked at the sight.

"This is my home, and no one disrespects me in my home."

The pain-laden shout came from the broken front doors. Lady Night leaned against Ayanna. Swirling lavender smoke hovered above her right hand. She whispered to it, then lobbed the spell at the overturned tables and chairs, where it exploded into a silver-and-lavender cloud. The effort nearly forced her to double over in agony.

Rumbling, scraping sounds filled the room, and the chairs and tables assembled themselves into five large figures that hurled themselves at Bear. The god roared his challenge and smashed the first two into pieces with his stolen hammer.

"I'm not going to be able to keep this up much longer," Lady Night grunted. She stood upright and shoved Ayanna toward the door. "You have to go now. Hurry! The magic will keep him busy for a while. Tristan, find your grandmother and Mami Wata and stop this before it's too late." She hurled another spell, sending a second wave of musical instruments crashing into Bear's face.

"Junior, let's go!" I called.

He glanced at me, then shook his head and redoubled his efforts. The stones he had already cast flew back into his hands and then across the room to pummel Bear again. How could I have missed the fact that he was one of Anansi's six sons? It was so obvious now. The same brown skin, the quirky smile, and then there was his special talent: throwing stones with laser-like accuracy. No wonder Nyame wanted to keep such a close eye on him.

I hesitated, then called, "Stone Thrower!"

The SBP buzzed in alarm in my pocket. I winced. Onstage, the boy smiled, then shook his head. "Go!" he shouted. "Just go!" Three stones pinged in quick succession, landing in a narrow gap between the armor on Bear's wrist. The god roared and the hammer dropped to the floor.

"Tristan, come on!" Ayanna shouted.

I limped to my feet and paused, torn. Junior tossed a few more stones, glanced over at me, and gave me a mock salute. "Do better, hero," he said, right before he hurled a stone that thumped me in the chest and sent me stumbling backward through the ruined door. "Someday I still have to tell my father that story."

Outside, the night sky had begun to lighten at the creases where the horizon watched from a safe distance. Gum Baby lay motionless on the ground, dust coating her still form. I scooped her up and limped to the pilot raft, hesitated, then climbed aboard. Nana was still out there somewhere, waiting for me. Ayanna followed and quickly took over, sending us up into the storm clouds. We both looked back in horror as another roar exploded into the darkness.

26
GET BACK UP

"TRISTAN STRONG PUNCHED A HOLE IN THE SKY," I MUTTERED, fists clenched so tight my fingernails threatened to pierce my palms. The pain from my right wrist raced up into my elbow, but I ignored it. "And let the evil in."

"Tristan?"

What was I supposed to do now? Bear was too strong. The other gods were scared to face him, and John Henry was barely clinging to his stories. What chance did a skinny kid from Chicago have?

"Tristan? Are you listening? Tristan!"

I lifted my head from my knees, which I was clutching to my chest while sitting in the middle of the raft. We floated above another dry riverbed leading north to the Golden Crescent. A further reminder of how Alke was falling apart and I couldn't do anything about it. When I tried to work with my friends to save people, I failed. When I tried to do things on my own, I failed. It felt as if a boulder had settled onto my shoulders, driving me to the ground and anchoring me in place.

"Tristan?"

Ayanna knelt in front of me, the SBP in her hand and a look of concern on her face. In my head I saw the juke joint collapsing, Lady Night and Junior inside, and my eyes welled up with tears. Lady Night had helped so many refugees from MidPass, and now she was gone. And I'd been so mean to Stone Thrower at first, when all he was trying to do was overcome his family legacy.

I knew something about that, and yet I'd failed him. I'd failed them both.

"Tristan!" Anansi peered out of the screen, a worried expression on his face as Ayanna leaned forward to put her hand on my shoulder. "We've got to keep moving."

"For what?" I muttered.

"Your grandmother! Your friends, your world, everything!" Ayanna threw up her hands. "What do you mean, for what? Your world and mine are in trouble if we don't stop that mangy-furred cretin!"

I looked around. The sun was just rising over the tip of Isihlangu to the east. It covered the mountain range in a gold-and-pink blanket of light that reminded me of Nana's quilt, a warm layer of comfort and reassurance. Somehow I was still wearing the backpack, though at this point I couldn't figure out why. For a brief moment I thought about flying to the fortress city of the Ridgefolk and begging them to hide me. But if everyone blamed me like Bear did, would they even open the door?

Ahead of us, the Golden Crescent sparkled like a polished crown. The gilded city was a distant glow on the horizon, like an early sunrise in a world of night. And yet the beauty didn't do anything for me. Who could care about beauty amid so much destruction? I couldn't look at it without remembering the iron monsters flooding the shores of the seaside city, the rotted corpse of the Maafa squatting in the bay like a hungry leviathan. I didn't want to see that happen again. But what could I do?

"Tristan. It's time to act, boy."

I looked down to see Anansi staring out at me. His face was so similar to that of the kid I'd just left behind to face Bear's wrath. For once, there was no mischievous smile or glint in the spider god's eyes. Only sadness.

"Is it true?" I asked, knowing the answer but wanting to hear the trickster god confirm it. I couldn't move until I did. "Was Junior . . . Is Junior your son?"

Ayanna looked back and forth between the phone and me, resignation warring with the need to keep moving, to keep busy, rather than deal with losing someone close. I knew that feeling well.

"It's wild…" I said. "The last story Nana told me, the only one I can still remember clear as day, was about Anansi and his six children. Whenever the trickster got himself into trouble, his sons had to come bail him out. He might've been eaten by a giant fish or a giant bird, but no matter the conundrum, his boys had his back." I shook my head. "I guess it's true… even when he's trapped inside a phone."

Anansi smiled softly. "Ah, yes. They're good boys, my sons. Trouble Seer, Road Builder, River Drinker, Game Skinner, Ground Pillow… and Stone Thrower."

Junior's face popped into my mind, along with the cross-body satchel he'd always kept close. It looked like he'd never be able to tell the story about his father.… Did Anansi know that Stone Thrower had sacrificed himself for their sake?

Just then, Gum Baby groaned and began to stir, which was a good thing, because I'd started to get worried about her, too. How long can a doll stay unconscious?

"*Unnngh.* Gum Baby needs to go easy on the chocolate milk next time." She sat up slowly while holding her head in her hands.

"Are you okay?" I asked.

"Yeah, Gum Baby's gone to rougher parties." Then she dropped her hands and hopped to her feet, her little fists balled as she searched the area. "Where is he? Where's that evil teddy bear? Gum Baby's gonna pound his face into mush!"

When she realized we were no longer in the juke joint, she

dropped her hands, confused. "What's wrong? Why ain't y'all taking Gum Baby to the next fight? Did we win?"

"No." I sighed and sat down on the edge of the raft, letting my legs dangle over the edge as I stared at the muddy remains of one of Mami Wata's rivers. "No, we didn't win. We lost. We lost Mami Wata, we lost my nana, we lost Alke. Bear won. I couldn't beat him."

"Did you try?" Gum Baby climbed into Ayanna's lap and cradled the SBP in her arms. Anansi stared unhappily at a smear of sap on the screen.

"She's right," Ayanna said. "Can't win anything if you don't try."

"What's the point? He can whip me seven ways from Sunday. He's done it twice already. He even beat John Henry! What am I supposed to do against that? Hope? I don't have any more of that. I'm clean out."

"What would your grandmother say?" Anansi asked, ducking under an app as the sap continued to roll down the screen. "Would she want you to give up without even attempting to fight?"

"I. Can't. Win." Why couldn't they understand that? This was when you threw in the towel. When you stopped the fight. I'd have to find some other hero to save the world. Nana would understand, wouldn't she?

Wouldn't she?

The sun finally rose above Isihlangu—maybe for the last

time. Bear was going to do something horrific, the gods of MidPass and Alke couldn't make up their minds about what to do to prevent that from happening, and I was useless.

Get back up.

The thought popped into my head like Nana herself was speaking in my ear. I shook my head and tried to ignore it.

Get back up.

"No," I said out loud. "Just to lose again? No."

Anansi and Gum Baby exchanged a look. They probably thought the stress was getting to me. Maybe it was. I was arguing with myself . . . and losing at that.

Get. Back. Up.

"He's just gonna win again, so what does it matter?" I folded my arms across my chest, well aware it looked like I was sulking, which was fine, because that's exactly what I was doing.

"Uh, Bumbletongue?" Gum Baby asked carefully. "Who are you talking to?"

But I flapped her question away and hopped to my feet, rocking the raft dangerously. "How am I supposed to fight against irrational outbursts? Or misplaced anger? Yes, I ripped open the sky the first time, but I didn't light MidPass on fire! That was the iron monsters, and King Cotton. And we beat them back to the bottom of the sea, together! But Bear won't listen to that. He's . . . he's . . ."

"Bear's dealing with trauma," Anansi said gently. "And he's not handling it well."

That stopped me mid-rant. Trauma. Nana had mentioned that trauma was a deeply distressing event. I guess I'd never really thought about it before, but losing someone you cared about was traumatic—it lingered with you for days and months. Years, even.

Eddie's death still lingered with me.

And just the thought of losing Nana was tearing my heart in two.

Everyone from MidPass who'd had to watch their homes burn or see their loved ones be ripped from them and taken away—that was traumatic.

And Bear . . . losing his children. His best friend. His home.

Yeah, all that was trauma.

"But," I said slowly, "how could he then turn around and inflict more trauma on others?"

Gum Baby hopped off Ayanna's lap and scrambled onto my shoulders as I knelt and picked up the SBP, wiping the screen on my shorts.

Ayanna pursed her lips. "Some of the folks from MidPass used to lash out in the days immediately after . . . well, when the iron monsters were defeated. Never like this, though."

Anansi nodded. "Something has wormed into Bear's head and poisoned his thoughts against the rest of the world. Both worlds. It's like he doesn't care anymore and just wants to cause as much mayhem and destruction as possible."

Something stirred loose in the back of my mind. "Poisoned his thoughts..."

The amber mask.

The oily shadow.

Poisoned his thoughts.

"Oh no," I whispered, horrified. I hurled myself at the rudder at the back of the raft, jerking it forward and shooting the vessel into the sky. I pointed it west—beyond the Golden Crescent.

"Hold it, Tristan, where are you taking us?" Ayanna shouted as we zoomed off.

I bit my lip and crossed my fingers and toes, praying that I was wrong. I so wanted to be wrong. But if I wasn't... Sweet peaches, I didn't want to think about that.

"Tristan?"

We sped through the breaking dawn. "I'm going to talk with an old friend."

Not too long ago, archeologists found the last ship to bring Africans across the ocean to America. The *Clotilda*, it was called, a wooden vessel of nightmares and horror. It was discovered in the Mobile River in Alabama. Wild, right? I'd thought about asking my grandparents to drive me to where they were planning to display it, to take a look at the tool of a terror that had severed families, friends, and communities again and again.

I never did ask, though.

Maybe the memory of another slave ship kept me silent. The hulls filled with disease and despair, the holds stuffed with shackled prisoners—those images still haunted me some nights. The folks I hadn't been able to save.

After learning about the *Clotilda* I'd wondered whether its reemergence all these centuries later had caused trauma in the descendants of abducted Africans.

Or what if it had the opposite effect? Sometimes, as Nana used to say, the only way to get rid of a boil is to lance it. (I think that means cut it with a knife and not with a jousting spear like I originally thought.) The point is, you have to experience some pain in order to begin healing.

Right now, if Alke was going to begin the process of healing the trauma caused by King Cotton and the iron monsters, we were going to have to lance a boil, and that boil was Bear.

But to do that, I had to raise another slave ship.

I needed to speak with the Maafa.

27
RETURN OF THE MAAFA

THE RAFT ZOOMED THROUGH PINK-TINGED CLOUDS AND THE COOL
dawn air. East of us, the towers and minarets of the Golden
Crescent began to emerge, shining like a bunch of Nana's
golden-tipped quilting needles had been plunged into the
earth. The sight made my heart lurch, and doubt tried to
creep back into my mind, but I forced it away. *She'll be all
right,* I said over and over to myself, clutching the scraps of
her quilt tight to my chest. Bear had said my grandmother
was safe—for now. But if the suspicion growing in my mind
was true, it was possible that soon no one would be safe.

The grand palaces of the Golden Crescent began to
appear, growing out of the horizon in all their splendor. Any
other time and I would've gawked at the sight. They had
never failed to amaze me before. This time I barely glanced
at them. My eyes were fixed on the smear of blue to the west
of them.

We zipped past the forest palace of the Mmoatia, the forest fairies who had healed many of those injured in the fight with the iron monsters. Ayanna had taken over, muttering something about flying without a pilot's license, and we soared by Nyame's palace, grander and larger than them all, with his giant golden statues that served as bodyguards. Repairs were still ongoing, and my eyes lingered just a bit as I sent good thoughts to John Henry.

Just hold on, I told him.

It seemed like I was saying that to everyone these days.

And then we reached the bay. Ayanna put on more speed, looking at me every so often so I could give her directions. We headed out over the still water, deep and calm. In the distance I could see a smudge of gray and glints of orange. MidPass, and the Burning Sea that surrounded it. Right now it appeared that the flaming waves were under control, but I didn't want to risk staying out over the dangerous water any longer than necessary. I still remembered the bone ships and their haunting cries as they chased me and Gum Baby.

Finally, I took a deep breath. "Here!" I shouted.

Ayanna raised her eyebrows but brought the raft down slowly, until we were floating just above the sea. A gust of wind swirled around us, setting several white-capped waves ablaze.

"I hope you know what you're doing, boy," Anansi said. I

clutched the SBP in my left hand. My right held the adinkra bracelet, and I rotated it slowly and made a fist every so often just to keep it loose. It still hurt, but not as much as before.

"I hope so, too," I muttered.

So . . . how do you call forth the disassembled wreckage of a haunted slave ship?

On the phone, of course. Anansi and I had worked it out, and it turned out to be really simple.

"Here we go." I opened up the Contacts app in the SBP, spelled out *M-a-a-f-a*, and then watched the icon of a small ship appear. It still tripped me out how the phone-that-was-absolutely-a-phone-and-not-a-magical-story-box worked sometimes. I tapped the icon, then sat the phone on the deck of the raft and clasped the imbongi bead I'd gotten from the Ridgefolk. "Maafa!" I shouted. "Maafa! I need to speak with you."

The surface of the water remained still.

I took a deep breath, focused on a mental image of the ship lying in pieces at the bottom of the sea, and shouted again. "MAAFA! I know you can hear me. This is long distance, hurry!"

Gum Baby scratched her head in confusion. "What does 'long distance' mean?"

I shrugged. "I don't know, but Granddad always shouted that when someone took their sweet time getting to the phone."

"Ohhh. It must be a threat. Gum Baby's gonna use that. 'These hands are long distance, thistle-head!'"

Before I could respond (everything was always so violent with that doll), the surface of the water bubbled a few dozen yards away. Then it started to steam, and fiery waterspouts began to form. I eyed our position nervously but didn't move. This would all be over soon. Hopefully.

Whoosh!

A giant beam of rotted wood erupted out of the sea and shot into the air like a rocket. Streams of burning water fell from it as it crashed back down and sent a giant wave surging past us. If Ayanna hadn't sent us shooting backward, we might've been roasted. I could feel the heat singeing my eyebrows. Another beam broke the surface, then another. Plank after plank rose out of the sea with eerie precision. Tangled ropes and slimy black seaweed snaked around them, knitting them into a strange jumble that began to look more and more familiar.

A curving hull.

A broken mast.

Tattered sails.

Soon, the bloated carcass of a slave ship floated in front of me. A jagged hole the size of John Henry had formed in the hull just above the water line, and with two broken spars jutting out near the remains of the top deck above it, it looked as if the Maafa had gained a face.

A sneering, hungry face.

Plus, the slave ship was huge. I'd forgotten how large it was. It easily dwarfed some of the palaces back on land. Still, I had business to handle and two worlds to save.

"Can you bring us in closer?" I asked Ayanna.

She shot me one of her patented *Are you serious?* looks but used her staff to move us a teeny bit nearer to the ship.

Thump. Thump. Thump.

Something heavy was moving through the wreckage. Even broken, the Maafa still had a deck that loomed over us, and we couldn't float any higher because of tangled rigging and jagged wooden masts that curled down toward us like claws.

Thump. Thump. Thump.

Whatever was up there sounded significant. I took a deep breath and prepared to face the worst thing I could possibly imagine.

"Ah, the Anansesem. Good. Good."

I froze. I hadn't imagined *this*. There, leaning over the edge of the deck and staring down at us with a sightless, featureless manacle head, stood a bossling. The overgrown fetterling, five times as big and ten times as vicious as the smaller, more common iron monsters, was a fearsome creature. I mean, four of them had succeeded in restraining the sky god at one point.

But even scarier—it was *speaking*.

"Are our stories being told?" the Maafa asked through

the bossling. It was weird talking to a ship via its surrogate mouth, a giant iron monster. Then again, it was weird talking to a ship at all. So . . .

I squared my shoulders and put one foot back in a boxing stance. It gave me balance and stability and made me feel a bit more secure. I glared at the giant iron monster and spoke with a confidence I didn't totally feel.

"I have told your story many times. In this world and beyond."

The bossling tilted its head. "You kept your word. We are impressed."

"You didn't think I would?"

"Recent events have left us . . . displeased."

That felt like an understatement. I could feel the hatred rolling off the ship in waves. Scuttling and skittering noises came from inside the giant hole, a maw of evil that looked ready to devour us, raft and all. I had to get my questions answered and skedaddle out of there.

"I'm sorry for whatever happened, but I have a question for you," I said.

Before I could continue, the bossling rattled menacingly, the sound of its chains dragging on the deck earsplitting. The iron monster screeched, and to my horror, answering calls emerged from inside the Maafa. There were more of them.

"YOU DO NOT GET TO DEMAND ANSWERS FROM US!" the Maafa/bossling roared. "There was a bargain.

You struck an agreement with us. The Anansesem tells our story, and we return to our slumber."

I nodded. "Yes, that was the deal. So—"

"So tell us why our sleep was disturbed, our resting spot ripped apart and looted? Your agents of betrayal, with the disgusting tools of your gods, entered *our* domain and took things that did not belong to them. Is the deal off, Anansesem? Shall our children return to punish those on land?"

The sound of hundreds of chains rattled in the darkness within the Maafa. A fetid smell, like swamp water and burning metal, rolled out of the submerged holds and nearly made me gag.

"No! The deal is still on. I am telling your story. And I don't know who—"

I stopped, midsentence and mid-cough. I *did* know who. The Maafa had just confirmed my worst fear.

"The one who took from you," I said. "What did he take? Did he . . . did he rescue King Cotton?"

The rattling stopped all at once. On the top deck, the bossling gave a final shriek and fell apart into a hundred fist-size chain links. I waited. This was a familiar routine. Sure enough, from inside the jagged maw of the Maafa came another set of heavy footsteps. A knotted wooden creature pressed forward, the light of dawn just falling across the monster's face.

A hullbeast.

When it spoke, I could hear the buzzing undertone of brand flies waiting to be belched forth and unleashed on its prey.

"The poisoned one's body," the monster rasped, "was not taken. His limbs were ripped apart by the currents, the bolls of his flesh churned in the burning water of our home until they burned to ash. No, that body could not be taken anywhere."

I sighed. That was a relief. Bear must've just salvaged parts of iron monsters from the sea floor to build his magic armor. Okay. I could deal with that. Defeating him would still be tough, but if they worked together, the gods of MidPass and Alke could—

"But..." continued the Maafa.

I froze as hundreds of fetterlings crept around the hull-beast, rimming the hole in the Maafa's hull like hungry fledg-lings waiting for their parent to bring them dinner.

I refused to be on the menu.

"But what?" I asked, shooting a glance at Ayanna. She gripped her staff, ready to zoom us away.

"But the angry one did take something."

The angry one. Bear.

More fetterlings began to cover every available surface on the Maafa. They leaned over the top deck, slithered around the broken mast, and clung to the tattered sails like rusted leeches. Gum Baby, unusually silent up to this point, tugged on my shorts leg.

"Gum Baby ain't afraid of nothin', don't misunderstand, but Gum Baby forgot to bring her beat-down boots."

"You don't wear boots," I whispered back.

"Because Gum Baby forgot them. Now seems like a good time to go look for them."

Ayanna glanced around nervously. "I agree with Gum Baby. Let's get out of here."

"Sounds wise to me," Anansi whispered.

The ship rumbled ominously. I stood and shouted, "What did Bear take?"

"Oh, we think you already know what it is. You just want someone else to speak it out loud, to take on the responsibility you so desperately try to avoid. It makes no difference to us. After we swallow you and the spider god whole, we will crawl forth from the sea again to the burned ruins of the angry one's lair and consume him as well."

"What did he take?" I shouted again.

"The mask of King Cotton."

Those five words didn't fade away. Instead, they combined with the thunder of the approaching storm and the howling wind. The Maafa suddenly lurched forward, spilling iron monsters over the sides like rats jumping out of a sinking ship. I'd been waiting for something like that—you don't enter the presence of evil and not expect to be betrayed—but still, the speed at which the fetterlings attacked nearly over-whelmed us.

Ayanna yanked her staff to the left, sending us swerving forward—straight into the Maafa's damaged hull. I don't think any of us expected that, not even Anansi or Gum Baby.

"Ayannaaaaaa!"

The raft dodged monster after monster. We ducked around tight corners, just barely avoiding leaping fetterlings and a massive swing of two of the hullbeast's four arms. Forward, into the darkness, into the damp rotten stench. We rocked left and right, the terrifying moans of the Maafa raising the hairs on the back of my neck.

At last I saw where Ayanna was taking us. An opening in the ceiling of the hold, and the deck beyond, and the freedom that was the morning sky. She angled the raft upward and I scooped up the SBP as it slid down the raft toward me.

"Hang on!" I shouted to Gum Baby, only to look back to see her firing sap balls at fetterlings that got too close.

"Sap attack!"

"You ain't got the reach!"

"Triple sap attack!"

We shot out into the air as the Maafa began to crumble around us. Fiery waves seemed to reach out, barely missing the raft by inches. Once we were about fifty feet in the air, we slowed and floated, watching as the ancient slave ship sank beneath the Burning Sea for the second time. My lungs were aching, and I realized I'd been holding my breath. Exhaling shakily, I collapsed to the floor of the raft and sat with my head in my hands.

"We made it," Anansi said, his muffled voice coming from my shirt pocket.

"Some help you were," I muttered.

"So what now?" Ayanna asked.

I didn't answer. Not at first.

The mask of King Cotton.

In our battle with the evil haint, Gum Baby had unleashed a furious barrage of sap attacks against King Cotton. The sticky amber stuff had covered King Cotton's head in a lumpy resin, and it had formed a mask. That's all that was left of him when the rest of his body drifted away, and that's what Bear had found at the bottom of the Burning Sea. While stealing iron-monster parts from the Maafa for his armor, he must've stumbled across the relic.

But I remembered the first time I'd seen the haint.

He was a slinking, oily shadow that had escaped from a bottle on the Bottle Tree.

And now that shadow was trapped in the amber mask.

King Cotton had gotten his hooks into Bear.

28
SHADOWS OF GREATNESS

THE ENCHANTED RAFT FLOATED ABOVE A BURNING SEA, MIDWAY between a coastal city of golden splendor and an abandoned smoking ruin of an island. On that raft sat a doll covered in sticky gum-tree sap, a magical phone with a trickster god trapped inside, and two exhausted rising eighth graders. At least, I think Ayanna would be in eighth grade. Did Alke have middle schools? Regardless, two worlds depended on their next move.

"Tristan, why are you talking in the third person?"

Anansi's question pulled me from my thoughts. I looked around. Gum Baby was shaking her head as she watched me, and the spider god peered out of the phone, a look of concern on his face. Ayanna had one eyebrow raised. Had I been speaking out loud without realizing it?

"What?" I asked.

"You were mumbling to yourself again," Gum Baby said.

"And Gum Baby *know* she didn't hear somethin' about a doll." The glare she fixed me with could've started a fire.

I shook my head quickly. "No, of course not. I must've... I must've sneezed. That's it. I have weird sneezes. They're more like cough-sneezes, so they can sound like words. I guess."

She looked slightly appeased, and I hurriedly turned back to Anansi, who had opened up another app on the SBP. It was Alke Maps, one of the first applications I'd seen when Nyame converted the Story Box into a phone. It was supposed to show every region in Alke. I studied it along with Ayanna. Gum Baby scrambled up onto my shoulder and peered down as well.

"So," Anansi said from the corner of the screen. "We need a plan."

I nodded and waited, but the spider god just kept looking at me expectantly. My jaw dropped. "You want *me* to come up with a plan? What about you? You're the god—can't you do something?"

"What, from my advantageous position inside this silly device? Sorry, my boy, but you've got to take the lead on this one. And everyone's counting on you, so, you know... no pressure." He flashed his easy smile, and I glared at him. He was enjoying this.

But maybe he was right. Oh, I'm sure he had some grand design, some scheme he was cooking up. At the moment, though, I couldn't see what it was. Unfortunately, there was nothing he could do except offer advice if I decided to confront Bear again. And . . . to be honest, I wasn't sure I was ready to do that quite yet. The knowledge that King Cotton was out and about—even if he was trapped in a sap mask—terrified me to the core.

I pushed the fear aside and tried to concentrate. *Think, Tristan, think.*

"Bear wants to go beyond punching a hole in the sky," I said slowly. "He said he wants to make it so no one, not haints or people or creatures or anything, could slip between the worlds again. But what does that mean? Is he out to destroy the tools of the gods, like John Henry's hammer?"

Anansi shook his head from his perch in the top corner of the SBP's screen. "Destroying a god's symbol, their essence, requires a massive amount of power and strength, and even Bear isn't that strong. No, he has to be doing something with them."

"And why kidnap Tristan's grandma and Mami Wata?" asked Ayanna. "Just to make us upset?"

The question hung in the air as the four of us thought about it. Well, Anansi, Ayanna, and I thought about it. Gum Baby had scrambled down from my shoulders and was hurling sap balls at the Burning Sea, watching little puffs of flame shoot up from the water's surface. I was tempted to nudge her off the raft to see what would happen, but I didn't. It was just a thought! I would never. . . .

Anyway.

I sighed. "Whatever his plans are, we need to stop them,

and that means finding where Bear has hidden Nana and Mami Wata. They could be anywhere. An abandoned palace in the Golden Crescent...Maybe in the foothills before we get to the Ridgefolk's territory...Anywhere!"

Anansi nodded. "We have to be strategic. Narrow down the possibilities and be smart about where we go and in what order."

That made sense. I tried to think while keeping an eye on Gum Baby, who was making bigger and bigger sap balls to generate larger flames on the sea surface. As I watched, the tiny terror rolled a sap ball as large as a melon, taking great care to make sure it didn't stick to the raft. She lifted it above her head, ready to cast it down as the ultimate sacrifice, when something wormed its way from the back of my mind and punched its way clear to the front.

Flames.

Burning.

"Sweet peaches!" I said. "I know where to go!"

"Where?" Anansi demanded. Gum Baby tried to turn around to face us, but the unwieldy sap ball plunged to the sea below, landing with a large splash that sent up a blazing curtain of fire before it quickly subsided.

"You better say something useful," Gum Baby said angrily. "Makin' Gum Baby waste a perfectly good sap balloon..."

I started to continue, then paused. "Um...sap balloon?"

"Did Gum Baby stutter? Larger than a sap ball and with seven times as much sap. Rebelutionary."

"You mean *revolutionary*."

"Gum Baby knows what she means! Sap balloons are going to change the game forever."

"What game?" Anansi asked, unable to help himself.

"The sap game. But Gum Baby wouldn't expect y'all dunderheads to understand. Big rebelutionary things are going on over here."

I looked between her and the replacement sap balloon she was trying to make. "Sure . . . okay. As I was saying, I know where to go. The Maafa basically told us. Remember? It said the angry one lived in the burned ruins of a lair. Well, where is the one place we know Bear had family ties, is currently a burned-out shell, and everyone was specifically warned to stay away from?"

Gum Baby, Ayanna, and Anansi stared at me like I had sprouted wings from my forehead. "Now, what are *you* babbling about?" the spider god said.

"Told you he was a Bumbletongue," Gum Baby muttered.

I shook my head, then scooted back to the rear of the flying raft and grabbed the rudder. "Laugh it up now. You'll see."

"Fine," Anansi said. "Where is Bear's hideout?"

I grinned. "MidPass."

MidPass.

I'd been to the island the folk heroes had called home, but I'd never seen it in its days of splendor. Before the carnage and wreckage. Before the terror and the lockdowns. My feelings of fear and failure were all I could remember about the place, and that fact made me sadder than expected.

I shrugged off my backpack and unzipped it. Inside, Nana's quilt pieces glowed faintly in the light of day. I pulled out a square, a warm orange-and-gold section with swaying fields of corn on it.

"Here goes nothing," I muttered.

Ayanna kept one eye on her steering and the other on me. "What are you doing now?"

"Chestnutt told me I could track my grandmother by using the Story Box with things associated with her. The memories and stories she put into this quilt of hers should do the trick." I held the fragment up to the SBP, a little unsure of what to do next, but a smile crossed my face as text crawled across the screen in gold letters:

New stories found.
Adding to database.
Author located. Plot route?

I tapped the acknowledgment button that appeared, and like some sort of magical GPS, the main screen of Alke Maps returned, this time with a glittering golden route guiding us forward.

"There we go," I said, holding up the phone so Ayanna could see.

As the raft sliced through the sky toward MidPass, I couldn't help but scan the sea below for bone ships. Somewhere down there was the exact spot Gum Baby and I had splashed into when we'd fallen through the hole in the sky. I still remembered the nightmarish sensation of falling forever, followed by the actual nightmare of the haunted skeleton boats.

Now the seas were calm—barely a flame sprinkled atop the surface. It felt . . . ordinary.

That was a good thing, right?

"Look," Gum Baby whispered.

The ruined island loomed out of a fog bank so gray it looked like a shield of smoke. Ayanna brought the raft lower and we skimmed over the tops of waves. Trees began to loom out of the distance, and I tried not to shudder. The Drowned Forest. Me and Ayanna and Gum Baby and Fox and the other Midfolk had fled through the soggy woods, desperately trying to escape the fetterlings chasing us. Trying, and failing.

"Gum Baby don't like seeing it like this." The small voice came from behind me, where the little doll had sat down crisscross applesauce and looked over the back of the raft as Ayanna steered. "It's so . . . empty."

"What was it like before?" I asked.

It was Ayanna who answered. "Before the iron monsters? It was loud. Good loud, not bad loud. Voices filled the air. You could hear laughter all over the island. Smell food cooking. See everybody playing. It was happy."

She fell into silence, and I didn't try to nudge her out of it. Truth was, I knew exactly what she meant. Some places just have that vibe. The feeling of good times tucked into nooks and crannies, spilling out of windows and doors. Chances are you know a place just like that. When you think of it, a smile crosses your face and memories appear like hidden treasures suddenly found.

That's how my grandparents' house had felt these past few weeks.

"Tristan, is that—?" Anansi's voice pulled me out of my thoughts. I held up the SBP, camera lens pointed out, so the spider god could see. Anansi alternated his gaze from the map to the world outside, looking at something off to the left. At first I didn't recognize it—that's how bad a toll the fire had taken. I just saw a lumpy mass as large as a building, with a tower emerging from its center.

Then it hit me.

"Oh no," I whispered.

A sharp gasp was all that came from Ayanna.

It was the Thicket. Or what remained of it. Low-hanging clouds hid much of it. And as we drew closer, the wind began to pick up, rocking the raft and making my stomach do flip-flops. We didn't have much time. The cooling temperature, the angry clouds—a storm was on its way.

We flew into a large clearing roughly the size of three football fields. The Drowned Forest had given way to scorched barren earth, still smoking in parts. Nothing grew. No animals moved. No birds flew in the sky above. The silence felt heavy, like a mass of soggy blankets, and it smelled . . . wrong.

The state of the Thicket squeezed my heart, and I felt tears prickle at the corner of my eyes. What used to be a beautiful and natural sloping tangle of woody vines, delicate flowers, and dangerous thorns—woven together into protective walls that sheltered an entire community— was now a black spiderweb of soot and ashes. Every so often a thin breeze would move harshly through the clearing, and the remnants of the magical epicenter of MidPass would rattle like bones.

Ticka ticka tickety ticka

But the most horrible sight protruded from the center of it all.

"Not too close," Anansi warned. His face was grim. Ayanna was biting her lower lip, and Gum Baby had gone ashen and silent. I watched them—the trickster god who'd come here in disguise, the girl who'd worked harder than anyone to save the people she loved, and the sap-covered doll who'd called this place home her whole life. Their faces were mirrors of my own, I was sure, as I turned back to confront the horror before us once more.

The Tree of Power stood out of the ruins of the Thicket, shattered.

And that was where the GPS route ended.

The top half of the tree was gone. Just gone. No canopy, no branches, just a splintered trunk that still towered over everything. A shadow of its former self. Its blackened tips looked like a ruined crown, hung on a spear planted in the ground where a beloved monarch had fallen.

And maybe it had.

But even that wasn't the worst part.

Greenish-white lines crisscrossed the trunk like veins of poison, and every so often they pulsed with a weird light. Thick clouds billowed out of the top, filling the sky.

I turned and stared at the horizon, at the storm that marched from MidPass ever closer to the Golden Crescent and the rest of Alke. The clouds were the same sickly greenish-gray color as what was leaking out of the destroyed Tree of Power. On a hunch, I pressed the adinkra flush against my wrist. Gum Baby turned around quickly at my hiss of pain.

"What is it?" she asked.

I stared at the tree as Ayanna pulled the rudder of the raft forward so we drifted closer. Those veins . . . they couldn't be. Could they?

"Tristan," Anansi said. "What are you seeing, my boy?"

I pointed at the ruined Tree of Power and took a deep shuddering breath. "That storm . . . it isn't natural. I think something in the ruined old tree is creating it."

Ayanna looked incredulous. "That's where you said your grandmother and Mami Wata are being kept!"

"Yeah. And I think I know why Bear collected all the remnants of the iron monsters. He needed chains powerful enough to restrain a god, just like the bosslings and the brand flies did to Nyame. And I'm starting to think..."

Gum Baby frowned. "What do you mean?"

"Let me show you."

I nodded at Ayanna. The raft picked up speed and Anansi looked worried. "Are you sure it's safe? What if Bear returns? I can't do anything to help you. You three will be on your own."

But I shook my head. Something had fallen into place, a puzzle piece I didn't even know was missing, and its addition completely changed the rules of the game. I didn't understand everything that was happening, but I knew one thing for sure. The storm, the kidnappings—they were all connected.

And if I didn't do something soon, both Alke and my world would pay, and pay dearly.

29

EYE OF THE STORM

AYANNA GUIDED THE RAFT TOWARD THE CORRUPTED TREE OF Power.

"How do we get inside?" Gum Baby whispered. She'd scrambled back to her perch on my shoulder and was currently gripping my hair. I was going to have to wash and rewash it for days to get the sap out. But I wasn't going to call her on it now. We were all frightened. Even Anansi looked shaken.

Because those weren't veins running up and down and around the trunk.

They were fetterlings, linked together like some horrible necklace. Or collar. Pulsing green as they choked the remaining life out of the magical tree. Bear had turned an area where the Midfolk had flourished into a prison.

Ayanna guided the raft carefully between the black tips of the trunk and dove into its hollowed-out middle, which was just wide enough for us to fit through. Darkness swallowed us, and I nearly panicked. Then the SBP flickered and the screen brightened.

"Here," Anansi said. He pointed at the bottom of the screen, where another app icon was materializing. "I thought you might need this."

I stared at the app's name: This Little Light. That sounded eerily close to a song Nana used to sing. The rounded square was navy blue with a yellow lantern icon glimmering in the middle. I tapped it, then gasped as light *unfolded* from the phone like origami made of moonbeams. It bathed the raft and everything inside the Tree of Power.

Including a figure slumped over at the very bottom of the chamber.

My heart skipped a beat.

"Nana," I whispered.

Ayanna, sensing the urgency, dropped us down in a tight spiral, ducking cobwebs and slipping around the moldy remains of the interior. The faint sound of a drumbeat danced in and out of my range of hearing, so I thought I could've imagined it. It sounded wrong. Offbeat.

As we dropped, the air grew thicker and staler, with the faint hint of a metallic tang, and the silver light of the SBP sent the shadows retreating. At last the raft hit the floor with a bump. I swallowed, then took a slow step forward, holding out the phone as I tried to figure out what I was seeing in front of me.

A rotted trough, roughly the size of a bathtub, sat in the middle of the damp, lumpy ground, holding a figure on a wooden stool. I couldn't tell if the figure was breathing. I couldn't tell if...

My foot kicked a clump of dirt and sent it skittering across the ground.

The figure sat up.

"Nana?" But as soon as I lifted the glowing phone clutched tightly in my hand, I knew I had the wrong person. In fact, it wasn't a person at all. No person I knew had shimmering blue-green dreadlocks that floated and swayed in midair as if in water. No person I knew had an iridescent shimmer on their dark brown skin like sunlight reflecting off a still lake. No.

This was a goddess.

I stood there for several seconds, confused. What had happened? The silly GPS was supposed to have led me to Nana. I took another step forward, and her head lifted, freezing me in my tracks.

"Mami Wata?" I called softly.

The question seemed to slip through the fog clouding her eyes, and the goddess of the rivers and lakes raised her chin so that her eyes could latch on to mine. Then, as if that effort had tired her, her head dropped and her eyes closed.

Wait.

I peeked over the edge of the rotted trough, then recoiled.

There was a pool of water at the bottom—a disgusting gray soup of fetterling chain links, brand-fly wings, and something lumpy that I didn't look at too closely. Mami Wata's feet and ankles were submerged in the glop.

"They're poisoning her," Anansi said. His voice was thick with disgust.

"Poison?"

"Like the brand flies on Nyame," Gum Baby added. She hopped up onto the lip of the makeshift tub and shook her head. "Just nasty."

"Mami Wata is a water goddess," Ayanna said. "She is one with Alke's different bodies of water and cares for them. By forcing her to take a footbath in iron-monster stew, Bear's keeping her too weak to use her powers."

"Even worse, the corrupted Tree of Power is sending this filth into the sky, poisoning the air." Anansi wore a grim expression. "It seems Bear has learned a lot of horrible things."

"The storm..." I said, my heart skipping a beat. "Bear's using Mami Wata to create it. When it hits Alke—"

"It'll destroy everything we're trying to rebuild," Ayanna finished. She shook her head. "We can't let that happen."

No, we couldn't. I rolled up my sleeves and gripped the side of the trough. It felt slimy and cold, and I tried not to shudder at the clammy sensation. "Okay, enough talking. Let's free her."

"Tristan, wait—" Anansi began, but it was too late. I heaved at the old wood, and it creaked stubbornly before a large chunk of the side ripped away in my hands. I fell back on the seat of my shorts, then scrambled aside as water began to spill out. First it trickled, then it gushed, splashing onto the ground and sending its rusty metal contents everywhere.

An ominous rumble echoed from somewhere near the top of the tree.

"Uh..." Gum Baby said. "What did you do?"

"I didn't do anything," I said, standing and wiping myself off.

"You did something. You're always doing something. Gum Baby thinks you need to start sitting down and learning to do nothing. Study it. Become an expert at doing nothing."

"First of all—"

Ayanna interrupted me. "Would you two please focus so we can avoid dying?"

We both glared at her, but at that moment another rumble sounded, and a piece of rotted bark the size of a surfboard hurtled through the air and landed like a spear in the ground next to me. Gum Baby and I stared at it, then at each other, then back at it.

"You know, not dying is good," I said.

"Gum Baby was just thinking that."

Something clanked in the nearly empty tub. A longer piece of fetterling chain had become entangled around

Mami Wata's foot. I tiptoed across the soggy ground and leaned into the trough to try to slip it off. The metal was cold. Bitter cold. More rumbles filled the dark space above our heads, as if the Tree of Power were expressing its pain from everything it had been through. Finally I managed to pull the snarled chain from around Mami Wata, and I tossed it to the other side of the tree. I stood, only to see two glints of light several inches from my face. Her eyes had opened. She was watching me.

With lightning quickness she lunged forward, her hair floating above her head and her face twisted into a grimace as she snagged my arm and yanked me close.

"You're too late," she whispered, just as the Tree of Power began to splinter apart. But instead of falling, the fragments remained suspended in midair as the world froze around me.

30

FREE MAMI WATA

MANY THINGS CAN BE TRUE AT THE SAME TIME.

I've heard that said several times by different people—Dad, Mom, even a few teachers. Loving reading and disliking the books I was given to read. Being hungry and not wanting to eat what was on my plate. The sun still shining bright in the sky and yet it's time for bed. (Thanks a lot, daylight saving time. Spring forward into the trash, why don't you.)

But never was that statement more real for me than when Mami Wata held my gaze for those few seconds. We were standing still and yet traveling everywhere at the same time.

One moment we were in the dead Tree of Power in MidPass, and the next we stood high on a grassy hill overlooking a mighty river as wide as a freeway, the roaring waters carrying canoes filled with brown-skinned families. Children waved and parents lifted their hands to honor the goddess on the bank, sometimes even floating gifts toward her that collected in the shallows.

Then we were sitting in a turquoise grotto behind a massive waterfall, the sound of it thundering through the mist. A group of girls sat on rocks nearby, laughing and talking as they braided each other's hair, sharpened spears, and made plans. Every so often one of them would stand, turn, and salute Mami Wata with a raised spear, the same kind of weapon I'd seen in Nyanza, with a long narrow blade at the top and rope tied to the shaft.

My eyes widened as I recognized Ninah, the river spirit who'd first warned us about Bear coming. That felt like years ago. Now she looked up, caught my eyes, and lifted a spear in greeting. I started to raise my hand, but the world went dark.

When sunlight returned, Mami Wata and I were floating above Nyanza. Not as I'd seen it with Ayanna and Junior and Gum Baby before, but as it was supposed to exist—a giant lake surrounded by several smaller ones, connected by a network of streams and floating bridges. People swam and played, fished, planted water crops, and lived their lives to the fullest.

"It is as it should be," a warm, musical voice said.

When I turned, the goddess was looking at me. Her long blue-green dreadlocks floated behind her as if we were underwater, and her eyes were as hard and black as the stones Junior threw. Seeing them made me think about the boy's sacrifice for my sake, and I looked away.

"You are worried about someone." It was a statement, not a question. When I nodded, she turned and stared out over the people living their lives below. Her people. Mami Wata stretched out her arms. "You are right to be. I am worried about everyone. What you are seeing is how it should be, but not how it is."

I frowned. "Yeah, the lakes are dry back in Nyanza. Everyone is scared, and no one knows what's going on. What happened?"

"You've seen my condition. I am the goddess of the waters. All waters. My rage is that of the Burning Sea, and my tears are the waterfalls in the Golden Crescent. I am tied to them all, and they are tied to me. My people, who carried me in their hearts while floating on my waters, have taken me across Alke."

There it was again, the concept of people carrying something from one place and taking it with them all over the land. Diaspora. All connected by origin. I remembered Chestnutt saying that Mami Wata was the source of Nyanza. I saw that now.

"So, if you're being poisoned," I said slowly, "then so is every water source in Alke. Or they would've been, if you hadn't cut off the tap. And that's why Old Man River was complaining to Keelboat Annie. You're connected."

"We are all connected. What Bear has done threatens all of Alke . . . and beyond." The hard black eyes turned on me again. "He knows not the implications if he continues."

"He's being controlled," I said. "By an evil haint."

"The seeds of hate can only sprout in fertile ground. Do not rush to blame all of this on the haint. But symptoms care not about who administered the poison. If the storm spreads, it will seep into the very fabric of this world and also into yours. It will corrupt all the stories, breaking them into fragments to be spread far apart and never heard again."

John Henry's condition flashed into my mind, and a chill wrapped around my spine. "We can't let that happen!"

Mami Wata nodded. "We cannot. But someone must step up. I kept this fragment of myself isolated from my corporal presence just in case help arrived. You *must* get me back to the Golden Crescent. Only there, with all the gods and goddesses of Alke present, can we stop the storm."

The picturesque scene of Nyanza flickered, then began to fade. I panicked.

"Wait!" I said. "How do I—?"

But she disappeared, along with the rest of the world, and I was left in darkness.

I blinked, and the Tree of Power was collapsing around us.

Mami Wata's grip held me in place.

We had to get out of there, and fast. But still the goddess of the waters held me tight, her deep black eyes boring into mine as if I were the one responsible for imprisoning her.

Which . . . you know, wasn't good.

"Uh, this ain't the time for a staring contest," Gum Baby

said. Ayanna already had the raft floating several inches off the ground, and Gum Baby had hopped on with the SBP in her arms. Anansi looked warily at the sticky hands slipping closer to the screen but opted to remain quiet since he was being saved. "Get on the good foot, Bumbletongue! Whichever one that is."

"Mami Wata, we need to go." I gently tugged her arm and the goddess shook herself out of her daze.

"Our world is ripping apart at the seams," she said, her words thick and full of pain. As if echoing her thoughts, the rotted baobab tree we stood inside groaned again, a thunderous sound that tried to shake my skin off my bones.

I slipped my shoulder beneath the goddess's arm and she leaned against me. She smelled like lemongrass growing alongside a stream. "And who...might you be?" she asked between gasps of pain. Really? I'd just talked to her—or some version of her. But before I could answer, a giant root as wide as a minivan ripped free of the earth, spraying clods of dirt everywhere.

"My hair!" Gum Baby wailed.

Despite everything, I laughed. "Really? You're worried about your hair at a time like this?"

"Some of us take pride in looking good." Gum Baby sniffed. "Not like you'd know anything about that."

"Hey!"

"Let's go!" Ayanna shouted.

Mami Wata and I stumbled forward and collapsed on the sturdy magical craft.

"Hold on!" Ayanna cried. She tried to take off, but the giant root had been joined by a second. And a third. I shook my head in disbelief. They were like sea serpents freed from a prison of mud and rock. Tiny fibers covered them all, soil and pebbles tangled in knots. The giant roots wavered in midair like . . .

A familiar pain started to throb against my left wrist.

I narrowed my eyes suspiciously. It couldn't be . . . Could it?

The tips of the roots had an eerie green glow, and I groaned. "For once in my life, can't things be easy?"

The raft tried to climb, but the roots were too quick, batting us out the air like gnats. We went spinning toward the ground, only just managing not to crash by the skin of our teeth. Well, my teeth, at least. Did spiders and animated dolls have teeth? Maybe if—

"Boy!"

Mami Wata's voice alternated between the soft babble of a creek and the rushing thunder of river rapids. She stood on the raft, wobbling a bit. The hem of her dress billowed softly behind her calves, rising and falling in waves, almost like the tail of a river dolphin swimming upstream. "The tree has been corrupted. We must—"

The largest of the roots hammered down on the ground next to us, barely missing crushing me like a roach. It was inches away, and I finally got a good look at the peeved appendage.

"Oh no," I muttered.

Thick chains choked the root, their rusty metal glowing the sickly green of the iron monsters. Even worse, wiggling bumps that oozed greenish-black liquid covered the poisoned tree. It smelled awful, like socks that haven't been washed in two months. You know the kind—the ones so stiff they can stand up on their own.

Blech.

I started to clench my fist, ready to use the adinkra bracelet to fight, then stopped. Not because of the pain—I could tolerate that now. But then why? What was I going to do, punch a tree? I'd done that once before, to disastrous results. Had throwing myself at Reggie worked? Had attacking Bear head-on worked? No, it hadn't.

We have to be strategic, Anansi had said.

Okay, then.

If Bear could steal the weapons of other gods to become more powerful, there was no reason I couldn't give their symbols to one of their own who needed them.

The giant root lifted into the air to join its two other partners in grime. I stood up as tall as I could and glanced at the river goddess. "How powerful are the waters you control? Will they do what you say?"

Mami Wata's gaze swept the hollowed tree, taking in the

poisoned roots hovering menacingly above the ground, the raft, and finally, the three of us. She studied Gum Baby, narrowed her eyes at the SBP in the doll's hands, and then focused on me. "Never question the power of a goddess, little one."

CRASH!

Another sharp splinter of bark fell through the dark to land just outside the SBP's light. I licked my lips and edged to the middle of the raft. Things were getting hairy in here, and I'd just about had my fill of close shaves.

"I'm here to help," I said. "My grandmother needs me. Alke needs me, even if it doesn't know it yet. But right now, I need you."

"The last time someone told me they were here to help, they poisoned my rivers, destroyed my streams, and locked me in a dying tree whose cries of pains were the only thing I heard for days!" Mami Wata glared at me, and when a god or goddess glares at you, you don't mess around. It's worse than that look your parents give you when you're cutting up in public and they're silently letting you know that it's on once y'all get back to the car.

The raft jerked to the left, and the smallest of the root trio slammed into the dirt where we'd been just moments before.

"Do something!" Gum Baby shouted.

"Trust me," I said to Mami Wata, putting as much honesty into my voice as I could muster.

I pulled the adinkra bracelet off my wrist and held it out

for her to inspect. Her eyes widened, then met my own. After a second that felt like an eternity, she nodded. I slipped the bracelet over her hand and she stiffened. Her hair began to sparkle. The brown skin of her arms began to gleam, and her dress whipped left and right around her ankles, as if she were standing in a current.

"I was born in the shallows of a mighty river," she whispered.

I grinned, despite everything. Despite the roots now constricting the raft like a giant python. Despite Nana not being here. Despite my hardly ever winning a fight. I knew this story. It was embroidered on the ruined quilt in my backpack.

"Or in the maelstrom of the sea," I said, speaking the next line.

"Or in the hurricane."

"Or in the lakes of the people."

"I am Mami Wata," the goddess said, her words a tide that would sweep aside all who stood before her.

My hand found hers and we spoke the final words together. "And this is my power!"

But when my voice ended, Mami Wata's rose. It was a slowly building roar, like a swollen river rushing down a mountain, not yet visible but terrifying in its approach. The ground trembled as she spoke. A fissure appeared in the earth just below the raft, the crack racing around us as if an invisible knife were stabbing through the dirt and trying to carve away our existence.

CRACK!

The roots reeled backward like wounded dragons as the earth trembled. The Tree of Power shuddered. With an agonizing rumble and a terrible groan, like it could no longer suffer the torture Bear had inflicted upon it, the evil role it was forced to play in betraying one of its own, the magical old baobab fell in on itself in a devastating avalanche of shattered bark. A dark cloud descended, a last-ditch effort of the poison desperate to smother us. This was it. I cringed, ducking and covering my head with a yelp while Gum Baby and Anansi shouted in fear.

FWOOM!

The ground shifted again and droplets of water misted the side of my face and my arms. I stood for a second, two, three, before realizing that I wasn't being crushed. I hadn't felt so much as a splinter. I opened my eyes, confused, then gasped.

The Tree of Power was gone.

Like it had never existed.

In its place, a fountain of water had erupted out of the earth in a perfect circle around us, rising into the air and arcing overhead to fall to the ground nearly a dozen yards away. Where the tree's canopy had been, there was now a foaming white spray, the leaves replaced by water droplets the size of my fist that fell to the ground so slowly they were like tears trickling down an invisible face. The storm clouds sped away until nothing blocked our view of the sky. We stood inside a shimmering blue cylinder, like a column of glass, a waterfall in reverse. (A water-rise?)

Mami Wata was in the center, her face upturned. Gum Baby scrambled over to me, climbing up to her familiar perch atop my shoulder to get a better view. She handed me the SBP, and I was so entranced by what was happening that I didn't even grimace at the sticky residue smeared all over the screen.

Even Anansi had been struck speechless by the goddess. That was impressive.

"What's Water Granny doing?" Gum Baby whispered.

Mami Wata stepped up to the wall of water and plunged her fingertips into it. Then she began to walk through, slowly, while tracing her fingers along the glimmering surface and humming softly to herself.

"Sweet peaches," I murmured.

"Oh my goodness," Ayanna said.

Gum Baby just shook her head, tiny droplets of sap splattering my shoulder, and Anansi stared thoughtfully.

Silver words appeared out of the ripples left in the wake of the river goddess's fingers. Shining cursive letters traced their way up through the wall of water in a spiral. I twirled around, awestruck. The words we'd just spoken, the beginning of one of Nana's many stories about the water goddess, floated in front of us.

The circle of water dropped so we could fly the raft out of it. As soon as we did, a geyser surged out of the earth where the Tree of Power had been.

"Now, then," Mami Wata said, wringing out her hair and eyeing the three of us in turn. "United we stand, hmm?"

I stepped forward on the raft and pulled her up. "Yes, ma'am." From my backpack I fished out the section of the quilt we'd used to guide us here. Parts of the words we'd just spoken still glimmered on the fabric. I shook my head. "I just don't get it. The SBP—I mean, the Story Box—was supposed to lead me to Nana."

"May I?"

I handed over the slightly soaked square to Mami Wata. She smiled as she examined it, rubbing the fabric between her thumb and forefinger.

"This is the story I told her."

"What do you mean?" I asked.

The goddess pursed her lips and handed the square back to me. Then, out of thin air, she produced a ribbon that looked suspiciously like seaweed and put her locs up in an elaborate bun. When she was finished, she placed both hands on her hips and cocked her head, looking just like Nana always did when she'd come to an important decision.

"I told your grandmother this story many years ago when she came to visit."

I shouldn't have been surprised by that statement, but it hit me like an uppercut. Then I recalled my conversation with Nana in her bedroom. She'd been to Alke, and I'd never had the chance to talk to her about it.

I pulled out several more tattered pieces of quilt, sorting them as I searched for the squares with writing on them, holding up one after another as I found them. "Do you recognize these? Did anyone else from here tell her stories?"

"Hmm." The river goddess tapped an aquamarine nail on her chin as she thought, before shrugging. "Two others that I know of. Their stories appear on those scraps you've got there. The boo hag from the foothills..."

"Lady Night?" I asked.

"And the loud woman who talks to one of my oldest rivers..."

"Keelboat Annie!" Ayanna said.

Wow, Nana had a pretty nice squad.

"Yes," said Mami Wata. "The four of us got together one time and—"

"I hate to interrupt," Anansi said, "but could you hold this fond reunion some other time, when we're not surrounded by death and decay?"

I swallowed the hundreds of questions threatening to spill out of my mouth and nodded.

"So the SBP tracked you down with the quilt," I said to Mami Wata, "because you are one of the authors who contributed to it. So even if we tried again, it might not take us directly to Nana. We're going to have to do this the hard way."

"Charge in headfirst like a blunder-head?" Gum Baby asked.

"Ignore the advice of those wiser than you and punch the first thing that moves?" Anansi asked.

"Beg someone flyer than you to save you?" Ayanna asked.

Mami Wata pursed her lips but thankfully didn't join in.

"NO," I said between gritted teeth, my neck flushing hot. "We need to find the other storytellers first."

"But Lady Night might be...gone," said Ayanna. "We don't know what happened to...people after we left."

By *people*, I knew she meant Junior, too, but she didn't want to say his name in front of Anansi.

My heart ached, but my voice was firm. "We don't know for sure, and until we do, they're still alive. If we can gather her and Keelboat Annie, then maybe..."

Anansi rubbed his chin with two of his six hands. "And, if you'll pardon my skepticism, just how do you plan on stopping Bear and the storm he is nearly ready to unleash? We don't even know where he is."

I grinned a fierce, toothy grin that was more feral than friendly.

"Oh yes we do," I said. "He'll be wherever Nana is. I know why Bear kidnapped her now."

31
THE GANG'S ALL HERE

OFF WE WENT.

Mami Wata knelt in the middle of the raft, her lips pinched and a determined look in her eyes. The goddess's dress had somehow transformed once we'd risen into the air, morphing into an aquamarine pantsuit with emerald bangles above each ankle. Her feet were still bare, but her toenails and fingernails were painted a vibrant shimmering blue. We were soaring over the Burning Sea. Beneath us, the waves were getting choppier, sending flames shooting up as the winds grew stronger. The storm clouds had moved on from MidPass once the tree was destroyed. I had no doubt that was what Bear had intended. The green-veined thunderclouds now raced us across the horizon. I shivered. The poison Bear had inflicted upon the Tree of Power was spreading.

It was headed for the Golden Crescent.

We were, too, but only once Nana's storytelling squad

had been assembled. It was still an absolute trip for me to think about my grandmother as a part of some interdimensional bridge club. (For the uninformed, which until recently included myself, bridge is a card game popular with grown-ups. I think it's rated PG for Parent Games.)

Right now we were going back to Lady Night's juke joint— or what was left of it. I had the location loaded in Alke Maps, and Ayanna had the raft speeding through the gray morning sky. I dreaded what we were going to find—or not—but it seemed I had no choice.

"So."

Mami Wata's voice dragged my attention away from the coming troubles and back to the present. "I believe some introductions are in order, right, young man? I already know Ayanna. Many times have I seen her flying through my domain."

"It's a pleasure to formally meet you," Ayanna said, managing to look respectful and reverent while also keeping us afloat.

"But the others..." The goddess raised an eyebrow, looking just like an aunt who was chaperoning your first date. The one who pretended not to notice when you did that arm-stretch yawn when she drove you and your date to the carnival.

No, I'm not talking about me, I'm just being hypothetical.

Anyway.

I cleared my throat and pointed around the raft. "That's Gum Baby holding the phone—sorry, the Story Box in phone form—and inside the phone is Anansi."

"The trickster?" She raised an eyebrow imperiously, like a queen studying her subjects. "Yes, I believe I did hear something about his . . . new form. And Gum Baby, your name has been spoken in my halls for some time. Impressive."

The little terror actually blushed. Blushed! Who knew sap-covered wood could do that? But before I could drag her for it, the river goddess turned to me.

"And you . . . Tristan Strong. You are your grandmother's descendant through and through. Stubborn. Hardheaded. Impulsive."

I cleared my throat but remained silent. It didn't seem like a good time to open my mouth. Things usually got worse when I did.

"And yet here we are." Mami Wata stared out over the sea. After a couple seconds, she shook her head. "Well, I'm glad you're stubborn."

Wait, what?

"I'm sorry . . . Did you just . . . Happy I'm stubborn? Being hardheaded is a talent now?" I couldn't believe it. Those words needed to be written on a T-shirt that I could wear twenty-four seven. It was the ultimate permission slip I could use anytime I wanted to do—

Mami Wata frowned, and her eyes flashed blue-green in

warning before returning to their natural black. "Don't get carried away now, hear me?"

"Of course not," I said, straightening up, even though I'd been doing exactly that.

"Good." Then, after a few seconds: "Your grandmother would be proud of you. *Is* proud of you. You're the only thing she ever wants to talk about, you know. 'My grandbaby did this, or went here, or helped with that.' She loves you."

Something prickled the corners of my eyes. "I'm going to get her back," I said softly, not meeting Mami Wata's eyes. "I swear it."

She nodded. "I believe you. It's not everyone who would give up their powers to save someone else." And with that, she gave me back my adinkra bracelet. Apparently, now that she was free and restored to her former glory, she didn't need it anymore. I thanked her and slipped it back onto my wrist. I flexed my wrist tentatively. . . . It still hurt, but I could manage.

We sat there in silence, the wind rushing around us as Ayanna angled the raft south. Gum Baby had stuck the SBP to the floor of the raft beneath her, and occasionally she and Anansi would shout at each other about directions before relaying them to Ayanna. Those two, I swear. Some people argue for no reason.

"Why would Gum Baby make a left turn there? The directions say go this way!"

"Because, my young sap-prentice, that way is a shortcut."

"Who you calling short?"

While they argued, we left the Burning Sea and crossed over rolling hills. Our shadow rippled on the landscape, and at any other time it would've been beautiful to watch, our height notwithstanding. But there was a growing tension that gripped my chest, like my nerves and dread were doing a group hug with my lungs.

Something bad was about to happen.

And when the compound with Lady Night's juke joint appeared on top of a hill in the distance and everyone on the raft gasped in horror, my fists clenched so hard I thought my palms would bleed. I realized then just how bad things were going to get.

The juke joint was no more.

Lady Night's juke joint had been obliterated. The walls had been blown apart, ripped to kindling and strewn up and down the hillside. Musical instruments lay scattered among the wreckage. A tuba. Half of a kick drum. I even saw the splintered remains of the stage at the bottom of a grassy slope.

Thank goodness Lady Night had gotten all her clientele out in time. But had she herself escaped? When I glanced up and met Mami Wata's eyes, I could tell she was wondering the same thing.

Ayanna set us down in one of the few spaces not covered in wreckage, and we stepped from the raft carefully. Gum Baby scrambled up to my shoulder, which Mami Wata raised an eyebrow at but didn't comment on.

I held up the sticky SBP so Anansi could get a good look, too. He scanned the area desperately. "I don't see him."

No one had to ask who he was referring to. I swallowed a lump and cleared my throat. "Maybe someone came to their rescue." I still hated the fact that we hadn't stayed to fight to the end.

"But how do you know?"

I'd never heard the trickster god's voice filled with such uncertainty and pain. I didn't answer but clenched my fists even tighter. From my vantage point on the hill I could see most of Alke and the storm gathering overhead. The poisonous clouds crowded over the Golden Crescent, flashes of green lightning illuminating them from within. We had to hurry and find everyone before it was too late.

"Tristan!"

Someone called my name from down the hill. I picked my way through large wooden beams and piles of trash to peer over the side. A giant sigh of relief escaped and some of the tension drained from my body.

Lady Night and a crowd of others waved from beneath a small copse of trees in front of the Isihlangu foothills. In fact . . . I squinted, then my eyebrows shot up in surprise. A few folks in the crowd were carrying familiar shields and beautiful clubs that ended with polished stones on the end—kieries.

It appeared Isihlangu had arrived to help.

I searched the crowd as I walked down toward them. My expression must've been pretty desperate, because when I reached the bottom of the hill, one of the Ridgefolk warriors stepped forward to say, "The princess isn't here."

I tried not to look too disappointed. Thandiwe would have been really helpful at the moment, but it seemed she was still on her mission with High John. Another god we could've used in the fight against Bear.

Lady Night greeted me warmly, then—to my surprise—strode forward and hugged Mami Wata fiercely. "How are you feeling?"

The water goddess squeezed the boo hag, then shook her head. "Better, thanks to the timely assistance of this boy here. If not for him and his . . . friends, this world and his would be doomed. Now at least we have a fighting chance."

Lady Night smiled at me, and my face got hot.

"Boy, is you blushing?" Gum Baby rapped me upside the head. "Act like you been here before."

I tried not to think about picking her up off my shoulder and throwing her into the trees. Instead, I looked around. The damage was sobering, almost depressing. No, it *was* depressing. "Junior?"

The boo hag hesitated, then shook her head. "While he was fighting Bear, I left to get help. When we came back, there was no sign of either one of them. Maybe..."

Her voice trailed off, but my mind finished her sentence. Maybe he'd survived and escaped. It was unlikely, but it was all we had.

Bear was responsible for all this.

The thought made my blood boil. And yet what could I do? Coming up with a plan that would save Nana, defeat Bear, and stop the poisonous storm from weakening and eventually severing the connection between my world and Alke—it seemed almost impossible. And time was running out, so every second mattered. The storm of the century was blotting out the sun, and lightning strikes cut through the air with searing flashes.

Mami Wata sighed, then turned to me. "We should summon Annie."

"Oh, right." I pulled out the SBP. Anansi made a *voila* gesture at a newly recharged Riverboat Rideshare app. The crowd begin to murmur as a familiar mist began to creep along the ground, spilling out of the trees and hiding the juke joint's wreckage from view. They shuffled closer, peering at the spectacle, and a worrying thought leaped to the forefront of my mind.

"Everyone!" I shouted. "Move up the hill if you don't want to be carried away." Just as I yelled the warning, a boat's horn blasted. The sound of trickling water emerged from the mist, and Mami Wata's face lit up as an enchanted keelboat launched out of the treetops.

Launched. Out. Of. The. Treetops.

"YAHOOOOO!" a voice boomed from the helm of the wooden boat, and the vessel landed with a mighty crash in the misty river. Keelboat Annie stood on the deck and waved to everyone. She wore overalls again, this time with a ripped pink collared shirt. Annie hopped down and—with a few giant steps—met us. To my surprise, the first thing she did was sweep up Mami Wata in a huge bear hug and twirl her around.

"Well, if this don't beat all," she said with a beaming grin. "And here I thought the old gang had seen its last days. Ha! Can't keep a good story group down." Then, as the mist faded, Annie saw the devastation around her and her eyes grew wide. "I didn't do that just now, did I? Sometimes I get carried away with my entrances and I have to tell myself, 'Annie,' I says, 'don't go too overboard with the shenanigans.' But I get so excited—"

Mami Wata caught one of Annie's massive wrists and patted her hand gently. "No, cousin, that wasn't you. It was the Masked One. Bear."

Lady Night shook her head, then embraced the two of them as well. It was a reunion I'd never thought I'd witness. But one was still missing. As if the thought had struck them all at the same time, they separated, their faces solemn.

"The gang isn't all together yet," Annie said with a frown. "We need our fearless leader."

My grandmother.

Mami Wata turned to me. "Well, young man, you've brought us together. There's a plan, isn't there?" Annie and Lady Night looked at me as well, and so did the former patrons of the juke joint and the warriors of Isihlangu. Then there was Ayanna, Anansi, and Gum Baby. They were all counting on me.

"There is," I said grimly. "Everyone is always telling me Alke is a story. My grandmother, the gods, you all. And Bear knows that, too. Your world is connected to mine by stories. Bear wants to destroy that connection. His storm is filled with the essence of the iron monsters who devour stories. If that storm washes over Alke—"

"The whole realm will be consumed," Anansi finished, his eyes filled with anger.

I nodded. "We have to get all the gods and goddesses together and—"

But before I could finish, a giant thunderclap rattled the sky and shook the ground. Seconds later, green lightning stabbed downward from the largest group of clouds hovering over the Golden Crescent. A bright flash lit up the evening, and everyone flinched.

Bear's storm had finally arrived.

32

BEACHFRONT SHOWDOWN

"SO LET ME TRY TO UNDERSTAND THIS SCHEME OF YOURS."

I kept my eyes glued to the screen of the SBP, ignoring the trickster god swinging in a hammock in the top right corner. I couldn't help it. The Alke Maps app was open, and I finally had a reason to use the weather-radar feature. Dark-green splotches spread from the west, creeping across the map in real time. It was little comfort that the storm had avoided MidPass. Mami Wata's fountain must have been protecting the deserted island.

"You want to enter a city at the center of a storm to confront a powerful villain who thinks you're responsible for everything bad in his life?" Anansi shook his head as he hopped down from the hammock and paced back and forth. "That boy Reggie must have knocked your brain clear out of your skull."

"It will work."

"And what's with the quilt?"

"It's filled with Nana's stories. She once told me that in order to repair it, we'd have to start from the beginning. I thought she meant just starting fresh with new squares, but now I know she meant recording the stories that she'd heard from these goddesses before. If we can use something powerful of hers, we might be able to break her out of Bear's story chains. It will work."

"And if it doesn't?"

I didn't respond. It had to work. I knew Anansi was worried about his son, so I was trying to keep his mind off the worst possibility, which forced me to mull over my own options. What if something went wrong? What if we weren't strong enough to challenge Bear?

I shook my head. We *were* strong enough. We had to be.

The storm-cooled wind ripped around us as we soared toward the Golden Crescent, and I had to struggle to keep my balance, even while sitting down. Ayanna's magical raft could expand when necessary, but still it was crowded, what with Mami Wata, Lady Night, Keelboat Annie, Ayanna, and myself taking up the front half with Nana's quilt sections spread out between us. I didn't know sewing was so tough! I'd pricked myself with the needle several times already, and I was struggling to maintain pace.

"Does he always talk this much?" Lady Night asked. Anansi was still muttering to himself and stalking back and forth across the SBP's screen.

I snorted. "You have no idea."

"Both of them are yappity-yaps," came Gum Baby's voice from behind us. She was standing on the rudder, steering the raft by leaning from side to side. I just...Sometimes I just can't with her. I shot her a halfhearted glare and then returned to the quilt sections in my lap.

My job was simple. Well, not that simple. But it was definitely easier than everyone else's, and I took a moment's break to watch them work.

Mami Wata whispered as she touched each square, infusing each individual image with the power of the sea, of a people stolen but unbowed, of a million faces gazing up from beneath the water. Blue-green crystals and emeralds materialized as she spoke quietly to the quilt, sweeping across the squares like a miniature tidal wave.

Lady Night sang softly as she sewed, and wove the song of Alke into the tapestry we were making. It was a wordless song, and yet one I instantly recognized. The drumbeat. The melody. The centuries of power and resiliency distilled into a rhythm that could be playing on a church piano or booming from someone's subwoofer. Everyone's head lifted a bit higher as she sang, and the quilt seemed to respond as she worked. Each square began to shimmer, the patterns and images shifting as I watched.

Keelboat Annie laughed as she stitched. It was like she was listening to a comedy routine in her earbuds and it was the funniest thing she'd ever heard. Her laughter was the kind that felt like it would split your ribs and make your face hurt. It was the sound of unworried determination. The sound of someone who had been told for years that she couldn't do what she had already proved she could, that she couldn't wear what felt comfortable to her, that she didn't belong. Her laugh gave the quilt strength. It wouldn't tear again, I was sure of it.

Ayanna, like the pilot she was, connected everyone's squares so they moved in the right direction.

And me?

I worked on the border that would hold it all together, all the while telling the quilt a story. I whispered and shouted and laughed and cried, willing each emotion into the fabric that represented Alke. I told a story relayed to me by a powerful woman who'd witnessed so many struggles, who'd given so much of herself, who'd empowered so many. And another tale about two plat-eyes desperate to reach their loved one.

The stories in each quilt square were unique, representing different places and experiences. The Diaspora. But when they were collected like this, they came together to make a beautiful artifact we all could appreciate. And the act of sharing it made us stronger. I had to make sure Bear understood that. I had to make sure Alke understood that.

If I didn't, we'd be torn apart, just as the quilt had been.

"Tristan?"

I looked up, my hands clutching a square of fabric. Everyone was staring at me. Was my fly open? Was there something on my face? Could it be—?

Mami Wata cleared her throat and nodded down at the SBP, where the Alke Maps app showed that we were nearly on top of the dot representing the Golden Crescent. I peered down from the front of the raft. Sure enough, we were flying over the bay. The few ships below were still moored, but the storm was tossing them about like toys, and trees were bent over nearly sideways as the winds howled. Gray-green clouds blotted out the sun and covered the land in shadow. Lightning struck an ivory tower, leaving black scorch marks and the smell of something burning in the air.

And there, in the middle of the beach, high waves battering uselessly against his armored form, stood Bear. John Henry's stolen hammer was clutched in his paws. But my eyes were focused on the person sitting on an overturned rowboat in front of him, her head held high and her hands folded calmly in her lap, staring straight ahead.

Nana.

"Take us down," I said quietly to Gum Baby. My words

were nearly lost in the wind, but for once the little doll and I were on the same page. We spiraled down and landed in the shallows, just as fat droplets of stinging rain began to fall. Everyone piled off the raft, spreading behind me in a semicircle.

Bear stepped forward, the mask of King Cotton shifting as he sneered. "Little hero, *grum grum*, I was getting worried you wouldn't make it. Welcome!"

I took a deep breath, then waded toward him.

No turning back now.

Who's that young girl dressed in blue . . . ?

The choppy sea sent waves to batter my calves and ankles. It took all my strength not to fall flat on my face, especially since I was holding the quilt above the water and my eyes were locked on Nana's. Bear loomed ominously behind her, squeezing John Henry's hammer, glaring at me through the eye holes of the poisoned mask.

It look like the children coming through. . . .

I don't know why that old spiritual was filling my thoughts right then. The marina gleamed in the eerie light of the stormy sky, and I could see Nyame's palace on the hill above. If I couldn't stop Bear in time, John Henry would . . .

I shook my head clear. Stay positive.

You don't believe I've been redeemed. . . .

I mouthed the words as I continued to march across the

beach. Nana was ten yards away. Eight. Five. Three. We were separated by mere feet and her eyes still stared blankly at something no one else could see. My fists clenched.

"Well, well," Bear rumbled as he stepped around the rowboat to stand in front of me. "What does the little hero have in his hands? A burial shroud? A sheet to drape over your body once I pound it into the sand, *grum grum?*"

Bear began to whirl the stolen hammer slowly, and the iron head started to glow a faint green as it made a figure eight in front of me. The air sizzled as the hammer passed by my face, and I flinched, stumbling backward and landing on the seat of my pants.

Bear laughed. "The great hero of MidPass! The champion of the Battle of the Bay! Scared. A coward, *grum grum.* Who would've guessed? Oh. Me. I've known it all along." The hammer dropped onto the sand as he threw back his head and roared in amusement.

I flushed and scrambled to my feet. I had to get him away from Nana. Once I rescued her, the others could take on Bear.

Just so the whole lake goes looking for me...

The words echoed in my head. I fumbled with the quilt, flipping it over until I found the square representing Nyanza. The last line of Nana's favorite spiritual was embroidered on it in spiraling golden thread.

The lake. The river goddess. Could it be?

I pulled out the phone, staring at Alke Maps while Anansi watched me incredulously. "Boy, have you lost your mind? You kids and your phones will be the death of us all."

But I was looking for something specific. A certain island in the middle of a storm, free of the poisonous taint and clouds.

The image of the geyser of cleansing water, the storm clouds blown apart, rinsed away by the power of a goddess.

"The fountain of Mami Wata," I whispered. "It cleared the poison from MidPass. If we can do the same here—"

"We just might have a chance of stopping Bear and his nearly invincible armor," Anansi concluded.

Bear had finished laughing and was staring at me suspiciously. I turned and threw the SBP back toward my friends. "Gum Baby, catch!" I shouted.

Without a second of hesitation, she leaped high into the air, not bothering to catch the spinning phone with her tiny hands. Instead, she rotated so that it collided with her back, sticking to her as she went tumbling out of the sky, only to land safely in Keelboat Annie's arms.

"Anansi knows what to do!" I shouted.

Annie nodded, then her eyes widened and she pointed behind me. I turned just in time to see a dark shape swinging at my head. I ducked, but the hammer clipped the side of my shoulder and sent me tumbling head over heels into the waves. Sand choked my nostrils and I swallowed some, coughing and rubbing my eyes with the quilt as I tried to stand back up. My arm felt numb, as if it was in so much pain my brain had simply shut down feeling so I didn't have to deal with it.

"Tristan Strong punched a hole in the sky," Bear sang, his voice muffled by the mask. Was it my imagination or was the mask glowing green, too? He stomped toward me. I struggled to my feet, but his paw shot out and grabbed me, squeezing my other arm so hard I cried out in pain. I dropped the quilt. "And let the evil in. Cities burned, now what did we learn?"

He turned and hurled me up the beach, and I landed hard, air forced out of my lungs with a giant *whoosh*. I groaned in pain as I rolled over, then froze.

Bear crouched over me, his iron-monster armor scraping together as the mask moved to within inches of my face.

"I will never," he said softly, "let it happen again."

His paw shot forward and grabbed me around the throat. He lifted me high in the air, then raised John Henry's hammer as well. I kicked helplessly, holding on to his paw with both hands in a futile attempt to free myself.

"See this, little hero? This is your twice-doom. This hammer will crush you like the bug that you are, and then, as your grandmother speaks the story of Alke, it will sever your world from ours. Forever!" Lightning forked across the sky, and to my horror, it didn't disappear. The bolts left jagged scars in the sky, like a crack spreading across glass. The sky was splintering. Alke and my world were being torn apart! If I couldn't do something about it, and soon, Nana and I would be stuck here, and we'd slowly fade away along with the rest of Alke.

"We have ... to be ... united," I gurgled. "Or we'll all die. I can help. We ... can help you."

The mask nearly touched my face as Bear leaned in even closer, and what little breath he hadn't squeezed out of me escaped in a gasp. His eyes were as green as the lightning, as green as the chains that had strangled the Tree of Power. The mask vibrated with poisonous energy.

I could almost hear King Cotton's voice as Bear spoke. "I would rather die," he growled.

He raised the glowing hammer high in the air. It was now or never. I dropped my hands and squeezed them into fists, ignoring the lingering pain in my right wrist. The akofena shadow gloves shimmered into view, and with a last-ditch effort, I swung with all my strength.

Thud, thud, thud.

A triple right hook collided with Bear's mask, knocking it out of place and skewing his vision. It barely hurt him, but it distracted him just enough that the hammer went whistling inches away from my head and Bear's grip loosened around my throat. I kicked off his hullbeast chest plate and slid out of his grasp, falling backward. I scrambled up and over to the quilt.

Bear growled and straightened King Cotton's mask, then stomped forward—

And paused.

"Look!" I shouted, holding up the blanket.

A golden light covered us both. Bear took a fumbling step, an armored paw reaching out, before withdrawing.

"What is this?" he growled.

"You don't recognize them?" I stretched my arms out wide, drawing Bear's attention away from the beach and filling his eyesight with the image on the quilt.

"It can't be," he whispered.

We'd worked feverishly adding a new square to the quilt. One new scene—the goddesses infusing the fabric with as much magic as they could spare, and me relaying the story of the plat-eyes as we worked. I'm sure it wasn't perfect, but it didn't have to be. No story is perfect for everyone, but everyone can find the perfect story when they need it most.

On the square, two bear cubs frolicked in a field while a larger bear stood watch over them, smiling.

Bear and his two cubs.

He raised his head, looking at me, and the green in his eyes flickered, as if he was trying to fight the poisonous hatred flowing through his system.

"Help me," Bear whispered.

33
HOSED DOWN

I TOOK A STEP CLOSER TO BEAR.

Lightning flared in the sky, illuminating the mask of King Cotton. A dark shadow slithered within the hardened sap—

And the mask re-formed, hardening, covering Bear's face completely.

Bear roared in pain, a muffled sound that vibrated the ground around me. He reared up, arms swinging wildly.

"No!" I shouted. We'd been so close. That mask had to come off—but it wasn't ready to relinquish its grasp on Bear's hatred.

I threw myself to the side, avoiding a flailing paw, and slid partway down a sand dune. When I stood, Bear's mask was back in its original shape, with slits for eyes and a gash for a mouth. His eyes were glowing green again, and he took a step forward . . . straight into a humongous stream of seawater that made him stagger back as it crashed into his chest. And then came another burst. And another. Each spray blasted the rogue god, knocking him off-balance.

Bear let loose a spluttering roar. "What sort of trickery…?" But his voice trailed off as he looked to the sea and stopped in his tracks.

This was the backup plan, just in case the sight of his cubs didn't work. We'd have to remove the armor the hard way.

Mami Wata stood thigh-deep in the sea, her eyes flashing blue-green, the flared hems of her pantsuit waving behind her like the tail of some mystical mermaid. Giant waterspouts, cyclones made of mist and vengeance, spun around her. Three, four, five of them! Her arms were spread wide as she glared at Bear. One hand flicked forward and a waterspout hurtled toward the beach, leaning until it was horizontal and striking Bear with the full force of a dozen firehoses.

Keelboat Annie had summoned her boat, and she, Lady Night, Ayanna, and Gum Baby were aboard. They raced on the back of Old Man River, leading miniature typhoons to the beach. There the swirling water combined into an explosive spray that hammered Bear.

His earsplitting roar shook the ground.

"Enough!" Bear shouted angrily. He shielded himself with one massive paw as another waterspout blasted him. His armor hung off him in ruins. The hullbeast chest plate was soggy and rotted, and the fetterling chains dangled like dull, tattered clothing. "You can't do this, *grum grum*!"

I sprinted forward and yanked off the chest plate, just as I'd ripped the wooden tub holding Mami Wata back in MidPass. Bear's fur was matted and singed underneath, as if it had never healed properly. He reached out blindly, one waterspout still hammering him in the face, and I skipped away before I lunged forward again to rip off an arm plate.

Piece by piece I stripped Bear of his poisoned armor. The gauntlets. The greaves. The rest of the chest plate. Ducking and dodging and slipping Bear's paws in a manner that would have made Granddad proud, I fought the round of my life. The shoulder guards. The leg greaves. All of it came off, until finally a waterlogged and weary Bear collapsed to his knees, wheezing and coughing up seawater.

The water attack ceased.

Only the mask was left.

And I hesitated to touch it. I just . . . Something inside made me recoil. I still felt the thorny tendrils of King Cotton's vines snaking up my wrist. I still heard his voice in my head. It was King Cotton holding me back in my nightmares, preventing me from rescuing the ones I loved.

Bear was right. I was a coward. I'd lasted this long and couldn't deliver the final knockout punch. I stepped back, stumbled, and fell.

I looked over and my gaze landed on Nana still sitting there, stiff as a board, but now she was staring straight at me.

Get. Back. Up.

She didn't say the words, but she might as well have. I turned back to Bear, to the mask with its oily blackness that swirled beneath the surface. I stood up, lunged at it with a cry of fury, and yanked it off. Then I hurled it as far as I could into the bay, which made my shoulder scream with pain.

When I turned back around, a patchy-snouted, crooked-eared face met mine, the green slowly fading from the eyes, leaving behind the haunted expression of someone dealing with a lot of anguish.

I recognized that look.

It was in every mirror I passed by.

"Where am I?" Bear whispered. "What's happening?"

I took a cautious step forward despite the hisses of warning behind me and stared him straight in the eyes.

"You're safe," I said.

The tension drained out of him, and his head drooped as his shoulders began to shake. I was about to offer him some comfort when I heard:

"Tristan!"

Gum Baby's shout had me spinning around looking for another attacker. An iron monster? The Maafa again? Was a mind-poisoned mob rushing forward, ready to stomp me into the sand?

No.

It was worse.

34
THE WORLD UNDONE

WE WERE TOO LATE. THE STORM HAD ARRIVED.

A streak of lightning, bigger and wider than any I'd ever seen before, split the sky in two before striking one of the boats in the marina.

As we watched, sickly green lines like snakes coursed through the water and then up the beach, turning everything dark gray, as if the essence of the world was being drawn out.

"Oh no," I whispered.

As if the poison had been injected into the veins of the city, it raced up the wide marble streets to the palaces. Everywhere it went, the world was ruined. Towers and minarets tumbled down like wave-swept sandcastles. Rivers and streams bubbled and boiled before turning into noxious steam. The ground shook as the jewel of Alke was consumed.

At this rate this entire world would fall piece by piece, and then mine, and there was nothing we could do about it.

Or was there?

John Henry's hammer rested in the sand a short distance away. I couldn't.... Could I?

A thundering sound filled the air. I whipped around to stare in horror as Nyame's great palace began to collapse in on itself, disintegrating into a cloud of fading gray story fragments and green clouds. Were the gods still in there?

My lips pressed tight together. I didn't have a choice.

I ran to where John Henry's hammer lay and, after a moment's hesitation, tried to wrap my hands around its giant handle. I waited for the throbbing in my wrist—but it never arrived. Finally, some good news. A tingling sensation rippled through my fingers, and I nearly let go. Before my very eyes, the hammer began to shrink, the engraved metal head morphing and the handle narrowing and shortening until it was the size of my forearm.

It reminded me of the Story Box, the way it changed shape to suit the wielder. This was a magical weapon, unique and powerful, which made what I was about to do hurt even more.

I squeezed my fists around the hammer shaft until the akofena shadow gloves appeared. I squeezed until the gloves gleamed in the air, and then I squeezed some more. I thought about the stories of Alke, the stories that belonged to this world and to my world and connected both, and I squeezed and squeezed and squeezed.

When I opened my eyes, the akofena gloves burned with

a black fire that danced up and down the hammer. The giant thundercloud squatted above us, leaking poison that drifted down and seeped into the land and sea. I had to stop it.

Sometimes there ain't no fixing something, baby. If you wanna rebuild, you gotta break it down and start all over.

Before I could talk myself out of it, I tossed the hammer into the air and cocked my right fist back as far as it could go. When the hammer began to fall back down, I hit it with the strongest uppercut I could manage. If I'd been wearing regular gloves, I would've broken my hand.

But these were the shadow gloves.

BAM!

John Henry's hammer shot into the sky. It streaked through the morning like a comet, trailing shining black fire as it punctured the storm cloud.

One second passed. Then another.

BOOM!

The thunderclap that followed felt like a right hook to my ears and knocked me off my feet. Then I couldn't hear a thing. Sand blasted my face and I squeezed my eyes shut as hurricane-force winds swept the beach. A wave slammed into me, sending me spinning farther up the dunes before it tried to drag me back. I had to claw deep furrows in the sand to hold on. Shielding my eyes, I stood and tried to find the others.

But I saw nothing but gray.

Had I made things worse? I couldn't even see my own hands in front of me.

"Nana!" I shouted. I took a step, then another half step, before stopping. What if she or the others were trying to find me? Maybe I had to stand still. I rubbed sand out of my eyes and tried to squint around. Everything was so blurry.

I cupped my hands around my mouth. "Nana!" Nothing. If only I could see....

"Wow, Tristan," I muttered, "you suck as a hero." Taking a deep breath, I pinched Nyame's adinkra and cautiously opened my eyes...

And gasped.

The power of the sky god's charm protected my eyes from the vicious storm. But, even more important, it showed them what the poisonous winds and devastating lightning Bear had unleashed were doing to Alke.

And it was terrible.

The land was outlined in words of silver, the people in twisted braids of copper and ebony cursive writing. The water glimmered the same color as Mami Wata's turquoise eyes in wavy handwriting, and the Golden Crescent... well, it was golden. (Not sure what you were expecting there.) Lines of golden script framed the city like a gorgeous skyline.

But the storm was ripping it all apart.

The story of Alke, the very fabric of the world, was being destroyed. Cruel winds tore apart the land and used the sea to drown it. Words, phrases, entire passages containing the origin of the realm were hurled into the sky, where they disappeared. The world was dissolving in front of my eyes.

A faint shout zipped past me. "Tristan?"

Nana! I spun around wildly and searched for my grandmother. There. A shimmering outline farther down the beach, surrounded by a maelstrom of fragmented silver sentences, huddled on the sand, hugging herself as if she was freezing.

She was fading, too.

I needed to find that quilt. Maybe, just maybe. But where was it? Bear had made me drop it, and I hoped it hadn't washed out to sea....

I desperately scanned the area and finally saw a faint glimmer on the sand under a big piece of driftwood. Could that be it? I sprinted toward it. Yes! The fabric was damp and caked with sand, but it was still in one piece, and the poison hadn't leeched its colors. I shook it out to dry it a little, then raced to Nana.

More glowing forms appeared as I got closer, including a large oblong object tossed to one side. But I only had eyes for my grandmother. I raced to her and draped the quilt over her.

Instantly the whirling greenish-gray fog disappeared, and with Nyame's adinkra I could see the quilt's golden aura slowly drawing the poison out of my shivering grandmother. The howling wind seemed to die down a bit.

"Are you okay?" I asked, skidding down beside her. With the poison draining out of her, Nana appeared as a coil of ruby-red script, as rich and powerful as the blood that we shared, the blood of the people. Her face, with the spectacles still perched on the end of her nose, turned to me.

"I'm fine," she said. "But this world is on its last legs if we don't do something."

"It's too late," I said mournfully. "Nana, we need to get home. Right now."

"And leave these poor people to their fate? I know I ain't raise a fool who raised a fool."

"But—"

"With all the powerful folks 'round here, we can't help those who need refuge from a silly storm? That's mighty sad, if you ask me."

I looked up to see other shimmering forms coming toward us. The wind, the same sickly green color as the poison, tried to batter everyone back, but they continued to push forward, and slowly I recognized them all.

The large oblong object I'd seen before was Keelboat Annie's boat. The goddess held it upside down, using her keel pole as a handle, so that it acted as an umbrella, sheltering everyone underneath. Lady Night, Gum Baby, and Ayanna were there, as well as a shivering Bear. Mami Wata was in back, doing her best to redirect huge waves that threatened to swallow the land whole. She pushed them off to the side to strike harmlessly at the base of the towering dunes.

"Look!" Gum Baby called.

Alkeans streamed down from the palaces above, including some familiar faces. A giant man crossed the beach in short, stumbling strides, outlined in powerful golden words that spoke of his strength.

"John Henry!" cried Ayanna.

His legs were restored, yet he walked with a limp and was struggling to pull a massive yacht through the shallows behind him. Golden letters swirled around his free hand in tight spirals. He caught me looking at them and nodded, then opened his fingers to show me what rested in his palm.

The pair of gloves he'd given me, which I'd left on his sickbed.

"Thank you," he said simply.

I nodded, then hesitated. "Your hammer—" I began.

"Later," he said, a sad, knowing expression in his eyes.

"Is everyone okay?" I asked him.

"I reckon most are, though it was mighty close." Many citizens of the Golden Crescent peeked over the edge of the yacht, the Flying Ladies among them. Miss Sarah and Miss Rose were using their wings to shelter people from the worst effects of the storm.

A harsh caw split the air, louder than the din of the storm.

Vast black wings flapped, and my heart swelled with happiness and relief. High John and Thandiwe rode on the back of Old Familiar, the shadow crow, along with others too sick or injured to walk...including Brer Rabbit. And then a line of golden statues moved stiffly down the dunes, carrying wooden palanquins with the injured and infirm inside. I had to shield my eyes—the statues appeared as blazing figures of white-hot cursive. Nyame, just as brilliant, stepped out of one of the conveyances. He had his hands full—literally. Several babies and a young crow were cradled in his arms, and his golden eyes latched on to me almost immediately.

We are out of time. His words boomed into my head. **Soon this world will be no more.**

Gum Baby scrambled up my legs and onto my shoulder. "So, uh, Bumbletongue, Gum Baby ain't scared or nothin', but you got a plan, right?" Her voice was tiny, her bravado stretched thin and fear beginning to seep out.

I looked around. Everyone wore scared expressions or put on brave faces. Another huge lightning bolt turned the entire sky white, then zigzagged to strike the top of the marina across the beach.

CRACK!

The building exploded in a blinding flash of broken words, and someone screamed. But before I could even let out a *Sweet peaches!*, a shout from Thandiwe made us all turn around.

"No!"

Far in the distance, Isihlangu was spiraling away into nothing. The shield of Alke was unraveling like one of Nana's wool sweaters.

I gritted my teeth. It was time to do some reknitting.

"Everybody!" I shouted. "Onto the boats! I *do* have a plan."

35

UNITED WE STAND

KEELBOAT ANNIE'S BOAT AMAZED ME AT EVERY TURN.

First, I thought it wouldn't fit all the refugees on board. Wrong. Then I thought there was no way John Henry, Bear (even as emaciated as he looked without his armor), Brer Rabbit, and the other gods would fit, too. Wrong again. We all managed to clamber aboard, soaked to the skin, teeth chattering in our mouths.

A ground-shaking rumble made the boat lurch to one side.

"Look!" someone shouted. The Golden Crescent seemed to *shudder* and heave up, then collapse in on itself. Golden braids of story—the contents of Nyame's Story Box, Anansi's trickster tales, and others were carried up into the sky, lost in the brightness of another lightning strike.

"We're going to disappear!"

"Help us!"

"Do something!"

The cries of Alkeans filled my ears as I dropped down next to Nana. She, of anyone, would know if my plan would work. If it didn't . . . well, I didn't want to think about that. The wailing around us wouldn't let me.

"Nana, I need your help," I said. The boat tossed and dipped as I described what I wanted to do, and her eyebrows nearly shot off of her face. She removed her glasses, rubbed her eyes, wiped her lenses, then looked up at me and shook her head. My heart dropped into my perpetually soaked shoes. But before I could lose hope, she put a hand gently on my arm.

"You don't need my help to do that, baby." She jerked her head toward the back of the boat, where the gods of Alke were trying to comfort the folks they were responsible for. "Seems like they're more your speed. Besides, I told you I was gonna get you to try your hand at this one day. Seems like now's as good a time as ever." She produced her golden needle—a spare quilting needle (Now, where had she been keeping that?)—and gave it to me, using both hands to fold my fingers over the shining tool. She smiled, then brought me forward into a hug. "Strongs keep punching," she whispered in my ear, then pushed me back and shooed me away. "Now go and save the world. I've got a bridge game at seven, and lord knows, if Miss Thang Ruby Lee James waits a second longer than she has to, the whole world will hear her complain."

I grinned, then stood and made my way carefully over to the others. I had to lean into the wind as Alke unspooled around us, the essence of this realm that was linked to mine swirling about like a sandstorm of magic. But I still had Nyame's adinkra activated, and the gods—my friends—stood strong in the encroaching darkness like statues of gold. I took a deep breath, then pulled out the SBP. Anansi was hiding under a makeshift lean-to he'd rigged out of a few apps and some spiderwebs. "Boy, I really hope you know what you're doing."

I shook my head, pausing as a vicious gust of wind nearly lifted me off the boat. "Nope. But when has that ever stopped me?" I told him my plan, and he whistled.

"That might actually...work. It's risky. Really risky. But...Oh, what's the use, you're going to do it anyway. Fine. Let me know when you need the Diaspor-app."

While he prepared, I got close enough to address the other gods. "There's a way we can save your world and all the people in it...but it will take all of us."

John Henry grimaced in pain as he leaned on Annie's keel pole as a crutch, the only thing big enough to support him. "What you figurin' on doing, Tristan?"

I took a deep breath. My heart was beating so loud I felt like *it* could be the rhythm of Alke on its own. "I...am going to stitch Alke into my world."

Silence.

In the space between, the storm raged, the winds howled,

and several gods stared at me as if I'd just loudly admitted to taking baths in peanut butter. I mean, if that's what you like to do, go for it. No judgment here. Just not my preferred way to bathe.

"You're going to stitch—" Miss Rose began.

"—our worlds together?" Miss Sarah ended. I nodded. If we didn't act soon, we'd all be swept away no matter what.

The boat heaved upward as a giant wave lifted us to the sky. My stomach flipped. We hung in the air forever, long enough for me to see something farther out on the Burning Sea. The sight was a punch to the solar plexus, robbing me of what little breath I had left before we crashed back down onto the water.

"Watch out!"

Before I could tell anyone what I'd seen, a second wave loomed overhead, a wall of white-capped gray curled like a fist ready to pound us to smithereens. Everyone grabbed something—a rail, a rope, John Henry's leg, anything that would keep them safe. People started screaming. But before the wave could batter the boat, it began to unwind, just like the rest of Alke, strands of the sea drifting up into the devouring storm clouds.

And what loomed behind it, what I had seen while we were in the air, was even worse.

"Is that—?" High John began.

"No!" someone shouted.

"Not again!"

"Sweet peaches," another person whispered, and I was half surprised to realize it was me.

Gum Baby's grip tightened on my shoulder; even Nana's face paled and her eyes widened at the glowing phenomenon. I pressed my lips tight together. From the outside I looked calm and determined, but really I was trying to hold back a scream.

There, at the edge of the bay, where the normally clear blue water met the fiery dark fathoms of the Burning Sea, framed in a swirling orange-red mist, was another hole in the sky.

It was as if someone had unzipped reality. A raging inferno gashed its way up into the clouds, and it was sucking up the poisonous storm like a vacuum, inhaling the maelstrom and sending it through to a new world fresh and unspoiled. It was a portal into a different realm—my realm. And through it I could see—

"Is that the farm?" Nana asked faintly.

I gritted my teeth.

No way was I going to let anything happen to my grandparents' farm. They hadn't put their sweat and blood into that land just to lose it to a stupid storm. NO! It would not happen.

"Grab the quilt!" I said, shoving one end at High John. He looked baffled, but there was no time for confusion, only action. "Grab it!" When his fingers finally closed over the border, I moved on down the line of gods. John Henry. Miss Sarah and Miss Rose. I tucked one corner into Brer Rabbit's feeble paws. The giant rabbit's whiskers twitched, but otherwise he didn't move. Even Bear grabbed hold. I handed the SBP to Gum Baby, then pointed. She scrambled onto the quilt and sat in a sticky heap near the center. At least I didn't have to worry about her blowing away.

I took one corner of the quilt, tugged at the thread I'd so carefully stitched at the border, and pulled it loose. I held Nana's golden needle just so while ignoring the storm screaming at us and the hole dragging us closer and closer. The angle of my wrist had to be right, or the thread—the magical essence that could tie two worlds together—might slip out of the needle.

Push down. Pull up.

The keelboat turned sideways as another wave surged beneath us. Someone screamed, but I didn't take my eyes off my work.

Push down. Pull up.

Sewing, as it turned out, was a lot like boxing. If that sentence doesn't make sense to you, it's cool, give it a minute. What I mean is, you need technique. Skill. Perseverance. It takes time to get good at it. If you rush, you'll just have to start all over, either from stitch one or round one of the next fight.

Push down. Pull up. Tie off the thread.

Almost finished. Just needed to add one more thing.

The opening between worlds was a few dozen yards away. It hummed with an energy of wrongness, like an untuned electric guitar someone was playing through an amp the size of a house. It made your teeth rattle and your eyeballs itch. I couldn't see the point where the tear met the Burning Sea, or the top, where it disappeared into the storm. Fiery mist obscured it all.

I ripped my eyes away and surveyed the boat of refugees. Keelboat Annie had one hand on the tiller and one hand on the quilt, straining to keep us straight. A few people were crying, and I think I saw Bear comforting a small hedgehog. Everyone clutched at one another, even the gods. There was something terrifying in that, but it was also reassuring. Even the strongest of us needed support, and that was okay.

"Mami Wata!" I called. The water goddess lifted her head from the other end of the boat, where she was working to keep us from being swamped with each newer and bigger wave. "When the next wave comes, can you direct it toward the hole?"

Multiple sets of eyes whipped around. "You want to go through?" John Henry yelled over the storm. I didn't answer. Instead, I looked at the Flying Ladies.

"Do you think you two, when I give the signal, could flap your wings as hard as you can in my direction?"

They glanced at each other. "You might—"

"—be lost to the sea!"

I shook my head. "I'll be anchored tight. Right, Gum Baby? Precoffinary measures."

Gum Baby stared at me like I was stupid, then her eyes widened. "Ooooh. Gum Baby smell what you boiling. One set of precoffinary measures coming right up."

I addressed everyone else. "I don't know if this is going to work like I want it to," I yelled. "I don't know if we'll make it through together. We might get split up. But Alke is a story. As long as we keep the threads intact, this world can be rebuilt. I believe that. You have to as well."

I looked each one of them in the eye before I spoke, and I put every ounce of Anansesem power I had into the promise. "So hold on. If we do get separated, remember this: I know your stories. As an Anansesem, I will find you. As your friend, I. Will. Find you."

I wanted to say something momentous. Something that captured the changes we were about to undergo. But I didn't have to. The storm did it for me.

With a great peal of rolling thunder, like an avalanche in reverse, the poison having seeped into the core of the land, Alke imploded.

The shoreline fell away. It just...dropped, caught in the jaws of an invisible shredder that ripped the world to its very fibers. As we bobbed on an endless sea, fragments of the land twisted away in the wind, great clouds of them. With Nyame's adinkra activated, it looked like glowing spools of silk being carried up into the sky, reds and greens and silvers and golds all slipping away to be lost forever.

Not if I could help it.

"Now!" I shouted at Miss Sarah and Miss Rose.

The winged goddesses let their gleaming black wings stretch out to their fullest extent, their brows furrowed and their muscles straining against the wind. Angels descending to provide aid. They shouted as one and unleashed a massive flap that ripped forward, sending fragments of Alke across the boat.

Right toward me.

At the same time, Mami Wata labored, pulling together a wave that was the queen of all waves, a towering behemoth of gray and white crowned in burning orange. It reared up beneath the boat, and Keelboat Annie struggled to keep the vessel straight.

And me?

The hero of Alke?

Champion of a dying world?

I quilted.

"Golden Crescent!" I shouted. Gum Baby, sitting on my shoulder, held out her arm and I plucked off a fragment of Alke's story thread that had become stuck to the little doll. I looped the material onto the quilting needle and went to work. When that piece had been added to the quilt, I looked up. "Nyanza next."

A blue-green strand was passed over.

"The Sands." A wheat-colored thread was attached to the quilt.

And so it went.

My needle went faster and faster, giving birth to a new world even as an old one died.

MidPass.

Isihlangu.

The Horn.

In my mind's eye I saw Alke from above as I'd seen it on the back of Old Familiar, when MidPass burned during my first adventure in this realm. It was a gleaming tapestry. That's what I was building.

I only hoped this would work.

Looking up, I caught John Henry's eyes. "I'm gonna need your help to give this some power," I said. "I'm gonna need everybody's help."

John Henry stared back in confusion.

"Remember when you and Brer Rabbit worked together to send Gum Baby through to my world? You had to give up some of your essence to make the trip between realms. For this to work, we need even more power."

"Tristan, we're getting close!"

Gum Baby, still covered in a few fragments of Alke,

pointed. The tear between the worlds was a stone's throw away. Time was up. I tied off the last stitch, stuffed Nana's needle back into my pocket, and beckoned everyone closer. Gods and Alkeans, people and animals, and a boy and his grandmother.

"Everyone, grab hold. You all," I shouted, looking at the gods, "put every ounce of power you've got into this quilt. What unites your world and mine are the stories we share. My grandmother told me that." Nana leaned against me briefly and I swallowed and forged on. "You are your stories, and your stories are Alke. So put your stories into these threads. Every tale, every lullaby, every joke. And hold on! Please, whatever you do, don't let go. I don't know how long this quilt will stay in one piece, but as long as we hold it together, we can bring Alke home."

The giant wave crested and we picked up speed. Keelboat Annie lashed the tiller straight so we pointed directly at the widening rip between the worlds. Behind us the last of Alke unspooled, consumed by the world-eating storm.

"Now!" I shouted.

If I'm totally honest, I wasn't sure what to expect. I didn't know what the others saw—the Alkeans and Nana. I don't even think the gods themselves were paying attention to anything other than infusing the quilt with the power of their own individual stories.

But, thanks to Nyame's adinkra on my wrist, I saw.

And what a story it was.

I saw words and moving images of all different colors. I heard faint echoes of songs, vibrant and powerful and achingly beautiful. Everyone holding that tapestry contributed. Yes, the gods, and me as Anansesem—we did our part, but so did the ordinary folk. Their tales went into the stitches, filling the squares with life. Children's laughter infused the quilt with the joy of a new generation, and elders shared their tears of sadness over the departed. Underneath it all pulsed the heartbeat of a nation, and it was a familiar rhythm.

We were united.

The keelboat plunged through the hole in the sky just as the sea disappeared out from under us.

All sound was silenced.

Darkness swept over us.

Only the flickering glow of the enchanted quilt cast any light, bathing the underside of everyone's face in soft gold. I had one last second to meet everyone's eyes, to send my hopes and prayers and love to my friends and family before even that small source of comfort was extinguished.

And then...

...there...

...was...

...nothing.

36

I WILL FIND YOU

I WOKE TO THE SMELL OF PANCAKES AND BACON.

I don't know why, but that fact made me angry. Those smells were for normal people. Ordinary kids could wake up and grab a plate while avoiding adults who were chatting and laughing and pouring their coffee, then sneak their way to the couch to watch Saturday morning cartoons.

Not me.

Bzzzt bzzzt

The SBP vibrated on the nightstand next to me, but I ignored it.

I rolled over on the mattress only to stop and let out a grunt of pain when my heavily bandaged ribs protested the change. I opened my eyes, glared at the bright sunlight spearing in through the bedroom window, and shoved my head under the pillow.

Someone knocked on the doorframe. "Heard you moving around. You all right?"

Granddad.

I removed the pillow. He wore his traditional work clothes—denim overalls with a cotton T-shirt underneath, and, sticking out of a side pocket, a faded brown bandanna for mopping his forehead. But there were new additions as well. His head was bandaged, as was his left arm, and he walked with a wince and a limp. He had a plate balanced in each hand, one heaped high with pancakes and the other holding a couple of slices of cantaloupe and a mug.

"Yeah. I mean, yes, sir. I'm all right."

He nodded, though his eyes lingered on my bandages as I carefully sat up and pushed back the covers. "Good. Was gonna bring your breakfast in, but if you're up, I'll leave it on the kitchen table for you." He turned to go.

"Hey, Granddad?"

He looked back at me.

"How is she? Nana, I mean. Is she...?"

I stopped talking when Granddad's shoulders slumped a bit. He didn't answer for a second, then turned his head away. I could still see one eye glistening. "No change, really. Made her favorite breakfast. I'm gonna sit with her for a while."

Bzzzt bzzzt

His eyes dropped to the phone, then looked at me, and

I braced for a lecture about it. But... Granddad didn't say anything except "Come on out when you're ready" as he moved on.

"Okay," I said. I slumped back onto the bed, staring at the magical phone, but my mind was elsewhere.

Two days had passed since we'd come through. My plan had partially worked. The keelboat had crashed into my world, landing in the middle of the Bottle Tree forest on the edge of Granddad and Nana's farm. Good thing it had happened after midnight and there weren't any neighbors within a ten-mile radius. The sudden appearance of a heavily damaged wooden boat straight out of the early twentieth century miiight have turned a few heads.

And the good news was there were only a few injuries. My ribs were one. Nana had sprained her knee, and after her previous collapse, the doctor had confined her to the bedroom for the foreseeable future. As for the others—

Bzzzt bzzzt

"Boy, if you don't check your messages," came Anansi's voice, "I will make your ringtone 'The Ballad of Gum Baby.'"

I looked over at the phone. The spider god, hollow-eyed and gaunt, sat in the corner of the screen. He hadn't moved from that spot since our return. Everyone had lost their home in Alke. But many, like Anansi, had lost something far more important: family and dear friends.

Bzzzt bzzzt

"Oh, for the love of—" I reached over, ignoring the pain in my side, and snatched up the phone. There was a golden dot in the corner of the Diaspor-app. I frowned. After a moment's hesitation, I tapped the icon.

Three pictures filled the screen. Captions scrolled beneath them, and I read the first one aloud.

"'Story fragment detected. Show location?'"

I squinted.

My eyes grew wide and I shot out of bed. "No way! Anansi, are you seeing this?"

He took a peek, then stood up suddenly and gripped the edge of one of the pictures, his voice raw and desperate. "Tell me this isn't a joke."

"I don't joke." I threw on a pair of basketball shorts and a T-shirt and sprinted out of my room. "Back in a minute, Granddad!" I shouted as I ran out the door.

The sun barely peeked over the canopy of the Bottle Tree forest. The heat wave had broken and the air smelled sweet, the aftermath of the storm that had poured in through the rip. My bare feet squelched in muddy puddles and then pounded the damp path that circled the farm's cornfield. A stitch in my side nearly doubled me over, but I forced myself to keep running. The SBP was in one hand and the other pumped through the air as if the information I needed would save my life.

And then I was there.

I skidded to a stop in front of the gnarled sentinel trees that guarded the Bottle Tree. I hesitated, but a gust of wind swirled around me and the leafy branches seemed to sway to the side, allowing me entrance. I bowed my head in thanks, then forced myself to walk calmly into the dim forest. A thick quiet covered the place, as if all noise stopped at the path outside out of respect.

The first time I'd entered the forest had been at night. Everything had looked scary back then, when the landscape was unfamiliar and I was chasing after a tiny terror.

The Bottle Tree stood in the center of the clearing, bright blue ornamental bottles hanging from the small weeping myrtle's stiff, straight branches. My eyes didn't linger on it long. Instead, I looked up, searching for something else. A new addition to the forest.

Near the top of the canopy, an oblong shape blocked the rest of the sun. I marched over to the tree that was holding it up and cupped my hands over my mouth. "It's me! Let me up."

A rope dropped down, a loop tied at the end. Gingerly, I stepped onto it and held on for dear life as I was yanked up twenty feet in the air. Gulping, I stepped off the rope . . . and onto Keelboat Annie's boat.

Well, I guess it was a tree house now.

Inside, a small group of exhausted and bedraggled Alkeans stared at me. Nyame. Bear. Annie. Lady Night and Mami

Wata. A few assorted citizens of the Golden Crescent. And, finally, Brer Rabbit lay on a homemade cot at the back of the boat. John Henry rested on the floor next to the large rabbit, bandages covering his legs, a rough woolen blanket in his lap.

So few here. So many lost, scattered across the country to who knows where.

Gum Baby.

Ayanna.

Miss Sarah and Miss Rose.

High John and Thandiwe.

Before I could tell anyone about what I'd seen on the SBP, Mami Wata stood. Her face was grim as she studied something in her hands. Actually, as I surveyed the deck, everybody's expression was wavering between fear and defeat. No one—not even Nyame—wanted to meet my eyes. I stopped, confused. I knew their situation was dire, but this was something else.

Something bigger, it looked like.

"What is it?" I finally asked. "Tell me."

But Mami Wata didn't speak. Instead, she walked toward me, her pantsuit shimmering as she moved, her hair corralled into a loose bun. She held up the object, and when I saw what it was, my pulse quickened.

A piece of King Cotton's mask.

"I found it this morning, at dawn," she said.

I took the shard of hardened sap in my hand and held it up

to the sunlight. There was no more sign of the inky shadow inside. "Maybe it . . . he's gone."

"That's not all." Mami Wata looked down over the hull. "There were shards of glass on the ground as well."

I stared at her, then sprinted to the edge of the boat. What I saw made my heart fall and land at the foot of the Bottle Tree below. Even from up here I could see the empty branches, the broken blue glass sparkling on the forest floor like gems.

Someone had broken almost half the bottles that had held trapped haints and evil spirits. And with King Cotton no longer imprisoned in his mask, I had a strong idea about who was responsible.

I squeezed the SBP tight, and it vibrated in response. Anansi peered at me out of the screen and nodded. He knew exactly what I was thinking. Now we had two jobs to do: tracking down the haints that had escaped into this world, and keeping the promise I'd made before we'd gone through the hole in the sky.

I was determined to keep that promise. And maybe I could start at that very second. I held up the phone, the pictures blown up on the screen. Everyone's eyes went wide.

"I hope you're all rested up," I said, "because we have work ahead of us. We're going to find King Cotton, bring him back to this forest, and recapture every single haint he freed. And that's not all. We have friends and relatives out there, and I don't know about you, but I plan on finding them, too. Starting with these three."

A brown-skinned Black girl was walking out of a gas station, a backpack slung over her shoulder. Her dark brown curls were tinted red at the tips, the sides of her head were shaved, and there was a zigzag part on one side. She wore a black leather jacket, skinny jeans, and gold flats. A golden baseball bat was strapped to her back, a glaring face painted on the barrel. In this world she looked completely different, but I recognized the Alkean pilot instantly.

A boy followed her, his dark brown skin gleaming from the camera's flash. He was in the middle of blowing a bubble with chewing gum, and he wore a sleeveless tank top with jogging pants, and multiple beaded bracelets on both wrists. Hanging on his shoulder was a cross-body satchel.

Anansi let out a ragged sob of relief.

But there was one more picture. Peeking over the boy's opposite shoulder was a tiny, sticky brown face I never thought I'd be so happy to see.

I looked around the room and let out a fierce grin. "Let's go get our friends."

Do you understand now?

I'm coming for you.

I've got the SBP alerting me each time it spots another Alkean here in the United States. It pings me whenever a haint shows its evil face. It's on, King Cotton. The final round. I've got powerful folks in my corner and a rhythm in my fists. And don't think we're limited to Alabama. Ha, nope! That'd be too easy. I'm going to find you, and I'm going to find them. Please believe, I will bring every single one of them back to their family.

Because Alke wasn't...*isn't* just another realm.

Alke is a story.

Each of us carries parts of it—chapters, scenes, even just a few words. And when we come together? That magical world is brought to life. And as long as we continue to pass on the story of its existence to others, it can never be completely destroyed. Maybe, just maybe, word by word and line by line, we can rebuild that special place we call our own.

So...keep your eyes peeled.

And if you're Alkean—from MidPass, the Golden Crescent, the Grasslands, wherever—remember this:

I'm coming to find you and bring you home.

ACKNOWLEDGMENTS

This book wouldn't have been possible without the help, support, encouragement, existence, persistence, strength, and tireless advocacy of the women and gender-nonconforming people in and around my life. There's a saying that goes: "Behind every strong man is a strong woman." What it should say is: "In front of every strong man are three stronger women, maybe more, so let's start with their story."

To my mother, carrying the torch alone and yet not alone.

To my wife, relentless in her passion for our children (your children, my children, the world's children) and their ability to learn without restriction.

To Jendayi and Carol, both leaders, examples, and sisters.

To Lauren and Nikki and Wobby, pillars of support in our family.

To Shani, Kylie, Kendi, Maddy, Nia, Aminah, and Zuri,

who will take over what we have left them and reshape the world.

To my aunts, my cousins, my grandmothers, my branches and roots on the family tree. Without you I couldn't grow.

To Dhonielle, Sona, Patrice, and Steph, thanks for believing in me.

To Nina, thank you for the songs "Four Women" and "Sinnerman," which helped inspire this story.

To her, she, they, them, and you . . . thank you.

Don't miss the explosive finale,

Tristan Strong Keeps Punching!

1
STAY STRONG

IT SHOULD BE PHYSICALLY IMPOSSIBLE FOR THE HUMAN BODY TO burst into flame. Aren't there rules against that? I'm pretty sure my Life Science class covered it last year. Call me old-fashioned, but I'm a firm believer that people aren't meant to be matches.

So that's why I stared in utter horror at the small silver flame popping out of my knuckles.

"I don't like that," I said, my voice sounding faint and distant to my own ears.

That was probably wrong to say. For several reasons. First, I was already trying my best not to lose my temper and attract attention. For some reason the tour guide kept shooting angry looks at our group and shushing us. And we weren't even being that loud! No more so than anyone else on the tour. Still, I was pretty sure my bursting into flame would get us more than a mean look.

We were stuffed in the middle of a crowd in a tiny museum crammed with fascinating exhibits. Granddad called it the Pharmacy Museum. From that name I expected to see some boring displays, like the history of headache medicine or something like that. Instead, I learned about century-old tools used to probe, prod, and investigate the human body. Pretty cool! But again, the place was jam-packed. Everybody in the French Quarter must've come for a tour. So I definitely didn't want to cause a panic because my fist had turned into a Flamin' Hot.

Yes, the Strongs were in New Orleans. One last adventure before I headed back to Chicago to start the new school year. It was bittersweet. I mean, I was looking forward to getting home, being back in my neighborhood, and seeing my parents. Still, I'd had fun with Granddad and Nana. I'd eaten a bunch of key lime pie, done a little boxing, fallen into another world with powerful gods, and made a bunch of folk-hero friends... You know, the normal summer.

I was excited to visit the Big Easy, but this trip had come with a few strings attached. And—

"What don't you like?" someone said over my left shoulder. "The artificial leech? C'mon! That's so cool! Apparently back then you'd jam that thing into your—"

"Thank you, Terrence," I whispered, covering up my burning hand.

The tour guide glared as Terrence continued to hiss facts at me. I shot a glare right back, and the guide huffed and turned around. Then I looked at the walking encyclopedia behind me. Terrence was a short, thin Black boy with a red-tipped lightning bolt dyed into his close-cropped hair. He was also one of those aforementioned attached strings.

"No more ancient surgery lessons," I said in a low voice. "Please."

He shrugged and continued to mutter trivia to the stranger next to him. I shook my head. Terrence was my nine-year-old cousin, Dad's brother's son, and the second reason I had to keep things to myself. The powers that be (Nana) had decided that Terrence needed a buddy, someone to partner with as we toured New Orleans, and guess who that was?

Lucky me.

Terrence wore an oversize lime-green T-shirt with an icon of a flexed bicep on the front and STRONGS ON THE MOVE written beneath it in bold black letters. On the back, BLACK IS A RAINBOW arced over interlocking hands in different shades of brown. Yeah. Brown and lime green. The message was great! The aesthetics? Eh. I (unfortunately) was wearing the same shirt, and four or five others in the Pharmacy Museum were sporting it as well.

You've probably figured out what was happening.

It was a Strong family reunion.

Relatives I hadn't seen in years—and some I'd never met at all—had made the trip. Great-aunts, cousins, their children. I met my Uncle Jeff-Jeff and what he called his emotional support pug (also, strangely, called Jeff-Jeff). In fact, it seemed the only ones not here were my parents. They'd been unable to make the trip—something about car trouble—and Mom had stressed the importance of me representing for the Chicago Strongs. What I did would reflect on them. So, you know how it goes. Best behavior and all that.

Which brings us to the third reason I had to avoid making a scene. I was on a mission.

Two weeks ago I had returned from my second trip to Alke, the magical world where storied folk heroes like John Henry, heroines like Keelboat Annie, gods like Anansi and Nyame, and goddesses like Mami Wata reigned.

Unfortunately, it was also my last trip there. Alke had been destroyed, and the only way to save its inhabitants had been to weave the story of their world into mine. Now Alkeans were scattered across the country, and it was my responsibility to help find them and make sure they were okay.

Whiiich you can't really do when you're a line buddy for your cousin.

"Where should we visit next?" Terrence asked as we exited the museum. "I could use some dinner first." He pulled out his phone and started scrolling different travel websites, then gasped. "Tristan, look! There's a pizza parlor that gives you an oversize spatula if you eat a whole supreme pie!"

He looked at me with way too much glee in his eyes (could that be a medical condition?) and I shook my head. "We're supposed to wait here for Granddad, then we'll move to the next stop." The hotel, I hoped.

My phone vibrated. I froze for a second before reaching for it. Fortunately, the flame had disappeared from my knuckles, and Terrence was still busy reading about pizza. I pulled a sleek black smartphone from the back pocket of my basketball shorts.

The SBP, or Story Box Phone, was the magical treasure chest of Anansi tales. Nyame the sky god had transferred the stories from an actual box into my phone and then trapped Anansi himself inside with them. That hadn't stopped the spider god from bossing and heckling me at every opportunity. The plus side? Anansi had turned out to be a talented web designer and had added all sorts of cool apps, including one that alerted us to the location of Alkeans. I now had the most advanced smartphone in this realm or any other.

The spider god stared out at me from the home screen. His expression was impatient as he pointed to the Maps app icon. "What's taking you so long? We've got to get a move on!"

"Okay, where's the alert coming from?" I asked Anansi.

I wanted to tell him about the knuckle flames, but just at that moment Terrence moved closer to me. I turned to prevent him from being able to see the SBP's screen. "I'm on the phone," I mouthed to him, pointing to the buds in my ears. He frowned but went back to scoping out which pizza he apparently wanted to cram inside his face.

"Hurry up, Tristan," said Terrence. "I've always wanted a pizza spatula. I'm going to be a chef, you know. Open my own restaurant and serve my famous teriyaki pizza." He licked his lips and I shivered. Some food preferences should remain private.

I looked back at Anansi. "Well? Where should I send Nyame?"

Hey, I was only twelve. I couldn't exactly go gallivanting across the country by myself to find every Alkean. But the sky god could.

Anansi shook his head. "No, you're not listening. Right here, just a few blocks away. There's an Alkean who needs help in the French Quarter!"

I inhaled sharply. Yes! We could handle this ourselves! All I had to do was give Terrence the slip, and then we could—

A tingling sensation pricked the corners of my eyes.

That was weird. I squinted. Rubbed at them. Blinked a few times, but the sensation wouldn't go away. I had just turned to ask Terrence if there was anything in my eyes when I saw someone I recognized. He was whistling while walking down the street in the opposite direction.

Tall.

Neatly dressed.

Evil.

King Cotton was strolling through the French Quarter without a care in the world.

The way I figure it, no one is owed anything. Not an easy life. Not a happy ending. Nothing. I learned that from Granddad. Life comes at you fast, like a flurry of jabs and hooks, and sometimes the only thing you can do is learn how to take a few on the chin and keep on standing.

And not every story is neat and tidy, either. Sometimes pages are missing, ripped out by forces beyond our control. Sometimes the villain wins. Sometimes the villain wins by a *lot*. And not every question may get answered. I mean, there are a hundred stories unfolding without our knowledge every day, and the details will never see the light of day because we either can't or won't seek them out. So, tough luck, the ending to that chapter is forever shrouded from view.

Until someone comes along and tries to tell it. Tries to tease out the answers, give folks some closure. That's my role as an Anansesem—a seeker, recorder, and teller of stories. I didn't ask for the title—the title chose me when I was in Alke. In fact, I didn't want the job. I didn't think I'd be any good at it. But I was wrong. And despite my best attempts to avoid the responsibility, the magic of my people's stories didn't care about my objections. Since I was the reason the characters in those tales were now scattered around the world, telling their stories was one thing that only I could do.

Maybe Nana had said it best the first week after we'd returned to our world. She'd been laid up in bed, recovering from being abducted, and the two of us were talking about Alke. And stories. When I mentioned it was hard to find the energy to speak about the world I had destroyed, she peered at me over the new quilt she was working on.

"You gotta find the pulse of the story, baby," she'd said.

"Let the rhythm beat like a heart, and hold on to that pulse once you got it. Don't change it, no matter what anybody else says. Even if they call you a liar or selfish, or say you lucky to be here, or tell you to go somewhere else if you so unhappy, you don't let it go. Then speak those words. Tell the story."

Tell the story. I wanted to do just that. But how could I when King Cotton, the haint who had corrupted everything in Alke, now had his sights on my world? I had to stop him first.

"Hoo HOOO! Boy oh boy oh boy."

I'd shoved the phone back into my pocket and was two seconds away from tearing off after Cotton when Granddad walked out of a seafood grill a few doors down from the Pharmacy Museum. He was licking his fingers and doing a little jig, something everyone in the family called his *good-eatin' shuffle*. Nana followed him, no stranger to Granddad''s apparent inability to say no to an order of battered clam strips. He had a bunch of take-out bags in his hand and Nana was scolding him.

"Walter, you done stopped at every restaurant selling fried clams. You ain't supposed to be eating those! What you gonna do with all them, plant them?"

Before I could duck away, she spotted Terrence and me and steered Granddad toward us. Granddad didn't look up from his clam strips. He'd eat two or three, smack his lips and exclaim how good they were, then roll the bag closed and open another. It was like watching a squirrel eat nuts, except this particular squirrel knew how to throw a mean right hook and could ground you.

"Maaaaaaaaaaan, let me tell you about these clam strips right here!" Granddad said when they reached us.

I rolled my eyes. Anytime he started with a *Let me tell you*, I knew we weren't going anywhere soon. Might as well unfurl a sleeping bag and put on your pajamas, you're going to be there for a while. Few things riled up Walter Strong more than a crisp, well-fried clam strip. Which would have been fine any other day (that's not exactly true, but what was I, a mere twelve-year-old, supposed to do?), just not when Cotton was on the loose.

My pocket vibrated twice. I checked to make sure Granddad was distracted (which was easy, since his eyes were closed as he bit into another clam strip) before pulling out the phone. Granddad hated how often I checked it. Meanwhile, Terrence told Nana about the pizza parlor.

The screen winked to life, and the worried face of a trickster god stared out at me.

On an average day, Anansi had a contagious smile and a twinkle in his eye. You never knew if he had your back or had a trick in his back pocket. He was the Weaver, the owner of all stories, from truths to tall tales, and his name was embedded in my title of Anansesem. But at the moment, the spider god looked far from his normal self.

I slipped in one earbud and his voice, normally melodic and lilting, was flat and strained. "Well, are we leaving or not?"

I peered around the crowded street filled with tourists just like me and my grandparents. It was early evening, but the Louisiana sun still beamed down on the French Quarter as if focused through a magnifying glass. My own reunion T-shirt (yes, still lime green) clung to my back, my black basketball shorts felt like they weighed thirty pounds, and my new all-black Chuck Taylors (*That's the second pair we bought you*, Granddad had grumbled) felt like their soles were melting.

Still, everywhere I looked, people were laughing, joking, shopping, eating, dancing, and carrying on their merry way through what was possibly the most vibrant square mile in the whole country. Music thumped from Bourbon Street a few blocks over while the casinos on Canal Street flickered to life. Adults and teens and children walked by with powdered sugar dusting their lips and fingers as they bit into soft, hot beignets and—if you didn't know any better—life was all good.

Yet a shadow lingered now, just out of sight. Cotton. The haint's specter hovered in my peripheral vision, waiting for the right moment to strike.

I shook my head. "Not just yet," I told Anansi. "But—"

"Time is running out, Tristan! We have to move!" There was resignation in his voice, like he knew what I was going to say next.

"I know," I said. "It's just . . . all my family is here."

Anansi didn't respond, and when I glanced at the SBP, I saw he was sitting with his back against the edge of the screen, slumped and depressed. I realized, too late, what I'd just said, and I opened my mouth to say more, but no words would bring back his family—specifically, his son—safe and sound, so I closed it. Sometimes condolences don't ease the hurt—they just make things worse.

"Hey now, what's with that face?"

Granddad's voice came from behind me. He cradled another container of clam strips as if it were a baby, but he wore a concerned look. Nana was speaking to Terrence a few feet away, both of them huddled over his phone as they picked the next destination for our Strong subgroup. "You look like you just got sucker punched, boy. What's the best way to defend against that happening again?"

I snorted, though there wasn't much humor in it. Granddad always had a boxing analogy ready to apply to any situation, and he'd quiz me at various points throughout the day to test my knowledge of the sport. History, theory, techniques—it didn't matter. He'd only let me go back to doing whatever I was doing if I answered his questions correctly.

If Gum Baby were here, she'd call it a Grandpop Quiz. I smiled, and then it faded from my face. The little loudmouth was lost out there somewhere, too. As much as I hated to admit it (and if you tell her, I will sing "The Ballad of the Gummy" nonstop outside your window), I missed the tiny sap monster.

"Well?" Granddad asked.

I sighed, stared into the crowd streaming past, and racked my brain. "Um, dodge it?"

"You take a sucker punch, you didn't dodge anything. Not for a good minute. Try again."

"Keep my head on a swivel? Make sure I'm always aware."

Granddad pursed his lips. "Better, but still not all the way there. Think about it. Sometimes an opponent will get the drop on you, and they'll send punch after punch at you. Those blows gonna land and land hard. Knock you back. Stun you. How do you defend against a flurry like that? How do you respond?"

I struggled to come up with an answer, but at that moment the SBP vibrated. Three times in a row. That wasn't a signal from Anansi. That was an alert.

"Tristan."

Granddad's voice jerked me from my thoughts. He loaded me up with his take-out boxes and bags so he could place both hands on my shoulders. Then he pulled me close, into a hug. My arms were too full to hug him back, but I was too surprised to respond anyway.

"Sometimes," Granddad said, squeezing me tight, "you just have to hold on. Clinch, and catch your breath. The world is going to hit you hard, son. Clinch and don't let go until you can keep on fighting. Hear me?"

"Yessir," I said, my voice muffled by his shirt.

Sometimes I forgot that Granddad had been violently introduced to the world of Alke when Bear—under the poisonous influence of the haint King Cotton—had attacked the farmhouse and kidnapped Nana. Had Granddad felt helpless while we were gone? Sucker punched?

The SBP vibrated again. Granddad sucked his teeth and stepped back. "Boy, who is that blowing up your phone? Tell them Stanleys to give you a break."

I groaned. "No, Granddad, no, no, no. They're called stans. *Stans*."

"Stans, Stanleys, Stanford Cardinals, you need to tell them to lay off." Granddad took back his clam strips and popped a few more golden-brown pieces into his mouth, chewing angrily. "I'm trying to teach here, and you, Mr. Popular, can barely focus. Go on and answer that, boy. I won't stand in the way."

I grinned even as I pulled out the phone and began to back up. "It's not like that, Granddad. I just need to check something real—"

"Tristan, watch out!"

Anansi's shout came from the earbud I still wore, even as the SBP was snatched from my hand. I whirled to see a kid running into the crowd.

"Hey!" I cried.

"Tristan—" Granddad began, but I was already tearing off after the robber.

"C'mon, Granddad!" I shouted and sprinted down the street.